ZOLA

ZOLA

JOHAN JACK SMITH

Translated from the Afrikaans by
Jaco Adriaanse

PENGUIN BOOKS

Published in 2019 by Penguin Random House South Africa (Pty) Ltd
Company Reg No 1953/000441/07
The Estuaries No 4, Oxbow Crescent, Century Avenue, Century City, 7441, South Africa
PO Box 1144, Cape Town, 8000, South Africa
www.penguinrandomhouse.co.za

First edition, first printing 2019
1 3 5 7 9 8 6 4 2

ISBN 978-1-4859-0386-4 (Print)
ISBN 978-1-4859-0397-0 (ePub)

Cover design by publicide
Text design by Fahiema Hallam
Set in Minion Pro

Printed and bound by Novus Print, a Novus Holdings company

Ook beskikbaar in Afrikaans

For Almerie

His lungs are on fire and his knee is aching fiercely. His left leg has started to drag behind him. It must be the adrenaline leaving his system. He stops and breathes heavily. With a heave, he trudges on, the body hanging over his right shoulder. Dead weight. He didn't expect such a small, fragile thing to weigh so much. The girl's head keeps knocking between his shoulders; he feels her hand swinging against his lower back with each step. He thinks he can feel the wetness of her lower body seeping through his coat. This one is difficult to carry, more uncomfortable than the others. It isn't far now.

Here and there, lights from passing cars illuminate the side streets of the city. It's almost four o'clock. Fortunately the siding is dark, and anyone driving around at this time of night is either drunk or themselves busy with something that requires the black of night.

He arrives at the spot he identified from below. He will leave her here. He looks around again, lifts her from his shoulder carefully and puts her down, propped up with her back to the railing. He takes the blue-and-white nylon rope from the back of his trousers. He'll have to be quick.

Then he hears a car on the M1 behind him. It's going fast. He stops, doesn't move a muscle. He crouches down next to her body when he hears the car slow down, probably to take the turn into Smit Street. The car lights fall blindly on his overcoat, are absorbed by it. The car passes. The driver doesn't notice him.

He goes to work, quickly now, ties the rope beneath her breasts and around her back, knots it in the front, just above her navel so that the marks on her back aren't damaged. Otherwise all his effort will have been for nothing.

He ties the rope to one of the short wooden struts on the barrier railing. He has become used to working with the white latex gloves; his hands aren't as clumsy as they were at the start. He lifts her up, then drops her over the edge. With a jerk, the body hangs limply from the pole. The girl's head is pressed into her chest, her arms loose at her sides. She sways slowly from left to right, turning to her left. He pulls on the rope one last time, checking that the knot will hold. It bothers him that the rope is cutting into the marks on her back. It's too late to do anything about it now. He looks around, making sure he didn't leave anything behind, then sweeps a shoe over the loose gravel and walks down Smit Street. He climbs back over the low railing that runs parallel with the turn-off. His knee is going to give him hell tomorrow.

Standing under the bridge, he looks back and up, taking in his night's work. It looks like there's something on the ground below the girl. He squints in the dark. Must be imagining things. He has to get out of here. He is satisfied. It won't be long before someone sees her. If they miss this one, he doesn't really know what more he can do. He couldn't believe his luck when he realised the condition she was in. If this isn't going to get their attention, nothing will. He has given them all the pieces; they just need to figure out it's a puzzle.

1

The coffee shop in Mayfair is quiet as usual. Captain David Majola taps his index finger beside his cup. A brown stain runs from the lip to the saucer. His cup is a quarter full, lukewarm, the *Daily Sun* open in front of him.

'Refill?' asks the waiter with the Malawian accent.

'I'm okay for now, thanks.'

The man nods and walks on to a table by the window where an Indian man is busy on his phone. He mumbles something to the waiter without looking up.

Majola looks at the waiter, takes in his neat white shirt and black trousers. He's wearing cheap shoes. There are many like him. Waiters. Gardeners. Even butlers, washing up, cooking and walking the dogs throughout the northern suburbs. All of them looking for a meaningful life. And a full stomach. Mostly a full stomach. He's heard that Malawi isn't the same any more. Fewer and fewer fish in the lake. Even after receiving land from the government, the people remain poor.

Behind the Indian, the traffic is bustling, vehicles filled with impatient passengers on their way to work – the occasional outburst at the taxis that stop without signalling or cram into overstuffed lanes. Their faces are grim, hidden behind dark glasses. One would never guess it's Friday by the looks of them.

'Do you think if you stare at that headline long enough it's going to change?' Warrant Officer Jason Basson pulls his chair back with a screech and sits down, blowing on his hands. 'Damn, it's cold this morning.'

'You have to really love smoking to be outside right now,' Majola says. He looks at Basson in his navy-blue, long-sleeved shirt and matching trousers. The shirt is a bit tight around the midriff, but it still looks stylish with the dark-brown tie and jacket. He can see why women find Basson attractive. Majola always teased him that it was his own fashion sense that had rubbed off on Basson when they'd started working together. Before that, Basson only wore those awful, baggy chinos with short-sleeved, checked shirts. Even Delia, Basson's wife, has thanked him in private for the change.

Basson winks the waiter over, who comes bustling with a refill. Steam rises from the cup as Basson takes the small silver jug and adds milk, stirs it in slowly.

'When last did you watch *7de Laan*?' he asks.

'It's been a while.'

'You haven't missed much. Don't you prefer *Generations*, anyway?' Basson asks with a mischievous smile.

Majola takes a sip of his coffee, somewhat taken aback by the direction the conversation is heading in.

'You think just because I'm a darky I have to watch the soaps for darkies? A bit racist, don't you think?"

'Whoa, no man. That's not what I mean. It's just a bit strange that you like Afrikaans soap operas.'

'That's probably my mother's fault. And Auntie Anne. I grew up with Afrikaans television. My mother believed the storylines were better. Probably why I speak Afrikaans in the first place. Well, that and Kappie, I guess.'

'Yeah, that's because he can hardly speak a word of English. But didn't Auntie Anne also send you to some or other larney Afrikaans school in Linden?'

Majola nods. 'Ja, Louw Geldenhuys. Then one year at Linden High. That was before I went to go find my real mother in Alex. Just in time too – I was about to go gangster on those little botterpieletjies.'

'I think you mean "botterbulletjies".' laughs Basson. 'Speaking of Kappie, how is he these days?'

Majola smiles over the rim of his cup. 'Hard-ass as always. But he hasn't had a setback in a while. Lizanne texted me about two weeks ago, asked me to swing by and bring a few movies. He's getting tired of rewatching everything on TV. And reading the Bible all day gets him down.' Majola looks at Basson, adjusts himself in his chair. 'I'm actually just trying to catch up on all the Oscar nominations this year; still a whole bunch I haven't seen yet.'

'I only got around to watching *Gone Girl* the other day. That Rosamund Pike is on fucking fire. Goddamn, what I wouldn't do for one hour with—'

'Isn't it a bit early to be thinking of sex?' asks Majola.

'Never, my man. When you're my age it's only in the mornings you can still get a half-decent erection. The rest of the day it's an uphill battle.'

Majola leans forward in his chair. 'Or maybe you walked past your fireman neighbour's window again?'

'No fucking chance!' answers Basson, feigning offence. 'I just look straight ahead and pretend I don't see a thing. You know, I spoke to a guy from action cricket the other day. He says he knows Wikus, worked with him in the city a while back. Everyone knows about his crossdressing, but everyone's too scared to say anything about it. Apparently one day a guy said something, and Wikus sorted him out right there on the spot, in front of everyone. Backhand to the ear, sent the idiot flying. Apparently he kicks ass as a fireman too. Hardworking, neat, even saved a bunch of people. So if he wants to walk around his house in a dress every night, I've got nothing to say about that.'

Majola listens with half an ear. He's got his eye on the man by the window who just jumped out of his seat when a passing taxi backfired. The man sees Majola watching him and quickly looks down at his phone, pretending nothing happened.

'Are you listening?'

'Ja, sorry.' He takes another look at the man before turning back to Basson.

'In any case, I always thought crossdressers were more hairdressers than firemen. You know, the kind who clearly bat for the other team.'

'Don't you think you're being a bit judgemental? And homophobic, come to think of it?'

Basson's cup clatters to the table. 'Shit, first I'm a racist, now I'm judgemental. And homophobic too, for good measure. Okay, I guess I am that. But I'm more of a racist, according to you, right?' Basson winks at Majola, who laughs back. 'Delia speaks to him quite often. Even got a recipe for fridge tart the other day. Jeez, that queen can bake. But they haven't been hanging out as much lately. He's been visiting new tenants on the ground floor. Lady with a young boy.'

'Does it bother you that an older transvestite is visiting a young mother and her boy?' Majola asks.

'I wondered about that in the beginning, but he looks totally harmless to me. Delia said he's been through some serious heartbreak. His boyfriend died in an accident close to Krugersdorp. Head-on collision with a taxi. No surprises there.' Basson searches a jacket pocket.

'You just went for a smoke,' says Majola.

'I'm just making sure they're there. But now that you mention it ...'

Basson pushes his chair out. The man at the other table looks up quickly.

'Before I go die of hypothermia again ... you said something the other day that I can't quite shake. About Radebe. Do you really think he's got his fingers in the cash register?'

'I don't know. There are some things that just don't make sense, though. He keeps ordering raids in Alex, even if it's outside his jurisdiction. He and the colonel from that area work together regularly. It's only the eastern side that he avoids.'

'Your mother lives there, right?' asks Basson.

'And my sister, yeah. About four streets away from that dealer, Calvin Mpete. I don't like that they're so close to him.'

Basson takes out his cigarettes. 'But isn't Radebe also from that valley? Don't you remember him from back in the day? Or was that too long ago?'

Majola thinks for a second. 'I remember him vaguely. He wasn't there long, maybe two years. He was a sergeant at the time. When the transition came, suddenly he was a colonel. Now he lives in Mondeor in a two-storey house with a pool and a six-foot wall. But I'm sure he was in the service long enough to make some connections. Did you know he has a degree in criminology?'

Basson gets up. 'Who the hell would give him one of those? The People's University of Bophuthatswana?'

Majola frowns. 'Wits, actually.'

'Sergeant Busi told me that Radebe's wife left him and took the kids too.

Second wife, much younger than him. Can't blame her if it's true; he's a moody bliksem. But you know Busi – she talks a lot of kak. Anyway, ask the guy for our bill. I think today is my turn if I remember correctly.'

Majola hears the man at the window raise his voice and sees him push his coffee to the edge of the table. 'Warm it up, idiot. Can't you feel it's cold? Are you stupid or something?'

The waiter nods apologetically and takes the cup, walks to Majola's table mumbling something under his breath.

'Can we get the bill please?' Majola asks.

The waiter smiles and nods, walks to the kitchen.

The man at the window notices Majola watching him and tries to look really busy on his phone. The waiter walks by, puts down their bill, and takes a fresh cup of coffee to the disgruntled customer.

Basson comes back in and sits down. Majola smells the smoke following him like a spectre.

Basson takes his wallet out of his back pocket. 'What's the damage?' he asks.

The man at the window gets up, takes out his wallet and drops a few coins on the table. The waiter, confused, places the fresh cup down in front of him but the man ignores it. The waiter is visibly disappointed when he sees the coins, but thanks the man with a smile. The man ignores him and walks away.

As he passes Majola and Basson, Majola says, 'Watch out for those gunshots out there – you might just have a heart attack. Or piss your pants.'

The man smiles reflexively at first, then gets angry. He is about to say something when he notices the z88 pistol protruding from Majola's jacket. He walks on.

'What was that about?'

Majola shakes his head. 'Nothing. Just a rude asshole.'

Few people know of this place. He and Basson come here at least once a week, sometimes to discuss cases before the day starts, other times just to shoot the breeze, like today.

Majola's phone rings shrilly. It's the theme from *The Exorcist*.

'Ah, you got it. Where did you download it from?'

Majola raises a finger. 'Hold up, it's Ramsamy.'

'Majola,' he answers, then listens carefully. 'Say again. Where?' He looks at Basson, who looks like he's just realised his Friday is going to be a long one. And that's not how he wanted to start his weekend.

'Okay, we're on our way. Hang tight.' Majola gets up, grabs his coat from the chair.

'They found a woman at the Smit Street turn-off on the M1 northbound.'

Basson sighs deeply. 'Well, at least it's on the way to the station.'

'Something doesn't sound right. Ramsamy sounds rattled, which is odd for him. Said something about above and below the offramp. Think it's a bit early for him to talk sense.'

Basson moves his chair back. Majola checks the bill, takes out his wallet and adds another twenty.

'Cheapskate.'

Basson grunts. 'A racist, a homophobe and a cheapskate. Sounds like your old president.'

'Go fuck yourself. That Zulu was nothing of mine. Give me the keys, I know a shortcut.'

Basson tosses the Corolla's keys to him. Majola says goodbye to the manager at the door and pulls his coat tightly around him against the icy Johannesburg air.

Traffic is going to be bad on the M1 North. They will have closed the offramp. Majola can smell Basson, a mix of smoke and Old Spice. It makes him queasy, with the exhaust fumes slipping through the chink in the window. They have an agreement that Basson can't smoke in the car. At first he was somewhat testy about it, but later conceded. Smoker's guilt – because these days, smokers are increasingly treated as criminals for their expensive habit.

Basson has the heater on high. The car is warming up fast, but the heat is making Majola anxious, which is why his window is slightly open. He considers using the police siren, but it's not going to help. Traffic has come to a complete standstill.

Majola takes in the businesses lining the street. Shops selling fabrics and electronics, cellphone repair shops. Just a few streets further down, on his right, is the Oriental Plaza, where you can buy damn near anything you can think of – delicious curries, fine fabrics, cheap clothing and shoes, fake sunglasses, you name it.

He hasn't been there in nearly twenty years. The last time was with Busiswe. Majola touches the scar on his throat absentmindedly, barely visible these days. But he still sees it clearly, as he did the day he woke up in hospital and went to look in the mirror.

'Switch on the siren. There's enough room on the side for us to get through,' Basson says. He is deliberately not talking about the scene that's waiting for them. 'Do you remember the time that busted old Cressida cut in front of us and I showed the guy my nine mill? Mother-fucker took out his AK-47.'

Majola nods. 'That wasn't funny. Don't bring a pistol to a machine-gun fight.'

The blue flashes from the Corolla's headlights reflect abstractly from the other cars. People start noticing them, peer curiously, and turn slowly to the right to give them space to pass. An old bakkie takes its time to move aside and Majola starts gesturing to the driver to get out of the way.

'Nyakaza wena, man,' he says, irritated.

He can feel that today is going to be special. And not special like a beautiful sunset; more like the kids in the special class at school, who were always ridiculed by the others. Those with the snotty noses, who cried or laughed when they shouldn't have.

'Up ahead,' Basson says, nodding at the orange, white and blue Metro police vehicle.

The M1 highway looms like a giant grey spaceship high overhead. The underbelly of the grotesque cement behemoth is intermittently illuminated by the flashing blue lights of the emergency vehicles below. Traffic is being redirected to the right to clear Smit Street. Graf Street and its access road are blocked off by four police vehicles. Some drivers make futile attempts to cut in from the left lane, and the morning air is cut by the shrill echo of angry horns. The whole scene is surrounded by yellow police tape.

'Look at all the rubberneckers behind the tape. They'll have to move them all back,' says Basson. Majola pulls in behind one of the four-wheel-drive police trucks and kills the engine. 'Are you going to put on your yellow jacket?'

'Fuck that,' says Majola, opening his door. 'I'm not taking off my coat. The guys here are from our beat. By now they should know who we are.'

Majola and Basson walk in the direction of the crime scene. To the left lies Braamfontein Cemetery, the crematorium rising ominously from behind the wall. Majola lifts the tape, indicates for Basson to duck through. Two uniformed officers are talking to each other, one rubbing his hands to warm them.

'Move the line ten metres back, up against the cemetery wall. And tell the people up front to put their phones away – this isn't the fucking Oscars,' says Majola, flashing his badge at the nearest constable.

Basson, hands in his pockets, stares at the constable. The spectators have their phones raised to take pictures. Majola looks on with frustration.

'Morning, Captain. Sorry, Captain, I'll sort it out right away.' The constable nods helpfully and walks to the crowd.

About thirty metres away, Majola sees more officers, gathered around something covered by a white sheet. Their blue uniforms contrast sharply with the white wall, which is surprisingly graffiti free. The people behind the yellow tape are being herded back reluctantly at the young constable's behest. Something bothers him. It's the angle of their phones – they aren't pointing down at the scene on the road; they're pointing up, into the sky.

Majola looks up. The scene hits him like a blow to the gut.

'Jissis.'

He hears Basson gasp as he too looks up.

'Yeah, like Jesus on the cross,' says the constable, who has returned to stand next to them.

Majola throws him a sharp look, is ready to berate him, but turns back to the naked girl dangling from the rope beneath the bridge. He shakes his head. 'Bastard is either really brave or really stupid. Johannesburg Central isn't even three kilometres from here.'

Basson doesn't answer, turns to the constable. 'What's everyone doing down there under the bridge, in the road? Investigating some roadkill while we're at it?'

'No, Warrant Officer, you'll have to go down and see for yourself. Forensics are already there. Ask one of them to explain,' says the constable.

'Captain Majola!' a loud voice calls from behind. Majola and Basson turn in unison. It's Martie Bam, journalist at *Beeld*. She's behind the yellow tape, in front of a crowd that's looking increasingly ill at ease. Behind her is a youngish black guy, at the ready with a video camera.

'Morning, Captain. The weekend seems to be kicking off with some action. What happened here?'

Majola shakes his head. 'Mrs Bam, your guess is as good as mine. If you don't mind, I need to go do my job.' He sees Basson checking out her legs, clad in skin-tight denim.

'Oh, come now, Captain, I'm also just here to do my job. And it's Miss Bam, as I've mentioned before,' she says with a smile.

Majola turns around without replying and walks on. Basson follows him, with a final glance back at her legs.

'That bloody woman is everywhere. I don't understand how she gets to the crime scenes so quickly. And what's with the guy with the video camera? I thought she was with the newspapers?' says Basson, trying to keep up. They cross the sidewalk, start climbing the slope.

'These days everything is filmed for social media and TV. People are too lazy to read. Newspapers are going the way of the dodo.' Majola turns to his right, sees the policemen gathered around the bulging white sheet in the road. They stare back at him in complete silence. 'What the hell happened here? Why two crime scenes?' Majola asks.

One of the men on the bridge starts making his way towards them. Sergeant Rahid Ramsamy is clean shaven, his hair gelled back. He's wearing a brown windbreaker under his blue jacket with the words *Crime Scene Investigator* on the back.

'Look at Head Girl with her lovely raincoat,' says Basson.

Sergeant Ramsamy transferred from Durban where he was a member of the Flying Squad, the first guys on the scene. He's been a detective under Majola for two years. He joins them and walks them back.

'Morning, Captain.'

Majola nods. Ramsamy doesn't greet Basson, just throws him a look. Basson looks dead ahead.

'Morning, Sergeant,' Majola says.

'I take it you saw the hanging girl from down there?' asks Ramsamy.

'I did. But what happened under the bridge? The other scene?'

Ramsamy looks at his shoes, shakes his head.

'What is it, Sergeant?' Majola asks again.

'It's a baby.'

'A what?' splutters Basson.

'According to Dr Lubbe, the girl was still alive. Then she went into labour. She was about six months pregnant.'

Majola feels his heart skip a slow beat. 'How the fuck is that possible?' He walks back to the railing and looks down at the bundled white sheet.

'Go ask Dr Lubbe yourself,' replies Ramsamy.

The men walk closer. 'Just as I thought this place can't get any darker. Fucking Jozi zoo at its best,' says Basson.

Majola sees the cars coming into view to his right as they walk higher. Traffic must be backed up all the way to Gold Reef City to the south, the Mooi Street turn-off to the east, and probably all the way to Roodepoort in the west. Just another day in Johannesburg traffic. The cold morning air burns his lungs.

Ramsamy walks out ahead, his breath fogging up around him. 'A hysterical woman called the Brixton station at 05:45 this morning. She had the number on her phone for emergencies, apparently lives in that area. She was on her way to work when she saw the girl. I don't understand how no one noticed it earlier. This road starts to get busy from 05:00.'

'If you're not coming from Seventeenth Street you wouldn't see her,' Basson says sharply.

Ramsamy ignores his comment. 'She'll come in later for questioning; she says she has to go to work first.'

'Make sure she comes in. What about the CCTV cameras on the M1? Where are they located?' asks Majola.

'There's one about 300 metres south of here, attached to one of the overhanging road signs. But it looks out over the Metro trains at Braamfontein station. The other one is on the footbridge further north, looking out over Wits University, and it's too far off to make out anything useful. I sent someone out first thing this morning to make sure.' Ramsamy looks impressed with his own proactivity.

'Good work,' Majola says. A deep dejectedness settles over him as he makes his way to the crime scene. 'What about eyewitnesses?'

'There's an old man who sleeps next to the cemetery wall. Considering all the strange garbage he has lying around him, I think he's a sangoma or something. But he's beyond drunk, probably from last night. Can't get much more from him than mumbling. Two of the officers are giving him coffee. He might be able to talk if we go down there.'

'A drunken sangoma? This morning just keeps getting weirder and weirder,' Majola says, shaking his head.

Various police vehicles are parked at the scene: two highway-patrol vehicles, an Audi, a BMW and a four-wheel-drive bakkie hearse. A gurney has already been wheeled out onto the road, a few metres from where the girl is hanging. Two officials from LCRC, the Local Criminal Records Centre, are busy documenting the scene. One is taking pictures, the camera flashing again and again. Dr Jaco Lubbe looks over the railing, like someone who is cautious around heights. About eight metres below, the other uniformed officials stand around the second scene.

Doctor Lubbe, or Doc, as nearly every police officer inevitably calls him, is dressed in his white overcoat and black beanie, a grey moustache sitting like a broom atop his lip. The Eighties-looking metal-rimmed spectacles always remind Majola of the American evangelist Billy Graham. He's wearing an orange jacket with the words *Forensic Pathology Services* on the back.

'Morning, gentlemen. Do you think I will ever see the day when our finest detectives show up at a crime scene before the forensics and pathology teams?' Doc teases them.

One of the officers looks up with a smile before going on with his work.

Dr Lubbe speaks to Basson, gives Majola only a brief nod.

Majola looks at the ageing man. He's one of the many who still don't trust black officers, even though he would never let on out of respect for rank and authority. He also noticed this with Kappie, even though he was a sergeant at the time. He has great respect for the doctor nonetheless: he has years of experience and is good at his job.

'Have you seen the goddamn traffic?' asks Basson.

Dr Lubbe smiles. 'I came all the way from Rosettenville too. Father of three decided to end it all with a bang; used dumdums, of all things. Probably because he knew what the traffic was going to be like today. It's okay though. Perhaps one day when you lot are grown up, you'll know all the back streets and shortcuts too.'

'I was almost ready to have her hoisted up,' Lubbe continues, 'then I saw you coming. Ramsamy told me to wait for you.'

Ramsamy nods in agreement.

Majola steps cautiously forward, doesn't want to disturb anything that might be useful to the forensics teams. 'What do you make of this, Doctor?' he asks, peering over the railing. The girl's head and shoulders are visible, as are the two nylon ropes holding her up.

'I guess we'll see in a moment. I'm not going to figure it out from up here. I take it you heard about the foetus?'

'We did, ja,' replies Majola. 'Have to say, this takes the cake.'

'Can I take her?' Dr Lubbe asks one of the investigators. 'You almost done? Any luck?'

The man shakes his head. 'Not much. It looks like there could be a footprint here, but it's difficult because of the gravel. And over here it looks like someone scuffed another print. And we can't determine if there are any tyre tracks – whether he dropped her here or dragged her from down there. No drag marks, no nothing. And that's it. We're going down below now. You can do your thing here. The video team is also done.'

'Come, Mbalula, make yourself useful.' Dr Lubbe calls his assistant over from where he is standing by the hearse. 'Captain, grab some gloves from the chest by the bakkie. I'm going to need your help. My old body doesn't cooperate in this cold, and it's even worse for Mbalula. You too, Warrant Officer Basson, I need you to cut the ropes. There are scissors in the chest.'

Majola and Basson step closer. 'All yours,' says Majola after taking out some latex gloves and giving the scissors to Basson.

Basson also puts on gloves, in case there's something on the ropes they can use.

'Come closer,' the doctor orders. 'This is what I need you to do. Captain, you and Mbalula will take her under her arms, here, by the armpits. If you've got a good grip, Basson, go in and cut the rope. Cut it with one hand, and give it to the constable. And in God's name, don't drop the rope. Once Basson has handed over the rope, we pick her up. I'll cut the piece around the pole later. Raise her high without bumping her against the railing. Then Basson and I will take her up here. Okay? Let's do it.'

Majola and Mbalula walk closer and bend over the railing. They both get a grip under her arms. Even through the gloves Majola can feel how cold her skin is. Basson comes closer with the scissors.

When he is satisfied, Dr Lubbe says, 'Okay, Basson, cut the rope.'

Basson takes the rope in his left hand and cuts it quickly with his right. The scissors are sharp. He passes the rope to the constable next to him, who places it into a perforated evidence bag. With one motion, Majola and Mbalula lift the girl. Basson and Dr Lubbe carry her to the gurney, where they place her on her back in the body bag.

The uniformed officials, the forensics teams, the doctor, Ramsamy, Majola, Basson, everyone stares at her as if hypnotised. Majola shakes his head. The expression on her face is peaceful. The cuts on her body make it clear, however, that her passing was torturous. Nearly her entire lower body is covered in blood.

Dr Lubbe steps closer. 'I don't want to poke around too much before the postmortem, but let's take a quick look.' He starts with her wrists. 'Well, she wasn't only tied around the body. Clear abrasions to the wrists. Same with her ankles.' He points at discolorations higher up her legs. 'Bruises, around the knees too, on the inside. Probably to keep her legs open. Could indicate she was in a sitting position, although she might have been lying down as well. Bruises around her neck. And these contusions to her breasts. They look like burns. Jesus, he really fucked her up. And that's just from what I can see with the naked eye.'

'Burns?' asks Ramsamy, who had been quietly standing to one side. 'So, he tortured her?'

Dr Lubbe looks at Basson first, then at Majola, then at Ramsamy. He talks slowly, his words clipped. 'Sergeant, a foetus doesn't simply fall from a woman's body.'

Ramsamy doesn't respond.

'The dry blood on her lower body … he did a lot of damage. I'll have to do this properly in the lab. The foetus must have come out when he tied her up and dropped her over the railing. Which means that she spontaneously aborted. To tell you the truth, I've never seen anything like this. Almost thirty years and still ...'

Majola looks at the girl. What must she have gone through? Was she mercifully unconscious when her baby was torn loose from her body? He can't keep the images from flashing through his mind: how she possibly saw her baby fall. Nausea and fury vie for control of Majola. 'Time of death? Was it before ... or after the—'

Dr Lubbe answers almost immediately. 'I'll be able to determine that at the lab. Let's wrap up here, I still have to go down below.'

Majola and Basson pull off their latex gloves and put them back in the box.

Mbalula approaches. He draws two paper bags over the girl's hands and binds them with elastic bands.

Majola has seen enough. 'Let's go down. Ramsamy, where's the man who apparently witnessed something?'

'Yes, you go see him, I don't think you'll find any clues with the foetus. Spare yourself that sight.'

Just before Mbalula puts the body bag onto the gurney, Dr Lubbe stops him. 'Mbalula, come grab here quick. I just want to check the back.'

Majola stops in his tracks, Basson and Ramsamy too. Dr Lubbe and Mbalula slowly turn the girl over onto her side. Lubbe bends over, leans in closer, his face only centimetres from her skin. 'That's strange ...'

Majola walks closer, stands next to the pathologist.

'Take a look at this: they look like numbers. Yes, numbers and letters,' says Dr Lubbe. Majola crouches to see better, Basson standing behind him.

'It looks like they've been carved in; deep lacerations on her back. O-N-3-4-5-0-6-1-9-8-6,' Majola reads. 'Or is that last digit an 8? And, under that, U-M-H-A 2-3-2-1.'

The pathologist carefully lowers the girl onto her back again. 'The murderer used her body like a canvas. He clearly had time on his hands.'

The detectives take one last look at the girl, while Mbalula removes the gum strip of the beige body bag and seals it.

Majola often wonders why the bags are beige; in American police procedurals they're always black. Maybe the beige looks slightly less grim than black.

Two guys from Forensics step closer, wearing their dark-blue overalls with white reflector strips.

'Captain.' Dr Lubbe cleans his glasses with his handkerchief. 'I don't want to jump the gun here ...' He shakes his head. 'My sister's laaitie helps out at the morgue in Germiston. Studies at UJ, pretty bright bulb. About a month or two ago, I went over for a braai at their place, and we ended up talking shop. The boy tells me about a girl they brought in from Orange Farm. Grievously injured. Burn wounds, from electric shocks. With numbers carved into her back.'

His eyes follow the gurney as they push it into the back of the bakkie. 'I hope for all of your sakes the two cases are not related. But I suggest you give Orange Farm a call. This looks like a statement. Especially with the police station so close by.'

Majola sighs audibly. Basson lights a cigarette.

'Who is the pathologist over there?' asks Majola.

'Bester, I think,' the doctor answers.

Majola sighs again. This is the very last thing he needs right now. A fucking serial. That means an incredible amount of pressure from the top. The media hounding you. Sleepless nights. It feels like yesterday that he solved the UJ-Rapist case. That took four months to solve, and he did enough legwork that he might as well have trekked the Drakensberg barefoot, like the whiteys did back in the day when they crossed the country. Before he draws any conclusions, they'll have to determine whether there are any connections between the victims.

'What time can we swing by the lab, Doctor?'

'I've got a lot of work. They're crammed into those fridges like sardines. But it seems like I'll have to take this one. Sooner rather than later. Come around four o'clock, I should be ready by then. I might start a bit earlier.'

'Thanks, Doc. There must be dozens that are on the list ahead of this one.'

'As I said, sardines. No worries.'

Majola joins Basson and Ramsamy as they make their way down.

'Sergeant,' Majola says, turning to Ramsamy. 'Go check the internal database; see if you find anything similar. Then you call all the other stations in Gauteng, the morgues too. Call me if you find anything. I don't care if you have to take the whole weekend.'

Ramsamy is visibly upset about this.

'Don't worry, Sergeant,' Basson adds. 'You can continue baking samoosas for Curry-Muncher Masterchef after the weekend.'

Ramsamy stops in his tracks and turns around with a loud 'Fuck you!'

'That's "fuck you, Warrant Officer", *Sergeant* Ramsamy,' Basson says scornfully.

'Enough,' says Majola, clearly irritated. 'Can you stop your bullshit just for one day?'

Basson looks away. Ramsamy shakes his head vehemently, clearly pissed off that he's being scolded too. 'Yes, Captain,' Ramsamy says, still angry. Basson flicks his cigarette butt to the ground, then the three walk on.

'I'll call the pathologist in Germiston and the station at Orange Farm,' Majola continues. 'Basson, you call Mbatho, Davids, Rikhotso and Mitchell. Tell them I'll see them in the ops room at six tonight.'

Basson nods.

The crowd behind the police line has dwindled. Only a few curious onlookers remain. Majola scans their faces. One thing Kappie taught him was that sometimes the murderer returns to the scene of the crime. 'You would think the bastard would be scared of getting caught, but actually he's afraid of missing out,' he used to explain. Nobody looks suspect, though. The traffic still hasn't moved. The morning seems to want to warm up, but it can't crack the cold.

Martie Bam and her colleague are still there. She's busy on her phone and the cameraman looks bored, leaning against the small white car with a cigarette in his mouth.

'Where's the old man?' asks Majola.

'Over there,' says Ramsamy, nodding at the police bakkies without taking his hands out of his pockets.

The man is sitting on the open hatch of one of the bakkies. As they approach, Majola can see that he has seen better days. Or perhaps not. Perhaps he's one of those who never saw any good days, who got dealt a poor hand at birth. Or even worse, was never offered a seat at the poker table to begin with. His chin is lowered to his chest and he's barely moving. Beads have been woven into his long hair and more dangle from his neck and wrists. A thin string hangs around his neck, with the skulls of rats or mice threaded on it. He's wearing a thick, grimy coat. His beard is grey and it looks as if his nose has been broken several times.

As they approach, they are greeted by the sickly-sweet smell of old alcohol and sweat mixed with tobacco. The two police officers make room for the three detectives to come closer. Majola identifies himself to the officers.

'Madala,' he says to the old man. No response. Majola switches to Zulu.

'The policemen tell me you saw something last night. The girl on the bridge? What can you remember?' Still nothing. Majola sees the nicotine stains on the man's fingers. Majola mimes at Basson to give the old man a cigarette. Basson, unamused, takes one out of his packet. The old man slowly lifts his head and puts the cigarette into his mouth.

'Umlilo,' answers the man, looking at Basson's hands.

'Give him a light,' Majola tells Basson.

Basson shakes his head but lights the cigarette dangling from the old man's mouth. The old man draws deeply, blows out through his nose.

'Madala, what can you tell us? What happened on the bridge?'

The man whispers something, almost inaudible.

'Say again?' asks Majola, stepping closer and bowing his head.

'Zola Budd.'

A silence follows. Then Basson speaks. 'Zola Budd? Did I hear correctly? Shit, Captain, if we move now, we might just catch her running past Vereeniging on her way back to Bloemfontein. Or wait, rather Walkerville – she's no spring chicken these days.'

Majola turns to Basson. 'The old people always talked about "Zola Budds". That's what they called the minibus taxis.'

'Well, fuck me running,' Basson says, astonished.

Majola turns back to the old man. 'Zola Budd? Iteksi?'

The old man nods almost imperceptibly.

'Zola Budd,' he says again.

'Where did you see him, madala? Under the bridge or above it? Can you remember the colour? Did you see the man driving it?'

The old man shakes his head. 'Mnyama.'

'Dark. Was the colour dark, or was it too dark to see?' Majola tries to clarify. No response.

Just as Majola is about to speak, the man says the word 'ukukhanya'.

Majola, irritated now, shakes his head. 'Light or dark; can't be both.'

One of the constables steps closer. '"Ukukhanya" can mean either "light" or "lights" in isiXhosa. He's not referring to the colour of the taxi.'

Majola frowns. 'That doesn't tell me shit. Can you show us where the taxi was parked?'

The man lifts his hand slowly and points at the wall running along the cemetery. Majola turns to look.

'There by the wall, under the trees?'

The man nods.

'It's pretty far from where they found the old man's belongings, beside the cemetery wall. He wouldn't have been able to see much,' Majola says. 'And the man that drove the taxi? Did you see him?'

The man shakes his head. 'Ukufa … ukufa.'

Majola stares at the man, then turns to Basson. '"Ukufa" means "death".'

He turns to the two officers. 'Keep him a while longer. Get some more coffee into him; maybe he'll remember something else.' It won't help leaving a business card, he thinks. The old man's so drunk that he probably won't remember this conversation anyway.

'Ramsamy, ask LCRC when they're done to go check if they can find any fresh tyre marks there by the wall. Maybe we'll get lucky today.' No response but smoke is blown from his nose. His cigarette is down to the filter.

'Thanks, madala,' Majola says to the old man.

'Sounds like ghost stories to me,' says Basson, more to himself than anyone else as they walk away.

Majola ignores him and turns to Ramsamy again. 'Sergeant, call me later and tell me what you've found. And make very sure about those cameras. Up there as well as down here. With Braamfontein train station on the other side there, we might just be in luck.'

Ramsamy nods and walks off to the LCRC team still busy under the bridge, the video team now filming.

'Do you think it's something to go on? A taxi? Or minibus?' Basson asks.

'To be honest, I hope it isn't. Do you have any idea how many of those are driving around Gauteng?'

'No, how many?' Basson asks drily.

'Fucking loads. And it's not like they're going to queue up to come and help us out.'

Majola quickens his pace when he sees that Martie Bam and her cameraman have spotted him.

'Captain!' she yells from the other side of the police line. 'Just a few questions, Captain.'

The cameraman lifts the camera to his shoulder. But Majola ignores her and gets into the car. She gives up, looking angry as she turns away. The cameraman follows her back to their vehicle.

'I hope Doc is wrong. Please let this be a once-off. Revenge. Jealous boyfriend. Or someone who doesn't want to be a daddy just yet. Or something like that.' Basson cups his hands and blows into them.

Majola stares dead ahead, then takes his phone from his jacket pocket. He has two missed calls. One is from Lizanne, the other from Colonel Radebe. He listens to his voicemail and after a few seconds puts the phone back in his pocket. 'It's Kappie. He's had a setback and Lizanne wants me to go to the retirement home with her when she finishes her shift at the Mediclinic. It's in an hour. It'll have to wait; Radebe wants to see me too.'

'Okay, I'll open a docket. It's still hours until we have to go to the lab,' Basson replies.

Majola nods and starts the car, pulls away slowly. 'Fucker is arrogant enough to hang a girl a few hundred metres from the station. Believe me, I also hope this is a once-off. But my gut tells me we're not going to be that lucky.'

'Not this time,' Basson replies, staring out the window.

2

It doesn't take Majola and Basson long to get to Johannesburg Central. It's almost directly next to the crime scene. The traffic is less heavy below the highway than above it.

Basson looks somewhat dejected, probably about all the paperwork ahead. Majola is irritated. Mostly about Colonel Radebe's terse voice message. 'Get to my office. This is going to be a media fuck-up.'

In the parking lot, he stares up at the blue, ten-storey building. World renowned. Or rather, reviled. Before the station was rechristened 'Johannesburg Central' in 1997, it went by the name of John Vorster Square, named after the former prime minister of the Republic of South Africa. The ninth and tenth floors belonged to the demons from the Security Police. The lift stopped at the eighth floor, and you had to climb the stairs to the last two levels. These were often the final steps of the captured; many would never descend again alive.

The bust of John Vorster was taken down in 1997, along with the legacy of apartheid. Majola often wondered what the old mlungu with the black hat would have said if he saw the parking lot strewn with rubbish. Or the broken police vehicles parked next to the highway, falling apart in the wind and rain. But God knows, rather rubbish on the tarmac than the bodies of fallen political activists.

Basson gives Majola a nod before going into his office. 'I'll open the docket, then I'll call the other stations. Someone might already have reported her missing. I'll start searching the database too, before Head Girl over here starts freaking out over all the work,' he says, nodding at Ramsamy. 'Good luck.'

Majola smiles.

'Come in,' Colonel Radebe grunts. His office is warm, the aircon on high heat. He sits behind a large wooden desk, three chairs in a row facing him. He is focused on his laptop, his glasses on his nose.

'Morning, Colonel,' says Majola. The mugginess in the office isn't helping Majola's sense of unease. He can't stop thinking of his school years – feeling like a troublemaker, caught for smoking by the bicycle racks. Dreading the painful hiding that was fast approaching. The whiteys always brag about the hidings they got at school as if they had it rough. That's before they realise that he went to a white primary school. He doesn't ever bother mentioning to them the beatings the kids received at the hands of the black teachers at his high school in Alex. If they got angry enough, those hands were often clenched into fists.

Majola scans the line of framed photos, starting with the president, the commissioner, provincial commissioner, general, lieutenant-general, major-general and brigadier, and finally Radebe himself. All of them look as if they know something no one else does. The frame and photo of Radebe look different from the rest, and Majola wonders if he had them made up himself. Radebe looks up at Majola with bloodshot eyes.

'So, vertel my van die sisi wat hang van die bridge.'

Majola can't decide what frustrates him more – Radebe's broken Afrikaans, or his pretentious English which makes him sound like just another politician on a pedestal.

He can't fathom why Radebe always insists on speaking Afrikaans to him. Perhaps he's poking fun at his friendship with Kappie, or at Majola's Afrikaans upbringing. Majola knows Radebe hates the Afrikaners.

'A woman on her way to work reported it at the Brixton station around 05:45. Bound with ropes to the railing of the Smit Street turn-off. Erg verniel. I've never seen anything like it. She went into labour while she hung there. The foetus was found lying under the bridge.'

Radebe's eyes widen. 'Sy het a baby? Terwyl sy dead is?'

'Dr Lubbe suspects she was unconscious. Apparently it's not possible for a woman to give birth after death.'

'Bliksem. Prints? CCTV footage? Witnesses?'

'No prints. The cameras are too far from the scene. We're checking to see if there are cameras at the Braamfontein Metrorail. And there's a drunk old sangoma who says he saw a van. Or taxi.'

Radebe snorts. 'Is he reliable? Jou sangoma?'

'Difficult to say. Warrant Officer Basson is calling the other stations to find out if anyone has been reported missing in the last day. Sergeant Ramsamy is checking the database for similar cases. The autopsy is at four. After that we'll call in the rest of the team for a debrief.'

'Wie wil jy sit op die team vir die meeting?'

'Warrant Mbatho and Warrant Davids, Sergeant Rikhotso, and then Pieter Mitchell from IT. And Ramsamy and Basson, of course.'

Radebe looks directly at Majola and pushes the glasses back up his nose.

'Do you suspect this is a serial?' Radebe asks.

'I hope not. I'm just about to go call the morgues at Germiston and Orange Farm. Dr Lubbe said there might be similar cases there. If that's the case, then we're probably dealing with a serial.'

Radebe takes off his glasses, rubs his eyes before going on. 'Question is: let us say, madala onder die bridge is reg. He did see a taxi. But whether that's an actual taxi driver is 'n ander issue. Is it someone wat pretend to be a taxi driver? Of drive hy net in specific zones? Taking a fat chance if he's driving in other drivers' zones.'

'We'll have to find out, Colonel. Maybe we get lucky with the cameras at the train station.'

'Kaptein, kom ons hope madala was drunk. If the taxi associations have to get involved, hierdie ding raak very complicated. Maar jy weet dit seker?'

'Yes, Colonel, I know.'

'Use whoever you need. Davids and Mbatho are busy met a hijacking; they can put that on hold. They hit a dead end anyway. Siphelile. Finished.'

Majola nods.

'Hierdie case is priority. What were you and Basson working on?'

'The last case was that couple who were murdered in the restaurant in Melville three weeks ago,' Majola replies.

'Put it on ice. And keep the media out of this. If they want to know something, let them speak to Cele. Let the media officer do her fucking job for once. Sy kan speak to me directly.'

'I will tell her that, Colonel.'

'I'm coming in tomorrow. Let me know what you find with the autopsy. En about the other case in Orange Farm.'

Radebe leans back in his chair, folds his hands over his stomach.

'How is your mlungu-daddy doing?'

Majola feels his blood rise but tries not to show it. 'Captain Loots?'

'Who else? Is he still upholding the commandments after he found Jesus?' Radebe asks, smirking.

Majola shakes his head. A man's faith shouldn't be something to laugh at.

'Not too well. His daughter called earlier to tell me he's had a setback.'

'The ghosts of the past are tenacious and will keep biting.' Radebe smiles smugly at his own wit. 'After he recovers van sy setback, ask him what he thinks about this case.'

'But he's a civilian now.' Majola can't hide his surprise.

Ja, I know. Maar he's not a normal civilian; daar's nie meer baie met sy experience and knowledge. I insist, actually. If this is a serial, you're going to need all the support you can get. Give him a copy of the report once you've got more information. I don't like the bliksem, but you can't ignore his skills. Let's call him a consultant, Radebe says with a slight smile.

'Right, Colonel,' Majola replies, somewhat taken aback that Radebe doesn't trust that he can get the job done, but glad that he'll be able to work with Kappie again.

'Kaptein, ek count op jou. Ons need some good publicity. The SAPS has been dragged through the shit the past year; the people don't trust us any more. Who knows, maybe you make colonel sooner than you think?'

Majola looks at him questioningly.

'Nou maar toe,' Radebe says, using the old Afrikaans platitude to indicate that the conversation is over. 'This boere language is giving me an even bigger headache than I already had. Catch up with me tomorrow on everything you find out. Dismissed.'

Majola feels like he's been rapped over the knuckles again.

Majola walks into the offices of the Serious and Violent Crimes Unit where Basson and Ramsamy both have phones pressed to their ears. Basson's legs are crossed on top of his desk, Ramsamy is sitting up straight, notepad on his desk, pen in hand. Basson signs off and drops the phone into the cradle.

'Nothing so far. Brixton, Mayfair, Melville, Sophiatown: none of their missing persons fit our description,' Basson says, looking up at Majola.

'Sergeant? Anything your side?' Majola asks Ramsamy.

'It's taking forever to find and pull the dossiers on the database. I'm working my way forward from six months ago. But I think we'll have more luck if we contact the other station directors directly instead of the detectives. We simply have too many murders on the database. But it's Friday, so I doubt anyone's going to be at their desks after lunch.'

'Good idea.' Majola shrugs off his jacket and sits at his desk. He starts his computer with a sigh. 'Ancient piece of shit.' He tosses the mouse aside. 'Sergeant, can you please find the morgue's number in Germiston? If I have to wait for this thing, we're gonna be here till the end of days.'

Ramsamy nods, finds the number on his computer.

Majola paces in the corridor while he waits to be put through to the right person. He's never liked talking on the phone in front of other people. He checks his watch. It's still some time before they have to go see Dr Lubbe. It feels like forever before a voice comes on the line.

'Bester.' The abruptness of the voice makes Majola start.

'Dr Bester. Captain Majola from Serious and Violent Crimes. Can you spare a moment?'

'Yes, I can talk.'

'It's related to a case we're investigating. I need to know if there are any similarities to a case of yours.'

'I'm listening.'

'Have you recently seen a victim, a young black woman, who appears to have been raped and lacerated with a blunt object? With a series of cuts on her back. Specifically, numbers and letters?'

Bester takes a moment to think. 'Rapes are very common. Attacks and molestation too. But wait, there was this one ...'

Majola tightens his grip on the phone.

'Couple of months ago. Young girl. Naked as the day she was born. The killer did serious damage to her lower body. I thought he might have used a broomstick. She bled to death. But she had these marks on her back. It looked like a date.'

'Three months ago?' Majola asks.

'More or less. There was another thing. There were burns all over her torso. Her breasts, to be specific.'

Fuck. It's him.

'Can I come and pick up the report right away?' Majola asks.

'I'm in the middle of an autopsy. Can you give me an hour? I'll scan the report and mail it to you.' Majola recites his email address to him. 'Tell me, does this have anything to do with the girl on the M1 today? I heard about it on the news.'

'It's still a bit early to tell, but let's hope not. Oh, and another thing, you don't happen to remember who the investigating officer was?'

'Sergeant Ntatane, if I remember correctly. We spent hours talking about the girl.'

'Thank you, Doctor.'

'No problem. I'll get that report to you in a bit. Good day Captain.'

Majola slips the phone into his pocket and goes back into the office.

'What does the pathologist have?' asks Basson.

'Dr Lubbe was right. Cuts on the back. Burns on the chest.'

'Fuck it. That can't be coincidence. Welcome to Serial Killer Central.'

'He'll send the report in an hour. We can only hope.' Majola checks his watch again.

'Who took the case at Orange Farm?' Basson asks.

'Ntatane.'

'That clown they caught using the police van as a taxi?'

'It can only be him,' says Majola, looking at his messages again.

Basson gets up, phone in hand. 'I'll call him, ask him to send that report immediately. You go. Go find out what Lizanne wants. I can see it's bothering you. We'll keep going here. If I don't get anywhere with Ntatane, you can go pick up the docket. I'll make sure Head Girl doesn't lose her shit.'

Ramsamy looks up sharply.

'Careful now, you don't want Head Girl to bitch-slap you,' Majola jokes, looking at Ramsamy.

'I know Hindi Karate, brother. And this is Joziwood, not Bollywood,' says Basson.

Ramsamy snorts and shakes his head.

'Okay, I'll see you guys later. Keep me posted about that dossier.' Majola takes his jacket and car keys and walks out into the cold.

Majola notices the reinforced railings as he drives across the Westdene Dam bridge. He was young when it happened, but he can still remember that every station on television – well, all three of them – covered the incident. Auntie Anne cried when they showed the crane lifting the yellow double-decker bus from the water, and the row of small bodies covered in sheets.

He casts his eye over the houses of Westdene, most of them dating back to the 1930s, all wooden floors and steel ceilings. He actually considered buying here at one point, before he decided on the apartment in Melville. He wanted a more upbeat environment, something more modern. He doesn't get white people's love of old things. Antique shops. Auctions for things well past their expiration date. Nostalgia.

Last week the uniforms had to come here to clean out a house where something like forty immigrants had settled. People buy the houses and then rent them out under the pretence of 'student accommodation'. Then dozens of people move in, forced to share two bathrooms. The neighbours start complaining, mostly actors and artists who bought here years ago, irate at the noise and the smell. But next week the same happens at another house, or the people just move back in. Everywhere you look you see the *For Sale* signs.

Still, Westdene has always been a melting pot of different people. Gays, interracial marriages, corporates and arty types. It's an interesting place: people here talk about good streets, not good neighbourhoods. And the people on these streets are ready and vigilant, with neighbourhood-watch groups on WhatsApp. Everyone's got everyone else on speed dial, that kind of thing. They're quick to mete out community justice before the police arrive.

Majola stops at the gates to the Rosewood Retirement Village, next to Westdene's leisure centre in Dover Street. The complex comprises twenty units, spread over six plots. The gardens are all well kept, even if all the grass died after the frost set in with the last cold front. The guard approaches with a clip-board and smiles when he sees it's Majola.

'Long time,' he says amicably.

Majola nods and greets him. Captain Daan Loots, or, as everyone calls him, Kappie, has been living here for two years, after being declared unfit for service by the SAPS. The report said that he suffered from serious post-traumatic stress disorder.

Majola only once saw him suffer an episode, just before he retired. It wasn't pretty. Kappie drew his firearm on an old black man crossing the road at a red light in Brixton. Majola stopped him just before he fired the shot. Something had gone wrong. Seriously wrong. There was something in his eyes, something dark and forbidding. He was talking strangely, as if with a different voice, and he didn't recognise Majola. Afterwards, when he had calmed down, he couldn't remember any of it.

Majola pulls up behind Lizanne's red Conquest under the awning. As he walks across the shrivelled grass, he sees her inside, getting ready to leave the apartment. She draws the curtains, then pulls the sliding door shut behind her. She starts when she sees Majola.

'You jumped. What, you think I look like a tsotsi these days?' Majola jokes.

Lizanne relaxes and smiles. 'Well, with that black gangster coat of yours, you could easily pass as one.'

Majola hugs her tightly. 'Where's Kappie?'

'He's taking a nap. The nurse gave him something to help him sleep.'

'What happened this morning?' Majola asks, concerned.

'Let's go sit in the garden, get some sun while we can; I can spare a bit of time,' Lizanne says. She jerks a thumb over her shoulder. 'That gloomy grey-beard doesn't believe in heaters. It's flippin' freezing in there.'

They go to the green wire chairs and table beside the cement bird-bath. Two sparrows fly off as Majola pulls a chair out for Lizanne, then sits down. The metal of the chair is cold against his hands. Lizanne still has her blue nurse's uniform on under a thick white sweater. Her blonde hair is pulled back into a ponytail. She looks tired; he can see faint traces of bags under her eyes through her makeup. Being the theatre nurse for a neurosurgeon has its challenges. Still, she's a good-looking woman.

Lizanne wraps her sweater more tightly around herself. 'These past few weeks have been so good. But this morning the nurse calls me to say that he's broken all the crockery in the apartment, that he's swearing like a sailor. Talk-ing strangely about Casspirs and dogs. Kept calling the nurse a stupid mei— Sorry, you know what I mean.'

'I do, and don't apologise. Has his psychologist been here yet?'

Lizanne shakes her head. 'Nope. He's off hunting with friends for the week-end. You know how it is here. In the winters he goes off hunting every chance he gets.'

Majola watches the sparrows, which have returned to the edge of the bird-bath. They don't seem to mind the cold at all.

'Is he still taking his pills?'

'The nurse says he does, says she always checks that he takes them after dinner. I don't get it. He hasn't had an episode in over a month. Just two weeks ago the psychologist said that the medication and the treatments seemed to be working. Now they're probably going to increase the dose. And the pills upset his stomach. And what if they start to think that he's a danger to the other old people? What if they want him out of here?' Lizanne's brow knots as she talks.

'The psychologist told me about a hypnotherapy session they had. Apparently, he opened up a bit. But he still only spoke of times long ago, of when he was a young officer. I can't remember much from that time; I was too young. Has he ever spoken to you about all that? You know, the apartheid stuff? All I can remember is that he wore a uniform back then. And that some nights he smelled of smoke and petrol when he came home.'

Majola looks at Lizanne, slowly shakes his head. 'Not a lot. He always talked more about his days as a detective. The years before that are a state secret. Sometimes I wonder if the old guard maybe took some kind of oath never to talk about it. I got the feeling he carried shame with him, perhaps because I'm a darky.'

Lizanne smiles.

'Once or twice, though, he said, "Those days are over – this is a new country with new problems. And we can help lift the burden by taking out the rubbish". I think the police frustrated him a lot after the transition. The discipline that slowly degraded. The corruption. Or maybe it was the fact that he knew he would never be promoted again. I never asked him,' Majola says, shaking his head.

'It's hard for me to see him like this,' he continues. 'He was the one who turned me into a detective. At first, he was pretty sceptical of his new colleague. But after four months it wasn't "Warrant Officer Majola" any more; it became "young man". "Young man, I'll carve a sharp detective out of you yet, just watch me." "Young man, this isn't csi, this is csd – Crime Scene Desperation," he always joked.'

Lizanne wipes a tear from her cheek.

Majola squeezes her hand. 'But when he was on a case, when he smelled blood, the wolf in him came out. I still remember the black hardcover notebook with the red binding. Some of the cases he ended up solving were the ones no one else wanted to take. Your dad was a hard-ass – he kept at it, relentlessly, until he found the one clue that pulled all the others together. "It's in the detail, young man. Try to see the bigger picture." He went back to old scenes over and over again. He would drop to one knee and just look at everything again, run through it all one more time. He taught me about legwork. Talk to everyone. Leave your contact details. There are no stupid questions you can ask a witness. Think like the murderer. Everyone makes mistakes. Everyone screws up. It's our job to see where they fucked up.'

Majola looks at Lizanne. 'Sorry. Are you okay? I'm going on and on.'

She nods. 'It's okay. It's hard for me too. I remember him very differently. I sometimes wish my mom was still alive. She would have been able to tell me more. I do remember them arguing a lot in those days. I sometimes fell asleep on her lap on the couch, where we'd sit waiting for him to come home. She said he'd been a much gentler soul when she'd met him.'

An old woman in a pink dressing gown comes walking out of her apartment with some bread in her hand. She doesn't look at the two of them as she shuffles past to the lawn some fifteen metres away from the wire table and chairs.

'Tweet, tweet, tweet,' she calls shrilly.

Lizanne smiles.

The two sparrows in the bird-bath flap over to her. They bob closer to the crumbs she's dropping, but get chased off by a big pigeon.

'Hey, you beast!' the old lady cries. 'Shoo, shoo, you little shit.'

Despite her protestations, the pigeon continues to peck at the crumbs as the sparrows watch.

Lizanne goes on, her eyes on the pigeon. 'Just before my mom died, I saw him sit outside in the garden one day, next to the yesterday-today-and-tomorrow bush he loved so much. He had a glass of brandy with him. By that point my mom was in a real bad way, busy with the chemo and stuff. I overheard him say, "Talk, you dog. Or do you want more of the tube? You saw what I did to your friend." So I took him to his room. Some nights he would stand by the living-room window, then he would say to Mom, "Can you see them, Annatjie? Do you hear them? They're coming for me, the bastards. They're coming to kill us.""

For a moment all is quiet. 'That was tough for my mom. She wanted to help, but wasn't in any condition to. *He* was the one who should have been helping *her*. I did what I could, which wasn't much. It got better when he stopped drinking. And joined that happy-clappy church. Luckily that madness didn't last. His conversion was all he talked about for a while there.'

The old woman in pink is surrounded by birds. The pigeons are still getting most of the crumbs, to her great frustration.

'I'm glad he quit the drinking,' Majola says after a while. 'I remember, towards the end, he could barely see a shift through before hitting the bar. Sometimes you could smell the alcohol on him in the morning. But I never asked; I knew about your mom's illness. It wasn't my place. I just heard the stories from the old days. Especially the stuff that went down at Brixton Robbery Homicide and the Security Branch – things got out of control there, if the stories are true. To be fair, the whole country was out of control at that point.'

Majola checks his phone on the table. He wonders how Ramsamy is doing.

'So how are things going with the booze? You still on the water wagon?' Lizanne asks him gently.

'The what?'

Lizanne smiles. 'Are you still sober? Still haven't had a drink?'

Majola shifts in his chair, uncomfortable for a moment. 'It's going well. I haven't had a drink in 250 days. Or nearly 250 days. I still watch a lot of movies when I'm off duty, and besides that I'm mostly just on duty. I need to get around to my mom and sister more often; I haven't been there in a while.' Majola hesitates for a second. 'Sometimes it gets hard. This morning we had a scene … really rattled my cage. Not far from here, near the M1.'

'Shit, were you there?' Lizanne asks. 'One of the doctors mentioned the traffic before I got off shift, said the M1 was a madhouse. He thought there was an accident somewhere.'

'If only it was an accident. It's stuff like that, days like today, that always had me hitting the bottle hard. It was all that helped. Of course, now I realise it just made everything so much worse.'

'I'll invite you to dinner some time. I haven't cooked for two in a while,' Lizanne says. 'When you live by yourself, you just live off two-minute noodles.'

Majola laughs. 'Ja, that would be lekker. Lekker boerekos. With red grape juice instead of wine.' Lizanne laughs with him.

'Listen, I have to hit the road. I'm sitting here like I'm on holiday,' Majola says, as he gets up slowly and picks up his phone. 'I'll try to come by again tomorrow if I can find a few minutes. If he wakes up, tell him I was here.'

Lizanne gets up. 'I will. I'm going to stick around for a while. I was heading home but it's better if I'm here when he wakes up. Maybe I'll see you tomorrow. I'll see what the operating schedule looks like.'

The old woman comes walking up to them. She looks highly pissed off. Her pink dressing gown is billowing behind her like a sail, her slip-ons slapping at her heels.

'Tata, do you see how those pigeons steal the crumbs? I'm going to kill them. Every last one. I'll get some Two Step. That'll do it. It kills everything. We always used it on the farm; put it in a wine bottle for those fokkertjies who stole the sheep. They take two steps, and then they die.'

Majola's jaw drops. 'What's that, Auntie?'

'Auntie?' Her hand shoots to her breast, her eyes widen. She turns to Lizanne. 'What happened to "Missus"? What is happening to this country, girly? If your dad could see you now. Shame on you!'

Lizanne wants to say something but the old lady is already bustling back to her apartment. Majola motions for Lizanne to let it go.

'Your dad's nothing on her. I think they should rather be worried that *she* poisons the whole bloody complex.'

Lizanne chokes back her laughter.

Majola takes out his phone and checks the messages. Basson has made pro-gress with Orange Farm: the dossiers have been faxed over.

Across the lawn, in the street, he can see a young woman walking with a pram. Majola thinks of the girl on the bridge. Her unborn child. Things could have been so different for her. But this city has a habit of cutting futures short. Cutting lives down. You don't even need to take Two Step.

Warrant Officer Jason Basson is waiting outside the station when Majola ar-rives, cigarette in one hand, brown folder in the other. Majola immediately gets his hopes up that these are the reports by Bester and Ntatane. Basson takes one last drag before flicking his cigarette aside.

He looks tense. It's not required that detectives should be present at post-mortems, but Majola prefers to go. Another thing Kappie taught him. It makes the investigation feel tangible, real, personal. If you can see the body yourself, see the damage that was done first hand, a fire is lit inside you to find whoever did it. That's how it feels to him.

'Is this the report from Bester?' Majola asks Basson as he gets into the car.

'Yes, just came through. Ntatane's was also quick. Maybe he didn't have any passengers to drive around today.'

'What do you see?' asks Majola.

'Brother, you're gonna have to give me some time to read it first. And I throw up if I read in the car,' Basson replies.

'Heard anything from the other branches yet?'

'We're struggling to reach them; the detectives are all out working. When I left, Ramsamy was looking excited about something. He said he would call if he hit the jackpot.'

'Is everyone on the team going to be at the meeting tonight?'

'Yes. Davids says you're fucking with his date night. Why do I suddenly feel like your secretary?'

Majola laughs. 'Thanks for my messages, Miss Basson. Tell Davids he can always call the escort agency again tomorrow.'

Basson snorts and rolls his eyes.

Majola is glad Dr Lubbe has fast-tracked this autopsy. There are dozens of other cases that were higher on his list. He appreciates that the pathologist wants to discuss the case with them instead of just handing them his report. He is, nevertheless, concerned. What does Lubbe want to show them? This morn-ing's been heavy enough; clearly it's affected Basson too.

He doesn't always get what drives Basson. Majola has noticed how he's more proactive when the victim is white, especially a woman or a child, as if seized by a newfound impatience to solve the case. He's always been a bit of a tough nut. Sometimes he looks jaded, dulled by the work; at others he's all vim and vigour. He can't hold it against Basson, though; his dad was known to have been a vehement racist. With a background like that, a son often struggles to kick off the father's shoes.

The Johannesburg morgue and the forensic pathology services are in Braamfontein, just a few kilometres from Johannesburg Central. Majola sighs and opens a window. Some afternoons, those few kilometres can feel like a trip to Durban. Everyone has the same intention: leave early to avoid the traffic. But it's just as chaotic as every other day, if not more so.

In this grey building, about twenty autopsies are performed by government pathologists every week, double that of nearly any other morgue in South Africa. Except for Hillbrow. And that doesn't include victims from car accidents, suicides or back-street abortions either.

The worst, and the busiest, is the morgue in Hillbrow. There, up to eighteen bodies can show up in a single day. He read somewhere that in 2015 they handled over 3 000 bodies. Beside the fact that it's not even safe for the police in that area, that statistic really murders the mood.

Majola remembers one morning at the Hillbrow Mortuary very clearly. At some point he couldn't stand it, and had to leave the building to go vomit in the street. The industrial antiseptic they use in morgues smells bad, but in Hillbrow it's worse. The smell of death permeates everything, from the chipped and flaking paint on the walls to the filthy grooves of the dull, tiled floors. It's as if God has forsaken the dead, leaving them there to rot. He's already reaped his souls. The remains he leaves for the police and the pathologists. Braamfontein is somewhat better: dishevelled but not in complete disrepair. And Dr Lubbe fortunately prefers this laboratory to those in Germiston and Hillbrow.

The white Corolla enters the virtually abandoned parking lot, parks between Dr Lubbe's bakkie with the red Lions sticker on the back and a white bakkie with a yellow stripe with the words *Forensic Pathology Services* running down its side. Dr Lubbe is smoking in a patch of sunlight in a corner of the parking lot. He waves when he sees the detectives. Majola climbs out of the car.

'I see the good doctor is working on his tan?' Basson jokes as he gets out.

Dr Lubbe tips the ash to the ground beside his theatre shoes, which he hadn't removed on leaving the building. 'Not nearly enough sunlight. Besides, my face is red enough from all the cheap booze.'

Basson also lights a cigarette.

'You know, this city has a ton of history,' says Lubbe, looking around him. 'Not far from here, just across the street there, is where they built Johannesburg's first hospital. Opened in 1886. Only three rooms. The first patient was a miner who'd contracted typhoid. He died shortly after being admitted. The second patient was also a miner, who' taken a serious tumble down the No 2 Reef in Doornfontein. Miners have always had a pretty shitty time.'

'How do you know all this stuff, Doc?' Basson asks as he takes another drag.

'Internet, boetie, internet. If you click around a bit, you'll see it's not all just Asian porn.'

Basson laughs. 'Asians, you say?'

Majola claps a hand on Basson's shoulder. 'Last time I checked his phone he was into Voortrekkers Gone Wild.'

Basson shakes his head. 'Once they take off those bonnets, brother, the beast is unleashed.'

They laugh, until Dr Lubbe breaks into a coughing fit.

'Listen, boys.' He interrupts himself with a final cough. 'Let's wrap this up. Otherwise my wife certainly won't take off her bonnet tonight.'

As they approach the building, Dr Lubbe's assistant Mbalula comes walking out, dressed in scrubs.

'Mbalula, go get the girl from this morning from the fridge,' Dr Lubbe instructs. 'When you're done, you can take off for the day.' He turns to the others. 'You guys go put on the outfits. I'll see you inside.'

The detectives quickly sign the register, before donning boots and rubber coveralls in the next room.

'It's probably too early to ask if someone called to report the girl missing,' Dr Lubbe says as he enters the room. 'Although I saw *News24* posted something about it on their Facebook page.'

Majola nods. 'Warrant Basson made the inquiries this morning. Though I think the chances are good that they'll start asking questions tomorrow. Dr Bester confirmed our suspicions: it looks like she's not the only one.'

'He did?' Dr Lubbe asks, surprise registering in his voice.

'Yeah. His report's in the car. We're going to check it over once we're done here.'

'Did he say anything about electrocution?'

'Electrocution? Like from a wall socket?' Basson asks.

'Close, but it's not that simple.' A sombre expression crosses the doctor's face.

The dull yellow glow of the fluorescents and the smell of antiseptics lead them down the corridor to the dissection theatre. The walls need to be painted, as does the ceiling. Staff have made an admirable attempt to keep the floors clean, but entropy is slowly taking over the place. Still, it looks like a Sun City hotel room compared to the Hillbrow morgue, Majola thinks.

Dr Lubbe stands at the steel table, clipboard in hand, the girl lying before him on her back. His face is pulled into a deep frown. 'Listen, I know you guys choose to be here for the autopsies. But I wanted to get this one done earlier so that I could go home. I did call,' he offers by way of apology. 'The last few weeks have been … rough. But I wanted to show you this in person, so that you understand what we're dealing with here. So, I'm going to run through the process again. Especially the scanning. This is not an open-and-shut case, gentlemen.'

Majola looks at the girl on the table. It all appears different this time. It's because they're doing it backwards. She's already been washed, closed up; her insides have already been inspected and returned to her. Stitches run from her pubic bone to her suprasternal notch, branching off to both shoulders.

Basson steps closer. 'So, let's hear it,' he says.

Dr Lubbe's tone is suddenly serious, none of the jocularity of earlier.

'This fucker is thorough. Nothing under her nails, no hair or semen, nothing.' He pauses. 'Maybe I should get something out of the way first. Captain, you asked me if she was dead when the foetus fell.'

'I did,' Majola nods.

'I figured everyone was freaked out enough this morning,' Dr Lubbe goes on, 'so I decided to wait.'

Dr Lubbe pauses, seems to be composing himself, before he goes on. 'Captain, a woman has to be alive to give birth. A foetus will not just fall out of her. He must have torn loose the umbilical cord with the object. She was assaulted so badly that her left hip was dislocated. She was not yet dead when he tied her up. She was likely unconscious when she went into labour. He must have thought she was dead – the bastard wouldn't have left her there if he knew she was still alive. If someone had found her in time, she would have talked.'

'Mother-fucker ...' Basson says, nearly inaudibly.

'She bled to death, gentlemen. Tied to that bridge.'

Majola shakes his head.

'So, here's my theory,' the doctor continues. 'The injuries were caused by a blunt object. Possibly a broomstick. During this part, her waters broke. She would then have gone into labour. And the other injuries, which I'll get to in a moment, were inflicted elsewhere.'

Dr Lubbe takes a step to his right, so that he is standing beside her lower body.

'The amount of violence he used is astonishing. There are contusions and lacerations on her thighs and pubis. The object penetrated her cervix; there's a hole in her bladder. Her perineum has been torn and her rectum perforated. The list, I'm afraid, goes on.'

Basson is looking pale. 'And the foetus? Did you discover anything there?'

'The foetus was male. About six months old.'

Majola is glad he is talking about it as a foetus and not as a baby. 'There was a dent in the foetus's skull which could have come from the object. But it's hard to say because of the fall. See, the head could possibly have been facing down if she had gone into labour. In the way of the blunt object.'

Majola can't hide his disgust any more. He's seen a lot. Might already have seen too much. But this monster doesn't belong here. He belongs in hell. Where he came from.

The whole scene feels off. As if he's slipped into unreality. Maybe it's because Mbalula isn't there with his flashing camera, which always brings him back to reality, flash by flash by flash.

'What about the abrasions?' Basson asks.

Dr Lubbe checks the notes he has pinned to the board, then lifts her left arm.

'On both wrists and ankles. Also on the inside of her knees. But that wasn't a rope; it looks more like a steel clamp. The diameter is about five centimetres. It's the same for the wrists and ankles. There is, however, a thinner line of bruising on her neck. She was prone, lying down, and her legs were spread wide when he started ramming the blunt object … See, if she was sitting, he wouldn't have penetrated as easily. The vaginal canal curves upwards.

'You remember I mentioned the possibility of electrocution?'

Basson nods.

'I was correct. The marks on both breasts indicate the presence of clamps.'

The pathologist points to her nipples with his pen. 'Crocodile clamps, to be precise, like those you'd use to charge a car battery. The internal examination indicated damage to the adipose tissue around her breasts, which is characteristic of high-current electric shock. Have you ever heard the term "parrilla"?'

Both detectives shake their heads.

'It's basically a Spanish word for braai. Or barbecue. In South American countries, they used it as a torture method. The word refers to the steel frame on which the victims to be tortured are placed – almost like a chop on a grid, to make it a little more local.'

Dr Lubbe walks away from the table and studies his notes. 'What I think happened was that the torturer placed the clamps on her breasts and administered the shocks using electrodes. You can control the intensity of the current with a power box. The electrodes would be connected to either a wall plug or a car battery. You choose the most sensitive parts of the body, even the clitoris if the victim is a woman. The pain is excruciating; the victim's bones can break from the contractions.'

'Did it cause her death?' Majola asks.

'No, it doesn't look like it. When I checked her heart, the muscle showed signs of ventricular fibrillation.'

'Which means?' asks Basson.

'That's basically the fast, uncontrollable quivering of the heart muscle. But if that caused her death, she wouldn't have gone into labour on the bridge. I'm just struggling to figure out why the son of a bitch would have wanted to electrocute and cripple her. Come, follow me for a moment.'

Majola flashes a look at Basson. Surely this can't get any worse, they both seem to be thinking. Dr Lubbe leads them to the room where the scanning is done. He switches on the light and walks to a computer. He wiggles his mouse and the screen lights up. After he has logged in, an x-ray immediately pops up on the screen.

'As you can see here, the ulna is broken in both her right and left forearms. That must have been as a result of the electrocution. She must have tried to pull free, but the clamps wouldn't give.'

He clicks to another x-ray. 'This is the left hip. You can see how it's broken from the trauma by the blunt object.'

Dr Lubbe turns to the detectives. 'Do you see why I asked you to come over? This guy had fun doing this to her. And he had time.'

Majola turns and looks back to the room where the body is still lying on the table.

'And the cuts on her back?'

The doctor walks past. 'Come and see.'

'Well, one thing's for sure,' says Basson. 'My braai plans for the night are fucked. I will never look at my Weber in the same way again. Every time I toss some ribs on the grill, I'm going to be thinking of parralla.'

'Parrilla,' Dr Lubbe corrects him, with the ghost of a smile. 'Nah, detective, nothing stops me from braaiing.'

The three men are back at the table. Basson pats his pockets, probably to check if his cigarettes are still there.

Dr Lubbe lifts and turns the girl so that they can clearly see the cuts covering her back and sides.

'The cuts were made with a thin, sharp blade, most likely a scalpel. More than that I can't say; I'll have to see if the swabs picked up anything. The numbers on her back read "ON 345061986", with "UMHA 2321" carved beneath that. I have no idea what that can be; you'll have to figure that out. It does look like there's a space after the first two letters of the top row, if that helps.'

Majola stands closer. 'Can it be a date? June 1986?'

'What about a docket number?' Basson asks.

'No, you're grasping at straws. Docket numbers start with "CR" or "IR" for "crime register" or "incident register". Maybe part of an ID number? Her ID number?' Majola says.

Dr Lubbe shakes his head. 'That would make her over thirty. This girl isn't older than 23. It could be anything. Lotto numbers. A date that has significance for the killer. For all we know it's the number on his vest from when he ran the fucking Comrades.'

'And the sequence at the bottom?' Basson asks.

'Can't make head or tail of that either. UMHA has to be an acronym of some sort. Maybe the fucker spelled "ouma" wrong. Hell if I know.'

Dr Lubbe lowers the girl again.

'I wouldn't focus on the numbers and letters if I were you, though. I'd focus on the time of her death.'

Majola and Basson perk up.

'The woman who reported the girl: the call came in around 05:30, right?'

Majola nods in agreement.

'It was 05:45, to be precise,' Basson confirms.

'According to the formula we use, which relies on the rate at which the body temperature of a dead body drops, she died somewhere between 04:00 and

05:30, if we keep in mind the cold morning we've had. To my mind, that means the son of a bitch must have been torturing her close to the scene of the crime.'

'But couldn't he have strung her up at three?'

'No fucking chance. Not with her injuries. She wasn't alive for more than thirty minutes after he hung her there. If I were you, I would start looking in the city. Even Fairlands, Brixton, maybe Mayfair. He definitely didn't drive through from Springs.'

Basson shakes his head. 'He must have driven her around first. No one's getting into a taxi at three in the morning. This kind of torture could have taken hours. Or he waited before he got started.'

'Not just an ugly face, Detective,' the doctor jokes. 'You've got a point there.'

The pathologist prepares to move the gurney with the body. Lubbe looks up. 'There's something else that's bothering me. Let's say he lives in the city. In an apartment, or a smallish house. Wouldn't someone have seen something? Heard something? She would have kicked up an enormous racket. The only place to pull off something like this is on a farm or a large plot of land. Somewhere remote. Where there's no one around.'

The detectives keep their eyes on the girl as she is wheeled off.

Majola has just tied his laces when his phone rings. Basson is waiting at the door to the changing room, an unlit cigarette already hanging from his mouth.

'Yes, Sergeant Ramsamy.'

Basson points at the cigarette, then at the door, before walking down the corridor.

It's cold outside the morgue, which makes Basson think of his dad. He always said, 'The coldest time of day is before sunrise and before sunset.' Every year, like clockwork, he would also announce, 'Today is the day the season changes. It's the longest night and the shortest day. Now you know, my boy, summer is on its way.' The solstice had been earlier this week.

He tries to remember as much as he can of what his dad taught him. Tries to pass some of it on to Nonnie. That's one way to keep him alive. Because he's not doing a terrific job of stepping out from under his dad's shadow as a policeman.

Basson watches the cars driving past the building, people who left the office after five, or those who stopped for a quick beer after work.

He and Reza had done the same thing a few times. Before they went to her apartment in Randburg.

Dr Lubbe disturbs his musings when he lights a cigarette and exhales the smoke slowly, staring into the distance. He is still in his rubber coveralls.

'This city is actually quite beautiful. Especially at night.'

Basson is still staring at the passing cars. 'Yeah. A pity all the sick motherfuckers come crawling out of their holes at night though.'

'Are you still going to braai tonight?'

Basson shakes his head slowly. 'Nah, Doc. I'll stop to pick up some fish and chips from that Chinaman at Cresta. The last thing I want to see right now is a grill. How that Chinaman is still so fucking cheap I don't—'

The heavy glass door opens behind them and they turn in unison. Majola comes out, phone still in his hand. He doesn't look at them.

'And?' Basson asks.

'You were right, Doctor. Sebokeng, Alexandra, Daveyton, Diepsloot and Thokoza.'

'And that's not counting Orange Farm, which is still waiting in the car.' Basson sighs deeply.

'Exactly. The whole of fucking Gauteng. That's not even all the satellite stations. Six open cases, stretching over a year. Seven if you add today's murder. All of them black girls between the ages of eighteen and twenty-four. Signs of electrocution on some, but all of them have signs of sexual assault with a blunt object. And cuts on their backs.'

Dr Lubbe whistles through his teeth. Basson listens attentively.

'Were they ... were they also pregnant?' Basson asks, carefully.

'Not according to Ramsamy.' Basson looks relieved. 'This looks like the only one at present. We'll have to work through the reports carefully tonight and tomorrow. Ramsamy just checked the basics, focusing on cause of death and the numbers and letters on the backs. But it's highly unlikely that these aren't related incidents.'

'Why are we only hearing about this now?' Basson wants to know.

'You know how it goes in the townships. Murders like this aren't new or newsworthy,' Majola answers.

'But why is this one different? Why hang her from one of the busiest highways in the city? Why not stick to the townships?' Basson steps on his cigarette butt.

Dr Lubbe takes another drag of his cigarette before addressing Basson directly. 'He's getting impatient. He wanted you to find her. Maybe he figured the detectives in the townships were too slow, useless.'

Majola looks at the two men. He can't shake his irritation at the fact that the pathologist keeps addressing Basson when he has something to say. It also pisses him off that he thinks all the township detectives are useless. They might be few in number, but at least they're there.

'And there goes my theory that he lives in the city, or close to this morning's scene. Your tickets to the shit show have been booked, gentlemen.'

Basson looks dejected at the new revelations; his second cigarette is lit and the tip glows brightly under the fluorescents on the morgue's veranda. Majola walks to the Corolla, putting numbers into his phone.

'I told Ramsamy to go around to the other stations first thing in the morning to pick up all the dockets that weren't faxed through. At least two of them were already loaded onto the central database. The rest were faxed or emailed this afternoon. Maybe he'll bring back more info from the other stations, but it's a Saturday, so I doubt it. Maybe Monday.'

Dr Lubbe walks to the door. 'Well, I don't want to keep you from your work any longer, gentlemen. And I've got to tjaila for the day.'

'Thanks, Doc,' says Basson.

'No worries, boys. I'll go get the report. Mbalula has already printed the photos.'

Majola is making a call, and doesn't see the doctor enter the building.

'Fuck,' Majola curses, 'now Radebe's phone is off.'

Basson smiles. 'What are you worried about? You'll see him tomorrow, right?'

'I'm trying not to give him more reason to shit all over me tomorrow.'

The parking lot at Johannesburg Central is quieter than usual as most of the personnel have left for the day. Majola stops the white Corolla next to a police bakkie. That's one of the perks of making captain – no one bats an eyelid if you want to take a police vehicle home. No need to wear out your own car. Although Majola hasn't taken his old BMW for a spin in a while; it doesn't do it good to stand idle for so long.

Ramsamy's silver Honda with the low-profile tyres is there too; hopefully he's busy prepping the ops room for the meeting.

'Fucking curry-muncher car,' Basson mumbles under his breath when he sees the Honda.

Ramsamy might get on Basson's nerves, but he can't fault him on his dedication. He's told Ramsamy the same, that he wished more of the officers had his passion for the job. There are still good people on the force, but in this city they're scarce. Maybe things are better in Cape Town and Durban.

A sliver of light emanates from the ops room. Majola can hear Davids laughing. He opens the door and walks in, Basson following him. Sergeant Ramsamy is busy distributing stapled stacks of paper, copies of the dossiers that were sent over by the other branches.

'Evening, everyone,' Majola says. The team greet him. Everyone's here except for Warrant Officer Mbatho. He's not surprised.

Sergeant Rikhotso is reading through one of the dossiers. With twenty-five years of service behind him, he's the oldest member on the task force. Rikhotso sweated bullets under the old regime with commanders who didn't want to see black skins donning blue uniforms. But he's streetwise and dedicated. And he's got patience unequalled by anyone else on the team. He's an old bachelor; it seems his only love in life is soccer.

Warrant Officer Davids and Pieter Mitchell from IT are watching something on a laptop. Ramsamy starts and looks up.

'Did you think it was the ghost of Verwoerd coming to get you?'

Ramsamy laughs. 'Evening, Captain. Hell, sir, you've heard the stories about this building. The voices on the ninth floor, the sounds of people screaming or crying late at night. And this case creeps me out enough as is.' Ramsamy's expression turns serious. 'I was going to tell you. Katlehong also faxed through their documents. Another one. With yesterday's girl, that puts us at eight so far.'

Majola shakes his head, even though he expected this.

'It's too much of a coincidence. These cases have to be connected,' Ramsamy continues. 'Cuts on the back. Naked. Sexually abused. I'm sure everyone's realised at this point, but we've got a serial killer on our hands. But assumption is the mother of all fu—, you know what I mean, Captain.'

'I hear you, Sergeant. And yes, we'll have to go see for ourselves before we jump to conclusions. The girls might be connected to one other in some way.'

'Some of the dossiers are incomplete. And all of them are still open. Some of the photos that were faxed through were very unclear too. They'll have to scan and email them, or we'll have to go and pick them up,' Ramsamy says.

'Did you find the woman who called in about the body on the M1?' Basson asks Ramsamy.

'Yeah. Didn't learn anything more than we got this morning. Just a whole rant about how unsafe she feels and how useless we are. And nothing useful came from the Metro trains. The only camera pointing in the direction of the crime scene has been bust for months.'

'Mbatho said she's on her way, stuck in traffic,' Davids says to no one in particular.

Majola doesn't reply. Everyone knows he's not happy with Mbatho's lacklustre work ethic.

'Let's get started. Sergeant Ramsamy, thanks for the copies of the dossiers. Can you get us a new map of Gauteng? There should be one somewhere in the storeroom.'

'Why don't we use Davids and Mbatho's map of the hijacking case on the wall? It looks brand new,' Basson says, looking at Davids.

'Fuck off. We don't just hang out in coffee shops all day long. A dead end is a dead end, my bru,' says Davids.

'Isn't that because you guys hang out in gay bars all day long?' Basson jokes.

Davids lifts a middle finger in Basson's direction. By the looks of his tailored suit and designer shoes, Davids could have just left an expensive restaurant in Sandton. Majola likes Davids. He left Cape Town for Gauteng because of a girl, just after Kappie retired. The City of Gold soon killed the relationship. Everyone suspects that he works as a private investigator on the side. That would explain the two phones he carries with him everywhere. And the new BMW 320i in the parking lot.

He's not the only police officer to do other work to supplement his income. A lot of them do stakeouts, usually a jealous husband or wife with some trust issues, third-party investigations for insurance companies, the acquisition of phone records, and the odd intimidation or two. It's so much easier when you can flash police identification.

Even if it is illegal, Majola doesn't interfere. Davids remains diligent in his actual work, even if the hijacking fiasco reached a dead end. And his colleague, Mbatho, is definitely holding him back. But it looks like he's figured out a way to manage her.

'I take it Ramsamy filled most of you in while we were in Braamfontein?' Majola asks. Everyone nods agreement.

'I'm just glad the other girls weren't pregnant too,' Pieter Mitchell adds. Again, all heads nod in grim agreement.

Mitchell is a typical IT guy, perhaps stereotypical. Checked shirt and jeans a few sizes too big for him. But he knows his stuff. Even pirated some rare films that Majola couldn't find himself.

The door opens and Warrant Officer Mbatho walks in. 'Sorry I'm late,' she mumbles before sitting down next to Sergeant Rikhotso.

'Sergeant Ramsamy, please give Warrant Mbatho a dossier.' Majola can barely keep the irritation from his voice.

He scans the papers in his hand and inhales slowly. 'Okay, everyone's got a copy of the case file. I'll work through Katlehong's tonight. Mitchell, you take Sebokeng; Davids, you take Alexandra.'

'Jesus, why am I the lucky winner who gets the rat farm?' Davids pleads melodramatically. Then it dawns on him that Majola's mother lives in Alexandra, and he swallows his smile. Majola ignores him and goes on.

'Basson, if you can take Diepsloot and yesterday's report, then Ramsamy takes Orange Farm and Sergeant Rikhotso takes Thokoza. Mbatho, you do Daveyton. Tomorrow morning I want to know everything you found.'

The team seem surprised that they can go home. But Majola knows they also have families whom they miss and who miss them. They'll have to work late into the night. He knows they'll be sharper tomorrow if they can work from home instead of being miserable in the cold ops room.

'What do you lot think is our first priority? What are we looking for?' Majola asks the room.

Ramsamy is first to speak. 'Eyewitnesses. Family and friends.'

'That's right, Sergeant. One of the most important things is to get clarity over the issue of the taxi or minibus. We can't base our whole investigation on the ramblings of a drunken sangoma. If you find something in the reports about eyewitnesses, you call me, I don't care what time it is.'

Silence. Everyone is busy taking notes.

'What else?' Majola asks.

'The numbers on the back,' Basson says.

'That's right. Mitchell, can you search the internet? Maybe something will pop up. An algorithm, maybe a date? Go see if something significant happened on those dates. Also look for the second row of letters, alone and in combination with the first row. If you find something in the reports that could explain the numbers, send it to Mitchell immediately. Don't wait till tomorrow. It's going to be a long night.' Majola takes a moment so his words can sink in.

'Mitchell, can you also check the internal database again? Maybe Ramsamy missed something. There could be more open cases like these. We can't assume the murderer has only been active for the past few months. We'll also have to send the pictures for handwriting analysis, even if only to determine if he's right- or left-handed. It's something.'

Mitchell drags his laptop closer and lifts up the screen.

'Warrant Mbatho, you'll do some research on the parrilla method mentioned in the autopsy report. Sergeant Rikhotso will go make copies for everyone.

'The what now?' Mbatho asks, surprised.

'The method of electrocution he used on the girl. It's all in the report.'

'Ah, okay.'

Basson smiles slightly and shakes his head.

'Contact all the stations close to the M1 scene again,' Majola continues. 'See if anyone has reported her missing at this point. Even if they don't know what happened, enough time has passed for people to have become concerned. A lot of people mistakenly believe you have to wait twenty-four hours before reporting someone missing because Hollywood told them so. Perhaps by now they've made the call.

'What else can you think of?' Majola asks. He is met with silence from the team.

'Tyre prints, fingerprints, correlations between crime scenes. See if anything overlaps between the routes and the crime scenes,' Basson chips in.

'Good stuff. That's how we'll catch this guy. One fingerprint. Then we can check the database. Maybe he has prior offences.'

'Can we assume it's a black man?' Mbatho asks.

'Well, if it's a taxi, then the chances are good. How many taxi drivers do you know who aren't black?' Majola asks.

Rikhotso laughs loudly. 'A mlungu driving black people around in a taxi. Can you imagine?'

'Just remember,' Majola interjects, 'at this point we don't know if it's a taxi or just an ordinary minibus. We're speculating. By tomorrow we should have a better idea. I want your reports by tomorrow morning. Summarise everything you find, then we'll compare notes. Colleagues, this case takes priority over all others. Colonel Radebe wants a suspect. Use all the resources at your disposal. Let's see how far we can get tonight.'

'And the media?' Davids asks.

'Stay away from them for now. I don't think they can help at this point. Maybe later when we have a profile or a sketch to show the public. With this last victim he clearly made a statement. To him this is a game. He leaves clues. He wants us to chase him, to catch him. The devil is in the detail, so pay attention to these dossiers. And don't just assume we've got a serial killer here – speak to everyone. Maybe it's an ex-boyfriend, a teacher, whatever. Maybe they were all in the same netball team. Take the dossiers home, or work here; I don't care. As long as I get my reports bright and early. I'll see you at morning parade.'

The team all sit back down and start paging through their dossiers. Rikhotso gets up and takes the autopsy report. Davids is preparing to leave.

'Kappie taught you well: "the devil is in the detail". Or did you get that from a movie?' Basson asks Majola under his breath. He smiles. 'Can't we throw Mbatho on the parrilla grill?' He takes out a cigarette.

Majola shakes his head and they walk out together. 'God knows that woman is going to drive me back to drinking. Uyavilapha, man.'

'Huh?'

'Lazy one, that woman.'

3

Basson is waiting impatiently for the security guard in his little booth to open the gates to the apartment block. Delia took his remote again after forgetting hers at work yesterday. The security guards at Greenbriar in Parkwood, the old building where they have an apartment, always greet him cheerily. Probably because they know he's a cop. Once he had to come and pick something up in passing and pulled in with his police vehicle. One of the showy Audi A4s with the modern lights on the roof. As he passed the gate, he stepped on the gas to make the wheels spin. Left the guard with eyes wide.

His dad bought the two-bedroom apartment back in the Sixties, when it was still relatively affordable to live in Parkwood, especially in an apartment. In those days a policeman would never have been able to afford a house in this area. Hell, today a policeman can't even afford an apartment. Except if you have some money coming in on the side.

He only ever crossed the line once. Okay, twice. When he was still new to the force, when he still wore a uniform, one night he chased a suspect across an open stretch of field in Ferndale. The guy dropped his bag. In it Basson found a laptop. The guy was so far ahead that a smoker like him, even young as he was then, would never have been able to catch him anyway. He didn't declare the laptop, and the owners never reported it stolen.

The other time was more serious.

It happened about two years ago. One of his informants, a wheeler and drug dealer around the city, Nigel October, once joked that he should sniff around the evidence locker to find something he could flip. October was from Mitchells Plain and had to flee the rival gangs in the area. He settled in Berea and quickly worked his way up. The administration at Johannesburg Central's evidence room was always a bit suspect. At first no one noticed that the kilogram of cocaine had gone missing. Two months later, R300 000 was deposited into Basson's account. He had a few sleepless nights, but after a new constable took the fall, things went better.

Not even Delia knows about it. She thinks the money came from somewhere else. His dad would claw himself out of his grave and beat the shit out of him if he could. Some Sunday mornings he sits in the Linden Dutch Reformed Church and feels shame and guilt wash over him. But by Tuesday, when the city's grime is back under his skin, he's over it.

After his dad's death, his mother stayed on in the apartment. And six years later, after her death and little Nonnie's birth, he and Delia moved back to the place he grew up in. The complex has three blocks. His block is three storeys high, with the super and the janitor's quarters on the top floor. There's a big garden which they keep in immaculate condition, as well as a pool and a splash pool for kids between his building and the other two.

The braai area is beside the pool. It irritates him that he has to use a communal braai area situated so far from their apartment. At the outset it really pissed him off, because they couldn't take Nonnie out in the cold if they wanted to braai. Later, he had to keep his eye on her constantly to ensure she didn't fall in the pool. The neighbours, an assortment of old Jewish tannies, rich hipsters whose parents pay their rent, lesbian and gay couples and the newly married, always stare at the odd people who insisted on braaiing so frequently. It doesn't bother him. They can slam their windows in protest at the smoke until they shatter – he's gonna braai, come rain or shine.

Any building that is home to a diverse multitude comes with its share of tales, trials and tribulations. But these three buildings have perhaps seen more than their fair share. They've seen a murder, the result of a love triangle gone awry, and a drowning in the pool.

But one event stands out in Basson's mind. His mom told this story at every opportunity from the day it happened, on the fifth of March 1979. Basson was still a young boy, barely seven at the time. At about 6.30 a.m. everyone in the apartment was woken up by a tremendous thundering noise from the building across from theirs. Balls of flame and thick clouds of smoke were spewing into the early-morning air. Everyone initially thought it was a missile or a bomb. Those were turbulent times in the Republic, and bombings weren't out of the ordinary. But this time it was a light aircraft. An elderly couple, Ken and Doreen Waddell, were killed instantly. As if this wasn't a bizarre enough situation, it later turned out that the pilot had known the old couple. The only thing Basson, his family and the other residents saw was one severed wing, lying in the garden, and one of the wheels next to a parked car in the lot. Speculation abounded, the leading theory being that the pilot, Ernie Christie, was on his way to crash his aircraft into the house where his ex-wife lived.

Basson sometimes stares at the building but he can't seem to remember what all the fire and smoke looked like.

He pulls his red Mazda 3 into the parking lot under the building, picks up the bag with the fish and chips and walks to the lift. A small silver car pulls into the spot next to the glass doors. He's too late to avoid them.

'Officer Basson! No rest for those strong arms of the law?'

The refined, almost feminine voice is at odds with the solid figure towering over the tiny vehicle. Wikus comes round the car towards Basson, followed by a youngish, plump, blonde woman. Basson greets them stiffly.

'Have you met Louisa?'

Basson sticks his hand across the low wall, shakes hers without having to come too close. 'So, I take it you're the one who's getting all the fridge tart now?' Basson asks. He can't think of any other conversational fallback.

Louisa laughs. She's quite pretty, Basson thinks, when he sees the dimples in her cheeks.

'Jis, Wikus, looks like we'll be fighting over your tarts any day now,' Louisa jokes. Wikus doesn't answer; he's busy lifting a little boy from a baby seat in the back. Looks to be about two years old.

'Bikey!' the boy yells, pointing a finger at the car boot.

'Ja, ja, relax your buns.'

Basson wonders why the kid isn't in bed yet. He is barely two and it's after eight.

'These days it's all he thinks about – cars and motorbikes.' Wikus takes the black tricycle out and puts it down on the tarmac. The boy immediately lunges for it.

'Okay, you can ride for a bit, then we have to go inside. It's cold outside and you need a bath,' Louisa says.

Wikus looks at the boy and points at Basson. 'Drive carefully, or the oom will give us a ticket. And watch out for the cars!'

Basson smiles and moves towards the door. 'Have a good evening, guys. That kid of mine is probably wondering where I am.'

Wikus and Louisa say goodbye, then turn to the boy trundling along on the bike.

Just as Basson gets into the lift, Wikus comes around the corner.

'You and Delia must come for dinner one night. I make a mean curry.'

'Um … that sounds great,' Basson struggles. 'I'll tell Delia.'

Wikus smiles, happy for having reached out. 'Right. I'll get in touch. Oh yes, little Riaantjie's birthday is next week. Little guy's turning two. You guys should come. I booked a room at that cute place down by Zoo Lake. He and Nonnie can have a jol on the jungle gym and the bouncy castle. There are people there to watch them. Almost like at the Spur, just with better food. I'll be baking myself. I dropped the invite in your mailbox, Delia's probably seen it.'

'Thanks ... Wikus, I'll see how things on my side are looking. I might have to work, but I'm sure Delia and Nonnie would love to come.'

One storey higher, the lift door opens. Basson feels guilty for being too lazy to climb the stairs. There's a gym bag in his trunk, just soaking up the exhaust fumes. But he can't find the strength to drag himself there in the mornings. Or any other time. Especially not in the winter. It's just R200 per month, though, so it's not like his laziness is bankrupting him, he tells himself.

When he opens the door, Nonnie's voice is the first thing he hears.

'Papa!' The little blonde girl, already in her pyjamas, comes running up and throws her arms around his legs.

'Hey, pretty girl, did you miss me?'

Delia comes in from the bedroom, also wearing her pyjamas and slippers.

'Hello,' she says, beaming. 'I thought you were coming earlier so we could braai?'

Basson hefts the bag onto the counter. 'Fish and calamari?'

'That'll do,' she says, hugging him tight. 'I'll warm it up a bit.'

Basson removes his holster and gun, puts it on the tall bookcase. Nonnie goes back to the TV. He sighs. *Frozen* again. Basson leans against the kitchen cupboard while Delia takes out two plates for them and a small one for Nonnie.

'You could have called, you know ...'

Basson can hear the distrust in her voice. It's been almost four months, but the resentment still runs deep.

'Ja, my bad. I just came from a briefing. Then I ran into your friend down-stairs.'

'Wikus?' Delia asks, without looking up. 'Did he tell you they invited us to Riaantjie's birthday? Look how pretty the invite is. Wikus made it. It's on the fridge.'

There's a picture of a car on it, neatly coloured in. Man with many talents, clearly.

'What a fucking day. We picked up a girl at the Wits turn-off this morning. Had to go to the Braamfontein morgue before the briefing. Tomorrow morn-ing bright and early I'm back at the station. I think there are a few late nights ahead.'

Delia squeezes a wedge of lemon over the food.

'Jan told me it was chaos on the M1. He only got to the office at nine.' Jan is Delia's boss, one of the partners at the law firm where she works as a secretary.

'Yeah, probably the same chaos I was in. But let's not discuss this now. I'm sure you don't want to hear about murder and mayhem on a Friday night.'

He prefers not to discuss his work with Delia, even though she's told him many times that he has to talk about it. He wants to keep that darkness beyond these four walls. But sometimes he just can't help himself. Sometimes it has to come out.

Basson takes a glass from the drying rack, half a bottle of brandy from the cupboard and a can of Coke from the fridge. He pours himself a stiff drink.

'Can I get you anything?'

Delia shakes her head. 'Not tonight, thank you. What about the market in Linden tomorrow morning?'

Basson takes a sip. 'Let's see what time I get back; maybe there'll still be time. Otherwise we'll go for a walk at Emmarentia Dam tomorrow afternoon or something. Maybe we can braai after, if we're lucky. Although I think this case is going to ruin my personal life for a while.'

Around the table they discuss Nonnie and the goings-on at her school. Basson listens with half an ear. He would be lying if he said that he doesn't sometimes think of Reza. He catches himself missing the impulsiveness, the lust for adventure. The sneaky text messages during the working day. Especially after a day like today – where he just wants to get drunk and have rough sex with someone he doesn't have any deeper feelings for. At least, he thought he didn't feel anything for her. Until he had to break it off.

He remembers the day Majola cracked a joke about the goofy grin plastered across his face after he received a text from her. 'Damn man, looks like your mistress just surprised you with a blow job.' That frightened him; he thought Majola suspected something. When Delia kicked him out and he had to stay at the Road Lodge for a month, Majola did find out. To his credit, Majola didn't judge him. The only thing he said was that it was none of his business. And that he needed to sort out his shit, because he had been drinking every night. He gave the same advice if Basson ever wanted to see his daughter again. So Basson broke off all contact with Reza and did all the emotional repair work he could with Delia.

After dinner he helps her to clear the dishes, and after a quick cigarette on the balcony, the three of them sit down in front of the TV. Nonnie gets comfortable with her head on his lap and Delia snuggles in close.

'You're restless tonight. What's bothering you?'

Basson worms his way deeper into the couch. Nonnie shifts on his lap. It looks like she's starting to doze off.

'Oh, nothing. It's just work. After today and that other girl we found at Wemmer Pan a while back … it's like this city has lost its mind. Too many people or something. Or too many bad people. And too few of us. Police.'

Delia waits for him to go on.

'You know, when the divers removed the bodies from the water, up by the dam wall, we saw the mother first. When they lifted her out, her hand was still holding on to her daughter's. They must have been holding hands the whole time, until they drowned. And that's how they died together. Hand in hand. The girl stared right at me all the while … until they zipped up the bag. I mean, fucking hell. Who rapes a—'

Delia looks pointedly down at Nonnie.

'Her lights are out.' He goes on, 'Who rapes a nine-year-old and her mother? Then ties their feet to concrete blocks and drops them in a dam? On a bright, sunny day?'

Delia moves closer. 'Jason …' After a few seconds of silence she asks, 'Don't you think it's time you spoke to my brother? I know you don't want to retire at this point. But you and Theuns get along well, don't you? And he said that with your background and skill set you would be in high demand. And they could use someone with your experience.'

Basson doesn't answer immediately. 'Uh-huh.'

'These apartments are selling for up to two million these days. That ground-floor one of Sylvia's sold like this.' She snaps her fingers. 'We'd be able to move into a house. With a garden. Maybe even a pool. And we've got the R300 000 from your mom's life insurance.'

Basson feels the icy hand of his lie grab his chest.

She hugs him. 'And even though I don't like the wind, I'll just have to get used to PE. And Nonnie would grow up by the sea, away from the city.'

'Port Elizabeth is a city,' Basson jokes.

'Yes, but it's not this city.'

'What about Jeffreys Bay? I'm used to driving and it's just over an hour from PE. And Theuns said I wouldn't have to commute every day. Maybe even save up for that boat …'

Delia turns to him, eyes widening. 'Jason Basson, do you want to tell me you're actually considering it?'

Basson smiles. 'I've been thinking about it for a while. When we visit in September, I'll speak to Theuns. Then we can put the apartment up for sale. Ja, man, it would be nice to live by the sea. A bit of fresh air will do us good.'

Nonnie lifts her head from her dad's lap, eyes barely open. 'Are we going to the beach?'

Basson laughs and musses her hair.

'Yes, little nosy Nonnie, you don't miss a thing. I thought you were asleep. Maybe yes, maybe we are.'

Basson looks at the television. A man and woman are embracing. A tear is rolling down her check as she climbs into a yellow taxi cab.

Before he can go anywhere, he has to catch the mother-fucker who's been doing this stuff to the girls. He has to. That will be his legacy, his contribution to the force and the country. This will be his time to shine.

Not Majola's.

Basson sits at the ball-and-claw dining table they inherited from his mother. Delia is reading in the bedroom and Nonnie is asleep by her side.

In front of him is the Diepsloot dossier. He's still working up the nerve to dig in. It reminds him of his school years and being saddled with homework; he usually left it until the very last minute – usually Sunday nights.

He gets up and walks to the bedroom. 'Do you want some coffee?' he asks quietly, not wanting to disturb Nonnie.

'No, thanks. Otherwise I won't be able to sleep. I think I'm just about ready to turn off the light anyway. How far are you?'

Basson shakes his head. 'I'm still gonna be a while,' he says, too ashamed to admit he hasn't even started.

He walks over and kisses her softly.

'Sleep tight.'

'You too. Will you go put Nonnie to bed?'

Basson picks up his daughter, carefully so as not to wake her, and carries her to her room. He tucks her in tightly and kisses her on the forehead. He goes to the kitchen, flicks on the kettle. While it's coming to the boil, he walks to the balcony and lights a cigarette.

From here he can see Brixton Tower and the blue-lit Hillbrow Tower clearly. With Nonnie's fragile little body fresh in his memory, he can't help but think of all the darkness he's been through on the job in this city. He should write a book about all the fucking terrible shit he's seen and experienced. He's had to use his service pistol a few times. A hijacker tried to shoot a woman after the car came to a stop in Bez Valley. A rich businessman in Houghton shot his wife and was threatening to shoot his children too. During a hostage situation in Southgate, he had to move fast and take out two Zimbabweans to protect the staff of a jewellery store.

And that doesn't take into account his early days in uniform, when the violence erupted between Inkatha and the ANC. His rifle must have claimed several lives amid the chaos. Especially at the roadblocks, where he mostly worked on a stop-and-search unit in Soweto. If motorists sped through a roadblock, it was his job to stop them. One night this young guy and his girlfriend, barely nineteen, in his dad's Cressida, didn't stop. So they started unloading. Shot it to shreds. When they searched the car afterwards, all they found was a baggie with a few grams of dagga. That one stuck with him for a while; it was the first time he had taken a life. Later that night, at the bar, his captain put a double brandy and Coke down in front of him: 'Suck it up, newbie. There's more of this coming. It gets easier. Your best friend, Klippies, will help you forget.'

The other incident that haunted him happened at Johannesburg's train station and bus depot. An older woman from Bloemfontein got stabbed in the stomach for her handbag. She had been waiting for her daughter's bus. She lay on his lap while they waited for the ambulance. Just before her pupils shrank and the last light of life left her, she whispered, 'Tell my son Sakkie that I forgive him. And I love him.' He never did find Sakkie. A week later it was the psychopath in Booysens who cut his daughter's feet off with an angle grinder. Said she wanted to run away and go live with her aunt.

Christ, that was rough.

His hope for this city started to dissipate. He knows that violence and crime are everywhere, but the monster that lives under this city tears at its people ceaselessly. And those who try to fight it are becoming breathless. This is not the City of Gold it used to be. This is the City of Blood. Cape Town might have it bad with the gangs on the Flats, but the demons are all here. From Houghton to Snake Park.

It had just gone ten o'clock one night when he went to buy cigarettes from the Quick Stop barely two kilometres down the road. He wasn't on duty but he didn't want to leave his pistol in the car. Then two robbers walked in. He was slow in reacting; they shot the cashier in the head. He identified himself and then opened fire. Four shots, two headshots apiece. Man of the hour, according to the flying squad who were the first on the scene. Despite the fact that he was there in his pyjama pants and slippers.

The drunk woman with her ribs kicked in who stabbed him with a knife when he ended up wrestling with her drunk husband, who had nearly beaten her to death, on their kitchen floor in Rosettenville. Another time he had to go on antiretrovirals when a junkie in Pullingerkop Park in Hillbrow stabbed him in the arm with a heroin needle.

The latest horror show running in his mind is the drowned mother and daughter at Wemmer Pan. And now the foetus on the M1.

The public blames you for everything. The promotions never come your way. Resources and assistance are always in drastically short supply. The way time is regarded in Africa. This isn't 'hurry up and wait' as they taught him in police college – this is 'take your time, they can wait'. The long hours. Shitty pay. Most of the time the brass don't have a clue what's going on. Not to mention the useless assholes at the very top due to haphazard cabinet reshuffles. One fucking idiot after the other. Talk, talk, talking away while not doing a goddamn thing. Only when the media get loud do they wake up. As with this case. Suddenly Radebe cares again.

Basson crushes the cigarette butt in the ashtray by the door. He goes to make sure that Nonnie hasn't kicked her blankets off and returns to his work.

He opens the Diepsloot dossier, beside it the M1 dossier that he got started on today. But he's still too distracted to start. His thoughts amble to Majola and how they met. Majola is hard working and they get along well – at least as well as can be reasonably expected from a forty-something-year-old white Afrikaner and a Zulu. They know which of the other's buttons not to push. Just before he died, Basson remembers his dad talking about the 'new SAPS': 'My boy, you may not be able to use the k-word any more. But you can still think it'. Since his death, Basson has had to make peace with the fact that his dad wasn't always right.

And Majola has a lot to do with that. Forced him to realise that a lot of his prejudices were based on misinformation. He still can't completely shake it, though. He still sometimes wonders if he can trust someone like Majola. And that's a problem.

After Warrant Officer Ben Viljoen retired and Daan Loots was declared unfit for duty, he was placed with Majola. He worked hard for the promotion when it became clear that Loots was on his way out and someone would have to take his place. But Loots stabbed him in the back. Fucking Judas. Should have looked out for his own people. It's hard enough being white in the force. One night in the canteen at the Norwood station, he very nearly came to blows with Loots. They were busy playing darts. Loots needed a trip to win the game or close the board. He actually got it – trip twenty. As he walked to the board to retrieve his darts, he said, 'You worked hard, but you didn't work smart. Just like your dad.' They had to restrain him or he would have broken Loots's neck that night. After that their relationship soured somewhat.

It took a few weeks for conversations with Majola to thaw a bit. Majola knew Basson was eyeing the job and was sensitive about the situation at the outset. The common ground, funnily enough, was found in films. One day Basson was talking about a pretty obscure Guy Pearce movie he'd watched over the weekend, *The Rover*. Majola had seen it too. Since that day, they have discussed movies a lot. They make recommendations, swap opinions, loan their DVDs back and forth. And until now it has been a pleasant shared interest.

Basson sighs and picks the dossier up again. A dossier has three parts: the first contains the reports, interviews, statements and pictures of the scene. The second contains correspondence with other branches of the force and interviews done with associates, like the victim's place of work and so on. The final part is essentially a diary of the investigation on an SAPS 5 form.

He's already craving another cigarette but he clenches his jaw and holds out. The date on the Diepsloot dossier is 11 December. The handwriting is untidy, almost illegible. The girl, who her parents identified as Bettie Khumalo, was 21 years old. She went missing one night after visiting a friend, Joseph Sabane. Her parents got worried when she still wasn't home by eleven. Joseph's mother testified that she went home alone, without Joseph, and had left around eight. She didn't have her own transport, so she made use of taxis.

That's good, thought Basson. The first connection. The girl must have jumped in a taxi on Orange Street, about 300 metres from Joseph's house. It's a pretty busy road. The security guard who patrols the grounds of the Rabasotho Combined School in Ajax Street found her body around five o'clock the next morning. The killer had about eight or nine hours to do whatever he wanted with her, which could have included going somewhere else to commit the atrocities.

The girl's body was placed right beside the school gates. The guard admitted that he had been asleep on the other side of the school grounds. No other witnesses, perhaps because it was a Sunday morning. There are no aerial photos of the area in the dossier. Basson opens his laptop, waits for the internet to connect and does a search on Google Maps. Diepsloot looks like so many other neighbourhoods – shacks everywhere, with a few houses scattered in between. The only trees in the area are the handful surrounding the school. It's not very far from William Nicol Drive, which would have given the murderer quick access to a major road. The school gate is surrounded by houses. No eyewitnesses. He must have taken a huge risk to dump the body there.

Basson takes a sip of his coffee and looks through the colour pictures of the girl again. She sits on the ground, her legs stretched out in front of her, chin on her chest. Completely naked. Her hair is short; she doesn't have extensions like the girl from this morning. Her arms hang limply at her sides. Blood has pooled between her legs. Another picture shows a close-up of her face. Her eyes are open and there is blood coming from her nose and running over her chin. Could he have been hitting her with something? The girl this morning had no damage to her face. There are dark marks across her breasts and nipples.

Basson takes a cigarette from his packet and puts it behind an ear. His attention is caught by a picture of a tyre print. A clear print. Fifteen-inch tyres. Quite worn down.

'Now we're getting somewhere,' he whispers as he inspects the picture. But his excitement is dampened somewhat when he realises the tyre prints are only of use once you've caught the culprit. Or if you want to connect the scenes to each other. But still, it's not nothing.

He pulls the pictures from the post-mortem closer. It was done four weeks after the murder was committed. Pretty impressive if you consider how many people they have on their staff. Bruises around the wrists and ankles, also around her neck. She bit off her own tongue.

'Goddammit.' His voice sounds hollow in the empty room.

It must have been from the shock. Cause of death: internal bleeding. She bled to death as a result of the damage to her abdomen. Nothing about electrocution. The burns to her breasts, the pathologist concluded, were probably caused by a cigarette lighter. Basson gets the feeling that this pathologist doesn't have the experience that Doc Lubbe does. A Dr Debbie Harris. Probably fresh out of university.

The cypher on her back is clearer than those on the girl from this morning. Paper-thin incisions. ON 342061986. The same 1986 at the end as the other one. It has to be a date. Beneath that the letters 'ABAZA' followed by a 12 and a 9.

Basson takes out the pictures of the lacerations from that morning.

'ON 345061986,' Basson whispers.

It's only the third letter that's different. And under that, 'UMHA 2321'.

'UMHA ABAZA.'

Could that mean something in Xhosa or Zulu? Or one of the other languages? He'll have to ask Majola or Rikhotso. Acronyms perhaps?

He looks up Pieter Mitchell's number on his phone. On the balcony he lights a cigarette. Almost all the other apartments are dark, lights out.

He texts, *Hi Pieter. Here's my docket's number (the lacerations on the girl's back). I hope I'm not interrupting your wanking session* ☺

Basson laughs at his own joke, takes another deep drag and zips his jacket up against the cold.

He thinks of the last time they were in Jeffreys Bay. He caught this monster of a grunter at the Gamtoos River. That was a good week: good weather, only light breezes in the afternoons. His phone beeps.

Wrong, asshole, I save the masturbation until after lunch. An afternoon delight with myself. Besides, go fuck yourself.

Basson smiles. Just as he's getting ready to go back inside another message comes through. He's impressed by how quickly Pieter can type. Fucking IT nerds.

Were you taking a nap? It's just you and Mbatho who haven't sent me anything. The numbers are definitely related. The first rows, in any case. It's just the third number that changes across dossiers. I suspect they could be docket numbers. But the 'ON' in front of each baffles me. And the second rows are fucking Greek. I'm sending this on to Captain Majola now.

Basson summarises his deductions in a Word document, along with all the other relevant information. It's well past midnight. He closes the laptop.

Suddenly Nonnie is standing in the passage.

'I'm scared, Papa.'

'Oh no, my girl.' He walks closer, picks her up and rubs her back. 'There's nothing to be afraid of, my love. I'm here, aren't I? Come, I'll come and lie with you till you fall asleep.' He carries Nonnie into her room.

But he knows. He knows all too well. There are so many good reasons for fear.

4

The fluorescent lights of the garage flicker a few times before they flash to life. He always takes a moment to inspect the vehicle after he switches on the lights. It astonishes him how such an everyday piece of machinery, which looks so mundane and gets used by so many people every day, can facilitate such tremendous pain and suffering. All of it behind tinted windows.

The interior of the vehicle determines how someone's life will come to an end. It's sublime, really. Holy, even. He smiles as he puts on the latex gloves and walks to the portable CD player.

After a few seconds, some generic boeremusiek blasts from the speakers, the only CD he owns in this genre. The sound of banjos and concertinas reverberates around the room. Something is scratching at the steel garage door; the sound of whining follows. He should have got rid of the cursed dog a long time ago. He doesn't understand what the thing is still doing here.

He switches on the compressor, opens the tap at the wall and picks up the hose lying under the stainless-steel workbench. He opens the sliding door of the vehicle and a sharp smell overwhelms him. He's angry at himself for not cleaning it out after the morning's outing – it's going to be much harder to get the blood off now that it's dried. He lowers the pipe to the floor. He forgot to remove the girl's meagre belongings, scattered on the floor. He picks up her bloody shoes, jeans, blouse, sweater, bra and panties, and drops them on the workbench by the door. The panties are bloodier than the other garments and still haven't dried properly. He holds the soft material between his fingers, hesitates for a few moments, then puts the panties on the pile with the rest of the items.

He turns the handle on the nozzle, and a thin, pressurised stream of water comes shooting out. He directs it at the inside of the vehicle and starts to wash out the blood. After a while he can't stand the dog's whining any more so he opens the garage door. The dog whimpers its relief and immediately starts to lap at the water pooling beneath the vehicle. The man props the broom up next to the bench, sees the panties, and can't resist picking them up again. He brings the pink material to his nose and inhales deeply. His left hand moves down his body almost involuntarily, starts to rub between his legs. Hard. Harder. Almost violent now. The dog comes closer and presses its snout between his legs.

'Fuck off!' he roars, hitting the dog on the head with his clenched fist.

The dog makes a shrill keening sound and scampers to the corner, where it crouches down on its front paws, watching the man. He hurls the panties back onto the heap of bloody belongings. After taking out a plastic bag from beneath the passenger seat, he places the scalpel and a police truncheon beside the clothing. Using a rag dipped in paraffin, he wipes first the scalpel, then the truncheon, which is much bloodier even than the blade. Carefully, he places them in the plastic bag and returns it to its place under the seat of the vehicle.

He struggles to remove the number plates with the screwdriver. His body doesn't like being prone on the floor. After replacing the plates, he gets up slowly. The dog comes hesitantly closer, but flees again when the man chucks the screwdriver at it. The CD has stopped playing. It's just him, the dog and the fluorescents with their low-key humming.

Behind the vehicle, he locks up the number plates and the girl's handbag and clothing in a tall double-door steel cabinet. Next to it is a large deep-freeze. He sticks the girl's ID card up on the cabinet door beside the others. Adjacent to the IDs hangs an A4 sheet of paper with two columns of numbers and letters. Eight of the rows have been struck through. With a pen he draws a line through the ninth row. All the girls on the cards stare back at him, unsmiling. As if they know something. Their eyes are colourless and dead.

'Soon …' he says hoarsely.

He removes the gloves, takes one last look at the vehicle. It looks like something from a horror movie. His script. He's the director. He decides who lives or dies. So far there hasn't been a hysterical scream-queen who got away.

The only difference is that his story isn't done yet. But he's getting close.

He hits the lights. The dog left the room a while back.

5

Majola unlocks the security gate and the wooden door to his apartment, hangs up his jacket and coat on the rack in the hallway. His balcony overlooks a new shopping centre in Melville. It has a bookstore, a coffee shop and a Vietnamese restaurant that sells sticky chicken on bamboo sticks. Below him are a few other shops too – mostly clothing outlets, an antique store, a laundrette where he takes his clothes to be washed and ironed. He insists on ironing his own dress shirts, though; they always mess up the collars.

A few hundred metres on, Melville turns into Parkview. Sometimes, on the last Saturday of the month, he walks to the market next to the old tennis courts to pick up cold meats and whatever else catches his eye.

He bought the apartment four years ago and has enjoyed living here so far. At least as much as you can when you harbour a deep love-hate relationship with your city. Maybe it's the friendly people in Melville, who keep themselves blind to the deadly, gnashing fangs of crime around them. Or the quaint shops and bars. Sometimes his street can get a bit too busy over the weekends, especially with drunk drivers trying to avoid the Beyers Naudé and Barry Hertzog main roads. He can't believe that people still insist on driving under the influence. He knows some officers aren't above being bribed, but all it takes is one night, one wrong turn and one roadblock. That's it for you. A night in the cells, lawyering up, and a criminal record.

His neighbour is an old Jewish lady who practically never leaves her apartment. At least she greets him when she sees him. On the other side lives a couple who are studying at Wits. Their bedroom is right next to his and often, late nights or early mornings, the banging on the wall can get a bit boisterous. All he can do is bang on the wall himself; they know who he is. They were first-years when he caught the UJ Rapist. They recognised him from the pictures in the newspapers. The guy, Themba, apparently had shared a res with Kevin Phosa, who would later be known as the UJ Rapist. Much later, after the hearing, the English media renamed him the Sneaker Rapist.

In the kitchen, he flicks on the kettle. He drops the dossiers on the table, takes off his shoulder holster and hangs it over the back of the chair.

It was thanks to that arrest that he made captain. It was during the same stretch that Kappie was declared medically unfit for duty. He and Basson were in line for the promotion. Perhaps he would have got it anyway because of affirmative action, but solving the case made him feel better about the promotion.

Colonel Radebe was hard to pin down from the start. Always busy with his own agenda. When he called him in that morning, he was mightily impressed. Perhaps even proud. You rarely see Radebe smile, but that day all you saw were his pearly whites. Went on and on about how Majola was 'upholding the good name of the Zulu nation' and 'now the boere can shut the hell up about the darkies just coasting off affirmative action'. But Majola knew it was going to piss off some people, especially Basson, who was older than him and had more years of experience. To make matters worse, Basson would later be made his partner. There were also rumours that Kappie insisted he get the job instead of Basson.

But Majola knew you don't look a gift horse in the mouth. He wonders what the mlungus would have done if they still ran all the state departments, like back in the day. 'Sorry sir, I can't take the promotion. That black man has been here longer and has more experience than I do.' Fat fucking chance. Your turn is your turn. Deal with it.

The UJ Rapist case was tricky, but he had inhlanhla; he got lucky. A case of being at the right place at the right time. Kevin Phosa raped seven girls over four months. Same modus operandi each time: he threatened them with a knife, told them to take off all their clothes, and then proceeded to rape them. He used his phone to take video footage of each assault, with his knife held against their throats. When he was done, he took their shoes. Not the underwear, the shoes. Just that. And all of them were wearing sneakers.

They had nothing to go on. He was careful, always wore a condom. Campus security was stepped up. The SAPS sent an undercover detective to campus, with no luck. The media started making things really difficult for them. The various feminist and gender-based-violence groups even more so. Girls were too scared to attend night classes or even leave the residences. The police were running out of ideas. Until one night.

On a Friday night, Kevin Phosa walked into campus security, clearly having had too much to drink. He claimed that he knew the rapist. It was a fellow student, James Cele, who lived in the same res as he did. He'd apparently seen him slip out one night wearing the same black hoodie and gloves as those mentioned in the newspapers.

Majola was despatched immediately to continue the questioning. With Phosa sitting cross-legged in front of him, Majola noticed the shoes. Expensive, imported Ewing basketball shoes. And the prints matched those they had found at the last scene, the only one where they had found any usable prints. Majola starting asking him about the shoes, and pushed him for alibis on the nights of the rapes. Phosa started getting panicky. Majola became suspicious and requested a warrant to search his room.

That night the police found a black bag in Phosa's room containing nine pairs of girls' sneakers, seven of which belonged to the Wits students. On his computer they found the phone footage he had taken, along with thousands of pornographic pictures and videos of girls wearing nothing but sneakers.

During the trial, Phosa's psychologist argued for a reduced sentence. She told of his traumatic years growing up in Soweto. The aunt who raised him was unhinged, had a mean, sadistic streak in her. Once, when he was seven, she caught him stealing, so she forced him to wear his sister's sneakers, which were two sizes too small for him. He also had to wear them on the wrong feet. This made him the laughing stock of the neighbourhood. To school, to church, everywhere they went, he had to wear the sneakers, for months. The aunt clearly favoured his sister, while he faced frequent beatings with her belt. As he got older, he developed something of an obsession with sneakers. Especially girls' sneakers.

The whole thing turned into a media circus. After a few weeks, everyone knew of the black detective at Johannesburg Central with a sharp eye for detail. And then he made captain, at the impressive age of 37.

The click of the kettle interrupts his train of thought. He makes a mug of coffee, pulls a chair up to the kitchen counter and opens the dossier.

Majola checks his watch. It's just gone two o'clock, Saturday morning.

He walks over to his favourite chair in the lounge, falls into it with a sigh. There's no point in going to bed now; his head is too busy. He's spent hours with the dossiers from Orange Farm and Katlehong. The incidents took place three months apart. He checked every detail. Read them over and over. No fingerprints. No tyre prints. No eyewitnesses. Just mayhem.

After all of that, the stuff that really sticks with him are the photos of the crime scenes. Colour photos. They're going to bother him for a while. The blood-lust on display. The seeming arrogance of the murderer.

He thinks of the chalkboard up on his fridge. *246 days clean.* Andy, his sponsor from the group in Melville across from the May's Pharmacy, told him to keep this tally. He now does this every morning while waiting for the kettle to boil, writes up his days without alcohol. He remembers his conversation with Lizanne from earlier, how close he came to letting the truth slip. Yeah, he's off the booze, but that was only ever the catalyst. To something worse, and more dangerous, and highly destructive. Which has had him so lost that there've been times he didn't think he'd ever make it back to himself.

It happened kind of coincidentally. One night, out by himself, watching a foreign film at the Cinema Nouveau in Rosebank, he ran into an old friend from Alexandra. Kabelo Mdele. He was out with a white girl with long, blonde hair. Said he was a partner at a construction company with two white guys. Majola called him later that week, curious to see where and how Kabelo lived. He found it inspiring to know that someone from their background had actually made it out, had actually made it. Kabelo invited him to a party that Saturday in Northcliff.

Majola paused to take in the house and the cars parked out front, BMWs and Range Rovers as far as the eye could see. He considered his own car and what he wore and suddenly felt out of place. The girls all looked like models and the blonde was draped across Kabelo again. He came over and immediately put a single-malt whisky in his hand. By the second whisky, he had started to loosen up a bit. The party was picking up speed when he realised something.

Every now and then some of the guests would go into one of the rooms, close the door, and come back a while later looking self-conscious.

Majola had his eye on a Sotho girl with long hair extensions all night. Kabelo noticed him watching her. He walked over to her and whispered something in her ear. She smiled, walked over and introduced herself as Mary. In one of the free rooms she kissed him, and took off her shirt and jeans. Just as things were starting to really kick off, she stopped him and took something from her wallet. She opened a small, transparent bag and tipped out some of the white powder onto her thigh. She handed the straw to Majola. 'You first.' He didn't hesitate for a moment. He wonders now, if he'd known back then how dark the road would get if he followed the little white line, if he would have. Darker, even, than it got after Busiswe.

When they rejoined the party, Kabelo came over, laughing. 'You didn't think I would offer a cop myself, did you?' And they went off to a room and did a line together.

Majola had found something that filled voids he had stopped trying to fill a long time ago. The feeling was surreal. Euphoria for a few hours. The confidence. All the horrors and nightmares the city dropped at his door, the first line gathered up and locked away in some dusty recess of his soul.

It made him forget the pain. Busiswe. He just remembered the good times. Later that evening he went home and stared at his ceiling until the sun came up. The dopamine his brain had released wouldn't let him sleep. But he didn't care. He spent the whole night thinking about Busiswe and wondering how much he'd missed out on before discovering this, this feeling. He was supposed to go visit his mother and Lulu in Alexandra the next day for lunch. When his mother started phoning him, he ignored the calls.

Majola casts his eye over the rows of DVDs lining the shelves beside the flat-screen TV. His collection is coming along nicely. He's found a lot of movies from the Eighties that he watched as a kid, mostly actions and thrillers. A few with Sidney Poitier. Vusi from next door proposed splitting the cost of a fibre-optic line, but he declined. How are you going to know what to watch if you could watch anything at all? He likes going to flea markets and DVD shops over weekends, looking for bargains and whatever catches his attention. He marvels at the well-designed covers, the stills from the film on the back cover. DVDs have become so cheap that every movie seems like a bargain.

Majola slumps down further in the chair. Feels his eyelids getting heavy.

He's standing somewhere in a park. The grass is dead and he is surrounded by eucalyptus trees. He starts. He's wearing only a pink nightgown. Someone is calling his name. Busiswe. She's wearing a black dress, and around her neck the purple scarf he bought her at the Oriental Plaza.

Her arms are outstretched, reaching for him. Then he sees the black, faceless figure behind her. He tries to run to her but he can't move. He looks down at his running shoes: his shoes are on the wrong feet. He sees the black figure close his arms around Busiswe. Tries to run again, but his left arm is bound by a rope. He tries to use his right hand to untie the rope and notices the numbers carved into his hand. Yellow pus seeps from the wounds. It's Andy's number. The figure wraps a raptor claw around Busiswe's mouth. He screams at it to let go of her. Somewhere a phone is ringing. It's the telephone booth on the other side of the park. He doesn't want to answer; he has to get to Busiswe. But the telephone keeps ringing …

Majola wakes up gasping, grasping the scar on his throat. It takes him a few seconds to gather himself. Then he realises his phone's alarm went off in the kitchen. He gets up, checks his watch. It's six o'clock. His body is stiff from sleeping in the chair.

6

On his way to the station, Majola catches the morning headlines hung from lampposts. On Empire Street, *Beeld* proclaims, 'Chaos op die M1'. But it's the *Saturday Star* that makes his spirits sink: 'Monster taxi on the loose'. His hackles rise. Someone in the department broke the rules and leaked some facts to the press. Or they got their info directly from the old sangoma.

'Come in.' Majola can barely hear Radebe's mumbled reply.

'What do you make of this?' Radebe asks, pushing the *Saturday Star* across the desk. The headline reads, 'Sho't Left – to Hell'.

Majola can't help smiling.

'It's the media officer and I who speak to the press. How many times gaan dit nog gebeur? Het ek nie gister this clear gemaak vir jou?'

'We talk to the team every time, Colonel, but the media offers them money. Or they enjoy the attention.'

Radebe removes his glasses and slumps back in his chair. 'Well, you'll have to start punishing them, because it can't go on like this. The commissioner het my glad gephone this morning, on his way to go play golf at his estate – now he's going to blame me for his kak handicap.'

Having slept for just four hours, Majola fails to register any sympathy for someone concerned about their handicap.

'They've already written about the murders,' Radebe says, leaning forward, pulling the newspaper back to himself. 'It pisses me off that the fucking tabloids have to do your work for you,' he goes on.

'Colonel?' Majola asks, surprised.

Radebe pulls a *Daily Sun* out from under the *Saturday Star* and reads the article. '"The naked body of a young woman was found in a field in Katlehong, mutilated and sexually assaulted with a blunt object."'

Majola shakes his head. 'It can only be speculation at this point, Colonel.

And sensation-seeking. There are many girls found dead and naked.' The sentence hangs in the air for a moment. 'I myself went through the Katlehong dossier.'

'What I don't understand,' Radebe says, starting to forget the Afrikaans, 'is how kak our internal communication has to be for us to only discover this now. Doesn't anyone use the internal database? How is it that a newspaper that reports on … fucking zombies who give girls AIDS and tokoloshes eating children, knows more than us? While you're at it, find out who wrote the original Katlehong article.'

Radebe starts tapping the table with his pen. 'Don't spend too much time on what the sangoma said. Focus on the girl. Relatives. Psycho boyfriend. And for fuck's sake, be very sure before you label this a serial.'

'We're still waiting for someone to identify the body,' Majola says.

'What did Lubbe say about the autopsy?'

'He says she was killed close to the scene. That's why we're on the asses of the departments close to the scene. He thinks she was in a sitting or lying position when the wounds were inflicted, which includes the electrocution. She bled to death.'

'Captain, what is your feeling?'

'At this stage it looks like a serial. That's my best guess. We worked through the dossiers last night, and there are seven cases that seem connected. Cuts on the back, sequences of numbers and letters. We're convening in the ops room shortly to get all our facts straight and look for connections.'

'Witnesses?'

'Still nothing.'

'We don't know if it was a taxi?'

'No, Colonel.'

'So why did I come in this morning?' Radebe throws his pen down. 'To be reminded of my sad existence?'

'Colonel?'

Radebe gets up slowly. 'I hear you sent detectives home to go work on this case. Now I have to sit here listening to your best guesses? You could have had that report done by this morning. And you're hedging your bets they won't just lose the fokken dockets.'

'The detectives are overworked, Colonel. They don't see their families. We need personnel to—'

'They should have thought about that before joining the service. I won't have useless people on my team, Captain.' He pauses. 'Dismissed,' he says, before Majola can answer. Majola salutes and makes for the door.

'Aren't you forgetting something?' Radebe asks, and points at the newspaper.

Majola turns around and picks up the newspaper. He's livid, has to bite his tongue not to say anything.

'And send me that report. Today. I'm waiting,' Radebe yells just before he closes the door. Majola stops, waits for him to finish his sentence, then goes. He recalls the stinging of his buttocks when he used to leave the principal's office.

Majola runs into Basson on the stairwell.

'You going for a smoke?' Majola asks.

'Yes. Do I have time?'

'Wait, I'm coming with you.'

They walk down the hall leading to the parking lot.

'What's Radebe got to say?'

'He just had to kak me out for allowing everyone to work from home last night.'

'Did he expect us to pull an all-nighter? Does he think this is fucking Hollywood? CSI?'

'I don't know what he's thinking. But he's taken a huge interest in this case.'

'Probably worried about his pension,' Basson scoffs.

'I doubt it. The brass always get themselves sorted. I think he could be getting a lot of pressure from the top.'

Majola and Basson stand under the awning, backs to the rain.

'What did you find in the Diepsloot dossier?' Majola asks, raising his collar against the cold and wet.

Basson fills Majola in, his breath and the smoke mixing in front of his mouth.

'The pathologist said nothing about electrocution but I don't think she's as jacked up as the good Doctor Lubbe. The victim apparently bit off her own tongue, and it looks like the killer broke her nose. No witnesses, but we do have a tyre print.'

'That's not much to go on but it's a start. What did the letters say? Can you remember them?'

'ABAZA,' Basson says almost immediately.

'ABAZA? That means "ask" in Zulu. I found the letters MAMM in the Katlehong dossier. But that doesn't say much either. I think the numbers after the letters might mean something. Or they might make sense when put together.'

'You know, I was also wondering if it's one of the black languages. We assumed the guy was black because of the potential taxi connection. Do you think he's working alone?'

'I also thought about that. Perhaps he has someone helping him. Because he would have to get his victims quiet somehow so he could do his thing. And they didn't find any trace of drugs in the girl. Or he's really strong. We'll just have to wait till we get more to work with.'

'He's been taking chances,' Majola says. 'And he's getting arrogant. All the other murders were in townships. The one yesterday is a sign that he's getting impatient, leaving her on a highway like that. He knows there are cameras; he knows there could be witnesses. I doubt these girls will have any connection to one other, but we'll have to send out Rikhotso and Mbatho to double-check. Radebe also insisted on it.'

'Yeah,' Basson says, 'he only leaves behind what he wants us to find. If we can't figure out who this is, what this is, he's not going to stop. I wonder when he's going to do it again. My gut tells me more is coming, and soon.'

'We're gonna have to hope for an eyewitness. Perhaps the investigating officers missed something. The problem is, most of the murders were committed months ago. We're already on the back foot. The detectives have so much work that they've forgotten about these cases. And at some point we'll have to speak to the press.'

'But first we need an eyewitness,' Basson says.

'Exactly.'

'Well, Martie is going to be thrilled.' Basson sends his cigarette arcing into a pool of water. 'I think I'm going to take that job in PE,' he says.

Majola is clearly taken aback. 'Have you already made the decision?'

'I spoke to Delia yesterday. I think it's time. I still have to speak to my brother-in-law, but I believe his offer still stands. I've been a Joburg boytjie for long enough. And I don't think I can afford to turn into any more of a bitter bastard.' He smiles.

'You? Bitter? Never!'

'Yeah, yeah, fuck you too. I'm going for a piss, I'll see you up there,' Basson says, opening the door. Majola watches him walk away. He would never have thought it, but he's going to miss that fucking Boer.

The ops room is stuffy despite the cold and the wet outside. Majola wonders when the power is going to go off again. Even the police aren't spared Eskom's mismanagement. And with the unexpected rain this winter, the demand for electricity isn't easing up.

Ramsamy has drawn up an organogram of the various dossiers on the whiteboard. Beside it hangs the old map of Gauteng that Davids and Mbatho worked on, with all the locations of the victims marked in red.

Everyone is here on this Saturday morning, looking tired. Except for Mbatho. 'Her sugar levels are probably a bit high again,' Basson jokes.

Ramsamy has been busy since Majola went to see Radebe. He has already put Majola and Basson's findings up on the board and the map. Everyone in the room is rather tense, he can tell. There isn't a lot to go on. Majola stands beside the round table, studying the organogram, which displays everything they could find: names, ages, employment, date of murder, place found, time of death, cause of death, investigating officer, the numbers and letters carved onto the backs and anything else relevant. It also includes a picture of each of the victims. Eight murders. Eight girls with eight families who haven't been able to say their goodbyes. And eight detectives without a fucking clue where to go from here.

Majola notices that the first two victims have numbers missing.

'Why are there fewer numbers in the Daveyton and Thokoza dossiers?'

'According to the Thokoza autopsy report, the body was only found five days after the girl's death. The body was quite decomposed at that point. He dumped her in a field. A passer-by found her,' Rikhotso answers.

'Mbatho had the Daveyton dossier, Captain,' Ramsamy reminds him. He rises and picks up the original Daveyton dossier from the table. He pages to the autopsy report. 'Four days. Four days before they found her. At a dump site,' Ramsamy says.

Majola nods. That confirms his suspicion that their guy is starting to take more chances. With the first few murders he was very careful. The time of death of the other victims confirms it.

As Mitchell said, the numbers in the first row are all close to identical. All the sequences begin with 'ON'. The first three numbers are different – and then they all end with '061986'. The numbers that differ do show a correlation, though – 345, 342, 341, and so on. All of them in the 340s. The second row, however, might as well be Greek for all Majola can figure out. ANG, ISON, SOTF, SHA, JISS, UMHA, ABAZA, MAMM, followed by numbers.

Majola sits down at the table, crosses his arms. 'Okay, what do we see here?' he asks, looking at the other detectives.

Mitchell is the first to speak. 'Black girls, all of them between eighteen and twenty-four.'

Majola crosses to the board and writes it down.

'What else?' he asks without turning around.

'Same tyre tracks at both Diepsloot and Thokoza: fifteen inch,' Basson chips in.

'Everyone's family members and boyfriends have alibis.'

'That's good, Ramsamy. What else?'

'All of them were abducted at night.' Davids sounds impressed by his own insight.

'Now we're getting somewhere.' Majola turns to the group. 'Yes?'

'I'll put money on it that all of them use public transport and that none of them own cars. Sergeant Ramsamy missed that.' Basson winks at Ramsamy.

'That's correct. Did everyone pick that up from their dossiers?' Everyone nods, except for Davids.

'There was nothing in the Alex dossier. But I'm sure if we go ask, it'll be the same there.'

Rikhotso shakes his head. 'Zola Budd. The sangoma might have been right. And it makes sense. Who gets into a stranger's car at night? A taxi is a different story.'

'Why do you say that?' Majola asks, sitting down. 'He could be asking them for help or directions, and then forcing them into the boot.'

'No fucking way. Most of these girls were picked up between seven and eight at night. There would still be a lot of people on the streets. Someone would have seen something,' Basson opines.

'Another thing that could be important,' Basson continues, 'is that Katlehong and Thokoza are practically right next to each other. Perhaps that means the killer lives somewhere in that area.'

'Good point. Sergeant Rikhotso, see if you can find the journalist who wrote the *Daily Sun* article.'

'Which article?' Davids wants to know.

'The one that got Radebe so worked up. It's on the table.'

'Yes, Captain.' Rikhotso picks up the newspaper, skims over the article in question.

A phone starts to ring softly. It's Ramsamy's. He checks the screen, gets up quickly.

'Sorry, Captain, I have to take this.' He leaves the room, closing the door behind him.

Before Majola can proceed, he hears voices in the corridor. It's Mbatho. She walks in, out of breath.

'Sorry I'm late, Captain. It's the girl they found on the M1. Her parents reported her missing at the Brixton station. I went over to check the photos they brought in. It's definitely her. Jane Semenga.'

'Did you contact the family?'

'I spoke to them, yes. We can go identify the body at Braamfontein at two. The mother was too upset to say anything.'

'Take Davids with you. Find out about her movements on Thursday – who she was in contact with, friends, maybe a boyfriend? Anything, anyone.'

'Got it, Captain.'

'And it's critical that we get the family to talk, even if they are distressed. Time is not on our side.'

'Yes, Captain.'

'Good work, Mbatho,' Majola says, almost grudgingly.

She starts to blush, unused to the praise, and sits down on an empty chair next to Rikhotso.

'Well, let's hope the family has something to add,' Majola says. 'Sergeant Rikhotso, I want you to contact all the families. Find out if any of the victims knew one other. Maybe we'll be lucky. It's worth a shot.'

Rikhotso nods.

'Let's focus on what's in front of us. So, the girls all use public transport. We can exclude the buses; they don't run at that time of night. Why do we think it's a taxi and not, for example, an Uber or something? Just because the victims all come from the townships and probably can't afford to use Uber?'

Basson hears Ramsamy coming back down the corridor. He's still on the phone, talking loudly. Majola's head drops and he sighs with frustration at another interruption.

Ramsamy is in the doorway, phone still in hand. 'I've got good and bad news.'

'You're out of the closet but you have AIDS?' Basson butts in. Davids starts to laugh.

Majola doesn't have the energy for this nonsense. 'Shut it. Let's hear what Ramsamy's got.'

'I just spoke to a friend who works at the Ga-Rankuwa station. He came back from leave today and saw my inquiry. There was another girl. Last month.'

'How the fuck is that good news?' Basson asks.

'That's the bad news. The good news is that they have an eyewitness. A good one.'

Majola and Basson look at each other.

'Yes?' Majola asks.

'She saw a red taxi at the crime scene. And the person who dropped the girl off next to a soccer field. She described everything in detail,' Ramsamy goes on, excitedly.

'Do you have her contact details?' Majola asks.

'Yes. She works at Nat's Liquor Store in Ga-Rankuwa. They're open until eight. She's expecting us, and sent a pin on WhatsApp.'

'Zola Budd,' Rikhotso says and smiles to himself. 'I told you.'

Majola picks up his jacket. Basson jumps up.

'Okay. We're going to Pretoria. Ramsamy, will you take over here? You were at the scene. Work over the correlations again. There has to be something. Update the organogram with Ga-Rankuwa's info when you get it.'

Ramsamy nods.

'Oh, and Mitchell, can you print us out some pictures of different types of taxis? Look for Quantums, Siyayas, HiAces, and that other shit the Chinese brought over ... what are they called again?'

'Amandlas,' Rikhotso answers.

'That's the one. Just send the pictures to my phone.'

Mitchell nods.

'Mbatho, you let me know the minute you're done identifying the body, and what you found out there.'

Majola stops at the door. 'Good work. All of you. This might be the break we've been looking for. Maybe we'll catch this guy before anyone else dies. Good.' He gives Ramsamy and Mbatho another smile each.

He puts on his jacket as they walk, Basson close behind him.

'Well, now we know for certain that it's a taxi. Or a minibus. It's a step in the right direction,' Basson says, out of breath.

'Yes, man. Isimangaliso. Just as I was losing hope too.'

'Let's just hope Mbatho doesn't break down with the mother, and actually remembers to ask the right questions,' Basson says.

But Majola doesn't answer; his thoughts are elsewhere. While they wait for the lift, he's still thinking of the dream he had of Busiswe.

The Corolla has come to a complete stop on the M1. There's been an accident at the Buccleuch interchange in Midrand, and another one at the Malboro turn-off. According to the traffic update, the N1 isn't looking much better either: two lanes have been closed at William Nicol. At least there's that. Basson told him to take the N1; Majola insisted on the M1. At least Majola doesn't have one more thing to feel bad about. And it's a Saturday, not even a working day. It's like everyone loses their fucking minds when it rains, all driving ability washed away by what's hardly been a deluge. To their left, a Quantum minibus has pulled into the emergency lane and switched on its hazards. The passengers are still inside, not keen to get out in the rain, even though it's easing up. There's a tense silence in the car. Anticipation. Hope. A clue.

'I don't think he belongs to one of the taxi associations,' Majola blurts out.

'Man, I hadn't thought about that. The thing is, everything I know about the taxi industry sounds dangerous as hell. Blame it on white privilege if you want,' Basson says drily.

Majola smiles. 'To be honest, I hope he is a member. It's going to take some legwork, but it improves our chances of catching him. There could be a chance that one of the patrol cars spotted him.'

'What – our patrol cars?'

'No, one from a taxi organisation.' Majola opens his window a crack. 'Allow me to explain the ins and outs of the industry, Mr White Privilege, or my understanding of it, at least. Most of the taxi drivers you see around, they're driving for someone. They call them "larneys", the guys who own the taxis.'

'I remember Rikhotso mentioning something like that.'

'Yes. Now, the larneys belong to the taxi associations. The associations own certain routes, and those routes get patrolled by unmarked patrol cars, to make sure that the taxis from rival associations, or "pirates", aren't poaching passengers on their routes.'

'Okay ...'

'So, let's say our sangoma and our witness from the liquor store are right – it is a taxi. If he picked up nine girls from all over the city, he must have been crossing over onto other routes. Those routes, or at least some of them, might have had patrol cars on them. Maybe someone confronted him. It would help if he belonged to one of the associations, because he would have had to give his details before he could pay the poaching fine. No one likes a pirate.'

'What do you think the chances are that he's working from one of the taxi ranks?' asks Basson.

'Well, if that's the case, our job is made even easier. They call it "binding" when the taxis pick up people from the ranks. The ranks are actually organised quite effectively. They have marshals who keep everything on record and make sure everything runs smoothly. They even have ranks, like the one at Mamelodi, where the guys can park their taxis overnight. They call it a "leshakeng". It means "kraal". We can try the ranks too. But I think he would probably float, which means that he'd just be cruising up and down routes, picking up people as he goes.'

'Do you think he drives for a larney or that it's his own taxi?' Basson asks.

'His own. If you drive for a larney, they make sure you work your ass off. The larneys expect a fixed amount of cash every day. If you don't make that, you cover the difference from your own pocket. Some of the taxi owners work differently. You work for them during the week; over the weekends you can borrow the taxi for your own business, and you get to keep the fare. Some of these murders were committed during the week, the one on the M1 too. But he could have a different arrangement with the taxi owner. But as I said, I think he drives for himself.'

'Sounds like a shitty job.'

'It is. The taxi owners do as they please. We don't have laws that regulate this stuff, so the drivers have to put up with a lot of shit. And the job is dangerous. Years ago, they had this saying: "Death from the back seat". The pirates would get on like any other passenger, and go sit in the back seat. Then they'd simply shoot the driver in the back of the head. The organisations are also at one other's throats. The government isn't helping. Many of the organisations get allocated the same routes by the courts. This causes complete mayhem. The drivers are lucky if they can take home R4 000 at the end of the month. And they work long days. First, they get the taxis from the owner's house, then they wait in the queue at the rank from three in the morning. If you're late, you miss a trip and make less money. Many work until eight at night. That's why the victims didn't have a problem getting in to one so late.'

'That explains why so many of them drive like lunatics.'

'Exactly. If people knew how the system worked, they would have a bit more understanding of the situation. Then you still have to bribe the Metro police. You have to keep the taxi on the road; if something breaks you have to fix it yourself, which includes the tyres. That's why so many of them are falling apart. And then you have the Rea Vaya and Uber stealing your business. Apparently, a lot of the guys use a herb, muti really, called "intelezi". They believe it makes them strong, keeps them safe. But it actually just makes them more aggressive.'

'Then you've got the passengers breathing down your neck too, I guess,' says Basson.

Majola nods. 'They shit all over you if they're late, they shit all over you if you drive like an idiot to get them there on time. You can't really win.'

The traffic starts to pick up speed after the Buccleuch interchange. In his rear-view mirror, Majola keeps one eye on the crumpled-up BMW being loaded onto a tow truck.

'Another thing just came to me. Do you remember in the Nineties, the government gave taxi owners R50 000 to scrap taxis because there were too many of them on the roads? And too many of them were skoroskoros, wrecks waiting to happen? They could also use the R50 000 to buy a new one.'

'I think I remember something like that.'

'There was a lot of corruption back then. Owners took the money and held onto the taxis, even though the records showed that they had been taken off the roads. Let's hope our taxi isn't one of those.'

'How the hell do you know so much about the taxi industry?'

'I've been taking taxis since I was a teenager. Still know the rules we had to obey. I'll never forget this sticker I saw inside one once: "I like your perm but not on my window".'

Basson laughs along.

'There are several unwritten rules too. Don't slam the sliding door. Don't sit next to the driver if you can't count the money. If a man and woman are sitting up front with the driver, then the woman has to sit in the middle.'

'Shit, I never would have guessed any of this was going on behind the scenes.'

There's a silence. The lanes at the Olifantshoek turn-off have been opened to those taking the left turn, after another accident

Majola sighs. 'I had a cousin who drove a taxi between Pretoria and Rustenburg for ages. One night on his way back, he had a head-on collision with a livestock truck transporting cows. Thirteen people died, him included. I was in two accidents myself as a teenager.'

'Fucking hell.' Basson whistles through his teeth.

They turn right just past Blue Hills, where the traffic seems to have calmed somewhat.

'I read the other day that something like 15 million people in this country make use of taxis. It's a R90-billion-per-year industry. If the taxis stop or protest, the country grinds to a halt.'

Basson steers the conversation in a different direction: 'How old were you when you learnt to drive?'

'Hm … I guess when I was around twenty, just before I left for police college. Had to make a plan with a borrowed car, this rusted-up, busted-up old Chev my mom's neighbour had. I get so fucking worked up when whiteys start talking about how poorly the darkies drive. You joked about white privilege earlier, but there's some truth to it.'

'Oh yeah?' Basson asks, lowering his voice slightly.

'A lot of these sisis with their new cars only learnt to drive once they could afford it, after working for a few years. That's why they're such nervous drivers. The whiteys start learning young, on a farm road with a bakkie or when they're still at school.'

Basson immediately goes on the defensive. 'Okay, but a lot of the darkies also buy their licences. In my day you couldn't do that, no such thing. I bought my first car, an old fucked-up Ford Escort, with a policeman's salary after graduating from college. My old man didn't have money to help.'

'I'm not saying this to piss you off, Jason. I'm just saying that people don't think about this stuff; there's a lot they don't understand. I know all of you weren't born with a silver spoon in your mouth.'

He can't remember the last time he called Basson by his first name. They don't usually use their names at all, as is so often the case between hot-headed men. They talk around it: you and yours. In meetings they refer to each other only by rank. Majola knows his promotion is still a touchy subject.

'No worries.' Basson stares out the window.

The rest of the trip is pretty quiet. Majola looks out at the plots and patches of bare field beside the road. He's never been crazy about Pretoria. The people here are still weird with each other. It's like they still haven't shaken the distrust. In most parts of Johannesburg, especially the city centre, people are much more likely to fall into conversations naturally, at restaurants and supermarkets. Here, people still eye each other with suspicion.

After passing Akasia, they take the turn-off onto the R566. Immediately there's more rubbish lying next to the road and the tarmac is riddled with potholes. Ga-Rankuwa is about forty kilometres from Pretoria. Though it's a region of Gauteng, it used to be part of the North West Province. During apartheid it was part of Bophuthatswana, the homeland under the rule of Lucas Mangope. Not many liked Mangope, seeing him as a puppet of the old government.

Majola parks the Corolla next to a banged-up bakkie. The parking lot is dotted with homemade gazebos and hawkers who sit in their shade selling all kinds of edibles. Nat's Liquor Store is situated beside the supermarket.

Majola pulls on his jacket before he locks the car. The rain has stopped but it's still cold and cloudy.

'Make sure it's locked; this is lion country,' Basson jokes.

'Not even the lions fuck with the Black Panther,' Majola replies.

'Wakanda forever, huh?'

'Damn straight.'

Just as they're about to walk in, Majola's phone beeps. Mitchell's come through with the pictures of the taxis.

'Just in time,' Majola says, showing the photo of the Quantum to Basson. Beside the door, there's a security guard on a plastic chair watching them. Especially Basson, as if he's never seen a white man. An older black man is behind the register.

Majola starts the conversation in English. 'Are you Nat?' he asks.

'No. Nat is next door. Who are you?' he asks, looking Majola up and down.

'I'm Captain Majola; this is my partner, Detective Basson from the Serious and Violent Crimes Unit. We're looking for Thuli Mokhebe.'

'Again? I thought you already spoke to her?'

'We need to speak to her again. Is she here?'

The man stares blankly at Majola, shakes his head.

'Thuli!' he calls to the back room. He gets off his chair and shuffles down the passage. 'Make it quick; this is on my time.'

Basson looks at Majola. 'Rude asshole. It's not like the place is exactly crawling with customers.'

They hear a shuffling from the back of the store.

Thuli is young, with a cheeky afro, light skin and a sharp look in her eye. About twenty-two, Majola estimates.

'Thuli?' he asks.

'Yes. Are you from the police?' There's a slight American twang to her English.

Majola introduces himself and Basson.

'I already told that Indian officer that I told Sergeant Molefe everything I know. Why don't you ask him?'

'Because there've been new developments in the case,' Basson answers. 'And we want to make sure we didn't miss anything.'

Majola does the rest of the talking. Basson has his notepad out.

She folds her arms. 'This can't take long.' She nods her head to the back room. 'He's full of shit.'

'We won't keep you long. Tell us what you remember of the morning you saw the taxi.'

'I was on my way to my sister. Friday morning. It was my one day off and we were going into the city. It was already getting light outside. You know that field at Tlotlo Mpho Primary in Zone 1? I saw a red taxi stop. It was a strange place to stop, I thought, among the trees, not really close to anything. So I stopped and watched from behind a tree. At first, I thought of asking for a lift to my sister's place; I still had far to walk. Then a man got out, opened the sliding door and lifted a girl out. She didn't have any clothes on. I thought she must be drunk. I saw him put her down carefully, up against a tree. He walked back, closed the door and drove off. When I walked closer, I saw the girl was full of blood. And her eyes were open. I knew she was dead. So I dialled 10111 from my phone.'

'What happened then?' Majola asks.

'Maybe half an hour later, a police van showed up. They asked me what I'd seen. I had to go back later that day to speak to the detective.'

'What can you remember about the taxi? Except that it was red.'

'It was an older type, not one of those big ones they drive these days. The windows were pitch black. The one mudguard was dented. The front one, on the right. It was pretty dark. But I remember the dent.'

Majola takes his phone out, shows her the picture of the Siyaya model, then the Super 16 HiAce.

'That one, ja.'

'You can't remember seeing a sign for one of the taxi associations or any-thing like that? Maybe on the door?'

'No, not that I remember.'

'And the man? Can you remember anything about him?'

'He was wearing black clothes. A hoodie. His hands were white, but it was probably gloves. They were too white.'

'Was there anything out of the ordinary about him? Big, small, the way he walked?'

'I think … he was struggling to carry the girl. As if he was tired or unfit. As if he struggled with her weight. And he was speaking to himself.'

'Could you hear what he said? What language he was speaking in?'

'No, it was too far off. But I heard him talking.'

'Could he have been speaking to someone else? Was there anyone else?'

'I don't think there was anyone else. Unless there was another person in the taxi.'

Majola looks at Basson.

'How tall was he? Skinny guy or fat? Average?'

She looks at Basson. 'About his height.'

There's a sudden silence between the three. The guard at the door is watch-ing the conversation with wide eyes.

'Is there anything else, Thuli? Anything you can remember that might help us?'

Thuli looks towards the back of the store, nervously. 'I can't think of any-thing else.'

Majola takes a business card from his pocket. 'Call me if you think of any-thing. Thanks for your time.'

She nods.

He shakes her hand and Basson puts his notepad back in his pocket. The two men walk to the door. Just before they leave, Thuli comes back up to them.

'Oh yeah, I remember the taxi had whitewall tyres. And black rims, I think. And I don't think the taxi had a reflecting strip on its side.'

Basson looks at Thuli. 'How do you remember this now?'

Thuli smiles. 'I've been taking taxis my whole life. And my uncle owns a tyre shop. And I've got a good memory.'

She turns serious. 'You know, I had a dream about that day. But not about the guy with the black clothes. Not about the girl either. I dreamt of that taxi. For days afterwards, I was looking out for it, everywhere on the road, but I didn't see it. When I go to sleep, I see it again. Always at night, with those tinted windows. Then I try to run away, but I can't …'

Warrant Officer Davids catches her just before she hits the ground. They are at the morgue in Braamfontein, and Jane Semenga's mother has just collapsed after seeing her daughter. Jane's father is sobbing uncontrollably. Warrant Officer Mbatho puts her hand on his shoulder. He turns around and drags her into an embrace.

His aftershave fills her nose; he smells good. That he has dressed smartly to come to identify his daughter's body makes her sad. Davids brings the mother slowly back to her feet and leads her to the door. The mortician pulls the cover back over Jane's face and leaves the room.

Outside, Jane's parents get into the back of Davids's BMW. Mbatho climbs into her own car. She turns the insulin pen slowly until it measures twelve units, then jabs the needle through her trousers to inject herself. She didn't want to do it in the morgue's toilets – the place gives her the heebie-jeebies. She doesn't understand why she's always the one who has to be there for the identifications, nor why Captain Majola insists that she should be the one to break the news to the families.

'Warrant Mbatho, it's easier for women: you're stronger than men when it comes to this kind of stuff.'

That's a lie. Leshano. It hurts her just as much. And it doesn't get easier. Every time she sees their faces when she tells them a loved one isn't coming back, her heart drops into her feet. Or like today, when they raised the sheet to show the girl's face to her parents and she had to watch as their last shred of hope died.

It's terrible.

From the lunchbox on the passenger seat, she takes out the three rolls she made. She knows she should stick to her diet and exercise regimen, but she's been struggling. And with the uncommon hours she works, it's almost impossible to get to the gym. Her membership at Curves expired two months ago. The bloody men don't understand – high glucose levels affect her mood, making her restless and cranky.

Sometimes she wonders what the hell she was thinking joining the police. After school she still thought she'd be able to make a difference. She was still healthy back then. She passed the entrance exams, then her uncle at the police college pulled a few strings, helped her to get placed at Randburg, where she promptly reported for duty, all fire and fury. Her heart was set on making detective, she passed those exams too and did well at first. Then she got sick. Type-1 diabetes.

'It's not an illness, it's a condition. If you can control it, you can lead a normal life,' the doctor had said.

She started out following the diet to a tee, no matter how hard she found it. To walk past the chocolate shelf in the supermarket was extremely hard. After a few years, the blood supply to her feet began giving her trouble. Then she started gaining weight. Some days she struggles to get out of bed. Her sick leave for the year has almost been spent and it's barely July.

She knows Captain Majola, Basson and all the rest don't like her. It doesn't bother her. A job is a job. Her colleague, Davids, is so busy with his own matters that he leaves her to her own devices most of the time. She doesn't mind at all. She received an official warning a while ago, but stepped up her game just enough over the next six months for it to expire from her record.

Sometimes she misses her old self, the one who still had fire in her belly, the one who wanted to change the world. But these days she's fine to do the bare minimum to stay out of trouble. And why should she put herself in the line of fire to catch murderers? Inevitably, there'll be another one next week. This country: sechaba se lahlehile. Gone to hell. But she has to ride it out a little longer, until her sister has her clothing business up and running. Fashion for the fuller figure. Not those dresses and blouses that hang like sheets in the wind` – sexy outfits. Because who said fuller figures can't be sexy? The business has been picking up nicely; sales are climbing at the little shop on Fox Street and through the website. By year-end her pension should be enough for her to buy half of the business. Maybe even sooner. Then she and her sister will be partners and she can help make clothing full time. She just has to be patient, keep her head down, and stay under the radar.

She takes a bite of one of the rolls. The butter has been slapped on and the four slices of salami are slathered in mayo. Then she puts it down: it tastes funny, probably stood in the sun for too long.

She looks up in time to see Davids pull away with the Semengas in the back seat. Another broken mother. Davids gestures to her that they're heading out. She slides the lunchbox under the seat. Davids can lead the interview at the station. She's not feeling very well.

7

Martie Bam is excited. Not as excited as she was for her first internet date, but she can feel the butterflies in her stomach, especially when she considers how this could pan out. Hell's Kitchen in Melville is busy for a Saturday afternoon. One would think everyone had had enough to drink the previous night. But for people from Gauteng, even partying on a Sunday isn't a big problem. In Harrismith in KwaZulu-Natal, where she grew up, you would never see that. The bars aren't even open on Sundays – only the Spur next to the highway and maybe one or two shebeens.

She likes Melville, the buzz of it. The only thing that gets on her nerves is the multitude of street vendors with their God-awful paintings and their wire animals. She avoids Xai-Xai across the road, where most of the other journalists hang out, drinking beer, eating pizza and shooting the shit.

Every now and then she'll see one of those hip young journalists. She doesn't mind them too much; they fawn over her anyway. And the guy from the *Huisgenoot* wasn't bad in bed. Jacques. Just a bit clingy. When he started sending her naked pictures after the first time they had sex, great as it was, she began to get bored of him. One night is enough, unless you have supernatural talents or superhuman endowments.

She doesn't really give a shit what her colleagues say about her, the gossip about how she gets her leads. Fuck 'em. She doesn't understand how people think. A man with a lifestyle like hers would be treated like a folk hero. Man of the hour. Player deluxe. But for some reason there's a taboo around women who go out hunting for sport. She hoped that the city would be different, hoped she could leave the small-town mentality behind, especially considering the times they're living in.

That's where she draws the line: somewhere between work and sex. Work is work, fun is fun. They dare to question her integrity. She's worked herself to the bone to get where she is, the wide-eyed girl from Harrismith who wanted to change the world. And that's what she's been doing. There are even talks of a book deal, though she doesn't know where she'll find the time. And she doesn't want to be like those crappy journos and writers who end up writing trashy gossip columns and filler pieces on rugby players and minor pop stars. Their books go straight to the bargain bin. Her book will have meat on its bones. She's still aiming for a position as editor of a newspaper. All her colleagues who are so concerned about the prospects of the traditional press should get out of the way – she'll stick it out.

She catches the eye of the bartender, who has been surreptitiously checking her out. Not bad. The tattoos on the muscular forearms, the beard, the slicked-back hair: it works for her. If today's appointment doesn't work out, he's a good fall-back option, although he's probably working late and she'd want the guy out of her bed by eleven.

Martie shifts on the barstool, crossing her right leg over her left, careful not to scratch her red stilettos against the counter. She bought the black tights to go with the shoes; they accentuate her slender ankles.

Martie lifts her glass in the direction of the bartender, gives him a smile. She moves her black-framed glasses up her nose, checks that her ponytail is still in place. The bartender comes over immediately.

'Another single J&B with water, please.'

The bartender takes her glass. She touches his hand lightly with her finger-tips. He smiles and walks away. She scans the faces of the people around her. The girls, mostly students or newly employed, look unkempt. Most of them aren't wearing makeup, and have unwashed hair tied loosely into buns. Like drugged-up librarians. That's what she calls this new trend. The men all have beards. Hipsters. A subculture so ubiquitous that it's become the mainstream. And almost everyone has tattoos. That's Johannesburg for you: every open surface has been graffitied over.

Martie considers the murder on the M1. The policeman put in charge of the homeless sangoma was hesitant at first, but she's learnt how to handle these types. Early mornings, that's when a man's resistance is at its lowest. David Majola will only be able to avoid her for so long. At some point he'll have to talk to her; the public has a right to know. That scene was screaming serial killer. She's already found an article in the *Daily Sun* that could have something to do with this murder. She'll get to the heart of it eventually.

David Majola interests her. The stern-looking Zulu who speaks beautiful Afrikaans. That's quite a rarity these days. Everyone just wants to speak English. During the Sneaker Rapist case, she dealt with him a few times. She tried everything she could think of, but the invitation for coffee or drinks never came. Perhaps he doesn't like white women. Or journalists. She's never had a thing for black guys, but she'd be willing to admit that she's fantasised about him a few times. Perhaps it's the Afrikaans. Martie smiles to herself. Her dad would turn in his grave. Her dad, who'd brush her hair and read to her in the evening after her mother ran off with another man. Her dad, who abandoned his dream of starting an engineering firm so that he could be at home more often and offer her security.

The bartender puts her drink in front of her.

'Should I run a tab?' he asks.

Martie drops her car keys onto the counter.

'Yes, please.'

She takes her drink and turns back to the people milling around. She wonders if some of these couples met online. She tried to do it the old-fashioned way but quickly realised that people have one appointment lined up after the other. And friends only have so many friends they can introduce you to. Internet hook-ups are just so much easier. After a few preliminary conversations it's easy to gauge whether someone has the same intentions as you do.

If they're too obvious about doing it just for the sex, she loses interest. They have to have something between the ears too. Have to know how to flirt, and for God's sake, they need to know how to spell. She's had one or two complete failures: one buffoon started crying when he spoke about his ex; the other clown went to the bathroom every few minutes to do another line of cocaine. When he returned without properly cleaning his nose, she excused herself, saying she was going to the ladies' room, got in her car, left, and blocked him on her phone. Can't be too careful these days.

There's a rumour doing the rounds in Pretoria that there's a serial killer there who finds his victims on dating apps. According to her sources, there have been three victims so far. She couldn't find out more, though. All of a sudden, no one wants to talk. But she'll break through. If she can solve the taxi-murderer case, and then find the dating-site murderer, her career is made. That could be the focus of her book, an omnibus of serial killers. Can you call two cases an omnibus, though?

The bartender interrupts her thoughts. 'More ice?'

Before she can answer, he walks into the bar. The well-built rugby player with the beard like a lumberjack and the warm smile hidden behind it. Martie ignores the bartender and gets up. She gives the guy a hug, brushing her cheek against his.

'Damn, boy, you're much hotter than your pictures made you look,' she whispers into his ear as she runs a hand lightly runs over his chest.

Basson glances at Majola. He looks equally tired of this shit. The fact that he's on the phone with Colonel Radebe probably isn't helping. Maybe it's the lack of sleep catching up with them. But they're full of plans and conclusions after speaking to Thuli.

'Yes, Colonel. I'll have the report on your desk first thing in the morning.' Majola wraps up the call. He lowers the phone and sighs.

'Hey, at least we've got enough to keep him off our asses for a few days,' says Basson, trying to lighten the mood.

Before Majola can reply, his phone rings again. 'Yebo, Davids?' While Davids talks, Majola nods occasionally.

'And? What did he say?' Basson asks when he's done.

'Jane Semenga's mother apparently said she had been seeing a guy, a young soccer player who plays for the Clever Boys. Studies sports management at Wits. She was at his place on Thursday night. He's also the father of the … That's the last time they saw her.'

'Ah, now we're getting somewhere.'

'Davids picked him up at Wits after practice. Now he's checking the CCTV footage at his apartment complex. And he's trying to find some of Jane's friends to see what they know,' Majola says.

'Davids is hustling,' Basson replies drily.

'I think you should do the interrogation this afternoon. I'll be there too. Rikhotso is apparently thrilled: the guy is one of his favourite players, so I don't think he'll ask the right questions.'

Basson nods but says nothing. He isn't looking forward to an interrogation with a star-struck Rikhotso behind him. But his captain has spoken.

At the station, they fill in the other detectives on their morning. Majola instructs them to contact every taxi association in the areas close to the murders on Monday, as they're not going to get anywhere on a Saturday night. And everything will be closed on Sunday.

Rikhotso is like a kid before Christmas. 'That boy's got talent,' he says, eyes wide.

Basson didn't mind the prospect of interrogating Benjamin Seketse, but now the long day is taking its toll. To make matters worse, he'll have to bum a lift home from Sergeant Rikhotso. Delia took his car this morning so she could take Nonnie to ballet practice, and Majola will be working late to get the report done for Radebe.

Rikhotso is starting to irritate him. He's acting like the guy's biggest fan. He's just sitting there in the corner smiling like an idiot, like he's waiting to ask for an autograph or something. When Rikhotso, who's from Rustenburg, heard Seketse was going to play for the Platinum Stars next year, he almost started applauding.

Just as he and Majola open the door to the interrogation room, Majola's phone rings. Majola switches to speaker and takes a few steps down the hall so Seketse can't hear.

'What have you got, Davids?'

'No man, Captain – not even a "good afternoon"?' Davids jokes.

Majola's silence prompts him to get to the point.

'We'll have his phone records by Wednesday. I checked the CCTV footage at the soccer star's fancy flat. There's a camera at the main entrance. It shows the victim arriving first, then Seketse, just after six. Just before eight she storms out. About ten minutes later he comes out the door, probably to look for her. After a few minutes he goes back into the apartment. He only leaves again the next morning. The neighbours said they also heard a fight, but later in the evening they could hear him showering and watching TV, till about eleven, they estimate.'

'Is there another way in or out of the building?'

'No, just the one entrance. No fire escape, nothing.'

'Did you speak to any of her friends?'

'Ah! Detective Basson. I did not know you were on the line too. That's where things get interesting. I spoke to one – her BFF, quite a hottie. She mentioned that Seketse apparently has a criminal record. For assault, actually. We checked the system. Gave his ex-girlfriend in Rustenburg quite a beating a few years back. And he's getting treatment for alcohol abuse. She says Jane was always a bit worried about that. But she also said Jane swore he never beat her.'

'What's your sense of him?' Majola asks.

'I don't know. Sounds to me like just another arrogant soccer player born with too much talent and a quick temper.'

Majola looks at Basson. 'Did she say anything about the other victims? Any mutual friends?'

'She tuned they don't know any of the others. And she and Jane have been chommies for more than ten years. And then she started crying. And that was the end of that.'

'Thanks, Davids. We'll talk again later.'

'Don't be all ruthless with him. Come Sunday he won't be worth shit against Bloem Celtic.' Davids laughs at his own joke and rings off.

Basson thinks for a few seconds, shakes his head slowly. 'I don't know.'

'Well, let's go find out,' Majola replies.

Basson and Majola enter the interrogation room. Basson takes a seat across from Seketse at the steel table. Majola leans against the wall with Rikhotso. Benjamin Seketse is clearly upset, though he's trying to hide it.

It's a pretty sombre room. Majola hasn't seen any interrogation rooms in South Africa resembling the ones you see on TV, with two-way mirrors. But he's heard they've got one like that at a new station in Soweto.

Basson takes in Seketse. The trainers and tracksuit alone probably cost more than the down payments on his car. He doesn't want to know what the gold chain around his neck is worth.

Basson introduces himself and Majola. Seketse doesn't respond.

'Okay. Let's start at the beginning. Tell me exactly what happened on Thursday.'

Seketse sighs, rolls his eyes, then turns towards Basson. He rests his arms on the table. Basson notices the TAG Heuer watch.

'Jane came for dinner. I had practice till late, so she took a taxi to my place. I ordered us some pizza. We got into an argument after we ate and she went home.'

'How much do you make at Wits? Or rather, how much will you make with the Platinum Pirates?'

'Platinum Stars,' Rikhotso chimes in from the corner.

'Jissis tog. Platinum Stars, then. Thank you, Sergeant,' Basson says through clenched teeth. Majola doesn't react; he's just observing the room quietly.

Seketse slaps a big, shit-eating grin across his face. 'Enough. More than you.'

'I imagine so. And you're still so young; you've got your whole life ahead of you. You've already got the money. Why the hell would you want a girlfriend and a baby right now? The girls probably line up at your door. Who's got time for cleaning shitty nappies, snot and vomit off everything in the middle of the night? That's not the life of a talented young player like yourself. You guys are drowning in pussy, aren't you? Did you knock Jane about a bit when you found out she was pregnant? That's your style, isn't it?'

Seketse's grin has faded. 'What do you mean?'

'They tell me you like beating up girls. Got yourself a criminal record for your efforts.'

'I was young. And I'm going for treatment. I don't drink any more.'

'Yeah, and now that you've stopped drinking, you probably need a new way to get rid of your frustration.'

Seketse just shakes his head.

'Where do you keep the red taxi?'

'The what?'

'The taxi you use to rape the girls.'

'Was Jane raped?'

Basson starts laughing.

'Detective.' Majola looks sternly at Basson.

Basson ignores him. He drags the dossier over. 'This is what I think: after you and Jane fought about the baby and your transfer to Rustenburg, you lost your cool. Hell, man, I can understand the frustration. Then you fucked her up badly.'

Seketse's face falls and his eyes widen.

Basson tosses a photo down in front of him. It's one of Jane strung up beside the highway. Seketse looks stunned.

'You won't let a baby get in the way of your fame and fortune, and even less a girl who bitches about you not being home enough. So, you carve a few numbers into her back, rape her with a broomstick and dump her by the side of the highway. Nice and close to the field where you practise – why make an effort? Look how pretty she looks. That's your handiwork.'

Seketse turns away from the photo, stricken. He looks to Rikhotso and Majola for help.

'Detective!' Majola barks and steps closer.

'You know you're our number-one suspect. Maybe I should call the *Daily Sun*. Great headline for tomorrow: *Soccer Star is m1 Monster*. And with that assault charge against you … I'm sure Platinum Aces will love that.'

'Aikona, man,' Rikhotso says.

Majola walks to the table and starts putting the pictures back in the folder.

'See me outside,' Majola orders Basson.

Seketse starts to tear up. 'It wasn't me. I told you. I'm not like those other players, those with the girlfriends in every town. Jane would come along. She just wanted the baby here in Joburg, close to her family. The fight was about that. God, man, take those pictures away. Take them away!' Seketse screams, close to hysteria.

Basson walks past Majola, who slams the door behind them.

'Was that necessary? To show him the photos? What the hell is the matter with you? You said you were uncertain about him.'

'You know how I feel about mother-fuckers who beat women,' Basson answers hoarsely.

'Or is it because he said he earns more than you do? Or is it because he's black and it's true?'

'Fuck you.' Basson holds Majola's gaze.

'Listen, we're all tired. But I don't want a lawsuit against us. I don't think it's him.'

Basson snorts.

'Let's wrap this up,' Majola says and opens the door for Basson.

Rikhotso is beside Seketse, a hand on his shoulder, but quickly removes it.

'You can go. But keep your phone charged. We'll contact you again about Jane, her habits, routines. Thanks for your time,' Majola says.

Basson doesn't look at Seketse.

'Come, Sergeant, you owe me a lift. He can call Uber. It's just around the corner,' Basson says to Rikhotso. Majola shakes his head.

Rikhotso takes his jacket and gives Basson a dirty look as he walks past him.

Seketse gets up slowly and walks to the door. He turns to Basson. 'Racist pig.'

'What was that?' Basson steps closer.

Majola grabs him by the arm. 'Goodnight, Mr Seketse.'

Basson glares at Seketse as he leaves.

'Go get some rest, Jason,' says Majola. 'When you feel better, speak to the investigating officer at Diepsloot tomorrow. Otherwise we'll talk on Monday if you don't find out anything.'

It's a long, quiet ride back to his apartment with Rikhotso. Just the sound of the wipers and Metro FM playing softly in the background.

'I'm glad you didn't show him a photo of the foetus,' Rikhotso blurts out.

'I may be a bastard, but I'm not a fucking bastard,' Basson replies resignedly.

'Could have fooled me. Don't you think you were a bit harsh on him?'

Basson takes his cigarettes from his pocket. 'You know, I've learnt never to underestimate people. I've seen people falling apart, in tears, wailing, the whole thing, especially after they see the pictures of the victim. They don't even ask for a lawyer. Five months later we catch them, usually with a higher body count than before. And a lot of these golden boys have it all – the money, the girls, the high life. That's why they have to find their kicks somewhere else.'

Rikhotso turns off the radio. 'That laaitie doesn't know anything. You could see it in his eyes.'

'Yeah?'

'Many years ago, we had these murders in Soweto, where I used to work. A Shangaan who was working on the mine in Randfontein came home earlier than usual that week. He had a wife and two little kids. When he got home, he caught her in bed with another man. The kids were asleep. The Shangaan decided to punish them. He bludgeoned the guy, his wife and his kids to death. With a brick. Right there, as they lay sleeping. Then he took a saw and cut all their heads off. The next morning the woman's sister shows up. She calls the cops, screaming, while the man calmly sits there, watching television with a quart of Castle in his hand and the saw right there next to him. When we got there, with the hysterical sister and the neighbours waiting outside, a ntja was already there, eating from the children's bodies.'

'Their dog?'

'No, one of the township dogs.'

Rikhotso shakes his head. 'The strangest thing was that we couldn't find their heads at first. We looked everywhere in the yard. The man didn't say a word. Gave himself up to be cuffed and calmly walked over and got in the back of the van. Sergeant Mgwene was smoking in the street when he saw it.'

Basson sees his turn-off and worries that Rikhotso isn't going to be done with his story in time. 'Turn left here, at the circle. Saw what?'

'The psycho had put the heads on the roof: wife, boyfriend, kids. Like flowerpots, between the stones keeping the shack's roof from blowing away. Probably why no one saw them at first. All four were looking in the same direction, out over the township.'

'Jissis.'

Rikhotso turns into Basson's apartment complex, puts the car in neutral.

'I looked into that guy's eyes and there was nothing. Lefeela. Fuck-all. The guy that we're looking for, with the taxi, he's someone like that. Something big has gone wrong in him. When I looked into that boy's eyes, I knew he wasn't a monster. He's just a moshanyana, a young boy who wants to play soccer. Our guy is still out there. And I hope we catch him. Because someone who feels nothing isn't going to stop.'

'You just missed Lizanne. She left ten minutes ago,' Kappie says, rubbing his hands together.

Majola looks at Kappie, sitting there on the same wire-mesh chair in the garden of the retirement home, wearing his blue bathrobe. He looks tired. His eyes are bloodshot, sunken, but still a bright blue. People always joked about his eyes, flattering him with comments that he looked like Paul Newman.

Is he imagining it or has Kappie lost more weight? His hands are shaky as they reach for the cup. The grey hair at his temples also seems thinner. Why are they sitting outside? The sun is almost down.

'I got a chance to speak to her yesterday. She says she's also working too hard. Those long hours can't be easy,' Majola says.

'Ja, young man. That child of mine. I wish she'd meet a good man. But I don't know how she thinks that's going to happen if she works all the damn time. Those surgeons claim their pound of flesh. Greedy bastards.'

Kappie settles himself more comfortably on the chair. 'Should have brought out some bloody cushions. We're both going to have checkered asses after this.'

'Why don't we sit inside? I'm more worried that we freeze them off,' Majola jokes.

Kappie smiles. 'The apartment stifles me a bit. And the cold air is good for you.'

Two squawking hadedas fly overhead. Kappie follows their flight over the trees.

'Damn things are all over the place. Did you know they're an alien species?'

'No, I didn't,' Majola responds half-heartedly.

'How's the job going? Is Radebe giving you grief?'

Majola sips the weak coffee. 'Well, Kappie, we're doing what we can. You know him – bastard doesn't sleep. I think I need to take some leave. But we're not here to talk about my health. How's yours? How are you feeling? Things were going so well for so long. I was worried yesterday.'

Kappie shakes his head. 'Your guess is as good as mine. Schoeman said things were looking better. We were talking about lowering the dose, if the psychiatrist agreed. He says I'm quite relaxed under the hypnosis; apparently a few things have come out of those sessions, from the past. He says it's good that

I'm talking about it all. But what does he know about what happened? Fuck it; most of the time I try to forget it.'

'You should try to do your part,' Majola says firmly. 'It's not going to help if you fight him.'

'The guy's away hunting more than he's here. And when he's here, he talks to you like you're a child. David, this thing is messing with my head. The only thing I can remember is how I felt before the episode: confused, forgetful. After that it's just nothing. It feels like sometimes I'm dreaming; images come back to me, stuff from the past. Riots. Masses of people. Sometimes it feels like I'm sitting in a train, but the train is going to derail and I can't get myself free. Like I'm tied down. There are people around me, old colleagues – sometimes you're there. Even the bullfrog, Radebe. Maybe I shouldn't read Revelations any more. I pray every day, asking God for some clarity. He must have a plan with all of this.'

Majola nods quietly, not knowing what else to say or do.

'What's bothering you?'

Majola is taken aback by Kappie's question. 'Sorry?'

'I can see something isn't right. You're staring into the distance, barely listening. How are things with your mother and sister?'

Majola is relieved that he doesn't have to start talking about the case immediately.

'I haven't been there in a while. I'll probably swing around tomorrow and take them some groceries. My mother's been complaining about Lulu; she's been hanging out with this Christine girl, and she's bad news. And she should be studying. My mother doesn't need that kind of stress. I feel bad – I should visit more often. But you know how the job gets sometimes.'

'Is that all?' Kappie asks.

Majola smiles. He's forgotten how sharp Kappie's instincts are. 'Did you hear about the mess on the M1 yesterday?'

'No. I was playing Santa Claus yesterday. My other persona.'

Majola ignores the joke and continues. 'They found a girl, tied up next to the M1, by the Smit Street turn-off. Very bad shape. She had numbers and letters carved into her back. Doctor Lubbe said it rang a bell, that he'd heard about something similar at Orange Farm. He was right.'

'Shit,' Kappie says. 'Do you think you've got a serial on your hands?'

'Exactly. Or it seems very likely. But we're still checking everything. I don't want to jump to conclusions,' Majola replies. He gives Kappie all the details he has. Kappie listens attentively, doesn't interrupt once.

When Majola goes quiet, Kappie says, 'Make doubly sure about the taxi first. To go on the word of a drunk old man is never a good idea. Double-check the girl's testimony as well. Any ideas about the numbers and letters?'

'No ideas yet. I asked Mitchell to search the internet. At this stage we don't have a lot to go on. Hopefully by Monday we'll know more.'

Kappie draws his robe tight around him. The sun has gone down. 'He's putting in a lot of effort. He rapes and sodomises her, electrocutes her and cuts her up. Masochist, my ass. This sounds like serious daddy or mommy issues. This sounds like a whole different level.'

Kappie rubs his chin while he thinks. The hadedas have settled into the nearby oak tree. 'Damn, some days I miss these cases. Wish I could see the report.'

Majola turns to Kappie. 'That's the thing. Radebe kind of insisted that I consult you about it. But that's only if you feel up to it. I won't run the risk of fucking up your health.'

Kappie shakes his head in disbelief. 'Radebe? He couldn't wait to get me out of his way and now he wants me to help? It's strange … I'm not a police pig any more; I'm a member of the public.

'That's what he told me. I think he wants to solve this case as soon as humanly possible. He's taking his pension one of these days. He probably wants to go out with a bang: engraved gold watch, the whole nine yards.'

'You know … he said the oddest thing the day I left,' says Kappie, 'in his office, in front of the commissioner and the general, when I went to say my good-byes.'

'Yes?' Majola leans closer.

Kappie shakes his head slowly. 'Ag, it's probably nothing. Bring me the report when you've got more to work with. I'll take a look. No wait, bring me all the dockets. I'm just sitting here wasting away with all the other geriatrics anyway. I swear I'm the youngest person here. PTSD, the doctor calls it; shit you see in the movies. Like the Yankees coming back from Vietnam. And this old lady who keeps chasing the pigeons around is driving me crazy. If I have to hear her lunatic screeching one more time, I'll have to borrow your pistol and take her down.'

Majola laughs.

'Surely he doesn't expect me to go to the crime scenes with you?' Kappie asks.

'No, no, just to check over the reports.'

Kappie sounds relieved. 'That's good. Maybe I can be useful one last time. And by the sound of it, you guys need all the help you can get. Not that I don't trust you, David. You had a great teacher, after all.'

Majola smiles. 'It's settled then. One last rodeo. I'll swing by again on Monday.'

8

On Sunday morning, just past nine, Basson calls the Diepsloot office. The investigating officer, however, isn't in, and isn't answering his cellphone either. Seeing the clouds lifting and the sun coming out, Basson decides that he'll finally have that braai. He'll check over the dossier later. Shit, a guy needs to kick back and relax every now and then.

At midday, he walks down to the braai area with a bag of acacia wood under one arm and a cooler box under the other. Nonnie is close behind him, carrying a pink ball. Delia has hung back to put the potatoes on the stove. The weather isn't bad for a winter's day, one of the few perks of Johannesburg. The week's rain was quite unseasonal, probably caused by global warming.

Just as they reach the low gate at the pool, Basson hears Wikus laughing. He stops in his tracks. He doesn't want to deal with other people in the braai area.

'Oh, come on. A bit of conversation won't kill you,' Delia says from behind him. She has an empty wine glass in her hand.

'Maybe *you* won't die. What are we gonna talk about? Cherries and tarts?' Basson asks.

'Isn't that what you and the other detectives talk about when you go to the bar?' Delia asks with a wink.

'Come, Daddy!' Nonnie calls, pulling his arm. Basson walks through the gate like a man on his way to the gallows.

'Ah! Our friendly neighbours!' Wikus yells from across the pool.

Basson lifts his hand in a slow greeting. Delia waves excitedly.

Wikus is propped up on a blue Camp Master chair with a pink cocktail in his hand. Louisa is sitting on a blanket on the grass, a safe distance from the Weber, also holding a cocktail. Little Riaan is next to her, fumbling with a rugby ball. His tricycle stands beside the pool.

Delia sits down next to Louisa as Nonnie rushes to join Riaan.

Basson looks at the glowing embers of the charcoal braai. 'Are you a bloody Englishman? Why are you braaiing with charcoal?' he asks.

'No, man. I just don't know where to find good wood. I'm not going to pay R50 for a bag of kameeldoring. But I see you've come to the rescue. Toss a few pieces on – some proper flames will add to the atmosphere.'

Basson lowers the cooler box and somewhat begrudgingly tears open the bag of wood. He was looking forward to making his own fire, not sharing one. After the first pieces catch alight, he pours a glass of wine for Delia and a brandy and Coke for himself. He drags a couple of the wire-mesh chairs over from the lawn.

'Ah, this is the life. The people here don't braai nearly enough. All these trustafarians think they're too fancy,' Wikus remarks.

'You've got a point there,' Basson agrees. 'And they're scared of a bit of cold.'

He looks at Wikus's hairy, muscular legs, at the grey arm hair revealed by his short-sleeved shirt. Clearly not bothered by the cold. You would swear he's a pumpkin farmer from Ventersdorp. Until he speaks.

'Cigarette?' Basson offers.

'No, I'm good thanks. If I start smoking at fifty-two, I'll die on the spot.'

'Really? Fifty-two? You look much younger,' Basson says, trying his best not to make it sound like a compliment.

'Ah, bless you, young one!' Wikus smiles at Basson.

Basson looks away and takes a long sip of his brandy.

'What do you think the Stormers are going to do in the Super Rugby? They gave the Sharks hell last night,' Wikus says.

'We'll have to see. That Kolisi is on fire. And with Etzebeth back from his injury, they're going to be difficult to stop,' Basson opines.

Again, he's surprised by how much Wikus knows about rugby. After the third brandy, and Wikus's fourth pink cocktail, the conversation has lightened somewhat. Basson starts to relax. On the other side of the pool, Delia, Louisa and the kids are kicking the ball around. The coals are almost ready.

'You said your old man was also in the police,' Wikus asks. His speech is slightly slurred.

'Yes. Thirty long years, at the Northwest station. He was also a detective. He got prostate cancer shortly after retiring. Died three years later.'

'Oh …'

The silence drags on. Basson lights another cigarette.

'What do you think of this new law? Outlawing corporal punishment, hidings, all of it.'

'I don't know,' Basson says, shaking his head. 'I think we need to question damn near every decision our government and our courts make. They can't even fix our schools; now they want to tell me how to raise my own child? My dad was pretty strict, as they all were back then. Didn't hesitate to start swinging his belt. I'm not saying I don't have any issues, but I can't blame it all on a fucking hiding. The times I fucked up, I deserved it. Even at school. The classes where the teachers didn't mind getting their hands dirty, those were the classes I always did my homework for. At least now I know the names of all the major rivers in South Africa and what the genitals of a grasshopper look like.'

Wikus cracks a smile while staring at the fire. He leans over and takes another sip of his cocktail. 'Yeah … mine too. But he didn't stop at the belt. And it had nothing to do with strict parenting. That's if the useless layabout wasn't out looking for other women to disappoint.'

Basson looks at Wikus. It sounds like a sensitive topic. 'Yes?' he says carefully, wanting him to go on.

'He was a right fuck-up. Not my real dad, my stepdad. My real dad had a heart attack when I was young. He was a train driver. Loved his booze, old Bernie did. That's the stepdad. If he wasn't raising his hand against my mother or sisters, then it was me. I couldn't sit and watch him beat them. Especially not my younger sister. The older I got, the worse the beatings became. I think he couldn't handle that I was a "pansy" or "camp" or whatever else he thought of me. Until one day. I knocked him clean through the lounge window with an uppercut. I think I was thirteen. But a big thirteen. Shortly after that, he upped and left us. We found out later he went to a girlfriend of his in Potgietersrus. My mother had to raise me and my four sisters on a hairdresser's salary.'

'That's heavy, man,' Basson says.

Wikus goes quiet for a moment. 'On the one hand I'm glad. Growing up I was used to a blow or a slap to the ear. When the first kid tried his luck at school, it was lights out for him. After a while the others realised they shouldn't fuck with the fag. It always made me think of the Johnny Cash song, "A Boy Named Sue". The only difference being I wouldn't have minded being named Sue.'

Basson laughs so hard he spills some of his drink on his lap.

'I was lonely after school, so I focused on my job. My mom had already died by then, my sisters all married. Shit, I missed her. I still have this lovely ball gown of hers. She kept it in the cupboard for years. Always told me how she and my real dad lit up the dance floor in Benoni. My stepdad didn't dance; he just drank. When he died, I took the dress. My sisters said it was old and smelled of mothballs.'

Basson wonders if this is the dress he saw him wearing that day when he walked past his kitchen window.

'That night,' Wikus goes on, 'when you saw me in the kitchen, I was wearing that dress.'

Fuck.

'It's not weird for me. When I have the dress on, it feels like she's still alive. I imagine I can still smell her on it. Despite the mothballs.'

Basson feels slightly better. As if he didn't intrude on Wikus's privacy when he saw him through the window.

'You know, then I met Hugo. I never knew an ugly old fag like me could be so happy.'

Basson doesn't know if he should laugh. It could be the brandy, but he has to admit, Wikus isn't as bad as he'd thought.

'Then, one night, three years ago, a taxi jumped a red light in Florida, and that was it for him.'

Delia had told him it had happened in Krugersdorp. He changes the subject while Wikus takes a long sip of his drink.

'You're not far from early retirement. What, eight years to go?'

Wikus gets up and rakes the coals. 'I know. It's around the corner. Then I can bake all day, every day. You know, Hugo taught me how to cook. He owned a coffee shop close to the Key West Shopping Centre. Now, that guy knows his stuff.' Wikus pauses. 'I still struggle to refer to him in the past tense. Sorry.' He shakes his head slowly.

'In any case, I've done my share of work at the station. These days I put in more time at the call desk, even though I'm acting platoon commander. But I'm not scared of the physical training, let me tell you. I can still kick the recruits' asses any day of the week.'

'Where is your station?' Basson can't remember if Wikus has told him this before.

'Randburg. I started out at Berea as an EMT, but I decided enough was enough when I transferred to Randburg.'

'EMT?' Basson asks.

'Emergency Medical Technician. It basically means I got trauma and emergency medical training. But I had enough of dragging the bodies of burnt children from wrecks and shacks. An old queen can only handle so much burnt meat.'

Basson can see he's going to struggle to get Wikus off this sombre tangent he's on.

'Do you remember how, back in the day, we had to drive around with map books? No GPS or Google Maps or anything,' Basson says to lighten the mood.

'Hell, yes, that was a to-do. And the brass would give you shit for getting lost.'

Wikus looks over at Louisa and little Riaan, running around on the grass. He cleans the grid with half an onion. Riaan comes running over and stands beside Basson's chair.

'Uppy!' Riaan says, arms raised at Basson. Basson picks him up onto his lap. Riaan rests his head on Basson's chest.

'Would you look at that?' Basson says, running his fingers through the soft, blond hair. He looks over at Nonnie playing with Delia and Louisa, not a worry in the world – sometimes Nonnie can get jealous.

'You know, after Hugo I was ready to end it all. I was tired of the cards I'd been dealt. I still had my dad's .38 special that I inherited from my mother. Kept it in a safe. Many nights I sat looking at the thing at the dinner table. I wanted to write a suicide note, but then I thought, to whom? Everyone is dead. Then I met these two. Maybe she reminds me of my mother. Her husband also left her with nothing. Asshole. I've only known them a couple of months, but the Lord knows, I would do anything for them. I know I shouldn't, but sometimes I hope that she doesn't meet someone new, otherwise they'll forget about me.'

Wikus's voice starts to tremble. 'Sometimes I wish I could take them to the country. This fucking city can eat you alive. So much darkness around us. Is that selfish of me? To want to keep them to myself? To want to protect them?'

Basson looks at Riaan, sitting calmly on his lap, untroubled by what's going on around him.

'I don't know, Wikus. But it's good that you want to keep them safe. Everyone needs someone who wants to do that for them.'

'Are we ready to braai, Wikus?' says Louise, walking over to them. 'It's getting a bit nippy for Riaan to be outside. And he has to have his nap soon.'

Wikus wipes his eyes. 'Yes. I'm starving too. And you, champ? Is my little Riaan's tummy growling yet?' The little boy gets off Basson's lap and gives Wikus a hug.

'Hungry,' he says. 'Tjoppie.'

While Wikus puts the meat on the grill, Delia comes to stand next to Basson as he pours himself another brandy.

'And, Jason Basson? Was that so bad?' she teases quietly.

'Not at all. We actually had a good time. And I didn't even have to talk about baked goods at all. And you know what?'

Delia shakes her head.

'Today you don't have to worry about me burning the steaks. It seems we've got a master chef in our midst.'

Delia smiles and kisses him on the cheek. 'Well, according to Louisa, we've got milk tart for dessert,' she says.

Majola carefully puts down the four bags of groceries and opens the garage door. He stopped in at Orange Farm and Katlehong just after nine to speak to the investigating officers. Sergeant Kane from Katlehong was still hungover from the previous night. But he made enough sense, and Majola feels confident that he's been thorough in his investigation. Sergeant Ntatane from Orange Farm is a smooth operator: the parts that were missing from his dossier, he could fill in for Majola in person, but his attention wasn't really on the job at hand. To him it was just another dossier. Just another unsolved murder.

Majola also visited the station during the morning to look at the organogram. He'd hoped that a fresh perspective might help. He even drove past the crime scene, noting where the old sangoma said he saw the taxi. Nothing. Their hope now lies with the taxi associations.

The sun is out and the afternoon has warmed up a bit. Majola's blood-red 1989 BMW 318is two-door coupé gleams in the garage. He runs his hand across the thin layer of dust on the boot. He unlocks the car, drops his bags on the passenger seat and gets behind the steering wheel. The smell of leather hangs thickly around him, and it's good. After a few attempts, the engine takes. Majola turns up the volume on the Boney James CD.

The CD player is one of the few upgrades he's made. And he had to fix the aircon. He got the car at a bargain from an older woman in Soweto, almost twelve years ago. It has nearly 200 000 kilometres on the odometer, but it still runs smoothly. He doesn't use it often, mostly uses his police car. That one he leaves out in the parking, to weather the wind and the rain. In Alexandra there are always people offering to buy his Beemer so that they can use it for spinning, but he can't find it in his heart to sell it.

Sometimes, usually after eleven at night, he takes the BMW onto the highway to clear his head. Then he'll take the M1, take the Sandton turn at the Buccleuch intersection, come back south on the N1 and then back onto the M1 past Gold Reef City. Forty minutes of peace and good music. He needs it at times.

It isn't long before he reaches the Grayston turn-off to Alexandra, and then he's on London Way. He is greeted by the smell of smoke almost instantly: peo-

ple trying to fight the cold. Rubbish, graffiti and hawkers selling candy, cigarettes and magwenjas dot the street. Here and there he sees people holding
church services in empty plots, mostly women in red-and-white uniforms. So
different to where he lives now, where Sunday afternoons and evenings are
calm and quiet. And such a contrast to what's going on across the highway, in
the wealthy suburb of Sandton, with its blonde housewives who believe their
shit doesn't smell and the dickheads driving up and down in Porsches and Fer-
raris. Like two different planets. Once he lost his cool at a white woman from
social services who expressed her surprise at the number of satellite dishes jutting from the Alexandra rooftops. Here there aren't any spas or coffee shops.
No craft breweries or ice-cream parlours. There's fuck-all else to do. Here you
watch TV. If you drink, you go to shebeens and play some pool.

Majola stops at a red light and an old man walks slowly over. He's already
shaking his head to show he doesn't have anything for the old man, who nevertheless knocks on his window. Majola rolls down the window in irritation.

The madala lifts an arm and points in the direction of Sandton, where some
of its buildings are visible. 'Baba, did you ever think heaven and hell would be
so close to each other?' he asks in Zulu, before walking off.

Majola's eyes follow him. A horn from behind makes him jump and he
realises the light has gone green.

Before buying his apartment three years ago, he was living in the Herders-
hof barracks in Sophiatown with the other police officers and their families.
But the place had fallen into such disrepair that he had to move. The lifts hadn't
worked in over a decade, and the building was fifteen storeys high. He was
lucky enough to end up on the second floor. Cars were being stolen from the
parking lot. There were weekly break-ins. What does it say about your country
when the people who uphold its justice are the ones who can't find any for
themselves?

His mother lives at 5224, Extension 7, East Bank, where she was fortunate
enough to be given one of the double-bedroom RDP houses eleven years ago.
He had had to pull some strings with Prince Sabisa to make it happen. Luckily,
they went to school together before Sabisa joined the township council. Then
again, anyone would probably jump at the chance to have a policeman owe
them a favour. They could have used this house when he was a teenager. He
had to sleep in the kitchen growing up, with the umkhukhu, or toilet, outside.

When he turned fourteen, he told Auntie Anne that he wanted to meet his
real mother. He had never felt that he belonged in Linden, always felt that
something was missing. Auntie Anne was heartbroken but she agreed to help
him look. After visiting countless orphanages, they found his biological mother, Thadie Majola. She fell to her knees and praised the Lord after she opened
her door. He left Linden behind, along with all his friends, the big house, the
pocket money, the nice clothes, and moved to Alex to be with Mama Thadie,
the woman who'd given him up because she couldn't care for him and her hus-

band didn't want him. At first he missed all of it. But it had never felt quite right there. The black kid with the white mother. The looks he got. The gossip. Something was always scratching at his insides, like a knife over burnt toast. It got harder and harder to ignore as he got older. He'd had to find his real mother. She had to teach him Zulu, as he could only speak Afrikaans and English. Luckily her Afrikaans wasn't bad.

It was difficult at first, but Auntie Anne and his mother helped him through it. He still doesn't regret his decision.

Jabulani Scrap Metals is on the corner of Second Avenue; further down is the famous Kings Cinema. Some of his best memories from his teenage years are of going to the movies with his mother. It's probable that this is where his love of movies started. His mother would buy them a Coke and a paper bag brimming with popcorn. They had to share but he didn't mind. Sometimes they bought chocolates with the money that Auntie Anne sent. The theatre closed in 2011, when Abraham Nkomo, who took over from his uncle, started renting it out for church services. The Kings Cinema is a national heritage building. He often wonders why the government didn't give money to keep it open so the children had somewhere safe to get off the streets.

The further he drives, the further he leaves behind his apartment in Melville, slowly swallowed by Alex. There is no shortage of churches. Ever since the Nigerians came to spread the prosperity gospel, the churches started to pop up like mushrooms. Names like *Lord's Chosen Congregation* and *God's Only Holy Church* are everywhere. And, of course, the more you donate to the holy pastor with one hand in the collection plate and the other in the underwear of someone from the congregation, the more God will bless you.

Majola has realised that the more desperate the people, the more churches spring up to take what little money they have left. Rosettenville is a good example. Lay preachers. Ama-charlatans. Give your virginity to the Lord and you'll be in line for eternal life. Spray the people with insecticide, let them eat grass and snakes. Insanity. Utter fucking insanity.

Yet Alex was his home for many years, even though he never felt quite at home here either. Perhaps it was because of his western upbringing with Auntie Anne. An upbringing wrapped in cotton wool, protected from the terrors of township life.

When he moved to Alex, he had to start standard seven at Eastbank High School. It was nothing like Linden High. He kept to himself mostly, away from the drugs and the gangs. His trouble with drugs would begin twenty years later on the other side of the highway. Go figure.

His mother was his compass. She kept him on the straight and narrow. Chased away the worse of his 'friends' with a sjambok. He never really excelled, but he did well enough to pass every year. Played a bit of soccer. Helped to raise his sister, the one his mother had at the age of forty-eight. He was barely fifteen, had just moved back to Alex, when she got pregnant. Lulu's father also didn't stick around. Just like his father. But he had no desire to track him down. Other than that, he spent his days reading, or watching movies on the new television his mother bought after saving up for a year, and the old video cassette player Auntie Anne donated. She transferred money quite regularly, and that helped to make things easier for them.

Alexandra was named for the wife of the mlungu farmer, a Mr Papenfus, who owned the land more than a century ago. Others say it was named for King Edward VII's wife. But he's always known it as Alex. The neighbourhood is rich in history: in 1941, Nelson Mandela rented a room on Seventh Avenue in Dark City – so named because the area had no electricity – while working as an articled clerk in Johannesburg.

The other thing that had made Alex infamous over the years was the amagundwane. The rats. A few years ago, what started as a problem became a plague. There were even fears that the bubonic plague would break out again. People told stories of the rats eating the noses, fingers and toes of sleeping babies. The *Daily Sun* even reported that the rats ate one gogo's chickens. The rats were an inevitable effect of overpopulation and accumulated trash. The Setswela informal settlement had the worst problem. No running water, no electricity, no toilets: the rodents caused havoc. At some point, the council tried to use owls to control the plague, without success. According to local cultural tradition, the owl was a bad omen, so people killed them, or worse, cut off their wings and claws. Later the municipality tried carbon-monoxide poisoning, which had better results. But the rats persisted.

Majola is still scared to death of rats. Back then, he could hear them at night. Especially on the roof. His mother put out poison but still they came. In the glow of the paraffin lamp, on his mattress under the kitchen table, he could see them scurrying, their shadows dashing across the wall. Despite his desperate prayers, eyes closed tight, they didn't go away. That's when he missed his double bed at Auntie Anne's.

The little yard in front of his mother's house is neat, despite the neighbour's Toyota Cressida propped up on bricks somewhat spoiling the scene. A mutt is sniffing at the overturned dustbin belonging to the woman next door. Some paving stones have been laid between the little houses, and the thorn tree out front is making a spirited attempt to stay alive.

He parks the BMW in front of the house, takes his pistol out from under the seat and gets the grocery bags from the boot. He double-checks that his car alarm has been set as he walks to the front door.

Mama Thadie opens the door just as he's about to knock. Her face lights up.

'Sawubona ndodana yami,' she says, throwing her arms around Majola.

'Sawubona, Mama,' he greets her tenderly.

The presence of her warm body and the familiar smell of herbs and Zam-Buk salve immediately relaxes him.

'Kuyabanda. Come inside,' she says happily.

'It's nice and cold, nè?' Majola says, sitting down at the green plastic table.

'I'm so glad you're here. I thought you'd never come visit us again. I thought you'd forgotten about us,' Mama Thadie says, smiling.

Majola drops his car keys and wallet on the table and puts his pistol on top of the cupboard against the wall so that his mother can't see it. She doesn't like weapons.

'Ngumsebenzi, Mama, always working; you know how it is. The criminals never sleep.'

Majola watches his mother as she puts on the kettle. It doesn't take long for the water to boil. He wonders what happened to the expensive stainless-steel kettle that he bought her. Just as he wonders what happened to the expensive pressure cooker and oil heater. Old people seem to stick with what they know. Like the asbestos heater beside the kitchen table, probably ten years old, burnt in places from wet clothes left to dry and forgotten.

His mother looks good. He smiles when he sees the green-and-white striped jersey he bought her two years ago. She has a bit of a limp; probably her hip giving her trouble again. These days she does domestic work at a flat in Sandton just once a week. The place is small and close enough. He happily pays R2 000 into her account every month to help out. And he covers her DSTV account.

'Thank you for the groceries. You know it's not necessary,' she says, pouring water into two cups. 'You've lost weight, David. Are you eating properly? Isn't it time for you to get yourself a wife?'

Majola doesn't feel like answering. He knows the conversation will inevitably turn to Busiswe.

'I ran into Busi's parents at the Plaza the other day.'

Well, fuck, that didn't take her long.

'They look well. But they didn't really want to talk.'

Because they're fucking heartless.

He tries to steer the conversation in a different direction. 'How is Auntie Liesbet doing? With the lung and everything?'

Mama Thadie takes a packet of biscuits from one of the bags Majola brought, tears it open and puts it in front of them.

'She's well. She's started working again. She still moans a lot, but now that she's working, she's not here all the time any more. So I don't have to listen to her go on all day.'

Majola smiles. He hears a car pass outside, music blaring.

'You should hear what the pastor has to say ...'

Majola lets his mother talk. Clearly, she misses company. He listens with half an ear, nods occasionally. At least she doesn't talk about the past too much. Old people get caught up in the details of their lives and thoughts. The older they get, the smaller their world becomes. When he has something to say, he could swear she doesn't really pay attention to him either. But he knows just being here means the world to her.

Mama Thadie gets up after a while to stir the pot of stew on the stove and put some rice in the microwave.

'How is Auntie Anne doing?' she asks, her back to him.

'Good, thanks. I spoke to her last week. Her sister is visiting from England.'

Suddenly Mama Thadie turns around. 'Why did you come back, David?'

Majola shakes his head. 'I've told you a hundred times. Mama is blood. And before Mama asks again, I understand why you left me at the orphanage. Mama was poor, there was no other choice. You wanted the best for me.'

Mama Thadie smiles shyly.

'Uphi uLulu? I thought she would be here tonight?' he asks to avoid having to discuss the topic further.

Mama Thadie pauses for a moment before turning the knob on the microwave.

'I don't know, David. She's out and about. I told her you were coming over, but she insists she's not a child any more. Christine came over earlier and they left together. That child barely greets me. I'm worried about Lulu: she's supposed to be studying. Exams are around the corner. But then she says hairdressing is only practical. They don't have to learn anything. But that's not what Agnes said, and she's at the college. She says they have to study too.'

He can hear the concern in her voice.

'But she works hard at the salon. Then at night she goes to college. Or so she says. It's hard to study after a day like that.'

Majola takes out his phone and calls Lulu's number. After a while he puts the phone down.

'She's not answering.'

He sighs loudly. He knows Christine. The one with the short skirts and the high heels. If he didn't know any better, he would have thought she was an isifebe. She certainly dresses like one.

'Ag, David, you know how she is. She has a mind of her own,' says Mama Thadie.

Majola is angry now. 'Ja, but I'm not going to waste my money. That course is expensive. And she has to make something of her life. I can't care for her forever.'

His mother tries to defend her daughter. 'She does make some money at the salon. She buys her own clothes and pays for her own transport.'

'I'm thinking of tomorrow. Or does she want to be an apprentice at the salon for the rest of her life? I'll have to speak to her.'

Mama Thadie takes off her apron, hangs it up.

'Can the two of us just spend the evening together? We'll leave Lulu for another day.'

Majola sighs again. 'Okay, okay,' he grumbles.

'I'm just going to the bathroom, then I'll come dish up.'

When he hears the click of the bathroom door, Majola gets up and walks to

Lulu's room. He opens the door and turns on the light. The bed has been made, probably by his mother, but the floor is littered with clothing. On her bedside table is a picture of the three of them: him, Lulu and their mother. It was taken years ago at Christmas. Everyone is smiling; it was a good day. He has a Christmas hat on and a beer in his hand. One wall is covered in posters of Tupac and Kanye West. He's never been a fan of Kanye West. Arrogant jackass.

He opens her cupboard. At least her clothing is neatly folded. At the bottom are some shoes and two boxes. He lifts the lids. More shoes. He closes the cupboard. He walks to the bedside table and opens a drawer. Inside he sees a pink book that looks like a diary. He pages through it quickly. There are diary entries but he's too embarrassed to read them, so he closes it. Just as he wants to put it back, he notices a CD case. It's by Black Coffee.

There's a slight scuffing, something sticky on the plastic container. The corners of the cover have a thin white film. He smells it.

Can it fucking be?

He licks the case. A bitter, sharp taste. It's cat. How could he ever forget the taste? A few times his dealer didn't have cocaine. He even spread it over his gums when he was too lazy to snort it.

Fucking Christine.

He hears his mother flushing the toilet. He searches the drawer and finds a straw, cut in half, with a white shine on the inside.

In his mother's fucking house?

Right under her nose?

He puts the case and the straw back, puts the diary on top. He flicks off the light and closes the door behind him. He takes a few quick steps and sits at the table again.

His blood is boiling. He's going to strangle her. Both her and Christine. He knows what that junk can do to you. It can nail you to the tracks as a train comes barrelling down. He still doesn't know by whose grace he'd been able to pull himself free before it was too late. But now he'll have to keep his cool. For his mother's sake. It would break her to know Lulu was involved with drugs.

'Do you want some Coke?'

Majola jumps, then nods, relieved when he sees the bottle in her hand. 'Please, yes.'

Mama Thadie pours him a glass. They eat their stew and rice in silence.

After clearing the table and putting the dishes in the sink, she comes to sit back down at the table.

'Can I help you wash up?'

'Don't worry, I'll do it after you've left. It's not like the two of us made a mess. Remind me to give you some stew to take home, otherwise I'll have too much left over.'

Majola doesn't want his mother to get suspicious, so he asks carefully, 'Does that Mpete still live on Mike Diradingwe Street?'

Mama Thadie stares at him for a moment.

'Yes, he does. The other day Auntie Teboho told me she saw Christine go in there.'

'Just Christine?' He tries not to sound concerned.

'Ja. I've asked Lulu if she's ever gone there but she says she stays away. He's bad news. I think he's dealing with nyope and all kinds of stuff.'

Of course Lulu would lie to her mother. Why would Christine go by herself if they're such good friends? And fucking hell, rather cat than nyope. He's seen people on that junk tear each other apart like animals.

Mama Thadie looks at Majola again before speaking. 'I'm worried, David. About you and Lulu,' she says, concern in her voice.

Majola wonders if she knows about Lulu's drug abuse. But how would she? She wouldn't recognise the white powder on the CD case. Unless gossip got around.

'Why, Mama? Because Lulu's never here? I'll speak to her, don't worry about it.'

Mamie Thadie hesitates before she speaks again. 'I went to the sangoma. Last week.'

Majola loses his composure. 'God, Mama, I told y—'

'David! Don't talk like that.'

He ignores her. 'I've told you before: you're just wasting your money. Bunch of nonsense. How much did he charge you this time?'

Mama Thadie shakes her head. 'Only R50. And R30 the first time.'

'You went twice? Why? What crap did the ancestors have to say this time?'

'David!'

He notices the pin with the ZCC insignia on her chest.

'What would the pastor say if he knew you were wasting your money on that charlatan, Mama?'

'David, wait. Just listen,' his mother says calmly. She pauses before she goes on. 'He saw something the first time. Then I had to go back to make sure.'

Majola shakes his head in disbelief.

'The first time he saw me and Lulu lying by the side of the road. It was dark. The second time he saw you lying there with us. We weren't moving.'

Majola smiles. 'Yup, and then? Then a rat came by and gave us all a lift to Durban?'

Mama Thadie looks hurt, disappointed in him for not taking her seriously.

'Okay, sorry, Mama. Please go on.'

Mama Thadie stares into his eyes again. Her own start tearing up.

'There was a taxi. A red taxi. And it was full of blood. It was driving away from us.'

Majola can feel his blood run cold and the hair on the back of his neck rising. The room starts to spin.

'What did you say, Mama?' His voice is almost inaudible.

'That's what he saw. I'm scared, David.'

He doesn't answer her. All he can see is his mother and sister by the side of the road, covered in blood, with numbers carved into their backs. How the hell is this possible? How does the sangoma know about the case he's working on? Is it purely coincidence? Or is there something to these predictions? He struggles to order his thoughts.

He feels an urge to stand up.

'David, is everything okay?' she asks.

He takes a while to answer. 'Ja, Mama. You shouldn't let these ghost stories frighten you. Why don't you stick to reading the Bible? Leave the taxi to me.'

Mama Thadie frowns. She doesn't understand.

'I have to get going. I've still got work waiting.'

In silence Majola puts on his jacket, picks up his keys, and gets the gun from the top of the cupboard. They walk to the front door, Majola with a stew-filled plastic container in his hand.

'Mama, don't come out; it's too cold.'

He hugs her tightly, holding her longer than usual.

'David, are you okay? What is wrong, my boy?'

'Just a bit tired. I have to go to bed early tonight. Tell Lulu I'll call her.'

Mama Thadie bids him farewell at the door and goes back inside.

Back in the car, Majola immediately switches on the aircon. He's struggling to make sense of what just happened. It feels unreal. Just as the week's horrors seemed to be coming to an end. The murders. Lulu. And now the sangoma's visions.

He dials Lulu's number again. He gets voicemail. 'Ngicel'ungithinte kusasa.'

And she'd better call tomorrow. His world has been shaken, violently shaken. He'll have to take a sleeping pill tonight.

Instead of taking London Way to the M1, he takes the turning to the M3. At the intersection he hesitates. On the corner of Mike Diradingwe Street, he looks at the grey double-storey house with the high wall. A black C-Class Mercedes with alloy rims is parked outside, a few men standing beside it. He can hear music playing but isn't sure if it's coming from the house or the car.

This is where Calvin Mpete lives. He wonders if Lulu gets her drugs here, and whether Auntie Teboho is telling the truth. But he knows Mpete wouldn't be selling it himself; he would have people doing it for him.

He pulls away slowly and starts to head for home, winding down a window. The three men standing next to the Mercedes turn to watch him pass. One has a beer in his hand. 'Ubheke ini?' yells the one closest to the car.

'I'm watching you, mother-fucker,' Majola mutters.

He wonders if the Z88 under the seat is cocked, but remembers he flicked the safety on before leaving Melville. He drives off slowly with the men still staring at him. He watches them in the rear-view mirror. One of them gives him the finger.

'You think you're God. I will bring the plagues down upon you. Watch me do it. You're fucking with the wrong Zulu,' Majola says to himself, shifting gears and picking up speed.

Aneni Masimba is getting cold. The man is late; it's almost seven o'clock. A Conquest with tinted windows drove past half an hour ago. Shortly afterwards, an Audi A1 with two young blonde women inside it followed. When the Conquest caught sight of the Audi, the driver accelerated and turned left at the end of the road. Bloody Nigerians. They're the ones giving the amakwerekwere a bad name in South Africa.

The alley is narrow and runs from Beyers Naudé in Melville. There's barely enough space for a single car to get through. He'll have to take an Uber to the McDonald's and walk from there. The man never meets him in the same place, but it's never far from this area. Sophiatown, Westdene, Melville, or a little further north, in Linden. He sends out the location on WhatsApp, from one of three different numbers. Then he delivers the package, with instructions on an A4 page. Always the same package, always same content, with the typed page.

Aneni pulls the black cap down over his head. His dreadlocks help a bit with the cold. He hopes the man will see him in the dark with his black tracksuit on.

In front of him is a wall full of graffiti. Aneni wonders where he'd be now if he had had the opportunity to study. But then he'd have had to finish school first. In Zim there's nothing. No work, no prospects, nothing. Fokkolo.

He had to buy his motorbike licence from a dodgy Metro policeman from Langlaagte. But it was worth it. Now he rides a delivery motorbike eight hours a day. The money isn't great but it's something. The man's payments help a lot: R2 000 a shot, throughout the past year. About as much as he makes in a week. He knows he should put more of it away, but he struggles with the booze. He's going to AA meetings now.

He has to piss, but it's so damn cold he can barely feel his hands. Just as he turns to the wall, he sees the lights of a slow-moving vehicle. Aneni blows into his hands. He is, as usual, a little nervous about the deal that's going to take place. The vehicle stops beside him and the electric window opens. They don't exchange greetings. The man hands him the parcel and the envelope with the cash.

Just before the man closes the window again, Aneni asks, 'When will you let me know about the next one?' Aneni can hardly see the man's face tonight.

'There won't be a next one. There is a little extra for you in the envelope. Make sure you don't fuck it up.'

Aneni watches the man's car as it drives away. Then he turns and walks quickly in the direction of Beyers Naudé Drive, disappointed.

***

Ayanda Mcayi crosses the open parking lot at Campus Square in Melville. She checks her phone: it's nearly ten. She scolds herself for not topping up her airtime, because then she could have got an Uber. But she doesn't have the R40 for the trip to Sophiatown anyway – she spent everything on gin and tonics at the News Café. It's quite late but she hopes she can still find a taxi.

Maybe she should have asked Peter to give her a lift; but no, he was way too touchy tonight. He would have suggested they exchange favours and she wasn't in the mood. He's the only one of her old school friends who still tries his luck, even though he knows she's been with Lungani for nearly four years, and happily so. The rest of her friends are still drinking, but she has class tomorrow. Exams are soon and she can't bunk. Besides, it's not like her mom would allow it.

Ayanda walks to the corner of Beyers Naudé and Kingsway. The streets are quiet tonight and it's cold, despite the rain having rolled on. The black leather jacket she's wearing over her dress isn't helping much and the gin and tonics are starting to wear off. At least she's wearing thick stockings.

Down the street at the McDonald's, she sees a taxi stop at the light. She steps to the curb, ready to hail it. There's a couple further down the road, who gesture to the taxi as the light turns green, but it pulls slowly away, leaving them behind. Ayanda drops her hand in despair. It's probably too late; it's not taking passengers any more. But when the taxi approaches her, it slows down and comes to a stop. Ayanda opens the sliding door, and it jams halfway, forcing her to get in the front row.

The first seat is broken so she moves to the middle and sits down, keeping her small black handbag on her lap. She notices that the seat to her right is also broken. She isn't in the mood to sit next to the driver and make small talk. She does feel she ought to say something about the seats, though.

'Don't you think it's time to fix the seats?' she says, her speech slightly slurred.

Dark glass separates her from the driver's side of the minibus. The glass extends to the ceiling above the front-seat headrests, and there's a small sliding window set into the glass panel, with what may be a latch on the driver's side, but she's not sure. She can hardly see the driver at all; it's almost pitch black. The taxi pulls away slowly, without anyone asking her where she's going or to hand over the fee.

'Hello?' she asks in the direction of the driver.

The cabin smells strange, like cleaning chemicals. The low light makes it difficult to see what else is in the cabin, and the windows are so dark that little light comes in from the outside. Ayanda feels panic rising as she looks around her.

She gets up and knocks on the window.

'Hello?'

She takes out her phone and the light illuminates the cabin. The first thing she notices is the rubber sheeting lining the sides, the seats and the ceiling. Ice runs through her veins.

'Can you please let me out?' she asks. She knocks on the window with more force.

There is no answer from behind the black glass.

'I said, let me out. Now!' But the sound of her voice seems muted, as if it is trapped inside the cabin with her.

The taxi comes to a sudden stop, throwing her against the window. Then it pulls away just as suddenly. She tugs on the door but it's locked. Not knowing what else to do, she sits back down.

'What the …' she trembles, unsure if she's just imagining this scene.

The backrests of both rows of seats fall forward, folding themselves in half. Then both rows move back in one mechanical motion to clear a two-metre gap between the glass wall and the retracted seats. She sees the tracks in the floor along which the seats run. She can't move. Her seat is the only one that didn't move.

Ayanda jumps when her backrest suddenly jerks backwards. She grabs the armrests of her seat, tries to stay upright.

As she does so, two steel clamps slam across her wrists, pinning her arms down on the armrests. Her handbag and phone fall to the floor. Ayanda screams from the shock and the pain. Again, she tries to get up, but two more clamps lock around her knees. The pain is agonising. She screams again. She tries to pull free, tugging at the clamps, but there is no give in them. She sits in the middle of the cabin. Alone.

'What do you want?!'

But there is only silence. All she can hear is the sound of the engine changing gear. The taxi comes to a stop at a red light. Through the dim window she can just make out another car stopped next to them.

'Help me! Please, help me!'

After a few seconds the car pulls away slowly. Her screams die in her throat. She knows this is the deepest kind of trouble. She can't make out where the driver is taking her. She looks down at her phone which starts ringing on the floor. She sees the name on the screen. It's Lungani.

She starts to sob in near silence.

'Please, God, please …'

After a while the cellphone goes quiet and dark again. Then she starts crying loudly. Her wrists ache, her knees too. The clamps dig into her, pull her into the seat.

'Lungani!'

But she knows she's alone.

Lungani is at home, waiting for her, probably wondering where she is.

She stops crying, tries to wrest back some control of the situation. She looks around her. Through the dark dividing glass, she can vaguely make out the lights of oncoming traffic. How long have they been driving? Where is he taking her? Is he going to rape her? Kill her?

She forces her mind away from the worst of these thoughts and looks at the clamps on her wrists. She tries to pull free again, but she can't get her hands free. The lights ahead have stopped coming. The taxi is slowing down. It feels like they're on a dirt road.

The taxi comes to an abrupt halt. A few seconds later the engine dies. The cabin becomes utterly silent. The only thing she can hear is her own breath and the faint ping of the cooling engine. She can't hear any other vehicles outside.

Here it is. Whatever is going to happen, is going to happen now. She tries again to break free but the steel bites into her.

'Please, God …' she murmurs through her tears.

She hears a door opening and being closed gingerly. She waits for the sliding door to open and for her abductor to show himself. Nothing happens.

Seconds tick by. Did the man walk away? Maybe he heard her praying? She's heard of instances where the victims prayed and the attackers let them go. Miracles still happen.

An iota of hope takes root. She tries to look through the window. She can't see anything happening outside. Did she imagine it or did something move past the driver's window?

The door slides open, breaking the silence. The man is standing in the doorway, silhouetted by the city lights. She can smell the field they must be in, moist from the rain. The man gets in and closes the door.

'Please …'

He sits down in front of her, on what looks like a black box, his back to the divider. He is dressed all in black. Underneath the hoodie he is wearing a balaclava; only the whites of his eyes are showing. She can faintly smell his aftershave.

Then she sees the white surgical gloves. Her breath catches in her throat and she starts to struggle against her bonds again. He picks something up off the floor and puts it down in front of him. She hadn't noticed him bringing anything in with him. He unfurls a black towel to reveal his tools.

Ayanda's heart drops as she sees the scalpel, the scissors, the truncheon.

'Please!'

The man doesn't react. He leans forward and unties her boots, slowly, even sensually, as if he's teasing her. Like a lover.

Suddenly he smashes a fist into her jaw. Her head jerks back like a rag doll's.

He fumbles behind her and ties something around her neck. She hears the sound of Velcro. Her legs and arms burn from the pressure of being restrained. It sounds as if he tosses her boots into a corner. Then she feels his hands underneath her dress, moving higher up, feels his fingers hook into the elastic of her stockings. The gloves are cold against her skin.

'God, please.'

He pulls the stockings off slowly. Then he rifles among his tools again. He pulls her dress up, puts one finger under the elastic of her panties and cuts it carefully with the scissors. His breathing starts to quicken. He smells her underwear and sighs to himself. He tosses it into the corner with her stockings and boots. Slowly, meticulously, he cuts through the leather of her jacket, then the fabric of her dress.

He sits down again and looks at her. She has only her bra on. Ayanda can feel his eyes crawling all over her naked flesh.

He stands up and leans over her, smells her neck. Ayanda starts to scream. The man steps away, pulls back and slaps her with the back of his hand. She tastes blood in her mouth. Ayanda weeps softly as he tears off her bra. She wants to close her legs but the clamps keep her exposed.

Ayanda can smell her own sweat and fear in the cabin. Her skin is crawling from the cold and the terror and her nipples stand out stiffly.

'Please. You can do whatever you want. I won't resist. You can have me. Right here. You don't have to use that.'

The man rubs the tip of the truncheon across her thigh. His breathing deepens again.

Then, with such violence that she thinks her lower body is broken in two, he rams the truncheon into her. She tastes metal on her tongue. With every blow, the sharp pain tears through her body. She feels her insides give way, get shoved around. She screams but she can't hear herself over the pain. It envelops everything, even the dull, rhythmic thudding of the truncheon. She feels one of her nails break on the armrest. She can feel her bottom and lower body getting wet. Her bladder is gone. Or is it blood? The man is getting exhausted from the exertion.

In that moment she gives up. She knows it is hopeless. Her lower body goes numb and there is a whistling in her ears. She wonders what Lungani will think if he sees what her body looks like now. Then her vision goes black and she no longer sees the man with the truncheon, rhythmically breaking her apart.

Ayanda is in her childhood home. Lungani is sitting with her mother and father at the kitchen table, talking, laughing. Lungani is wearing his police uniform. He looks great in it. Ayanda tries to join them at the table but can't seem to make it past the door. She calls out to Lungani but her voice doesn't reach him. Lungani shows her mother the engagement ring. She cries with clear joy. Her dad is impressed, smiling and nodding his happy assent. Lungani's expression changes. He's sad. He looks directly at Ayanda standing in the doorway. She sees his tears start to flow.

She comes to in the seat. Her vision is hazy. She can see movement in front of her, then her eyes find their focus. She looks down, sensing discomfort on her breasts. Crocodile clamps are hanging off her nipples. The cables run to the black box beside him. She looks at him, her chin on her chest. It sounds like he's moving through a puddle of water. She knows it must be her own blood.

She can't feel her lower body any more, and she can't move her legs. The pain is gone; everything below her waist is numb. The man bends over and flicks a switch on the box. The ceiling light flickers and dims as the stream of electricity shoots through Ayanda.

Her whole body spasms, her body contracts, and she starts to shake uncontrollably. She tries to scream but she can't. It feels like her neck is about to snap. The nerves in her body all catch fire simultaneously. It feels like lava is flowing through her veins. She feels cold, then warm. But through it all, she feels the dread. Suddenly it stops. The man has killed the switch.

Ayanda is thirsty. And she feels numb. Not just her lower body. Everything. Perhaps this is God's way of saving her from the suffering. She looks at her breasts again. Smoke rises from the points where the clamps bite into her flesh. She can smell meat burning. Her meat. She hears her breath heaving. She looks at her left hand on the chair. Her hand is in a spasm and two of her nails have broken off. She is so tired. Dead tired.

'Please ...' she mumbles, but the sound barely escapes her lips. She can't get her tongue to work.

The man flicks the switch again.

After a few seconds he turns it back off.

And on again.

He enjoys this.

It feels like an eternity. When does she die? Ayanda is losing consciousness. She doesn't know how long she's been lying there. She feels her heart jump in her chest. Violently and arrhythmically. Then it stops. A whiteness surrounds her. She is relieved. It's over. She exhales her final breath and her body goes limp.

The man puts two fingers on her neck to feel her pulse. Then he removes the clamps and returns them to the box. He walks around the girl. He removes the strap from around her neck and raises her torso. He wipes the sweat from her back and reaches for the scalpel.

9

Majola sits at the kitchen table, having turned the heater down a notch. It's still cold outside, but he's just showered. He studies his laptop screen – yesterday was a good day. Not only did Jane Semenga's family give them an identifiable victim, but the Ga-Rankuwa eyewitness is going to help a lot.

In the meanwhile, he's told Mitchell to knock together an image of the taxi as Thuli Mokhebe described it. The team can take it along when they do their questioning. He finished his report for Radebe this morning before going to Orange Farm and Thokoza, only to have Radebe tell him on the phone that he's going away to Hartbeespoort Dam, and to bring it in on Monday. His head is too busy.

Majola's phone rings. It's Lulu. It's past 11 p.m.

He hits the green button on the screen: 'Sawubona, Lulu.'

'Hello, David. How are you?'

'All's well, just busy.'

There follows an uncomfortable silence. Majola isn't sure how to broach the topic.

'I hear I missed you today. Mama told me you were here.'

'Yeah, I was. You always complain that I don't visit enough, then when I do come over, you're not there. Where were you?'

Another silence.

'Did you go through my things?'

Majola is caught off guard. 'You're playing with fire, Lulu.'

'What do you care all of a sudden? You just visit us to stop feeling so fucking guilty!'

'Lulu.'

'What? You think if you bring groceries every now and then, everything's just fine. Then you drive off to your white suburban lifestyle and leave us in this hellhole.'

'You know I'm busy. It doesn't mean I don't care.'

'Yeah, right.'

'If you get involved with that stuff, it's hard to get out. Do you buy from that Mpete asshole? On the corner?'

'I don't know what you're talking about.'

'Come on, Lulu. What do you think Mama's going to do if she finds out you're on drugs? You'll break her heart.'

Silence.

'When can I come see you? Or should I fetch you, then we'll go for coffee? Then we can check out the shops in Melville. How does that sound?'

'Bye, David.'

'Lulu, wait. Talk to m—'

But the call's ended.

Majola calls her number again but her phone is off.

He tosses his phone onto the table, opens the balcony door and steps outside. The air is fresh; he breathes in deeply.

'This is fucking ironic,' he says out loud, shaking his head.

Now the same devil he has to fight day in and day out has its claws sunk into his sister. It's only a matter of time before she backs herself into a corner. He wonders what's worse, and what scares him the most – the damage the drugs will do to her body, or the damage she'll do to herself and her loved ones to get her hands on it? He shudders to think what Mpete will want when Lulu can no longer pay for it. The day she exchanges her body for a fix. Or the day Mpete walks into their mother's house and takes or breaks whatever he wants. He doesn't know what he'll do if it comes to that. Will he be able to control himself if something happened to his mother or sister?

Majola closes the sliding door to the balcony and walks back to the kitchen. He knows he's only fooling himself. It almost never stops there. You can bullshit yourself for a while, but deep down that little voice is telling you: the difficult days of addiction might not be at the front door yet, but they're walking up the garden path.

Majola puts the kettle on while he checks his phone. Maybe Lulu's got back to him. Nothing. He's also waiting for a message from Kappie. Majola sent a text earlier to let him know he would bring the dossiers over tomorrow.

The weekend after his first run-in with cocaine, he went back to Kabelo's house for another party. The girl from the previous weekend was there again, this time with someone else. The blonde who'd been draped over Kabelo wasn't there. But Majola wasn't really there for the girls. He couldn't wait for Kabelo to invite him to the room. Later, at around four in the morning, Kabelo handed him a few prescription sleeping pills, saying, 'Take one before going to bed. Just one, though, otherwise you might not wake up again.'

When he woke up that Sunday afternoon, he felt awful. But he ascribed it to all the whisky they had drunk. By Monday the depression had him in its grip. He promised himself he wouldn't do it again: what goes up must come down. The blues only lasted until the Friday afternoon, when he and Basson went for a drink at a bar in Braamfontein.

He called Kabelo the minute he got home that night. He was on a game farm in the bushveld. Kabelo said he'd call him back in a few minutes; he just had to let his contact know to expect Majola's call. The dealer called himself Kevin. Majola always found it ironic that the dealers chose English names – Kevin, Kenny, Mickey, Tony, even Prince. Later he had a whole selection of these names saved on his phone.

'R500 for a nice big one. Meet me in ten minutes.'

On his way there he could feel an almost childish excitement. He laughed at the irony: the detective who makes a living putting dealers behind bars is about to go support one in his business venture.

He could feel the goose-bumps running down his spine. The R500 didn't bother him. He waited in the parking lot of a KFC in Melville. After what felt like forever, a red Toyota Conquest with tinted windows pulled up beside him. The man just sat there for a minute before getting out and walking over to Majola's window. Majola handed over the five blue notes and the man handed him a small transparent bag filled with white powder.

'Next time, roll up the bills before you hand them to me,' the man said and walked back to his car.

When Majola got home, the first thing he did was pour himself another whisky and tip the cocaine out on the counter. He hesitated for a moment before he crushed the powder with his bank card. A vision of the Marshall Street junkies came unbidden to his mind, heroin needles hanging from their arms, unaware of the time of day or even where they were. He saw his mother's face, concerned, warning him of the danger of nyope when he was a teenager. And he remembered Al Pacino's words in *The Devil's Advocate*: he'd told Keanu Reeves's character that no line of cocaine would ever compare to that first one.

Majola rolled up a R20 note and snorted a line.

By Sunday his hangover was worse. By Monday, Tuesday, the depression was nearly unbearable. He couldn't concentrate on his work. Basson saw that something was wrong. Majola pretended to have flu to explain the sniffing and the runny nose. Again, he promised himself, this was the last time. But that only lasted until the next two beers or whiskys hit his stomach the following weekend.

He saw Kabelo less and less. Most nights he would just hang out at home watching movies after calling his dealer. Other nights he went out in Melville, even met a few girls who went home with him. He lost ten kilograms.

Always the same story. By Monday he was ready to cut his wrists. He even considered tipping off the narcotics bureau to go raid the dealers. But he was scared that the dealers might know his licence plate. He tried deleting their numbers from his phone, but by this point he knew them all from memory.

He always blamed his habit on work or Busiswe. Or on the fact that he didn't really have any friends. Or that he was too shitty to go see his mother more often. Or that he couldn't talk to anyone about his problem. A brokeass cop with a drug habit? Who would believe him – Basson, who thinks that dagga smokers are all child molesters and rapists? Majola always found an excuse not to quit.

Cocaine didn't come cheap. He had to take out a loan, which only lasted three months. At one point he even considered selling his car.

He started fucking up at work. He was constantly pissed off and aggressive towards everyone. Basson made a few comments, opining that Majola was 'worse than a woman having her period'. Majola even had disciplinary action taken against him for calling a female constable 'an incompetent bitch'.

The big one happened in the evidence room one Monday. Majola had been using from the Friday all through the weekend, without sleeping more than four hours in total. The Monday started with another phone call from his mother, bawling and accusing him of not loving her or his sister.

And then he hit rock bottom. Later that morning, there was a knock on his office door. A kilogram of cocaine had been taken from the evidence room. Everywhere he went, he sensed people suspected him of being the one who took it.

Even Basson seemed to be asking a lot of questions about the matter, asking Majola if he knew anything that Basson didn't. That evening everything came crashing down. He went to meet Kevin in an alley off Beyers Naudé Drive. The dealer saw his SAPS ID in the inside pocket of his jacket and started running.

Majola ran after him, trying to explain. In the process his pistol fell from its holster into the road. He tried to call Kevin but he wouldn't pick up. When Majola got home, he drank half a bottle of whisky and took two sleeping pills to calm down.

He didn't go to work the next day. He only woke up at three in the afternoon. Without giving it much thought, he walked to a centre for drug addicts in Fourth Avenue. There he spent two hours talking to Andy, who led a group for recovering addicts. Andy helped him to realise where the real problem lay. The problem wasn't the cocaine – it was the alcohol. He never felt like buying drugs when he was sober. When he was sober, he felt too bad and too guilty. The trigger was the drinking. He listened to the other recovering alcoholics talking about their own struggles before Andy gave him a lift back home. Andy put a packet of Flagyl in his hand and wished him luck and fortitude.

That night there was a knock at his door. It was Basson. 'Radebe's looking for you. You have to go see him in the morning. I told him you have a stomach bug. And David … get your fucking shit together. I can only cover for you for so long.'

He knew he had to sort himself out.

The first few weeks were hard. One night he lost the fight and grabbed at the closest bottle. He started calling his dealers. Kevin's number no longer existed. But Prince picked up. Nothing particularly bad had even happened that day; he was just sick of trying. He drank through the nausea the Flagyl caused when mixed with alcohol. After the third line, he smashed the mirror in the bathroom, took one sleeping pill and went to bed.

Three days later, he was back to day one at the group in Fourth Avenue. The second attempt went better, even though all the junk food he started eating meant he picked up all ten kilograms he had lost while using. He started jogging, only going around the block at first, then two blocks, until he could run five kilometres without all the wheezing. He started eating better, though Basson didn't help with his insistence on always stopping for breakfast or grabbing a quick 'ou burgertjie'.

He feels good these days. He doesn't miss those times when he felt he could actually kill someone. Himself included. He doesn't miss worrying about where the money for the next gram would come from. He does miss the occasional single malt, but it's something he has to live with. When it gets bad, he usually puts on a movie or goes for a run.

His mouth still waters when he sees someone doing coke in a movie. He wonders if that feeling will ever go away. Twice he's had to swallow his pride and call Andy when he was having a hard time saying no to a whisky and a line.

But it's been worth it. Basson probably knew but he let him off the hook. Maybe he also thinks it was just the alcohol, like Lizanne. One day he just said, 'You look better. Next time I'll go drop you off first if I feel like a drink.'

Basson's had his own demons. They've just usually worn dresses and haven't come in plastic bags.

10

Lulu is sitting at a small table, surrounded by cigarettes and plastic packets of crisps bought from street vendors. She has a glass in her hand and a plate in front of her. There's no one else at the taxi rank. Majola watches her from his police car. A pigeon walks up to her table, then flaps its way onto it. Ignoring the pigeon, Lulu turns the glass upside down and puts it on the plate. She starts to move the glass over the plate. Two more pigeons land at her feet. Majola tries to open the car window but it's stuck. More pigeons land. Then a car pulls in behind her. The windows are black. Majola can't see the driver. He tries to open his car door but it won't open. The car is a busted-up old Ford Escort. Its door opens and a man in black gets out, a hoodie covering his face. Lulu is unfazed, still absorbed in whatever it is she's doing with the glass. The man walks up to Lulu. Majola starts to panic.

'Lulu!' he screams from the car but she doesn't hear him. The man is behind her now. And Majola sees the scalpel in his hand. He takes out his pistol and smashes it against the window, but the gun shatters into pieces. The man has the scalpel against Lulu's throat, looks directly at Majola. It's Basson.

'I bought her with my own money. I didn't get her for fucking free,' Basson says and drags the blade across her throat.

Majola wakes up yelling. It takes him a few seconds to realise he's in his bedroom. Relief washes over him.

'Fuck, man.' Still rattled, he gets up and walks to the balcony to open the door. He checks the wall clock: 5.35 a.m. Well, looks like he's up now. Might as well make coffee and eat breakfast. He rubs his eyes, the cold air fresh on his skin. In the kitchen he turns on the light and fills the kettle. What's got to him is how real the dream felt. The other night it was Busiswe; now Lulu. If it goes on like this, he might start believing in omens.

A car hooting down the road makes him jump. The balcony door is still open. He walks over to close it. Down on the street, at the traffic light, he sees it. Its lights are off, the windows pitch black. It's just standing there, idling, even though the light is green. Even in the dim street light, Majola can see it's red. Only the back is visible. He tries to make out the plates but the lights above the plates are dead too.

Majola runs to his bedroom to get his phone from the side table. He imagines hearing the vehicle pull away. He grabs the phone and runs back to the balcony, almost tripping over his shoes as he goes. He types in the number for the Flying Squad, but when he looks up, the taxi is gone. He leans over the railing to peer down the road, but there's nothing there. As if it disappeared into the cold morning air. Or wasn't there to begin with.

Did he dream it? Is he starting to lose his foolish mind? But he's sure there was a taxi at that traffic light. Maybe he's not quite awake enough yet. For a moment he stands there, looking over the balcony railing. The road is still wet from the rain and he can hear city traffic. A cold shiver slithers through him. His feet are wet from standing in a puddle. His breath comes quick, expelling puffs of mist.

He shakes his head, closes the door and walks back into the apartment, laughing at himself. Then he starts to run a bath before putting on a tracksuit over his white vest. His breathing calms while he makes the coffee. Then his phone rings. It's Davids. He drops the spoon to the kitchen floor.

11

'No fucking way.'

'Jason!' Delia is at the bedroom door, a towel wrapped around her, steam rising from her hair. She looks pointedly at Nonnie, who's sitting on the couch, eating cereal in her pyjamas, watching *Frozen* again.

'Sorry.' Basson is already dressed. He was on his way to go smoke his first cigarette of the day while he drank his coffee. Then Majola called.

He puts his cup of coffee down on the bookcase. 'There's another girl. ADT found her next to Westpark Cemetery.'

'Good lord. So soon?' Delia asks.

'Yup. The time for games is over. He's killing with purpose now.'

Basson quickly adjusts his tie in the mirror before grabbing his jacket from the dining-room chair.

'What about Nonnie?'

Basson kisses Delia on the cheek. 'I'm sorry, angel. Will you take her to crèche today? They're waiting for me.'

He walks over to Nonnie and kisses her on the forehead, then picks up his z88 and shoulder holster from the top of the bookcase and shoves his wallet and police ID into his pocket.

'What about your lunchbox?'

'I don't think I'll be taking lunch today. I'll pick up a pie or something on my way.'

Just as he's about to close the door, Delia says, 'Be careful.'

Traffic is gridlocked before the Barry Hertzog crossing, where Basson is coming from the direction of Victory Street. Probably another malfunctioning traffic light. That's the problem with Johannesburg: every time you discover a shortcut, other people are quick to discover it too, and you're forced to go back to the usual route again. He tries to listen to the radio but switches it off after a while. The music of these young pseudo-intellectual DJs gets on his nerves. And the jackasses on the English-language stations just spend their time making fun of Afrikaners. He doesn't have a lot of time for English South Africans. Fucking cultureless exiles who have pardoned themselves for the country's past. But when it comes to crime, they're the biggest racists.

Basson lights another cigarette, takes a deep drag and leans back in his seat. Majola will just have to wait. He can get going with the pathologists in the meantime.

He wonders why today, of all days, he can't stop thinking about his father. Maybe because the murder is at Westpark Cemetery, where his dad is buried. That was a bleak funeral. Pictures of his dad, old and recent, were shown on a projector while 'Green, Green Grass of Home' by Tom Jones played in the background. Basson had to hold back his tears. His dad's old colleagues from the force were all sitting there wiping their eyes. Flip Burger, the old station commander from Linden, couldn't give a damn if anyone saw him crying and sat there bawling his eyes out. Some of the old guard were dressed up in their uniforms. Only Daan Loots wasn't there. They never really saw eye to eye. After the funeral at Westpark, Sergeant Dirk Grové from the Randburg station came over with his red face to commiserate with Basson, who stood with his arm around his mother.

'Let's go raise a glass to your pops at the Buck and Hog,' he whispered with a mischievous grin.

Basson was reluctant to leave his mother and Delia at the apartment alone; they had made tea and laid out snacks for the funeral guests. But his mom gave a slight smile.

'Go. Go have fun with the boys. You never know when it will be their turn. Delia and I will manage, don't worry.'

Delia wasn't impressed when she had to come and pick him up after ten that night. That was after the police had called her. The afternoon had started out quite calmly. But by the third brandy and Coke, the policemen had shaken off their melancholy and shots were poured. The funeral was quickly forgotten and, try as Basson might, they wouldn't let him leave. 'To Jos Basson!' the guys cried every few minutes, before downing their drinks. Old Koos Viljoen from Boksburg threw up all over the bar counter, then the retired Jaco Minnie from the Pretoria SAPS College chucked his glass at the head of the old Englishman who was singing John Denver songs, just because he didn't know 'Green, Green Grass of Home'. Then Sergeant Piet van Hoven shoved his hand down a waitress's trousers and licked her on the cheek.

At this point, the burly manager had had enough of this drunk and mostly aged crowd of policemen, and tried to kick all of them out. But Dirk Grové ran at him like a bull, slamming him into the pool table. Bleeding, he walked from the bar with his phone to his ear, while Dirk got onto the counter and screamed, 'To Captain Jos! May his memory live on!' Everyone else had left the bar; only the policemen were left. Minutes later the Metro police showed up, and Jaco Minnie wanted to fight them too.

Basson was outside on the curb, his head between his knees, in the grip of drunken despair, when Dirk came to sit beside him, drink in hand, John Rolfe cigarette hanging from his lips.

'Do you get it now, young Jossie? Now you'll always remember your dad's funeral.'

Basson vomited noisily onto the ground.

'I don't know how your mom put up with this shit for so long. But listen to me carefully, Jason Basson, I certainly won't,' Delia hissed furiously when she had him in the car. Basson was breathing heavily, trying not to throw up again. He and Delia had only just got married.

Most of the old crowd have died. Dirk Grové too. Four years before his retirement, a guy shot him in the head and torso with an AK-47. The detectives blamed it on hijackers from a syndicate he was investigating. Uncle Jaco Minnie hanged himself in his garage. When they found him, 'Green, Green Grass of Home' was playing on repeat from an old CD player on his workbench.

The sound of a horn pulls Basson back into the present, where the traffic is moving. The guys from OUTsurance in their green-and-black outfits have finally shown up. Basson is relieved the rain has abated somewhat. He's driving against the traffic today, which would have helped if it weren't for the broken light. If he was in his police car, he would have turned on the sirens right about now. He crosses Emmarentia Dam in the direction of Roosevelt Park. His thoughts keep returning to his dad; he's struggling to focus on the scene that awaits him. Maybe he's subconsciously trying to avoid it.

Occasionally, his dad used to take him fishing at Emmarentia Dam. His mom would pack them some sandwiches, boiled eggs and a thermos with coffee. It wasn't really about the fishing, more about the stories about fishing his dad would tell. Those memories are worth more than gold to him. The older you get, the more life turns into a complete clusterfuck.

He knows he doesn't spend nearly enough time with Nonnie. It's the job. The long days, the plans he has to cancel when something comes up. Seeing Wikus and Riaantjie together the other day made him wonder what it would have been like if they'd had a boy. Nonnie doesn't really care for fishing or rugby. He always feels a bit uncomfortable around her, as if he doesn't really know what to do with her. He's decided: he'll take a few hours on Thursday to slip away and attend Riaantjie's birthday party. The distraction will do him some good. He's tense, he can feel it.

It's going to be chaos from here on out. Weekends are something of the past. Packing up once five o'clock comes around is wishful thinking. Radebe and the media are going to descend on them like lions on a wounded springbok. At least they've made some headway since the first murder on the M1. A red taxi with black windows and whitewall tyres with black rims. They'll just have to keep their wits about them, forget about the numbers carved into the victims, focus on the vehicle. Somewhere he's going to slip up, long before they've solved that riddle. The taxi associations are going to get restless, people will start avoiding red taxis like the plague. That's what they need:

proper collaboration with the associations and the public. Then they'll take him down.

Just this side of the botanical gardens, Basson turns into John Adamson Drive, to avoid the morning traffic on Beyers Naudé. As he joins Visser Street, he sees the Metro police with their flashing blue lights. In front of him a bakkie makes a U-turn when the driver sees the road is blocked; the guy's clearly fuming.

Basson slows down as he reaches the Metro vehicles, flashes his ID. The constable's face is barely visible behind the folds of his blue scarf. He nods and motions for Basson to pass. With West Park Road closed, the motorists from Albertville are probably spewing fire this morning. At least Metro did a better job of cordoning off the area this time, with a wide half-moon of yellow tape.

Basson feels the way he always does before entering a crime scene: excitement, with a touch of tension. At least that's something he hasn't lost yet. Today, however, the tension is riding high, as it's the second victim in three days. He pulls in behind Majola's police Corolla. Majola and Ramsamy are next to Doc Lubbe, deep in conversation, their attention on the cemetery wall. Beside them, three members of the LCRC are busy doing something on the ground.

He smiles when he notices that Majola is wearing his official crime-scene jacket today. Basson's own is still in the police car and he doesn't feel like asking Majola for the keys. He takes a few final drags of his cigarette, stamps it out next to the car and picks his coat up off the back seat. A few civilians have gathered some distance away, across the road. Two middle-aged guys on mountain bikes are busy on their phones. It doesn't look like the media have arrived yet.

'Well, at least it's stopped raining,' Basson says cheerfully as he approaches the men from behind.

Majola and Doc Lubbe turn.

'Is this the time to show up? We're about ready to zip her up,' Doc says with a smile.

The men greet each other sombrely. Basson can see, though, that they're not as upset as they were at the previous scene. There's more tension this time, less shock.

'Traffic on Hertzog was a nightmare.'

Mbalula and another forensics assistant push a gurney past him towards the girl lying against the steel gate.

'Her position is different to the other girls. All the rest were found sitting, weren't they?' Basson remarks.

'No, we think she was sitting upright and toppled over at some point after he left her here. We checked the gate for fingerprints too,' Majola says.

Basson notices the blue powdery residue on the black gate to the cemetery, and the padlock that keeps the gate locked. The cement has started to crack and weeds are pushing through wherever they can. One of the forensics guys is taking a cast of a footprint found in the mud.

'He left a footprint? A bit unusual for him.'

'Yeah,' says Majola. 'Looks like a Converse or Levi sneaker, a size nine or ten. I haven't forgotten everything from the Sneaker Rapist case. And there's another tyre print. If you compare it to the picture on my phone, then we're looking for the same killer.'

Basson smiles. 'Ramsamy, don't you wear this brand of tsotsi takkie? Where were you this morning?'

Ramsamy pretends not to hear him. Basson studies the body. The black girl is light skinned, of medium build, her hair cropped short. He can see the damage to her full breasts. Burn wounds. Her legs are splayed out in front of her, covered in blood, as is the ground between them. Her torso slouches to one side. Every few seconds the flashes from the cameras of the forensic unit wash the girl in a pale light, giving her a ghostly look in the grey of morning.

As if he can read Basson's mind, Doc says, 'Three of her nails are broken. I'll swab her later to see if there's anything there.'

'What's different? How is this one different to the other crime scenes?' Basson asks, pulling his coat tight around him.

'I had a quick look at all the other dossiers that Sergeant Ramsamy brought over on Friday. All I can say is that Debbie Harris either has to get a refund for her university fees, or she has to start stripping at the Lollypop Lounge. She doesn't have a fucking clue.'

Basson has to choke back his laughter.

'It looks to me like this one's been put through the same wringer as the others: tied up, tortured, electrocuted, cut. The numbers on her back look very similar to the other cases. There are clear injuries to her torso and vaginal area, bruises on her wrists and knees, and burn wounds on her breasts from the electrocution. It feels like fucking déjà vu. But there's another thing.' Doc looks down at the girl.

'Yes?' Basson is getting irritated. It feels like they're keeping something from him, as if they're punishing him for being late.

'I found a black hair on one of her eyelids. On her left eyeball, to be precise. It looks like a dog hair. It's too thick and long to be a human hair. Or that's what I suspect. We'll send it to Onderstepoort for analysis. But that's going to take forever, and I don't know if it will really help.'

'How do we know it wasn't just some mutt who came sniffing around her early in the morning?'

'Unlikely. We didn't find dog tracks. We looked. I'll find out if Radebe can speed up the process,' Majola says. 'If we were CSI Miami, this murder would be solved here and now.'

Majola looks at Basson. 'The other thing … the letters under the first row: well, they're concerning.' Majola turns to Dr Lubbe. 'Can I show him?'

The pathologist steps closer to the girl.

'Hold up, Mbalula. Before you load her up,' Doc says to Mbalula and his assistant as they're ready to zip up the body bag.

Carefully, Doc lifts up one of the girl's shoulders and angles her forward to reveal the cuts. Majola and Basson lean in closer.

The word 'Maduze' has been clearly carved in beneath the numbers.

'What does that mean?' asks Basson.

'Very soon,' Majola replies. 'In Zulu.'

'Thank you, Doctor,' Majola says and walks back to the road. Doc indicates for Mbalula to proceed.

'Very soon?' Basson asks when he joins Majola. 'Very soon what? Very soon he'll be done, or very soon we'll find another of these awful surprises?'

'That we'll have to find out. But it's a clear message.'

Majola looks up and down West Park Road.

'I sent Mbatho to speak to the people from that house,' Majola says, pointing across the road. 'The tracks show that the vehicle came from Albertville's side, from the west, not from the Beyers Naudé side. Many of the people have private CCTV cameras set up on their properties. Maybe we'll be lucky. The Jewish cemetery down there has a security guard, about fifty metres from the gate. There's another camera there too. Seems like they're more worried about their dead than the municipality is. Hopefully we find something.'

'Isn't it a bit early for Mbatho? I'm impressed,' Basson says.

'She's been living in Northcliff with her sister, just around the corner from here,' Ramsamy answers.

Doc joins them after removing his gloves at the bakkie. 'Gentlemen, I don't want to stick my nose into this investigation of yours, but it seems like you can use all the help you can get.'

Majola nods his head and smiles thinly. 'Let's hear it.'

Basson has already lit another cigarette.

'Okay, according to Captain Majola we're looking for a taxi. From the temperature readings I took, I put her time of death at around 4.30 a.m. The guard from ADT found her just before six.'

'I know what you're going to say,' Basson interjects.

'Why don't you consider the possibility?' asks Doc.

Majola and Ramsamy look questioningly at Basson, still in the dark.

'With the other murders, there was enough time to take the victims somewhere else to do the torturing and the killing before dropping them off. But to do all of this inside a vehicle? Seems a bit much, doesn't it, Doc?' Basson asks.

'I'm with Detective Basson. How the hell do you electrocute someone to death inside a van?'

Doc looks at Majola, surprise in his eyes. 'It's not that hard. A strong battery or generator will do the job. All the victims have bruises to the knees and wrists, as if they were held down with clamps or something. He could have bound the girls to a chair inside the taxi. If you're lying there strapped in, he can do whatever he wants to you. Look, he's killing them all across Gauteng. Let's say he lives in Hillbrow, or wherever. He picks her up all the fucking way out in Ga-Rankuwa, drives her back to Hillbrow and then takes her all the way back?'

'I hear you. But jissis, it sounds like something from a movie. He would have to have some help. Unless he drugs her. And all of this has to happen while he's driving too.'

'The girl in Ga-Rankuwa said it looked like he was talking to someone. Maybe he does have help. But at this point, none of the scenes show any evidence to suggest that's the case. He's too careful to leave anything behind. Or they're too careful.'

But Majola doesn't buy it; Doc's story seems too far-fetched.

'Why would he drop the girls off close to where he picked them up? If he lives somewhere else, why not just drop them anywhere?'

'Maybe he wants them to be found quickly. Or he does it so the families can identify them,' Majola says.

'Why?'

'God knows, Doctor. Because he wants them to be found. So that we can solve his riddle.'

Doc takes his car keys from his pocket, looks over at Mbalula putting the body away. 'Leave the numbers. They'll get you nowhere. Look for the taxi. He's gonna make a mistake. This road is busy; he took a fat chance here.'

Basson nods in agreement with the doctor's assessment.

'Another thing: you'll have to wait a while for this one. There was a hijacking in Lenasia. Two Muslims were shot in the head. Their bodies have to be buried within a day – one of their customs. So that's going to keep me busy. What is today? Monday? I'll probably only get around to her tomorrow morning. And it's just me and another guy on duty. I'm sorry.'

Majola sighs. 'I understand.'

'Let's hope his "soon" means that this nightmare is nearly over,' Doc says, lighting a cigarette as he walks.

Majola, Basson and Ramsamy head back to Majola's car.

'I hear what Doc is saying, and he could be right. But we can't just ignore the numbers,' Majola says.

Ramsamy nods his agreement, to Basson's chagrin.

Basson stares past the scene towards the cemetery.

'You know, I was just thinking. The murder on the M1 was right next to the crematorium in Braamfontein. Now we're at Westpark Cemetery,' Majola thinks out loud.

'Yes, but the rest weren't. What are you thinking?' asks Basson.

'Sergeant, go ask around at the cemetery offices. They should keep some kind of register. Name, identity number, et cetera. Take the numbers from the girls' backs and compare them to the register. Maybe there's something. And call Rikhotso: let him go check up on our soccer star, see what he's up to this morning.'

'You don't think he's asked Seketse for his autograph yet?' Basson jibes. 'Maybe he can get his Wits Celtic ball signed too.'

'It's Bloem Celtic,' Ramsamy corrects him.

'What does it matter? They're all fucking terrible at the game.'

Ramsamy shakes his head in disbelief. 'Right, Captain, I'll go see what I can find,' he says and walks off briskly.

'Seeing as we're talking about Hollywood, we can probably throw in the grave numbers too,' Basson says jokingly.

'Yeah, I know. I don't know. Maybe it's a bit optimistic, but it's worth a try.'

Basson lights a cigarette as the body is driven off. LCRC are done. Soon they'll open the road back up to the public, pull down the police line, and people will drive by, none the wiser. They'll go to work and moan about the traffic and the road closure, but by tonight it will have slipped their minds completely. While somewhere, a girl's family will start to wonder where she is, why she didn't come home or go to work. And their lives will be changed forever.

'I'll talk to Radebe. It's the second murder in three days, and practically in the same area. We'll have to pull in Metro and everyone who can help. We'll have to put up blockades in this area: Empire, Beyers, Ontdekkers, everywhere we can.'

'Good luck with that one. You know how difficult it is to get Metro to lift a finger,' Basson replies.

'I don't care how many fucking bribes they take, as long as they get the name of every driver of every red taxi in the city. We've got enough info to cast a net. If they can get everyone's names and details, we might be able to connect them to the numbers. They can even check the vehicles. If Dr Lubbe is right, they might find the clamps on the seats, or something to show that our man has converted his taxi into a torture chamber – anything that looks suspicious. At this point, we have to follow the leads we have. Everyone has to hit the taxi ranks, speak to the marshals, see if the associations can help.'

'Well, the media haven't been here – we made quick work this morning. But they'll pick up on it soon enough. I've already seen some meerkats with their phones held high. Radebe might be able to swing his dick around, help us solve this thing. Hopefully we'll get the resources we need. Is Mbatho still not back from visiting the homes?'

'I haven't seen her. She's probably drinking coffee with someone's grand-mother or something.' Basson stares blankly at the muddy footprints near his feet. The clouds have rolled in again, turning the sky grey and threatening worse weather.

'You know,' Majola says quietly, 'I saw him this morning.'

'Who – Radebe?'

'The taxi. In front of my apartment, from my balcony. Probably just after five.'

'You're sure you weren't dreaming?'

'I thought so too. Now I'm not so sure.'

'You need to take it easy. This case isn't different to any of the others we've worked on. We do what we can, with what we have. We can't work fucking miracles.'

'I know, I know …' Majola sighs. 'Are you superstitious?'

Basson is taken aback by the question. 'How do you mean?'

'Superstitious. Do you believe in omens, spirits, that type of thing?'

'Shit, I don't know. Not really. Were you watching some horror movies over the weekend or something?'

Majola smiles. 'No, not at all.'

'Listen, I won't say I don't believe in any of it. But before my dad died, he used to say this thing: in his whole life he never encountered anything he couldn't explain. And neither have I. But I will say this – I won't go messing where I don't need to. A cousin of mine, when we were young, told me he once played Glassy Glassy.'

Majola looks uncertain. 'Glassy Glassy?'

'Yes. It's something like a Ouija board.'

Majola nods. 'I see. Like in the movies.'

'Exactly. But you play with a glass turned upside down. You cut out the letters and numbers yourself, place a finger on the glass, and then the spirit, or whatever, moves the glass to answer your questions. Anyway. He said they made contact with something. And every time one of them would try to get up from their chair, something would smack them back down. The thing only disappeared at sunrise. That shit freaked me out as a kid. But I don't believe in, like, prophesies and that kind of stuff. Why do you ask?'

Majola tells Basson about his mother's visit to the sangoma.

'Shit,' Basson says, whistling through his teeth. 'That seems like a really big coincidence. And weird. First the one under the bridge; now your mom's personal sangoma is in the mix. Do you think it'll help to go speak to the sangoma? Maybe it's the same guy.'

Majola shakes his head. 'No, I know this charlatan. I hope it's just a really odd, admittedly creepy, coincidence.' Majola's phone beeps in his pocket. He takes it out, looks at the screen and puts it back.

'Speak of the Zulu devil.'

'Radebe?'

'The one and only.' Majola's phone beeps again. 'What the hell?' He takes it out again, stares at the screen.

'Who is it?'

'It's Lizanne. Kappie's had another setback.'

'Shit, didn't he have one on Friday too?'

'He did, yeah. Lizanne is very upset. Two in such a short time.'

'Hm.' Basson takes another drag.

'Hm what?'

'Do you want to hear a Hollywood script idea? We'll send it to Quentin Tarantino.'

'I'm listening,' Majola says, smiling.

'Okay. Here's the plot: retired captain from the apartheid-era police service abducts young black girls in a taxi and does all kinds of unspeakable things to them.'

Majola laughs loudly. 'Fuck it, I think you should rather send that one to Leon Schuster.'

'Don't you think it's a bit weird?' Basson asks.

'Are you serious?'

'I'm just wondering, that's all.'

'Fuck man, that madala can barely get out of bed, never mind kill young girls.'

Basson tosses his cigarette aside and lights another.

'Anyway, I'll see you at the station. When I'm done with Radebe, we'll swing by the taxi rank in Bree Street. Then we can go look for Zola parked in between all the Volkswagens and Anglias at the retirement home.'

Basson laughs. 'Okay, see you later. I'm going to need coffee for this Monday.'

Martie Bam is sitting at a table in the Media Park cafeteria in Auckland Park. It's still raining. She can see a brittle little journalist from a glamour rag smoking outside. If you don't like pap or jellied cow hooves, you should probably go find your food elsewhere.

What used to be the bastion of the Afrikaans print media now looks like a haunted ruin. The people at the top are still trying their damnedest to make sense of digital media but just can't seem to crack the recipe for success. The internet is different from print media – if you don't find your news in one place, you can find it in a million others, whether in Afrikaans or not. The spectres of defunct publications line the corridors. After the circulation numbers started dwindling, so did the staff, some of their own accord, others not. That's the reality of the press these days.

It's bloody freezing today. Whenever it rains like this, she misses Harrismith, where it could get properly cold. It didn't even have to rain: when the sun went down behind the Platberg, you started shivering. And then it was time for a movie and a hot Milo under a blanket beside dad on the couch, the fire crackling.

She rubs her stiff legs. The rugby player didn't disappoint. Not her usual type, this one – not much between the ears – but good lord, he took her in a way she hadn't been taken since her English lecturer at university. Young, dumb and full of cum, as the saying goes. A five-minute pause, then he was standing to attention all over again, stiff as a schoolboy. And he took the lead, which was new for her. She usually likes being the one in charge. There was no time to find a good position; he went ahead and put her in the right one. At one point she had to go fish some back-up condoms out of the kitchen drawer. She even considered letting him sleep over, so that she could start the next day blushing, but decided against it. Rules are rules.

Fortunately, she'll be seeing him again tomorrow night. Then she'll take back control. She'll put up with about twenty minutes of his stories about supplements, sports and shots with teammates before leading him to her bed. And there she'll make the schoolboy play along. He doesn't look like someone who gets offended easily. And she promised she'd do a profile of him in the sports section. She just has to speak to Dirk.

Patrick Baloyi walks over from the main building. Wearing a baseball cap and black jacket, he looks like he's just come off the set of a music video. But if you work for the *Daily Sun*, you're almost like a celebrity. It's the biggest publication in South Africa, with circulation numbers somewhere in the hundreds of thousands. Someone once said that the *Daily Sun* could topple the government, if it wanted to. Most of the journalists work in the townships; only a few come in to the office. It's a nightmare for the editors and proofreaders, but the stories are raw and honest. And sometimes, of course, a little far-fetched, unless you believe in the tokoloshe or zombies. Patrick is carrying a cup of coffee he made in the office, and comes to sit beside her.

'Morning, sisi. You look good. Did you sleep well?'

'On the contrary, I look so good because I barely slept at all. And it has nothing to do with a story,' she says, winking at him. 'How are you?'

'Ai, Martie,' laughs Patrick. 'I'm pretty busy. How can I help you?'

Martie leans forward in her chair. 'The taxi story. Thank you for giving me details for Saturday's *Beeld*. You've got better connections with the uniforms than I do.'

'The pleasure is mine. We've got to help each other out, right?'

'Have the police contacted you yet? About the Katlehong story?'

'Yes, I got a call from Captain Majola yesterday. Basically told him what I know, but it's mostly what I put in the article.'

Patrick avoids eye contact.

'And? Why do I get the feeling there's something else?'

Patrick smiles. 'Jesus, Martie, you don't miss a thing.' He mulls something over for a moment. 'There was a witness, the cousin of the girl who was murdered. Her name is Angie. They had an argument at a shebeen, about a boyfriend. The girl who was murdered, Doreen, she left first. Angie left a few minutes later. Doreen crossed the train tracks and walked into the field, then waved a taxi down in the next road. She got in and then she was gone. The cousin doesn't think Doreen saw her. After picking her up, the taxi slowly drove down a path that crossed the field. Angie thought it was strange, so she walked after them. A few hundred metres on, she saw the taxi stop under some trees. She heard screaming, screaming so horrific that she knew she had to get away. And she ran. She was hysterical when she got home, told her mom about the devil and evil spirits. She was too scared to tell the police anything, because she thought the family would blame her for Doreen's death. And she said Doreen was already in her grave, so it wouldn't have helped. I promised her I wouldn't tell anyone.'

'The bastard picks them up in a taxi? Did she describe the taxi?'

'She said it was red.'

Patrick moves uncomfortably in his chair. 'Sisi, you have to keep this quiet. I could get into big trouble, not just at work, but with the police too. This counts as withholding evidence.'

'I won't get you in trouble.'

'Promise?'

'Promise,' Martie says, smiling sweetly.

'Okay, I gotta run. See you later.'

Martie remains seated. The numbers. A taxi. She can feel a best-seller brewing. Now all she needs is for Majola to play along, otherwise she'll have to do the legwork herself. Maybe Warrant Officer Basson would be easier to play for information.

'I guess you'd better come inside then.'

Officer Mbatho walks past the old woman after showing her police ID. The woman's lips are drawn tight and she looks at Mbatho with suspicion. Mbatho is sweaty from the walk, despite the cold air. It's started raining again too. There were four houses with cameras set up. At three of them, no one came to the door, but this old woman came to stand at her security gate to see who was ringing the bell after her Yorkie began barking furiously. Mbatho had to yell over the racket, trying to explain who she was. Only then did the old lady open the electric gate for her.

Mbatho is relieved: the camera is in a good spot, pointing almost directly at the crime scene.

The Jewish cemetery didn't yield any insights. The guard who was stationed at the gate, and had spent the morning watching them work, hadn't seen a thing. Their camera had been broken for more than a week. They were waiting for someone to come fix it.

'Sh! Minki!' The woman shouts at the dog baring its teeth and growling at Mbatho.

Strange name for a dog, Mbatho thinks. She can't stop looking at the woman, the thin grey hair, the faded pink dressing gown, the sheepskin slippers. She appears to be around seventy.

'The computer is in the spare room; you'll have to come and check for yourself. I don't know much about these things. My husband is in Pietermaritzburg, visiting his brother for the week. He usually leaves the thing on.'

Mbatho follows the woman. The place smells like dog pee. They pass a room to the left and something catches Mbatho's eye. She stops in her tracks.

'Is that a Bernina 570?' she asks, indicating the sewing machine on the table, as excited as a schoolgirl.

The woman stops and turns around, smiling. 'Indeed. It's the Quilter's Edition. I bought it last year. Cost me a damn fortune Do you know anything about sewing?'

Mbatho walks to the dresses draped over the couch. 'They're beautiful! This fabric, the quality, the pattern …'

Mbatho remembers that the woman had asked her a question. 'Excuse me. Yes, my sister and I own a clothing store in the city. Well, really, it's my sister's. But I make some of the dresses. It's my passion.'

The old woman relaxes visibly.

'Ah! Yes, I get the fabric from Dubai, dirt cheap. I just send them my designs and they print them for me. I sell all my dresses at a store in Menlyn Maine in Pretoria. Their biggest clients are foreigners. They can't get enough of stuff with an African motif. What kind of clothing do you make?'

'Mostly dresses and blouses. But for the fuller figure, like me. I love these designs. They're so earthy. And the colours …'

'The madam in Pretoria doesn't pay me much. I just take forty percent of the selling price. They do help with buying the material, at least.'

Mbatho lifts up a dress, purple with yellow diamond patterns. 'Would Auntie be interested in displaying some of her dresses at our place? We won't take much, just something for the shelf space. We're not that busy yet but we're getting there. We can put your designs up on our website too.'

The woman's expression brightens. 'My dear, of course I'm interested. The more people who see my dresses, the better.'

'That's right, Auntie. Let me go talk to my sister, then we'll get in touch soon. Do you have dresses in stock?'

'I have some, yes. The madam sometimes sends back work that didn't sell. But I can make new ones too. You must just come, then we'll talk business.'

Mbatho grins. She digs in her handbag for a card. 'These are my police contact details. But just call the cell number, not the one for the office. Otherwise just leave a voicemail and I'll get back to you.'

'I'll do that, my dear. I'll leave this here, next to the Bernina, then I won't lose it.'

Mbatho gets ready to leave before she remembers why she came in the first place. 'Haibo! Almost forgot about the footage.'

The woman laughs. 'Come, I'll show you. Would you like some tea?'

'That would be great, thanks.

The woman walks to the study and points at an office chair behind a cluttered desk. Mbatho moves the mouse and the computer comes to life. The program is already open, and she can see a view of the gate with a time-stamp in the bottom corner.

'Old Karel is a little paranoid, you know. We don't really use the computer for anything else – this and every now and then when he wants to play Solitaire. It doesn't even have the internet on it.'

Mbatho smiles and opens the recording software. She's relieved: she knows this system, has worked on it before.

'This is going to take a while, Auntie. I'm sorry.'

'That's fine, dear. Milk and sugar?'

'Milk, please.' Mbatho hesitates. 'And two sugars.' She feels guilty about the sugar, but she's left her sweetener at home. The stuff is so damn bitter anyway.

'Okay, I'll be back in a few minutes.'

Mbatho sets the time to view footage from four o'clock that morning, then lets it play at double speed. The black-and-white footage shows the disused gate and the small field behind it, with the wall of the cemetery visible next to the gate. The disused gate where the girl was found is clearly visible. At ten to four, the first car drives past from left to right. Mbatho zooms in so that the cemetery gate fills the screen. She zooms back out when the footage becomes too grainy. She plays back the footage and sees that it's a sedan, light in colour. She continues. Six more cars come past, one of which is a private-security bakkie. The old woman comes back into the room, two red cups with matching saucers on a tray.

'What are you looking for, my dear?'

Mbatho barely looks up. 'A taxi, Auntie.'

The woman shakes her head. 'The scoundrels. One of them hit my Daisy and killed her, right here, in front of the gate. Didn't even stop. I saw it all through the window from the lounge. Bliksems.'

'That's bad, Auntie,' Mbatho says, eyes still fixed on the screen.

At 4:45 a van comes to an abrupt halt. Immediately Mbatho pauses the footage, rewinds a few seconds and starts watching again at normal speed. The van looks to be dark grey in colour on the screen. Black rims. Whitewall tyres. Black windows. Unmoving.

'Is that him, dear?' the woman asks, leaning forward to see more clearly.

'It's him, Auntie. Zola Budd.'

'Zola Budd? Lord in heaven, what's she doing in Johannesburg? I read in the *Huisgenoot* that she lives in Bloemfontein.'

Mbatho wants to explain, but the sliding door is being opened. It's too dark to see what's happening inside.

'There he is,' she whispers. 'The bastard.'

A man in dark clothes and a hoodie is slowly putting something down on the floor of the taxi. Two legs can be seen dangling from the doorway. Then he gets out of the taxi, bends over to pick the girl up, and throws her over his right shoulder.

'I don't think you want to see this,' Mbatho tells the woman, but she doesn't seem to hear.

The woman stands closer to get a better look.

'The child he has there – is she dead?'

'Yes, Auntie.'

The woman clicks her tongue.

Mbatho sees the dark figure close the sliding door and get in on the passenger side. After a long pause, the taxi pulls away slowly. In the grainy light of the colourless image, she can see the girl sitting against the wall.

'My God, did that happen outside my house?'

'Yes, Auntie,' Mbatho says, pulling her phone out of her handbag so she can call Captain Majola.

Basson walks into Café De La Crème in Melville. Breakfast will do him good after the morning's events. It's just past nine and the place is quite busy, despite the light rain. According to the forecast, rain wasn't expected until the weekend. For Wikus's sake, he hopes the weather improves by Thursday, in time for Riaantjie's birthday.

He reminds himself to stop at Cresta on his way home to pick up a gift, and get something for Nonnie too while he's there, although she's got more than enough toys. Her room is knee-deep in dolls, but she won't be happy if he shows up with something for the boy and she gets nothing.

Basson's phone rings just as he wants to place his order. It's an unfamiliar number.

'Basson.'

'Morning, Warrant Officer.'

The voice sounds vaguely familiar. 'That's me. Who's this?'

'What would you say if I tell you I have information that could help you with the taxi investigation?'

'Well, all I can say is that if you withhold evidence, that's obstruction of justice, which will earn you a nice pair of cuffs.'

'Ah. Kinky.'

Basson is perplexed by the reply.

'Who is this?'

'Martie Bam.'

Now he recognises the voice. For a moment he's speechless. 'Now you call *me*? I take it Captain Majola didn't want anything to do with you? Where did you get my number?'

'Oh, come on. I'm a journalist. Tracking people down is my forte. And you're much sexier than David Majola. So, do you want to hear me out or what?'

Basson smiles. 'Well, Martie ... I'm flattered that you called. But by now I've figured out that nothing in this life is free. So, what is it you want out of me?'

'Smart for a boer boy. You know the Katlehong dossier? Doreen Matetwa. It's incomplete.'

'All the fucking dossiers are incomplete. That's nothing new.'

'Yes, but you're missing a juicy piece of info that my friend at the *Daily Sun* withheld.'

'I'm listening.'

'Let's rather meet in person. The phone is so impersonal.'

'Where?'

'I'll get back to you. And keep this between us for now. Or do you want Captain Majola to steal the limelight again?'

'It's not like I can keep information from him. We're working on the same case.'

'I'm sure you'll figure something out. This might just be your breakthrough.'

'Whatever.'

'Oh yeah ... Detective? The murder at Westpark this morning? Was that our Zola Budd? The story is going to get out anyway. Tomorrow you'll read another bullshit hack-job in the newspapers.' She waits for her words to sink in. 'And another thing: you'll have to make this story public. Today was the third victim that I know of, presumably by the same killer. If this gets out, your names will be dirt. Again.'

'We're at a sensitive stage of the investigation. Bye, Martie. We'll speak soon.'

Basson puts down the phone. So now everyone is calling the killer *Zola Budd*.

He orders the full farmhouse breakfast, with extra bacon and filter coffee. He mulls over the conversation with Martie Bam. How important will her information be to the investigation? Or is she just trying to play him to get information for a story? Although, he has to admit, he doesn't mind playing her games. He'd be lying if he said that he didn't feel a thrill rushing up his spine when he realised who had called. Her voice is just so sensual. He scolds himself when he realises he's smiling like an idiot.

This is how all the shit with Reza started. A naughty thought. A spark. Reza, ten years younger than him, used to live with her mother next to his parents when he was in police college. He saw her once in a while when he went to visit. Back then she was an eleven-year-old tomboy hanging around by the pool, listening to the Backstreet Boys. Puberty did all kinds of things for her, left her transformed. He'd catch himself looking from time to time, but she was still way too young. It stopped at small talk by the stairs or while sharing the lift. She was in matric when he heard a ruckus by the stairs one night. It was Reza, and she had some muscled knucklehead with her. The guy was all fired up, yanking her around. Basson whacked him on the ear before twisting his arm up behind his back until he was screaming. After being made to apologise to Reza, Knucklehead left with his tail between his legs. She fell into his arms, crying. He couldn't ignore her toned back and slim waist, despite the tinge of guilt. Then she tried to kiss him. He pulled away immediately, more from shock than anything else. She went back to her apartment still crying.

After that he didn't see her again. She moved to Randburg with her mother.

About a year ago he was at the bank in Cresta. Across from him he saw a woman wearing black shorts and a golf shirt. Her legs were flawless and tanned and Basson kept trying to sneak a peek. He felt her staring at him and looked up self-consciously.

'Jason Basson, you should be ashamed, staring at your neighbour like that.'

Basson was gobsmacked. And then he recognised her.

'Reza? Reza from 105? Son of a ... the last time I saw you, you were still a girl.'

They both got up, unsure how familiarly to greet each other. Reza gave him a light hug. She smelled like suntan lotion and flowers.

'Give me your number; let's go get coffee some time,' she said. 'You know, I always wondered what happened to you and your mother. I even looked you up on Facebook.'

Basson gave her his number. She called him on the spot so he could save hers.

In all the years he'd been married to Delia, he had remained faithful. He was serious about his marriage, and when Nonnie was born, even more serious about making it work.

He thought about Reza constantly. He even had a wet dream about her one night. But he never called her. Every night, when Nonnie fell asleep in his arms watching TV, with Delia snuggled in tight, he would decide not to make that call.

Their sex life was good, maybe not as good as it had been before Nonnie came along, but Delia was still a beautiful woman and he was still attracted to her.

One Friday night, about two weeks after bumping into Reza, he got a message. *I'm going to the Irish club with a friend tonight. She's leaving for the airport at 7. Come join me for a glass of wine?*

Basson thought about it over and over. He was sick and tired of the work and he needed to get out of the house a bit. Nonnie and Delia were both bed-ridden with colds. For the first time in his marriage, he stepped over that line: *I have to work late, I'll get myself dinner. Hope my ladies feel better. Give Nonnie a kiss. xxx*

Bastard. Liar. Dickhead. But fuck it, a man has to relax too, he tried to justify it to himself. The whole time they were at the bar, he kept looking around to see if anyone he knew had come in. Reza looked incredible. She had on white cotton shorts that were practically see-through, with an olive-green shirt, unbuttoned just far enough to show off her sensual neck and her sun-kissed cleavage. After the second double brandy and Coke, the fire in his loins was raging. Reza kept moving closer to him. She put her foot up on his bar stool, her leg between his. They shared looks that lasted longer than they should have, she started touching him when she spoke. He could smell her sweet perfume and it was driving him crazy. He knew he was in trouble. Big fucking trouble.

Just as he was going to walk her to her car, he got a message: *Nonnie has a fever. Where are you?*

At the door of her red Mini Cooper, she kissed him hungrily. He kissed back, his hands on her ass. She stroked a hand over his crotch and he got an instantaneous erection. Then he took her by the shoulders and pushed her firmly back.

'I can't. Not tonight.'

He got in his car and drove home, concerned that Delia would smell Reza on him.

At home he got into bed with his sleeping wife and daughter. He gave himself hell and promised that that was the last time. He deleted her number from his phone.

Basson tried to forget about her. But it was hard. A few days later, Reza sent a picture of herself, topless, wearing only red lace panties. He blushed brightly and deleted it immediately.

A week after their drinks, bolstered by Klipdrift bravado and a burning, insatiable horniness, he drove to her apartment complex. To his frustration, he couldn't remember which number hers was, so he drove up and down looking for her car. Just as he was about to pull out, as fate would have it, she came pulling in.

Reza was surprised to see him, but she smiled at him.

'Are you going to turn around? How did you know where to find me? And how did you get inside in the first place?'

'I'm a detective, remember?'

Basson turned his car around and parked behind her. She didn't say anything as she opened the door, her sports vest wet with perspiration.

'I'm just going to jump in the shower; I had a spinning cla—' but he was already pulling her close.

He laid her down on the leather couch in the lounge and ran his tongue over her body like a deranged animal. They had sex twice that afternoon.

And so it went for two months, mostly at her apartment. The sex was so good that he couldn't stop himself, despite how guilty he felt about it. But after he and Delia ran into a very uncomfortable Reza at the supermarket one day, he knew that Delia suspected something. Women have a sixth sense about these things.

Then the bubble burst.

One Thursday night, Basson was building blocks with Nonnie on the carpet when he heard his phone beeping in the kitchen. Delia would always hum a tune to herself while she cooked, and suddenly she stopped. He could feel something rising in his gut as he headed to the kitchen. When he walked in, she was talking on his phone.

'Hello Reza. No, it's Delia. I read your message. You probably want to speak to Jason?'

Without a word, she gave the phone to Basson. He ended the call and read the message.

I had keys made for you. Now you can let yourself in one afternoon and take me like a burglar. Tick another fantasy off my list. xxx

Delia slapped him, hard. Basson was speechless. There was no getting out of it now.

She ordered him to leave immediately and he had to book into the Road Lodge in Randburg for a month. It took three weeks for her to speak to him. He told her everything at a coffee shop in Cresta mall. He was in tears, a strange feeling for him. Delia had never seen him cry before, not even at either of his parents' funerals.

She didn't say anything, just wiped her own tears every now and then. When he'd stopped talking, she got up. 'I've never been this disappointed in my life. You know my dad had affairs. You know what it did to my mother. Then you go and do it too. Bye, Jason.'

Basson remained sitting, lost. She didn't even take the roses he had bought her.

Three days later she showed up at the hotel. Basson had just got out of the shower and was sober for the first time in weeks. He was on his laptop, looking for garden flats to rent. She came and sat next to him on the bed.

'You can come back. For Nonnie. She misses you. I still don't know if I can forgive you. But I can try. It's going to take a lot of time. And if it happens again, I swear you will never see me or Nonnie ever again.'

Basson nodded his agreement in quiet confusion, with surprise, gratitude and joy.

'But first …' she said, unwrapping the towel from around his waist, 'you're going to take me like a burglar.'

Basson smiles when he thinks of that night. He calls the waiter over.

'The bill, please. Put two coffees to go on there too. It's going to be a long day.'

Majola's attention isn't on the road. He can't get Basson's theory out of his head. For a split second there, while Basson was talking, Majola could feel his blood run cold. Is it pure coincidence? That Kappie's setbacks would coincide with the murders? Is Kappie really capable of something like this? He looks at himself in the rear-view mirror and laughs. He'll have to park it; Colonel Radebe is waiting for him and he still has to update his report.

The lift at the station isn't working again. On the first flight of stairs he sees Colonel Radebe slowly descending. His navy-blue tailored suit sits snugly; the matching tie flaps with each step. Two uniforms see him coming and quickly stand against the wall to get out of his way.

'Bloody lifts. As hulle loadshed, dan work hulle nie; as hulle nie loadshed nie, dan work hulle ook nie. Die back-up generator is ook broken. Someone will have to answer for this,' Radebe says, out of breath. Majola wishes he would just speak plain English.

Radebe stops beside Majola. 'Is daai my report?'

'Yes, Colonel,' Majola answers, somewhat uncomfortable to have Radebe standing close enough for him to smell the sourness on his breath. He hands over the document.

'Now come, loop with me. Kan jy guess where I'm going?'

'No, Colonel.'

'To the commissioner. Hy soek a progress report. I wanted to work on it this morning, but then the shit hit the fan at Westpark. Now I'll have to do it in the car, or at the airport before I meet him. He's on his way to Cape Town.'

Majola walks at Radebe's side to the underground parking lot. Everyone makes room for them as they pass.

'Fill me in on this morning, en maak gou. Did you include a synopsis of this morning's scene?'

'Yes, Colonel.'

Majola tells Radebe about the similarities to the other murders and his concern that it followed just three days after the last one.

'Warrant Officer Mbatho found CCTV footage this morning. We're going to watch it now. We're almost a hundred percent sure the murderer is dropping these girls off in a red taxi.'

'En die Wits striker? Where was he this morning?'

'He's been in Bloemfontein since yesterday; they have a game against Celtic. His alibi is solid.'

'So, julle next step is die taxi ranks and the associations? You haven't figured out anything about the numbers and letters?'

'No, Colonel. I told Ramsamy to go look at the grave register at Westpark. Maybe it's not coincidence that the last two girls were found near a cemetery and a crematorium.'

'You're chasing a spook?' Radebe laughs at his own joke.

Majola ignores it. In fact, he's glad that Radebe's in a relatively good mood. He'd been expecting another dressing-down.

'I want to know if we can start putting up roadblocks, Colonel. If this morning's footage corresponds to what the girl from the liquor store in Ga-Rankuwa told us, I think we should start casting our net. We also have clear tyre prints from multiple scenes. He wears a size-ten shoe. We're still trying to determine if he's operating by himself. But I need some support.'

Radebe shakes his head without looking at Majola. 'Ek het bad news vir jou, Captain. Metro will be on a wage strike from tomorrow. And if the unions don't hear what they want to hear tomorrow, the strike might go on until next week. And the guys in uniform are busy with other stuff. We can't take them away from their sectors; things are bad out there.'

Majola is caught off guard. What happened to the extra units he was promised on Saturday? Their fucking hands have been cut off. Can't he see that?

'What about the media?' Majola asks, grasping at the last shred of hope for cooperation.

Radebe stops in his tracks.

'Captain, do you know how sensitive this case is?'

Majola looks into Radebe's eyes. He knows what's coming.

'Imagine the newspapers all starting to write about these victims, picked up in a red taxi all over Gauteng. At this point they're just speculating. They only know about three cases. Imagine what the taxi ranks will look like if no one wants to get into a red taxi. Niemand. I don't know if you've noticed, but besides the white ones, the red ones are everywhere. It's not a green or a pink taxi we're looking for. Weet jy what the associations will do?'

'They'll cause a lot of kak, Colonel,' Majola says, as if he's telling a teacher he didn't do his homework.

'Dis reg, Captain. They'll cause a lot of kak. The taxi owners will strike. The pirates will start to push their luck on the routes. Then the taxi owners will start fucking up the pirates, and vice versa. And then we're in the kak again, because we can't catch the murderer. Never mind the political backlash from the strike.'

Majola nods.

'Do you have an extra report ready for Daan Loots?' Radebe asks, walking to his car.

'Not yet, Colonel. He's been sick again. He's not doing well.'

Radebe stops again, turns to Majola. 'I don't give a fuck if he has AIDS and is lying in a ditch. Today, before you go to the taxi associations, you will take him a report. And he will look at it.'

Majola frowns at Radebe's outburst, but nods quietly.

Radebe takes out his phone. 'Hier's die contact for the main brother at the Faraday Taxi Association. He's got a klomp taxis in the area. They worked with us that time we were trying to catch a rapist in Muldersdrift. Tell the others to start working nicely with the other associations. Not everyone is as helpful as he is. Especially not the guys from the Baragwanath association or Dorljota.'

Majola's phone beeps as the contact details come through.

'Tell him I sent you. Don't say I never do anything for you,' Radebe says smugly. 'Captain, solve this case. I don't care how you do it – I'm not going to sink my career because you fuck up. Or I'll hand it to the Hawks. Maar ek het faith in jou. You're my man.'

Majola is worked up. How the fuck is he supposed to do this without any support units? With only the help of a psychologically disturbed old man? And how the hell will Captain Bok Louw and the rest of the cowboys from the Hawks help?

In the dark parking lot, Majola looks at the row of officers' cars. Mercedes, Chrysler, even a Bentley for Colonel Musake. Radebe's black bmw is parked at the end. Majola remembers the day a new sergeant from Pretoria parked in that spot. Radebe had Metro tow the car and the sergeant had to pay the R500 fine to have it released.

A uniformed sergeant stands idly by the car. He jumps to attention when he sees Radebe.

'Can you drive an automatic, Sarge? This is not a fucking manual Toyota Venture,' Radebe barks as he unlocks the car. The orange lights flare.

'Yes, Colonel,' the sergeant answers sharply as he opens the door for Radebe.

'Then let's get going,' says Radebe, climbing in. To Majola he says, 'Captain, keep me informed. You've made good progress. Bring him in quick, before this explodes in our faces like one of those Molotov cocktails I used to throw when I was young and handsome. En ek is serious about Loots. Get that report to him. I don't want to hear any excuses from you or him.'

Radebe closes the door and the car's rear lights come on. Majola gets out of the way.

Politics. That's what it's all about. No one cares about young girls getting killed. His spirits drop as he contemplates how to break the news to his team.

'How the fuck do they expect us to catch him? Should we all take our lawn chairs and cooler boxes and camp out by the side of the road every night?' Warrant Officer Davids asks, hugely upset, while sitting on the corner of Majola's desk.

'Isn't that what you do on your driveway every weekend there in Eldo, anyway?' Basson jokes as he puts Majola's coffee down in front of him. Majola is in the process of loading the footage from the old woman's house.

'How do you know that? Did you drive past my house when you went looking for prozzies?'

'I've got your mother's number on speed dial, my bru. I don't have to go looking; I just park my car outside her flat,' Basson retorts.

Davids can't think of a comeback, so he just laughs.

Basson pulls up a chair and moves in next to Mbatho. Mitchell is also there, behind Majola.

Suddenly the grainy black-and-white footage pops up, showing the unused gate in the dim street beside Westpark Cemetery.

'We got lucky with the angle,' Mbatho says.

The detectives wait in silence, their attention fixed on the screen.

'Did you bring the whole video or just the relevant part? How long do we have to wait?' Majola asks, not wanting to waste any time.

'Just a moment – he's coming,' Mbatho says.

A few seconds later the taxi pulls into view. Everyone leans closer.

'Mother-fucker,' Davids says under his breath.

'I thought the girl from Ga-Rankuwa was laying it on thick with her description. I stand corrected,' Basson says. 'Black rims, whitewall tyres, black windows, no reflecting strip. And I think we can assume it's red.'

'And it's a third-generation Toyota HiAce Siyaya,' Mitchell adds. 'You see those small, square lights in the front? That's the one. Toyota stopped making them in 1989.'

No one replies. The group appears hypnotised by the footage of the taxi. The thought, the image of something evil just became tangible.

On the screen, the door opens and two figures can be seen.

'Do you see what I see?' Basson asks, looking at Majola.

'I see it. He didn't get out of the front passenger door. That could mean he's not working alone.'

'Or it could mean that he climbed over the seats.'

'Why make the effort? It's not like he knew about the camera,' Majola says.

'He didn't? How sure are you? Maybe he's arrogant enough not to give a shit, so sure that we won't catch him,' Basson replies.

'Jirre, my man, we're not that useless,' Davids chips in.

'He's handling her carefully,' Basson remarks after the killer picks the girl up and disappears around the taxi with her over his shoulder. The man closes the sliding door and gets in on the passenger side.

Less than a minute later, the taxi pulls slowly away. The only thing left behind is the girl against the cemetery wall.

'Can we assume now that someone else is driving?' Davids asks.

'Might be. Either that or he's fucking with us,' says Basson.

'Or does he sit in the back with the girls from the start?' Majola asks, taking a sip of his coffee.

Sergeant Rikhotso comes to join them. 'Here's the copy of the report you asked for, Captain.'

'Thanks,' Majola replies without taking his eyes off the screen. 'Mitchell, play it back for us, from just after he stops.'

Majola moves his chair back to let Mitchell move in behind the computer. He plays it back for them.

The detectives all stare attentively at the screen.

'Stop there,' Majola orders.

'I don't see an emblem. I went to check – Faraday Taxi Association has a green circle emblem. There's nothing on that taxi. Should we not waste our time by going there?' Basson asks.

'We'll discuss that later. It could be on the other side. Mitchell, keep it going.'

Majola makes Mitchell stop again the moment the door slides open.

'Can you zoom in?'

The image loses too much quality though, and the inside remains pitch black.

'Slow it down, but keep the image zoomed in,' Majola instructs.

'He's wearing a balaclava underneath the hoodie,' Mitchell notes. 'And he's wearing gloves, probably light ones, like surgical gloves. I can't make out what race he is.'

'And we can't see a damn thing inside the taxi either,' Basson adds. 'At this stage we can only speculate about there being a driver.'

'Why would he get in on the passenger side then?' Mabatho asks.

'He could easily slide to the other side,' says Basson.

'He doesn't move like an old man,' Majola remarks.

'Who said anything about an old man?' says Mitchell.

'Thuli Mokhebe from Ga-Rankuwa. She said the man was huffing and heaving, as if he was struggling to carry the girl.'

'Maybe he's just unfit? The angle doesn't give us a licence plate,' Basson says.

Again, they watch the taxi pull away slowly. Majola turns his chair to the other detectives.

'As you guys heard this morning, there won't be a lot of help with this one. But if we can get the aid of the taxi associations, we might just catch this guy. Dr Lubbe thinks he's killing them inside the taxi.'

Davids, Rikhotso and Mbatho all look at him in surprise.

'Inside?' Davids inquires. 'With those types of injuries? How would he do it?'

Majola shakes his head. 'Dr Lubbe thinks it's doable, even the electrocution. He thinks the time of death and the time of discovery are too close. I'm still not entirely convinced. But we have to investigate the possibility. If we can find the taxi, chances are we'll find some DNA from one or several of the victims.'

Davids is astonished. 'It's like a fucking horror movie or something. Who is sick enough to turn their taxi into a slaughterhouse?'

'Someone we'll have to catch as soon as possible. Okay, this is what we're going to do,' Majola says. 'Go search the areas where the murders were committed. Find out who drives a red Siyaya minibus. Go ask car guards, petrol-station attendants, those guys who sell tyres and exhausts by the side of the road. Maybe it's not a taxi driver. Then go check the routes, see who patrols which ones. Find out who the drivers are in those areas. Compare the descriptions of their vehicles with what we just saw. Red taxi, dent in the right mudguard. Whitewall tyres. Tinted windows. No branding on the side. That's what we're looking for. Take some pictures of the tyre prints with you. Then talk to all the drivers of the patrol vehicles on all those routes. Don't make too much noise; we don't want to scare them. At this point they're our best shot. It's going to take a while. It's going to take time. The best step is to start by contacting the chairmen of the associations, then following the right channels as far as we can. They can refer us to the marshals at the ranks. Maybe we'll get a lucky break.

'I'll find out if there are any extra uniforms who can lend a hand, but I doubt it. Detective Basson and I will approach Faraday first. Warrant Officers Mbatho and Davids will go to Baragwanath. Chances are that one of them will be on the M1 or the Westpark route. Sergeant Rikhotso, when Ramsamy gets back from Westpark, you guys head out to Dorljota. And please, for now, keep the media out of this as far as you can. Just one spark in the wrong direction and Faraday and Dorljota will be at each other's throats again and then we've got a blood-bath on our hands. Keep me in the loop. Good luck.'

Everyone adjourns except for Majola and Basson. Basson tosses his empty coffee cup into Majola's bin.

'Why are we still wondering if the driver is black?' Basson asks.

'Well, we still can't be sure. I assume you think it unlikely for him not to be black?'

'Don't you think so too?'

'I do, but we have to be sure before we make assumptions.'

'Were any of the girls prostitutes?' Basson asks, looking over the report knocked together for Daan Loots.

'No. All of them were working or studying. Why do you ask?'

'Well, if they were prostitutes, they wouldn't have minded climbing in with a white guy who drives a minibus taxi.'

'You're right,' Majola agrees.

'See, I figure it's like this,' Basson explains. 'If the media get wind of this, the pressure from the top will be too much for Radebe to refuse us the help we need. So we kind of want them to find out. After the next murder, they will anyway. And if we've understood the message he carved into the girl this morning, that could come sooner than we think. Then we'll have to sift through thousands of telephone calls from the public with their made-up bullshit and useless nonsense, because you can be damn sure they're going to start ringing us. The story has already picked up a sensational twist among the team members. Everyone's talking about Zola Budd. If the public picks up the story, then we've got a soap opera on our hands.'

Majola nods his agreement.

'Hopefully we'll get something before then. I'm pissed off about the road-blocks. But he might not dump the bodies in the same areas. My hope is with the marshals, or the drivers of the patrol cars, or another witness who saw the red taxi. That tyre print could still come in handy. I just wish we had a bit more to go on at this point.'

Ramsamy enters the room.

'Morning, Captain.' As usual, he ignores Basson. 'I went to check the grave registers. People were buried on the dates that coincide with the markings.

Mostly white names, considering it was the 1980s. They also have the ID numbers associated with the grave numbers. What do you want me to do?'

'Follow this angle. Go check in with Rikhotso and then swing by Dorljota. Maybe they know something.'

Ramsamy looks at the computer, notices the footage of the gate at Westpark.

'Did I miss something?' he asks excitedly.

Basson rolls his eyes.

'It's definitely the taxi we're looking for. We're still unsure if we have one or two killers. You can check the footage if you like. Mitchell will also go over it again,' says Majola.

'As long as the taxi associations don't think you're another foreigner looking to take over one of their spaza shops at the ranks,' says Basson. 'The Bangladeshis got it bad when their shops were burnt down.'

Ramsamy gives Basson a look.

'Thank you, Sergeant,' Majola says.

Basson sighs and gets up. 'Well, the associations aren't going to come visit us of their own accord.'

Majola doesn't respond. He's staring at the screen.

'What's wrong?' Basson asks.

'The girl from this morning ... that road is busy. But the patrol cars don't really go there. Is that because Montgomery Park and Albertville fall under different jurisdictions? Do you think the murderer knew that? Is that a possibility?'

'What are you saying? That he could have information the public shouldn't have?' Basson asks.

'Or maybe he isn't a civilian.'

'Sjoe, David. That's a wild statement. One of us?'

'He left practically nothing on any of the victims or at any of the crime scenes. Maybe the hair this morning; that's all. The bodies are virtually clean. No DNA, no fingerprints. Nothing. As if he knows what we'll be looking for. I think you're right: I don't think he missed the cameras. He's too thorough. He's playing with us.'

'You can learn that stuff on the crime channel – how to clean a crime scene. Or on the internet. And what about the tyre print?' Basson protests.

'That could be ... I don't know. My gut tells me it's closer than we think. Even the numbers. It could be something specifically aimed at drawing out someone from the SAPS. I just can't put my bloody finger on it.'

Majola gets up.

'We have to go to Daan Loots first. That's why Rikhotso made a copy of the report. Radebe absolutely insists.'

'Still? Did you tell him he's sick again?' Basson asks, surprised.

'Yeah, I did. He didn't want to hear it.'

'Does the fucker have that little faith in us?'

Majola shrugs. 'Well, I'm going to stop there first. Are you coming, or do you want me to pick you up when I'm done?'

'I'll come along. See where I'll end up one day, while I'm at it.'

'I thought you were off to go surfing in PE?'

'Oh yeah, almost forgot about that plan. But who's gonna cover your ass when I'm gone?'

Majola laughs. 'Mbatho's working so hard these days, she'll have to take your spot.'

'Shit. Until her sugar levels drop again. Then she's off dead for another week. Come on, let's roll.'

As Basson and Majola weave through the morning traffic, two things keep running through Basson's mind: Martie Bam and Majola's suspicions.

He isn't too hopeful about Martie's info. Perhaps it's another witness who saw the taxi? If she doesn't have the licence plate or someone who can identify the killer, it's not going to be much help. Still, it might be worth hearing her out. If he's being honest, he feels a bit guilty for not sharing their conversation with Majola, but the feeling is fleeting.

Majola's suspicion that it could be someone on the force has got him thinking, though. He has a point. It does seem as if the murderer has more inside knowledge than the public. On the other hand, that's only true of the M1 and Westpark murders. It's impossible that he would know all the routes of the patrol cars in the other areas.

Hell, the last time he heard anything like this, his dad was telling him the story of the Norwood rapist. It happened back in the Nineties. His dad had spent a few nights drinking with Jaco Geldenhuys in the canteen of the Norwood station, where Geldenhuys was stationed. As happens with hard-drinking policemen, the conversation inevitably turned to the womenfolk. Geldenhuys didn't say a word on the subject. His dad had found it strange, the fact that on this subject Geldenhuys didn't want to say anything. He started to suspect that he was either way too proper, or that he was batting for the other team. Little did he know that Geldenhuys had killed three women and a teenage girl, and raped two of them. He shot three of them through the head at close range.

After Basson had finished his training, his dad sat him down one night and told him that he couldn't trust all policemen. It took a few years, but Basson learnt the lesson: the officers who load flashlight batteries into their tear-gas canisters so they do more damage to protestors, or the detectives who chuck suspects into a drainage hole behind the station, then lob a gas grenade or two in there.

He'd thought he was untouchable after graduating from the academy, thought the blue uniform and the Z88 made you invincible. He was heading out for a drink in Hillbrow with some of the other officers one Friday night.

Old Sergeant Jorrie Buys, the oldest among them, drove a small Mazda 323, and they were all crammed in, a pre-mixed bottle of cane and Coke being passed around. On their way to a club, a Greek in a baby-blue Ford Cortina stopped beside them at a light. He looked at Jorrie, waited for the light to turn green, gave him the finger, spun his wheels and tore off. Old Jorrie gave chase in the struggling Mazda, the other officers urging him on. At one point, the Greek hit a red light and had to stop, so Jorrie pulled up next to him. Stefan Muller got out of the passenger seat and heaved a brick through the guy's window, hitting the Greek in the head. Kurt Bakker shot all four of his tyres out with his service pistol. So it went. The camaraderie between the officers was something you couldn't find anywhere else. That is, until you started raping women and shooting them in the head. And white women too, his dad noted.

Basson looks over at Majola, who's focusing on the rain-slicked roads.

'Weren't you looking to buy a house in Westdene at one point?' he asks.

'Yeah. I had to decide between Westdene and Melville. I'm glad I chose Melville. I hear the student accommodation here gets the other residents furious.'

Basson smiles.

They stop in front of the gate of the retirement village. The security guard walks out of his booth, clipboard at the ready.

'This place is neat,' Basson remarks.

The guard looks at him suspiciously. Basson glares back.

The paving is still wet, despite the rain having stopped three hours ago. Beside the road, flower beds are thick with orange and yellow daisies. Majola stops next to a white Toyota Cruiser with a hunting chair bolted onto the back.

'Looks like Kappie's psychiatrist is finally on the job again,' Majola says when he spots the Cruiser.

'Are you coming?' Majola asks when he sees Basson loitering beside the car door, poised to light a cigarette.

'I'm going to stretch my legs. See you later.'

Majola walks to Kappie's unit, the report tucked under his arm.

When Majola disappears around the corner, Basson walks back to the security gate. The guard notices him but stays seated. He slides open the little window to his booth.

'Morning,' Basson says, looking out over the terrain. 'Do you know Daan Loots? The retired policeman?' he asks, jutting his chin in that direction.

'I know of him, yes. He lives in unit 14.'

'Does he have a lot of visitors?'

The man gives Basson another suspicious look. Basson puts the cigarette to his lips, reaches into a pocket and places his police ID on the windowsill.

'Only his daughter, with the Conquest. And sometimes the doctor.'

'He never leaves with someone else? Is there no one else? Only his daughter?'

The guard nods.

'It sounds like you're from Zim. Do you have a visa to work here?'

The guy's eyes widen. He looks down at his feet, begins fidgeting. 'Yes, I do. I'm just looking—'

'Are you sure it's only the daughter and the doctor who come to visit?'

The man nods again.

'Does this place have a service entry? To take out the rubbish?'

'Yes, behind the apartments. There's a gate. I unlock it every Tuesday morning. Then they pick the rubbish up around ten.'

'Does anyone else have the key?'

'The manager also has one.'

'Do you work nightshift too?'

'I work a twelve-hour shift: six in the morning to six at night. Petrus works nightshift, then we switch every two weeks.'

'I see. Thanks.'

Basson turns around and walks past the parked cars, back towards the apartments. Next to the first row he sees the small entrance that leads to the rear of the units. A narrow path runs there, beside the tall electrified fence bordering the street. There's a gate at the bottom of the path, and black bins dot the back doors of each unit. He walks towards the gate, wondering which one belongs to Kappie.

It's quiet as the grave, the only sound that of a far-off radio. Basson can't hear any voices. Is this where we all end up? The home stretch? The Lord's waiting room, surrounded by criminals and covered in graffiti? Drops glisten on the wire along the fence, which thrums faintly in the morning air. Basson checks the large padlock on the gate. It's solid. There are no cameras at the back here. He walks back to the road, smiling to himself. Does he really think Kappie has anything to do with this, or is his own distaste for the man clouding his judgement? Or is the desperation of this case making him overly hopeful of a solution? His father's advice about policemen keeps playing through his mind.

As he rounds the corner, he hears two voices at the police car. Majola is talking to an older man wearing jeans and a khaki shirt. The man sees Basson and stops talking.

'Johan Schoeman,' he says sternly, offering his hand. 'Psychologist.'

'Warrant Officer Basson.'

Basson notices the fine blue veins criss-crossing the man's face. An old drinker then. And why the fuck does he have to announce his occupation?

'Jeez, Detective,' says Schoeman, 'I thought I had all the whiteys declared medically unfit after 1994. You know, that bunch who wanted in on the full medical coverage and the fat pensions? Seems like a few are still roaming around.'

'A few of us didn't want to become private investigators and spend our days following cheating housewives around,' Basson answers sarcastically. Based on first impressions, he's not a fan of this guy.

Schoeman turns back to Majola. 'As I said, I asked the nurse if he's been missing his daily doses. I checked her file. He gets his mood stabilisers every evening and his antipsychotics at the right time. I don't understand it either. I can't find a cause for his setbacks, unless the medication is no longer working.'

'What are our options?'

Schoeman looks at Basson. 'If it goes on like this, I'll have to have him committed to Akeso in Parktown for further evaluation. I'm just worried that he might hurt himself or someone else during one of his episodes. I asked his psychiatrist to up his dose, for what that's worth. He'll have to go see her too; maybe she can help to figure out what's going on.'

Majola, who still has the report under his arm, looks across at the residences.

'Last time he told me you had him under hypnosis. Did anything strange come out during the session?'

Schoeman smiles. 'I can't tell you much about that. Doctor-patient confidentiality and all that, even though I'm not actually a doctor. What I will say is that, as with so many of the other officers from that time, he didn't walk away from his years of service without scars. He's got serious PTSD. But you know that.'

Majola nods. Basson looks at the hunting chair.

'Do you hunt, Detective?' asks Schoeman.

'Only people,' Basson answers gruffly.

Schoeman looks uncomfortable. 'Well, alright, gentlemen, I need to get going. Feel free to call me during office hours if there's anything else you want to know. You can get my number from Lizanne. Cheerio.'

Schoeman gets into his bakkie, puts on his sunglasses, and turns the ignition. Majola and Basson wait and watch the Cruiser pull away.

'Haven't you been inside with Daan yet?' Basson asks, pointing at the report.

'No, he's sleeping. Let me just go and drop it. I'll call him later and tell him I left it here. I'll be right back.'

Basson lights another cigarette.

Majola walks over to Kappie's studio apartment. The old lady who yelled at the pigeons is sitting on her porch, eyeing Majola suspiciously. He ignores her. Majola, who found Johan Schoeman in front of Kappie's door, knocks quietly on the glass door.

'Captain?'

No answer. Slowly he slides open the door and goes in.

The room is dark and smells like a hospital. Clinical. Kappie is lying on the single bed with his back turned to Majola, half covered by the sheets. He's snoring softly.

Kappie's Bible is on the floor beside the bed. Majola places the report on the kitchen counter and picks up the Bible. Couldn't Schoeman at least have taken it off the floor while he was here? He puts the Bible on the bedside table, next to a picture of Kappie and Lizanne.

The built-in cupboard in the corner is half open. Majola walks over, trying not to make a sound. He opens the door wide to have a look. It's full of clothes and shoes, painfully neat. The kind of clothes that men of Kappie's age inevitably wear, nothing particularly stylish. He notices an old dark-blue police uniform, the one members of the force used to wear on parade. Majola touches the material; the shirt's wrinkled. Strange, as all the other shirts hanging next to the suit are neatly ironed. He knows Kappie irons his own clothes. Majola looks around the tidy room; even the floor shines.

At the back door he notices footprints. Mud. It's been smudged so he can't make out the detail of the print.

Majola returns to the cupboard, bends down to check if any shoes have mud on them. A pair of black Parabellum police shoes is muddied.

Kappie mumbles something in his sleep. Majola replaces the shoes, feeling guilty for going through Kappie's belongings. Above the shirts he notices a large box. He takes it down, and quietly puts it down on the floor. He lifts the lid. It's empty.

What's going on with him? Did Basson's ridiculous theory turn him into an imbecile? He returns the box to the cupboard.

'Kappie?' Majola says again, looking at the old man lying in the bed. He thinks about what Dr Schoeman said about PTSD. Kappie's breathing is slow and even from the medicine.

Majola can't help but feel sympathy. The years of service claimed their pound of flesh. The old South Africa too. The once-great detective is now a shadow of his former self. What a complete waste of a human being.

12

Majola slides his phone into his pocket before walking into Johannesburg Central. He still can't get hold of Lulu. And last night, when his mother called, Lulu refused to speak to him even though she was there. Kappie hasn't called about the report either.

They didn't accomplish much at the Faraday Taxi Association the previous day after leaving Kappie. The chairman was in Polokwane, and his assistant was home sick. At ten this morning his team were at La Rochelle for their meeting. After they'd been waiting for an hour, Paul Motha showed up in his white BMW. Majola had to tell him that Radebe had sent them before he was prepared to have anything to do with them.

Rikhotso and Ramsamy haven't had any luck, as he suspected. Dorljota just pointed the finger at Faraday, as he knew they would. At least they now know that Faraday's taxis run the routes between Thokoza, Katlehong and central Johannesburg. The majority of Dorljota taxis run between Dobsonville, Doornkop and Tshepisong, mostly on the West Rand, but also doing Bram Fischer Drive in Randburg. It's not far from Westpark Cemetery, but none of the taxis fits the description.

Davids and Mbatho spent about three hours in traffic trying to get to Boksburg. When they finally got there, they were told to check out the taxi ranks themselves and sort it out with the marshals if they found the right taxi.

Faraday's administration, however, was like a well-oiled machine, every driver's details meticulously logged and filed. Within an hour, Motha's secretary had printed a list of all the drivers of red taxis, and compiled it into a folder with the green Faraday emblem on the front: when they were employed, former violations (such as those issued by marshals, complaints by passengers or traffic violations) and which routes they drove; also the taxi models and licence plates. Motha advised them to start with the taxis that did the Katlehong/ Tokhoza route, from the rank in Bree Street in the city centre. He also said they were welcome to give the tyre prints and taxi descriptions to the marshals, so they could compare them to the red taxis working at their ranks.

Majola was heartened by the progress. To make things even simpler, Motha provided the contact details for forty-four patrol drivers. His only request was that if they did find evidence that could lead to an arrest, they should keep him in the loop so he could avoid a media circus. But he also sounded convinced that it wasn't one of his guys.

What did bother Majola was that Motha said the marshals wouldn't have allowed a taxi without a reflecting strip to pick up passengers. Without it they were considered unroadworthy, and therefore a liability. But the years of sitting in traffic has also taught Majola that even Faraday's taxis probably weren't all up to Motha's standards.

The media had picked up the story – although it seems they knew less than last time. Only the *Daily Sun* hit the lampposts – 'Did taxi monster strike again?' – with a minor article on page four, accompanied by a crappy picture of the police vehicles at Westpark Cemetery. Probably one of the eyewitnesses. It seems that his warnings to the other officers helped. Or the person who kept talking to the press was on leave, or working a different shift. Nothing in the *Beeld*. Martie Bam was probably breathing fire.

Majola walks over to Basson, who's leaning against the Corolla as he smokes. Basson has been quiet today. He has days like this, when he withdraws into himself, and Majola knows not to probe. Maybe it's just the prospect of working through the hundreds of documents Motha had sent them. To find the model that fits their description is going to take weeks.

'I think we need to start with the patrol drivers. Then we can work through the folder with the models,' Basson says when he sees Majola.

'Do you still think he doesn't belong to an association? That he's a pirate?'

'I don't think he's stupid. I think our killer drives a taxi or a minibus, but I don't think he's a taxi driver. Fuck, I don't know any more,' Basson says despondently.

'Even if he isn't a taxi driver, they might know about a private vehicle that looks like a taxi, especially if they've seen him on their routes.' Majola tries to sound optimistic.

Basson's phone rings in his jacket pocket. He glances at the screen. 'It's Delia,' he says, surprise registering in his voice. He takes the call.

'Hold on ... slowly. Say that again? Where?'

Majola looks inquiringly at Basson.

'Murder?' Basson asks loudly. 'Where's Nonnie? Is she okay? I'm coming.' Basson ends the call.

'Fuck me.'

'What is it? Was there a murder?'

Basson shakes his head. 'At Greenbriar, our apartment complex. The caretaker told Delia. The Parkview police are already there.'

'Who was killed?'

'No idea. She's hysterical; I can't make out what she's saying.'

'Take the Corolla, you'll get there faster. Turn on the sirens. I'll Uber home if you're not back.' Majola tosses him the keys.

Basson drops them.

'Are you sure you're okay to drive?'

'Yes. I'll see you later,' Basson says quickly, bending to pick the keys up.

As Basson speeds off with screeching tyres, Majola mutters, 'Fucking week from hell.'

Basson flicks on the emergency lights as he takes the turn into Empire Road. Luckily the traffic isn't too bad and motorists get out of his way as he picks up speed.

His mind is in turmoil. Why is Delia so upset? Because the murder was so close to their apartment? Or rather, inside their complex? He's shocked: they've had break-ins, yes, and the aeroplane fiasco. That was years ago, though. But murder?

It starts to drizzle again. Ten minutes later, Basson is already close to home, passing the golf course in Parkview. What the hell has happened? In the light of day? Burglary? Was it the couple in 101 who argue constantly? One of the cleaning staff's husband or boyfriend?

A Metro police vehicle is parked at the gate to the complex, its lights flashing blue against the white wall of the adjacent house. The security guard and a uniformed officer stand in the driveway.

Basson shows his police ID and the officer tells the security guard to open up. The guard waves when he recognises Basson. The entrance to Greenbriar's parking lot has been closed off with yellow tape and he can't see the parking bays or the doors to the apartments. Basson parks in front of the tape as another uniform walks over. Basson is out like a shot, lifting the tape and flashing his ID.

The uniform nods and indicates, 'Down there. On the ground floor.'

As he approaches the front of the building, ice grips his spine and his legs go weak. Please let it not be what he thinks it is. He sees the ambulance, the two paramedics.

'Please ...' he says again, his voice breaking.

A cluster of people with umbrellas stand in front of the apartments. Delia is among them, her hand covering her mouth, along with three of their neighbours and the caretaker.

Basson stops.

He can't breathe.

Time slows to a halt.

It's Louisa and Riaantjie's apartment.

Delia sees him and comes running over. 'Jason,' she says, throwing her arms around him. Her umbrella falls to the ground.

'How the hell? Where is Riaantjie? Is he okay ...'

Basson loosens her hold on him and heads to the front door. He shows his ID to another uniform without glancing at him and walks in without waiting for permission. Another officer comes from one of the rooms; Basson shows him the ID too. Delia is still out in the rain.

'Warrant Officer? What does your section have to do with this?'

'I live here. I know these people,' Basson says, walking to the main bedroom.

'I don't want to disturb the crime scene until the Parkview detectives arrive.' He stands aside to let Basson through.

Louisa is lying on the bed. She is still in her pyjamas, but her pink top is now red. Her blonde hair is stuck to the left side of her face; the right side of her head has caved in. Her whole face is covered in blood and her eyes stare lifelessly at the ceiling. Beside her on the bed, he can see a bloody mess. Blood spatters the wall above the bed. Her left leg is folded awkwardly under her body. Her right hand is a bloody pulp, probably from trying to shield herself. At least she still has her pyjama pants on. Lying on the carpet, bringing everything together, lies a bloody hammer.

Then he sees the tracks. Small footprints. Two little feet walking from Louisa to the other side of the bed, to the window. As Basson carefully treads closer, he can hear his heartbeat, the ringing in his ears.

'Detective,' the uniform calls out, concern in his voice. 'Are you sure you want to ...'

But the voice doesn't reach him. It's somewhere else, in a vacuum. The first things Basson sees are Riaantjie's feet, lying side by side, toes pointing up. He stops. They look like a doll's feet: unreal, as if made from plastic. But the blood on their soles pulls Basson back into the moment.

'I think he might have been trying to help his mother. That would explain the tracks coming from this side of the bed. They must have hit him here,' the officer says quietly from a long way off.

'He's not even two years old. How the fuck is he going to help his mother?' Basson asks, hysteria rising in his soul.

He turns around. He's seen enough. He's seen way too much, today and on so many other days.

'How long ago was this reported?' Basson asks the uniform in the hallway. His hands are shaking.

'Sixty minutes, maybe eighty. We got here quite quickly. The security guard heard screaming – he went to check, saw three guys running towards the other block of flats, one with a laptop bag. He saw the one's face: shaved head, big physique, with a long cut on his cheek.'

'Do you have a unit on their tracks?'

'Two patrol cars are out on Emmarentia Avenue and Greenside Road next to the golf course. And First Avenue up here. Three officers are at the golf course's main gates, on foot.'

'Have you called the dog unit?'

'They're on their way from Randburg.'

Basson shakes his head as if trying to dislodge something.

'What were the woman and child doing at home?' he asks.

'The caretaker said it was her day off. He spoke to her this morning.'

'Why are the three officers on foot?'

'They didn't want to climb over the devil's fork, detective.'

'They didn't want to fucking climb over the fucking devil's fork, Detective?' Basson parrots. 'Jissis.'

The uniform gapes at him, caught off guard.

'Do you think these mother-fuckers were too scared to climb over the fucking fence?' Basson's anger starts to ignite as he points at the bloodied room behind him. He storms from the apartment. The constable at the door jumps out of his way.

'Jason, what now?' asks Delia, who's standing with the neighbours and two paramedics.

'Has someone called Wikus?'

'No, I don't think so.'

'You'd better let him know.'

Basson takes his pistol from its holster, drops the magazine, checks it, slams it back in.

The neighbours stare at him with wide eyes.

'Where are you going?' Delia asks, concern growing.

'To do what these useless mother-fuckers won't,' he says walking towards the building opposite. 'Call Wikus.'

'Jason!'

Basson walks on without answering. His hair is wet from the rain; he has to wipe his eyes. Rivulets start running down his neck, slide under his collar. But he doesn't feel the cold. His body is driven by adrenaline and fury as he crosses the soaking lawn to the fence. Here he finds a skinny, wiry little uniform hiding under an umbrella. A ratty yellow rug has been thrown over the spiked fence. Basson beckons the constable.

'Come, Constable. Let's go. Up and over.'

'Sorry?' The constable appears dumbstruck.

'I said, get up there. That's an order!'

The constable hesitates, probably wanting to ask Basson for identification, but the 9mm at his side visible under his open jacket seems to convince him. Basson bends over, locking his fingers, so the constable can step up. The constable raises his foot with uncertainty, then carefully pulls himself over, his hands on the rug. He drops to the other side, shoes sinking into the mud. Basson steps back, takes a run-up and hoists himself over in one movement. The rug moves and one of the spines stabs his palm. He loses his balance and falls on his ass in the mud.

'Fuck!'

The rug has fallen off and is also lying in the mud. The constable looks nervously at the drenched, pissed-off man before him. Basson's palm is bleeding.

'Pistol out, safety off, Constable. And then follow me. Just don't shoot me in the fucking back.'

Basson scans their surroundings. A few metres away, he can see fresh tracks leading through the mud in the direction of the short kikuyu grass of the golf course.

'Do you see these tracks? I bet you they lead to the Braamfontein Spruit,' Basson tells the constable.

Basson looks at his name tag. 'Monyane?'

The constable nods.

'Okay, Monyane, keep your eyes open and follow me.'

The constable follows close on Basson's heels, his gun clasped tightly in both hands. Basson's own pistol is still holstered. He's walking at a quick pace, his shoes drenched in muddy water. His shirt and tie are already soaked under his leather jacket.

Basson comes to a halt in the open field and looks to his left. About 400 metres to the south, he can see three men walking their way. Two of them are carrying something – shotguns. It's the three officers coming from the entrance to the golf course.

'Useless,' he says again, more to himself than to the constable.

He walks on towards the stream, whose banks drop a few metres down.

Pine trees line the banks, with a few palm trees scattered among them. Here and there he can see the roots of the pine trees through the mud. The tracks turn north, towards Parkhurst. The constable's phone starts to ring.

'Turn that fucking thing off!' Basson hisses.

Constable Monyane obeys, slips his phone into his pocket.

'Come. We'll follow the spruit. Just point that thing away from you while you're climbing down.'

Basson heads down first, gripping the tall grass with one hand to control his descent. His feet sink ankle-deep into the thick mud beside the stream, now swollen from the rain. Pieces of rubbish and building material are washing down. The tracks are clearly visible in the mud; Basson stops from time to time, listens. All he can hear is the rain on the trees and the traffic running along the edge of the golf course. The constable stands still when Basson stops, his pistol trained on the ground, water dripping from his blue police cap. They walk on.

At one point they have to climb back up as the stream's banks are too narrow for them to avoid walking in the water. A patrol car drives past slowly, about 150 metres away, and stops. When the occupants see the constable behind Basson, they wave.

Fifteen metres further, they climb back down into the stream bed, where it takes a turn away from the golf course towards the neighbouring residential area. There is more open ground here and the walking becomes easier. Basson picks up the pace. He knows there's a park coming up; he's taken Nonnie there many times. This is the first time he's followed the stream, though.

He wipes the rain from his eyes. He can feel a headache coming on. The image of the two little feet beside the bed fills his vision, making it difficult to see. He's struggling to focus; it's as if the stream in front of him is shaking, and with every jab of the headache he can see those small feet again.

'Everything okay?' the constable asks from behind.

Basson watches the stream running past. Then he sees the girl who was murdered at Wemmer Pan rising from the water, her eyes locked on his. She stands on top of the water, her arms at her sides. Her white dress is sopping, clinging to her body.

'Why?' she asks, almost inaudible through the rain.

Basson shakes his head vigorously.

'Everything okay?' the constable asks again.

Basson ignores him and walks on.

His lower back is starting to bother him. He's tired from trudging through mud and is starting to shiver from the cold. Every few metres, the embankment gives way and they sink knee-deep into the water, and he can feel its strong flow tugging at him. His pierced hand throbs. But his instincts tell him to push on. These dogs didn't plan ahead. The chance of their having a getaway car waiting seems slim. They must be on foot. And the stream is a good choice, as long as they haven't climbed out and jumped over the golf-course fence at some point. He prays that they're still here. Today he will kill every last one of them. The thought steels his resolve.

Behind the tennis courts of the Pirates sports club, rows of pines line the stream that cuts a straight line to the road bridge. Basson slows down, gives the sign for the constable to stop. Basson inspects the bridge but it's too dark to make out anything going on underneath it. The constable takes a step closer. Basson looks around him; they're exposed out here in the open. There's nothing but a lonely fern a few metres ahead. Basson hears muffled voices.

'Did you hear that?' he whispers to Monyane.

Monyane nods.

Basson unholsters his gun and releases the safety catch. Fine drops of water glisten on the barrel, but the holster has kept it mostly dry.

He raises his gun, lets it lead the way. His right elbow is raised higher than the left, the barrel pointed at the ground five metres ahead of him. He turns sharply to Monyane, then looks back at the bridge.

'Okay, stay ten metres behind me. If I shoot, you shoot. And you don't fucking miss.'

Monyane nods nervously.

As Basson walks closer, he hears the voices again. Maybe it's just some beggars taking shelter from the rain or rubbish pickers with their trolleys. It's Wednesday, refuse day. He regulates his breathing, blinks quickly against the rain. Twenty metres. He's out in the open now. If one of them is armed, he's in trouble. He's a sitting duck. He steps on an empty two-litre cooldrink bottle. He stops. He can still hears the voices. They haven't heard him. He walks closer. His hand is throbbing painfully around the gun's grip. Ten metres. He raises the z88 higher. The opening beneath the bridge is in his sights now. He can see the light coming through from the other side. His finger moves to the trigger, lightly.

Then a man appears under the bridge. He looks Basson straight in the eye. There's fear in his face. He doesn't blink. Basson can clearly see the scar on his cheek, the shaved head. Basson aims his gun at the man's head. His finger starts to tighten around the trigger.

'Stop! Police!' Monyane yells from behind Basson. The man doesn't move; neither does Basson. Slowly the man raises his arms.

'On the ground! Police!'

This is the moment, he has to decide. Yes or no. Life or death. He takes his finger off the trigger.

Suddenly Basson sees movement, figures under the bridge, hears shouting, the barking of dogs. The man slowly lies down on the cement, his eyes still on Basson, his hands still raised. Is he imagining it or did the guy just smile at him? Two policemen with r5 assault rifles come walking from under the bridge. Two more follow. He can hear an altercation behind them, someone screaming. Orders. Fear. An officer comes out with the laptop bag, raises it high.

'We got them,' he says triumphantly.

Basson just walks past them without looking around, without answering, his head down. The gun hangs limply from his hand.

When he's out of sight of the bridge and the other police, he sits down on a concrete slab next to the stream and drops his head into his hands. Above him in a tree, a hadeda announces its displeasure. Basson looks at his gun. Flips the safety catch back on.

A tear falls on the z88. It dissolves in the raindrops and disappears into the water and the floating debris of the spring.

'Come, we'll give you a lift,' Monyane says beside Basson.

He didn't even hear him approach. Basson gets up listlessly and holsters his gun. The area is lit rhythmically in blue. He barely hears the barking of the dogs or the crackle and hiss of the police radios. A sergeant helps him get up the embankment, and he climbs through the fence that leads to the road.

As he passes the police bakkie, one of the suspects calls out: 'Hey!'

Basson stops and stares through the barred window. The guy with the shaved head, the one he had his gun aimed at, looks at him with mockery in his eyes.

'That kid pissed himself after I hit him. Like a dog,' he says. The other two laugh. Basson wonders if he's dreaming. Something inside him breaks.

'Shut the fuck up!' Monyane yells, hitting the side of the van.

Basson walks on to the bakkie out front.

'This one here,' Monyane says to Basson, then tells the driver something in Sotho.

Basson gets in and the driver pulls away.

'A woman called us, one of the rich ones whose house overlooks the golf course. She said she saw three men walking in the stream. We were just about to climb down under the bridge when we heard Monyane yelling,' the sergeant explains as they drive.

Basson doesn't say anything. He just watches the regular swaying of the wipers over the windscreen.

The sergeant catches a quick glimpse of Basson before turning back to the road.

'What is a guy from svc doing here?' he asks carefully.

'I know the woman and boy. I knew them.'

'Eish. This is an ugly thing,' the sergeant says. 'Their getaway driver got cold feet. That's why they tried their luck in the stream.'

They drive on in silence until they get back to the apartment. The sergeant bids him a hesitant farewell. Basson doesn't answer him.

He feels tired but not from the cold or the muddy pursuit. It's a different kind of tired, more akin to defeat. He feels it in his bones. Laid low by creeping evil. Asphyxiating in the absence of justice. He looks again at his injured hand, which has stopped bleeding. Blood on his hand. Blood on his hands. The image of two tiny feet. Feet still getting used to shoes, feet that hadn't figured out the finer points of walking yet, feet that will never walk again. For a fucking laptop. That's how low the price has dropped for a child's life in this city. Maybe it's best that Louisa is dead too. Hopefully death came quickly. The words of the scarred man echo through the hallways of his head. He feels nauseous.

Basson spits in the street. The forensic vehicles are parked at the scene, LCRC and three new police vehicles that weren't there earlier. But it's not Doc Lubbe's. These are from Hillbrow. Dented, in disrepair.

Delia sees him from the porch and comes rushing over. She throws her arms around him.

'Are you okay? What happened? We need to get you into the shower or you'll get sick.'

'They've got them,' Basson says wearily.

'Really? That's good. That's good news, Jason.'

'Is it?' he asks without looking at her. He's staring at the van with the bodies in it.

They hear a voice coming from near the building's entrance, someone loudly berating the police officer where they've closed the road. Delia lets go of Basson and walks towards the voice.

'It's Wikus,' she says quietly.

Basson remains standing in the rain. When Wikus comes walking around the corner, Delia goes to him and grabs his arms.

'God, no. What is going on here? Did someone get hurt?'

Delia tries to keep him calm. 'Wait, Wikus. Come with me. Just wait a moment.'

'What's wrong, Delia? Where's Louisa?'

Basson sees Wikus's face turn to stone. He sees the gurney with Louisa's body under a sheet being pushed out by a member of the forensics team.

'Wikus, come here. Let's go have a cup of tea, let's talk.' Delia tries to usher him away.

Then he sees the other gurney. The bundle underneath the sheet is considerably smaller than the first one.

'No, my God, no! What is going on here? Where is Louisa? Riaantjie!? Tell me, Delia!'

Wikus falls to his knees. He starts to sob uncontrollably. Delia squats beside him, puts her arm across his shoulder.

'There now, Wikus.'

'No. No. This can't be. Where are they? Who's that under those sheets?' Wikus is gasping for breath through the tears.

A neighbour who has been watching them from the porch comes over. She drops to her knees beside them, overcome, crying. Tears run freely down Delia's cheeks too.

Basson turns around and walks to the lift. He's done. He's going to retire.

Basson is standing in front of the mirror with a towel tucked around his waist. The wound on his hand doesn't look as if it will need stitches. Darkness circles his eyes. Today was the final straw.

He goes to the kitchen and switches on the kettle. He's too nauseous to eat. Delia isn't back yet; she must still be with Wikus. The shower did some good, if only to drive away the worst of the cold. He picks up his phone: two missed calls from Majola. He dials his voicemail.

Jason. I heard about the murders. I take it you knew the people? Parkview told me they're holding the guys there. I'll swing by tonight. If something comes up and I don't make it, take the morning off tomorrow. Don't worry about the car. I'll get started on those patrol vehicles. We'll talk later. Keep your chin up.

Basson gets the brandy from the cupboard and pours himself a quarter of a glass. He knocks it back. His stomach burns. He pours another and does the same. Then pours himself another stiff drink, adding Coke and a few blocks of ice.

He walks out the front door and looks over the wall. The van with the bodies has gone, most of the police vehicles too. Only one police bakkie remains, probably someone taking statements. LCRC is still there. The yellow tape that hung across the entrance is lying in a puddle on the tarmac. Just another reminder of pointless violence, a yellow scar forever burnt into the minds of those who knew the victims.

Basson closes the front door and heads back to the bedroom, takes another deep swig and puts on a tracksuit. It won't surprise him if he gets sick from fucking around in the stream all afternoon. He covers the wound with a plaster, one of the *My Little Pony* ones they give to Nonnie. He laughs at how ridiculous it looks on his big, clumsy hand. His leg is troubling him, feels numb.

Then he hears the front door open. It's Delia, standing in the doorway.

'How do you feel?' she asks with concern in her voice.

'Better after the shower. How's Wikus?'

'Not good. He can't stop crying. I gave him something to calm his nerves. He's talking very incoherently. I'm really worried about him.'

'He'll be okay,' Basson says, drinking deeply again.

Delia's composure slips. 'How can you be so sure? Everyone isn't as emotionally stunted as you are.'

He hurls his glass; it shatters against the wall. The brown liquid splashes over the wall and carpets, and glass shards fly all over the room.

'Stunted? You didn't see that kid's bloody body next to the bed, did you?'

Basson stares at her shocked expression, his breathing heavy, his fists clenched. Then he collapses onto the bed, his head in his hands.

'I'm sorry. I didn't mean it like that,' Delia says and sits down beside him. She rubs her hand across his aching back.

'It's so fucking unnecessary. That child … Jesus.'

Delia doesn't say anything, just holds him closer.

'I'll get you one of those pills too, help you to calm down. I have to go pick up Nonnie. I'll bring some pizza back.'

'Okay. I'll clean this up,' Basson says, laboriously getting up from the bed.

'I'm going to bring Wikus something to eat too. Will you take it to him? I'm sure he'd really appreciate it. Maybe he needs to talk to another man,' Delia says carefully.

Basson sighs. 'Okay.'

Delia gets her handbag from the table. 'I'll be right back.'

Once she's out the door, Basson gets the dustpan and brush and a wet cloth and starts to pick up the glass shards.

When he's finished, he goes back to the cupboard for the bottle of brandy.

'Wikus?' Basson realises he's not very stable on his feet. Perhaps he should have taken more time over that last brandy. But when he heard Delia and Nonnie coming home, he had to do something.

'Why does Papa look so sad?' Nonnie had asked with sympathy as they ate pizza in front of the TV.

'Oh, nothing to worry about, little lady,' he said.

While dishing up dinner in the kitchen, he and Delia had decided to wait till the right time to tell her about Louisa and Riaantjie.

'Are we still going to Riaantjie's party? Can I go with to get him his present?'

Basson got up, picked up the extra pizza box and walked to the front door.

'Jason?' Delia said, worried.

'I'll be right back. I'm just going up to Wikus.'

Now he's standing in front of Wikus's door with a tongue as thick as his mind and a Hawaiian pizza in his hand.

'Wikus?' Basson hears a shuffling from the living room. He can smell something baking.

He turns the door knob and walks in.

Inside, the whole kitchen is covered in cookies, all decorated in a *Cars* theme. Wikus is icing them, his hands stained blue and red. Brown paper bags full of popcorn and sweets, all decorated with the smiling face of Lightning McQueen, fill one corner. One bag has Nonnie's name on it. Riaantjie's name is written the biggest of them. Basson has to choke back his tears.

'Look in the fridge,' Wikus says when he notices Basson.

Basson reluctantly opens the fridge. A huge ice-cream cake covers one shelf, another smiling car plastered over it, with the words 'Congrats Champy!' written beneath.

Basson closes the fridge and turns to Wikus. 'Wikus, you have to listen to me ...'

'I will Jason, but you'll have to excuse me, I still have a lot of baking to do,' he says, turning his back. 'It's Riaantjie's birthday on Thursday. I want to get ahead with the baking. Don't want the little thing to think I'm neglecting him. Right, Detective?' Quickly wiping his eyes, Wikus draws a line of red icing across his wet cheeks.

'Jason, where are you going? Haven't you had too much to drink?'

'I know what you think, but that's not where I'm going. I'm done with all of that. I just need to go have a chat.'

'Who with?'

'The three friendly gentlemen from this afternoon.'

'Please don't. You're going to get in trouble. What good will it do? You know it was them.'

'Probably nothing. But it might help me feel better.'

'Please, Jason. You've barely eaten, and you've been on the go all day. I need you here. Now. Stay. Let's go to bed.'

Basson ignores her and pulls his coat over his hoodie and tracksuit pants. He takes his police ID and keys from the table and places his gun on the bookcase.

'I'll be back soon,' he says, closing the door behind him.

Delia looks on helplessly. Then she grabs her phone.

'Hello, Delia,' Majola says hesitantly.

'You have to help. Jason just went to Parkview to talk to the murderers.'

'I'll call him.'

'That won't help. He left his phone here.'

'Okay. I'll go over there. Did he take his weapon?'

'No. But he's drunk a lot. He's not himself.'

'I'll go right away. It's going to take me a while to get there – I'm in Fordsburg.'

Basson parks in Ennis Road, around the corner from the Parkview station. He reaches under the seat and takes out the bottle of brandy he bought on his way here. He cracks the seal and takes two big swigs. The alcohol burns in his stomach. That should get him back to the level he was at when he walked into Wikus's place. Dutch courage.

Basson replaces the bottle, opens the door and gets out. Pulling his coat around him against the wind, he walks across the street to the complaints office.

It looks like all the others: walls plastered with clichéd warnings, potted plants somehow still clinging to life – the same smell too, like post offices used to smell: wood polish. But judging by the granite countertop, this place hasn't had a good clean in a while.

Basson walks up to the counter, careful not to stand too close in case they smell his breath. Two officers staff the office, a policewoman in uniform and a large policeman in civvies, wearing a denim jacket and a golf shirt.

'Can I help?' the man asks.

Basson takes out his ID.

'Serious and Violent Crimes? What can I do for you, Warrant?' he asks.

The other one looks up from her magazine.

'Who's in charge tonight?'

'That would be me. Sergeant Molebe.'

'The three from this afternoon, from Parkwood: I have some questions for them. We suspect they were involved in another murder in Randburg. They killed a pastor.'

The sergeant's eyes widen.

'His wife too.' Basson lays it on thick for effect.

'Eish. Fucking Zimbos. Rubbish.'

'Will you take me through?'

'I'll have to talk to the colonel first.' Sergeant Molebe takes out his phone.

'I won't be long. Twenty minutes in and out.' Basson banks on the sergeant not wanting to complicate his evening more than necessary.

The sergeant hesitates, looks at the woman, back at Basson. Then he picks up the office phone and says something brief in Xhosa. He puts the phone down and goes on with his work.

A young constable in uniform walks in from a door behind the counter. He holds the door for Basson and tells him to come through.

'Thanks,' Basson says to the sergeant, who doesn't look up from his writing.

Basson follows the constable down the hall, past a few offices to the back of the building, through a steel door and into a courtyard. The constable unlocks another steel door with a key from a bunch dangling from his belt. The familiarity of the grey walls and fluorescent lights of the cells strikes Basson for a moment. It's very quiet.

As if the constable is reading his thoughts, he says, 'There are only four of them in there: a drunk and the three from this afternoon.'

Basson walks downs the passage, past the first empty cell. He feels his heart rate accelerate. In the next cell a guy is passed out in a corner. In the next, the man from this afternoon is sitting on a thin mattress. He gets up the moment he sees them.

He recognises Basson. The man is wiry but strong, about half a head taller than Basson. His face drops; the bravado from earlier drains away.

'That one. Unlock his cell for me.'

'You don't want to take him to the interrogation room?' the constable asks.

'No. Cuff him while I go in. Then lock the cell.'

152

Basson takes his wallet from his inside pocket, takes out three blue bills.

'Go buy us some Cokes. Keep the change. Then come back in twenty minutes.'

The constable looks at the money, then at Basson, then at the man in the cell, who is watching them attentively.

'Eish.' He pockets the money. 'Okay, twenty minutes.'

The constable calls the guy over. The man hesitates. Then he laughs, walks up, turns around and puts his hands through the bars. The constable cuffs him, then unlocks the cell door.

Basson steps inside. He takes off his coat and gives it, along with his wallet and keys, to the constable. He goes to stand with his back against the wall while the constable locks the door and uncuffs the man. The man stares at Basson, defiance in his eyes. He rubs his wrists where the cuffs were. Then he yells something at his two partners in the other cells.

'Twenty minutes, nè?' the constable reminds him before leaving. Basson can hear him locking the steel door from the other side. The other two are whispering in their cell. The only other sound is the buzzing of the lights.

Basson takes off his hoodie, tosses it into a corner of the cell. Untucks his shirt.

The man shakes his head and smiles.

Basson raises his fists and drops his chin, puts his left foot forward and turns his body.

'Let's see if I also piss myself. Like a dog.'

The man's smile disappears. He glares at Basson. They've got twenty minutes to kill.

Then he rushes at Basson.

He tries to grab at him, but Basson sidesteps and lands a punch to his temple. The man groans as he stumbles past him, then turns to face Basson again.

He touches the side of his head. Then he rushes in again. His partners cheer him on loudly, despite not being able to see what's going on.

Basson throws a hook but only barely touches his chin. The man grabs him by the neck, holds him from behind. Basson bends his knees and whacks the man in the groin. He relaxes his grip long enough for Basson to break free. Basson comes in with an uppercut, and hears the man's jaw rattling. Follows with a left hook. The man goes down on one knee.

'Kwenja!' the man yells, groaning.

Basson aims a hard kick at his head but misjudges his footing, loses his balance and falls over backwards. The man comes in quickly, diving at Basson. Basson's head hits the floor hard. The man sits on Basson's chest, punches him with a right to the head.

Then he puts his hands on Basson's throat. Basson sees the white of the guy's teeth and grabs him by the wrists. He has to break out of this, fast. But his grip is strong and Basson can't break it. He tries to turn his body but he can't buck him off.

Then he relaxes his grip and lowers his arms. The man is too strong. He smiles at Basson. The fight is almost won. His sweat drips onto Basson's face; he's starting to lose consciousness. The light is starting to dim around the man's head.

Then Basson sees those little feet beside the bed.

In one movement, he stretches his arms to his sides and slams them against the man's ears. This shocks him enough for Basson to twist his body and throw him off. Basson lunges down to sit on the man's chest.

The first blow breaks his nose.

The second one breaks something in Basson's left hand.

He punches the guy's mouth with such violence that he smashes his head on the cement. He can't stop. The man's eyes close.

The other guys start yelling when they hear the rhythmic, deadly blows. Both of Basson's hands ache. The man's mouth is a bloody mess. His teeth are gone, his gums a bloody pulp. Both his arms lie limply at his sides.

'Who's the fucking dog now?!' Basson asks between blows.

He sees the slow breaths still being sucked into the bloody chest below him. He wraps his hands around his throat.

'This is for the boy,' he heaves.

He hears voices at the door. Keys jangling in the lock.

Basson releases his grip and gets up. He spits in the man's face, but there's no reaction. Basson walks to the corner and picks up his hoodie.

'Jason! What the fuck?' Majola yells when they get to the cell door and see the man on the floor.

Basson is taken aback when he sees Majola. He looks at the constable and the sergeant behind him.

'Can I get my Coke, please?'

The constable warily hands the can through the bars.

'Thanks,' Basson sighs resignedly and cracks the tab with a bloody hand.

The constable opens the cell door and checks the man on the floor.

'We'll have to call an ambulance,' he says to the sergeant, who turns around quickly and rushes off.

'Do you know how much shit you just caused?' Majola asks, looking at what's left of the man's face. 'Turn him on his side; he's going to choke on his own blood.'

Basson looks down, rubs the hand that's holding the Coke.

'I'll take whatever comes my way,' he says to Majola without taking his eyes off the man bleeding on the floor.

13

Majola pays the Uber driver and walks over to the Greenbriar apartment complex. It's still overcast, but hopefully the rain will stay away today. Wednesdays have always been good days in his book. Today, however, he doesn't feel it.

Last night was a mess, to say the least. Radebe called him at eleven, fuming. The Parkview station commander had called him directly and given him hell about svc being the shame of the police force.

Basson has been suspended until further notice. No matter how many times Majola explained how much he needed Basson on the taxi investigation, Radebe refused to budge. He didn't even want him coming close to the station; went on and on about police brutality and white racists who still think they can do whatever the hell they want. Basson is the Independent Police Investigation Directorate's problem now. It's in their hands.

Basson didn't sound surprised when Majola told him about Radebe's reaction. He can thank his lucky stars they didn't arrest him.

Majola sees the yellow police tape across the door to apartment 10. He can imagine how this must have hit Basson, but damn it, to get yourself drunk and then go assault a suspect isn't the right way to go about it.

The white police Corolla is parked behind Basson's car. Delia's Getz is also still here; she's probably taking the morning off.

Majola knocks on the door and hears Nonnie's voice inside. Delia opens the door, dressed for work. She looks tired.

'Morning, David.'

'Morning.'

Delia steps aside for him to enter, and Nonnie comes running up.

'Uncle David!' She hugs him tightly.

'Hi Nonnie! Look how big you're getting, girl. Where's Jason?' he asks, scanning the living room.

Delia's face turns serious. 'He's on the balcony. Go sit down, I'll make us some coffee. Milk and two sugars, right?'

'Please, and thank you.'

Majola walks through the living room, where Nonnie is now watching TV. Basson is sitting on one of the Morris chairs overlooking the garden. He's unshaven and wearing a black tracksuit. His left hand looks badly swollen.

'How's the hand?'

Basson must have heard him come in but doesn't look up. 'I think it's broken. Delia's taking me to the doctor later. The painkillers are helping, at least.'

Majola pulls up a chair and sits down. The garden is beautiful, the lawn still green despite the freezing nights. Four guinea fowl waddle around a palm tree.

'What's next?' Basson asks with a sigh.

'Well, IPID will do an investigation. And then there'll be a hearing. I'm going to insist you see a psychiatrist – the last few months have been rough. It could help your case.'

'How is the saintly murderer doing?'

Majola's brow furrows. 'His jaw is broken. And you probably know this, but you knocked out most of his teeth. At least he woke up in the hospital last night.'

'I should have beaten him to death.'

'Really? And then what? Then they arrest you for murder?'

'They?' Basson asks, defiantly.

Before Majola can answer, Delia comes out carrying a tray with two cups of steaming coffee and a plate of rusks. She places it on the table between them and goes back inside. Basson takes his coffee but leaves the rusks.

'Look, this thing with the taxi murderer is already a complete fuck-up. And now I have to make do without you. I can imagine you were upset, but—'

'Upset?' Basson's cup clatters as he puts it down on the railing. 'They were too chicken-shit to climb over the fence; they walked all the way around to the golf-course entrance like a bunch of little girls, scared of getting hurt. But why worry about a white woman and her little boy, right?'

Majola wants to chip in but Basson keeps going: 'When we had them in the van, the poor, innocent murderer told me that Riaantjie pissed himself like a dog when he bludgeoned him to death with a hammer. Tomorrow would have been his second birthday. Two fucking years old. So yes, you could say I was upset.'

'We can mention all this as motivation at the hearing,' Majola says.

This is followed by an uncomfortable silence.

'Fuck, man. If you'd really wanted to, you could have done something. You've got an in with your friend Radebe, haven't you?' says Basson. 'And IPID is only as independent as the colour of your money or the strength of your connections. But I know how it goes. Things work differently these days, don't they?'

'What are you trying to say?' Majola asks. He can see Delia sitting on the living-room couch, listening to every word they're saying.

Basson gets up. 'I'm saying you can't trust a fucking k—'

'Jason!' Delia says loudly. She is standing in the doorway, arms crossed.

Majola shakes his head and gets up. 'I think it's time for me to go.'

'Just don't break your back with all the effort,' Basson says sourly. 'And you can take my badge and gun from the table.'

Delia shakes her head in disbelief as she follows Majola, who picks up the police-issue gear on his way to the door.

She touches his arm. 'I'm so sorry. He isn't like that. You know him better than that.'

Majola smiles wryly. 'You know, Delia, some things will never change. I'm not stupid either. Good luck.'

'Here – take these,' she says quietly, handing him the keys to the car.

He takes them without a word, closes the door and walks down the stairs.

Delia goes back to the living room. 'Nonnie, can you go read in your room for a little bit? I need to speak to Daddy.'

Nonnie gets up and looks at Basson with confusion and concern. He's sitting down, sipping his coffee. She goes to her room.

'Was that necessary?'

Basson ignores her.

'The man I married is not your father, Jason. You're not a bloody racist.'

Basson smiles. 'I'm not? How many of my friends are black?'

'Stop that! You and David are friends, not just colleagues. You're going to call him and apologise.'

'No fucking chance. I'm done crawling. Every fucking day I'm on my knees in front of this bunch. My dad would turn in his grave.'

Delia sits in the chair opposite Basson.

'You think what you did last night was right. You think you can solve everything with violence. And now what? Now you'll probably lose your job, or go to prison. And the only one who still supports you is David. Then you call him … that? Did you think about Nonnie, for just one moment?'

Basson stares into the distance. 'I thought you'd be happy. Now you can go live closer to your brother, get out of this awful city.'

'The work is killing you, Jason. Look at you. Listen to yourself. You said it too: you come home at night and you don't say a word. You're becoming a shell of a man. You've got nothing to prove – not to your dad, not to me. I want to get out of here for us, Jason.' Her voice is trembling.

'You've got a lot to say about my father all of a sudden,' Basson says, taking another sip.

Delia doesn't respond. She just picks up the tray and the cup that Majola didn't touch. 'Go shower. I'm taking you to the doctor. I need to get to work. And you *will* call David, whether you want to or not.'

'How did it go?' Davids asks, sitting down on one of the desks in the ops room.

The rest of the team have already left, gone back to the taxi ranks to continue their search. Mbatho has been put in charge of confirming Ayanda Mcayi's identity and has taken Lungani Thlobe to the Braamfontein morgue.

'He didn't take it so well,' says Majola. 'You remember that case at Wemmer Pan? I noticed then that work was starting to get to him. At the M1 incident too, he kept staring at nothing, had this far-off look on his face. And then he went and made some racist comments out of the blue, too. I'm pretty fucking pissed off at him.' He pages through the Faraday documents again.

'What's next?' asks Davids.

'Now IPID have to do their investigation.'

'Can't you put in a good word with the colonel at Parkview? Look, Basson is full of his fair share of shit, but we can't really lose him now if we want to solve this case. And I'm sure this wasn't the first case of police brutality at Parkview.'

Majola shakes his head. 'Even if I could, it's not going to help. IPID is independent.'

Davids's phone rings. He answers it and listens for a moment. 'Okay, I'll come and get you.' He turns to Majola. 'It's my witness from Tembisa. I'm going to bring him here.'

'No, take him to the office next door. I don't want him to see what's going on in the ops room.'

Davids leaves to meet his contact at reception. Majola is feeling queasy and miserable. This morning was sobering: he feels like he's been stabbed in the back. The race issue has always been there between him and Basson, beneath the surface. But they've always managed it. Or so he thought. They should have talked the whole thing through at the start. He knows Basson is a racist, despite his attempts to hide it behind jokes and wisecracks. His insecurities, easy to mistake for bravado by those who don't know him, Majola has always swept under the carpet in the name of friendship and reconciliation. Maybe he thought that Basson saw something else in him, after months of fighting side by side through the dark Johannesburg streets. More than just a *kaffir*. How naive was he? Stupid. Basson is on his own now. He'll have to sort out his own shit.

Majola hears his phone beep. It's Kappie.

'This is Captain Majola.' Davids is in the doorway, introducing his contact. Majola gets up and they go to the office next door. Majola shakes the patrol driver's hand, looks him up and down. His pants are riding low and he's wearing a black beanie. The man looks suspicious. He sits at the table across from Majola.

'You drive one of the patrol cars for the Baragwanath Taxi Association. Please tell Captain Majola what you told me on the phone this morning.'

'Wait, hold on,' Majola protests. 'Who are you?'

The man jumps. 'Jacob Dube.'

'Okay. Aren't you working today?'

'No, it's my day off.'

Majola nods.

'It was last week Thursday. I came off duty at eight. I went to ChesaNyama, to get something to eat, you know. When I drove home, I saw him on Chris Hani Road, about two kilometres from the hospital. Most of our taxis were back at the rank by then. I thought he was busy poaching. We don't have any red taxis on that route.'

'And then?' Davids urges him to continue while carefully watching Majola's expression.

'Then I followed him. All the way to Southgate. I kept my distance, so that he wouldn't spot me. I thought it was strange that all his windows were tinted, even the windscreen.'

'When did you pull him over?' Majola asks.

'I didn't. He stopped just after Southgate, at Columbine Avenue, under the trees. I think he saw me then. He switched off his lights and just waited there.'

Davids indicates that Dube should continue.

'I drove up a bit closer to take down his licence plates. I always keep a log; you can't take chances. And it's not like he picked anyone up. But that taxi wasn't poaching. He drove past a bunch of people, even if he was going slowly. As if he was looking for someone, someone specific to pick up.'

'Did you happen to see the driver?'

'No.'

'And then?'

'Then he switched on his lights and drove on. I lost him at the M1.'

'That's probably when he went to Melville to pick up Jane Semenga,' Majola says.

'What were the numbers on his plates?' Davids asks.

Dube takes a small notebook from his shirt pocket and tears out a page.

Majola hands it to Davids. 'Go run this through the licensing department. You never know.'

'Was there anything else about the taxi, Jacob?' Majola asks. 'Did it have a reflecting strip? Any dents?'

'No, Captain. The only thing that caught my attention were the windows. I can't remember anything about dents or reflecting strips. I knew he was trouble. Now I'm glad I didn't give him a fine.'

'How did you know it was a taxi?' Davids asks.

'How many people do you know who personally drive a Siyaya?'

This gets a smile from Davids.

'Thank you, Jacob. And nothing about any of this to the newspapers, right?'

'That's right, Captain.'

'What do you think?' Davids asks, after seeing Dube out.

'He drives around until he finds someone. It's a long way from Soweto to Melville. Which doesn't get us closer to figuring out where he lives. Without roadblocks, our hands are tied.'

Majola's phone beeps. 'It's Mbatho,' he says. 'The girl from Westpark Cemetery has been identified. They're back at Brixton. I'll go see what's up. Are you coming?'

'No. I'll run these plates. Shit, man, imagine that – if the idiot never changed the plates.'

'We don't get fairy tales in Johannesburg, Warrant. Only there, under the pretty mountain in Cape Town. Here it's just blood and shit,' Majola says pointedly before leaving the office.

'Jesus, he's in a kak mood today,' Davids says to himself.

***

Lungani Thlobe is clean shaven and wearing a tracksuit from the police college. His eyes are red from crying.

Majola feels sorry for the man. But there's something else he can't quite put his finger on. Something is making him uncomfortable.

Mbatho has already gone over most of the important questions.

'I reported it on Monday. Why am I only hearing about this now?' Thlobe asks, looking first at Mbatho, then at Majola.

'Sometimes the communication between stations can be a bit slow. Because SVC is investigating the case, the file isn't at the station,' Majola answers.

'Did the taxi murderer get her?'

'Unfortunately I can't share that kind of information with you,' Majola answers, plunging the room into silence.

'At least tell me – did she die quickly?' Thlobe's eyes plead with Majola.

Majola looks at Mbatho, then leans forward in his chair. 'She did. She didn't have a lot of pain.'

Mbatho looks out the window.

'You know … on Monday I went to get permission from her parents to ask her to marry me. They said yes. I have the lobola ready and everything. I saved up for three years for the deposit. I even bought an expensive bottle of pula molomo before going to speak to her uncles.' Thlobe starts to cry. 'Her whole life was ahead of her. Our lives lay ahead of us. We wanted her to finish her studies before we …'

He goes on, but Majola isn't listening any more. His thoughts are elsewhere. Years ago, just before he went to police college. Now he gets why the young man makes him uncomfortable – it could have been him sitting in that chair.

After school he started working at a store as a security guard. He met Busiswe through a school friend. They were both quite shy and it took two chance social encounters for him to work up the nerve to ask her out. They clicked immediately. They had common interests, they both liked movies and spending quiet evenings in, and neither had many friends.

Busiswe had wanted to change the world, and got a bursary from Anglo American to study law. Majola wanted to study too but it had to wait. Maybe that was the problem from the start: Busiswe's parents didn't think he was good enough for her. After they had been dating for two years, Majola had gone to ask them for her hand in marriage. At first, they didn't want to agree to it, but Busiswe threatened to leave home and never speak to them again. The negotiations for lobola were disastrous. Majola's uncles were all dead, and his dad had disappeared completely. It took three days and four bottles of brandy before her uncles started to relax. They agreed to R30 000, of which he had to pay ten percent immediately. The fact that he had no family who would help him pay certainly helped to keep the amount low.

Busiswe just laughed, but it was important for her that her family was happy too. Their future was starting to look rosy.

One warm February Sunday afternoon, they went for a picnic under the bridge on the banks of the Jukskei River in Alexandra. Just the two of them. She was wearing a red dress and the purple scarf he had bought her. It was nearly sunset when five men came walking their way, talking and laughing loudly, clearly drunk or high on something.

He tried to stop them when they grabbed Busiswe by the arm and pinned her to the grass. But one guy grabbed him from behind and tried to slice his throat before sinking his knife into Majola's abdomen. He fell to the grass with blood seeping through his fingers from the wound in his neck. He saw them tear the red dress from Busiswe's body. She called out his name.

Three days later he woke up in the emergency wing of the Johannesburg General Hospital. The knife had missed his jugular and his windpipe, and none of his internal organs had suffered significant damage. He was lucky, the doctor told him. Busiswe was in a different ward; she had survived.

Later that night, he got up and went to check on her himself. In the room, an old woman was lying in one of the beds. Her eyes widened when she saw him come into the room. Beside her was an empty bed with bloody bandages on the floor, and a trail of red leading to the bathroom. She shook her head at him when she saw him walk to the bathroom. He carefully opened the door and saw Busiswe's reflection in the mirror. The men had cut her lips off after raping her. Her face looked like those of the skeletons you see in cartoons. She saw him and tried to say something, but she couldn't form the words. He turned around and walked out. She didn't follow him.

Majola was sitting in the parking lot sobbing when Busiswe jumped from a window on the fifth floor. She died on impact. A few days later he checked himself out of the hospital.

Busiswe's parents blamed him for her death. They still wanted him to pay the lobola after everything that had happened, but he refused. He didn't even go to the funeral. Then he turned his back on his Zulu culture, to his mother's great regret.

Eight months later he passed the fitness test for the SAPS, but failed the psych evaluation. Busiswe's suicide and the attack at the river had left their mark. Later that month, they called him up, out of the blue, and told him that he'd been accepted. He could join the police college in Pretoria the following week. Why had they suddenly changed their minds? No one gave him an answer. He thought he could make a difference; maybe he hoped to catch those same guys one day, because the investigation into the attack didn't go anywhere.

His world fell apart that year, and ever since he has been trying to put the pieces back together in a way that makes sense.

'Captain?'

'Captain Majola?'

Mbatho and Lungani Thlobe are staring at him.

'Is it okay if Mr Thlobe leaves?'

Majola awkwardly adjusts himself in his chair. His body is stiff. 'Yes. I'll be in contact if there's anything else we need to know.'

Just before Thlobe leaves the room, Majola gets up and turns to him. 'It gets better.'

Lungani looks at him blankly.

'How would you know?'

Majola puts his hand on his shoulder, looks into his eyes. 'I know.'

14

Basson is smoking on the balcony after taking Nonnie to school. He had to lie to her about why he wasn't at work. They haven't told her about what happened yet. Delia barely spoke to him last night or this morning. She has little concern for his fractured hand, and responded badly when she found out that he hadn't yet called Majola. But what would he tell him? How sorry he is for standing up for what's right?

He's already decided to pursue the Zola case himself. Fuck, he has to leave some kind of mark, break out from the shadows of the bastards who took what's his. Then he'll retire. He still has his old police ID. Or rather, the one he declared missing before finding it under the seat of his car. And his dad's z88. Between Martie Bam, Kappie's psychiatrist and his contact, Nigel October, he should be able to pull something off.

He just can't shake the hunch that Kappie is somehow involved. And he's learnt to trust his hunches. That sick old fuck has something to do with this. Fuck coincidence – there's a snake in the grass. Figuring this out would restore his honour in the eyes of these imbeciles. But actually, he's doing this more for himself. And it's not as if he has anything better to do with his time. You can only watch so much shitty daytime TV.

Basson flicks his cigarette over the railing and goes inside. In the bedroom he puts on his thick jacket and running shoes. Nothing like some fresh winter air to start the day off right.

Wikus's car isn't there. Maybe he's gone to work. Basson went past yesterday, but there was no one home. The apartment was completely silent.

At the gate, he stops to speak to the guard. 'Morning. Have you seen Wikus this morning?'

The guard shakes his head. 'That man. He went out here maybe one hour ago. He was wearing a dress. A red dress.'

'A dress?' Basson blurts.

'Yes. And his car was full of cakes.'

Basson takes out his phone as he walks back to the apartment.

'Morning,' Delia answers frostily.

'Wikus left this morning wearing a dress. I think he went to Zoo Lake. I'm going to check. He shouldn't do something rash now.'

'He's probably on his way to Riaantjie's birthday. God, Jason, we have to do something.'

'Call Doctor Malan and ask him what we should do. Maybe it's best to have him committed,' Basson says, unlocking the front door.

'Okay. Be safe. Keep me posted.'

'I will. Bye.'

Basson turns into the Zoo Lake Sports Club. The parking lot is empty, apart from five cars parked in front of the Panettone Café. One of them is Wikus's.

Basson stops his Mazda next to a delivery van and looks out over the empty cricket pitch, then towards the gate. It feels like he's on another planet. Everything around him feels surreal despite looking so very normal. The last few days have been absurd, to say the least – actually, the last few weeks. Johannesburg has finally decided to detonate its grand finale, bells, whistles and the kitchen sink, in the middle of his life.

He walks up the steps to the restaurant's entrance. A brunette in her thirties is sitting at the door. She gets up when she sees him.

'Morning.'

'Table for one?' she asks when no one follows him.

'Are there other people here?' Basson asks, quickly surveying the restaurant.

The woman is caught off guard by the question, but reacts when he shows her his ID. 'Two tables outside. And there's a man in the private room who's waiting for some people. I should say, I think it's a man. He's wearing a dress.'

'Do you have his name?'

The woman looks up the booking. 'Wikus Coetzer. He was here yesterday to get the room ready for the party. He even left some of the baked things here overnight, said he wouldn't have time to bring them all today.'

She points to a door at the back leading to the private room.

'Thank you.'

Basson hesitates at the door. He can hear Wikus talking to someone.

'Morning, Wikus,' Basson says quietly as he peeks around the door. The room is covered in *Cars*-themed decorations, everything in red, blue and yellow. There are enough baked goods to feed a school dormitory. The birthday cake Wikus baked stands in the middle of the room, its two candles already burning low.

Wikus starts when he sees him, but then he smiles.

'Detective! Welcome. You're a bit early.'

Basson sees the dark circles under Wikus's eyes. His hair is messy and his hands dirty. The red dress looks dishevelled, wrapped tightly around his hairy body. Basson tries to see if Wikus has any weapons close at hand, but it looks okay.

Wikus turns to the empty chair to his left.

'Say hello to Uncle Jason, Riaantjie. He came to wish you a happy birthday.'

Basson looks at the empty chair, then at the table. Two small handprints are slowly evaporating from the tabletop, as if a boy with warm hands had placed them there a moment ago.

Basson blinks in confusion, a chill cutting through him.

'Do you see, Detective? Riaantjie is here with us.'

Basson pulls himself together. 'Wikus. Will you come home with me?'

'But Nonnie and Delia aren't here yet. And I still have to give Riaantjie his new tricycle. I want to wait for the others.'

There's a wild look in his eyes and his left hand trembles where it rests on the table. An uncomfortable silence fills the room. The restaurant is completely quiet, the only sound the shuffling of a solitary waiter's feet.

'I'm sorry I couldn't protect them, Wikus,' Basson whispers.

Wikus's smile disappears. He stares, unmoving, at the wall. 'They didn't give me a chance to try.' Wikus's voice is low, almost inaudible.

Basson pulls out a chair and sits down.

'That's Riaantjie's chair,' Wikus says firmly.

'Excuse me,' Basson says, getting up immediately. He sits on the next chair along.

'You must think I'm crazy,' says Wikus.

'I don't think that at all. But I do think you need to speak to someone.'

'But I'm talking to Riaantjie, aren't I? But he's gone quiet now that you're here.'

'Wikus, please. Let me take you home.'

Sadness washes over Wikus. After a few moments he folds his hands together. 'Okay, Detective. Give me five minutes to say goodbye. Will you help me carry all this stuff?'

'Of course,' Basson gets up. 'I'll be outside, smoking.'

When Basson walks past the manager, she steps closer.

'Is everything okay?

Basson hesitates, then sighs. 'Not really, he—'

A shot reverberates through the restaurant.

For a moment Basson and the manager lock eyes. Then he turns and sprints to the room. Wikus's head is lying on the table, his eyes open wide. It looks like he's smiling. His left arm hangs limply at his side. The .38 revolver is on the floor. His right arm is on the table, hand open, as if he is holding someone's hand. The chair to his left is pulled out. Suddenly, the candles on the cake go out.

'Fuck, Wikus. Fuck, man,' Basson says and leans against the door jamb.

The manager appears behind him and starts screaming.

***

Basson is smoking on the front porch when his phone rings. It's Majola. He hesitates, then takes the call.

'Remember when you asked me if I was superstitious? If I believed in spirits and stuff?' Basson asks.

A body-removal bakkie pulls slowly into the parking lot. The manager is on her phone. The rest of the staff are standing around, not knowing what to do.

'Yes?' Majola replies.

'I swear there were two handprints on that table this morning, as if someone was sitting beside Wikus. A boy's hands. And it was like he was holding someone's hand when he blew his brains out. Fuck, I think I'm starting to lose it.'

'I think you need to rest,' Majola answers.

Basson takes a long drag. 'I should have been more thorough looking for weapons. I remember he told me that he had his dad's old .38 Special.'

'Delia asked me to call, to find out if you were okay.'

'Jesus. After what I said to you?'

'I'll give you the benefit of the doubt – although I still think you're a fucking asshole.'

Basson tries to smile. 'Fair enough.'

For a moment both men are quiet.

Basson changes the topic: 'How's Zola Budd doing?'

'One of the patrol drivers spotted him in Baragwanath the night he killed the girl on the M1. I picked up the pathology report today. Same story. The girl from Westpark's boyfriend is a trainee at the police college. And we have a number plate. Davids is on it.'

'So he drives around looking for victims?'

'It looks that way. Have you heard anything from IPID?'

'Nothing yet. You know how it goes … Listen, David—'

'We'll talk again. Good luck that side.'

Majola is at his desk, paging through the pathology report. The rest of the office is quiet, everyone still out asking questions at the taxi ranks. The system was offline the day before, so Davids hasn't traced the plates yet. They promised they would have the problem fixed by this afternoon. They've given the uniforms and the detectives the registration number, told them to be on the lookout. To his and Ramsamy's deep regret, the grave registers from Westpark turned out to be a dead end. The contact details for the families of the people buried on those dates are all out of date or missing.

Majola is halfway through the list of patrol drivers at Faraday. Most of them have merely been complaining about the taxis from Dorljota poaching on their routes. One or two of the taxis were red, and the patrol guys had given them fines, but nothing else seemed suspicious about them. The taxis had all been full of passengers too.

He dreamt of Busiswe again last night. He finds it strange that he keeps coming back to her. Usually she comes and goes, but she's been ever present the past week. The young police recruit was what did it. Then there was Basson's ordeal at Zoo Lake this morning.

According to Doc Lubbe, Ayanda Mcayi died of electrocution. She didn't bleed to death like Jane Semenga on the M1. He looks at the list of injuries: perforation of the rectum, torn perineum, shattered pubis. The list goes on. This time there weren't any broken limbs, though.

Does he really kill them in a taxi? If that's the case, all they have to do is pull over the right taxi, and then they have him. There would be enough evidence. But how do they do that without roadblocks? Basson's question is valid too: how do they know it's not just a red van? But he doubts it. Those models are almost exclusively used as taxis.

Majola studies the pictures of Ayanda: the bruising to her wrists and knees, the burns on her breasts, the numbers on her back. He looks again at those incisions. They're neatly done, finely cut. According to the handwriting analyst, the perpetrator's right-handed. What goes through his head as he does this? Does he reach orgasm?

If they understand the words on her back, then the next murder is around the corner. Then Radebe will have to jump. Give them what they need. Or, with some luck, whoever keeps feeding the media will keep quiet. About all the murders. Then all he'll do is shrug and tell Radebe that he warned them not to. Out of desperation, he's considered doing it himself.

His phone beeps. It's a message from Lulu. *Call me please.* Majola smiles. Has she decided to bury the hatchet? He calls her.

'Hey, David.'

'Hello, Lulu. How are you? This is a pleasant surprise.'

'Okay, David.'

A silence follows.

'I'm in trouble.'

'Are you pregnant?' Majola asks nervously.

'No, come on. It's not that.'

'Then what?'

'I owe someone money.'

'Who?' Majola can guess, but he's hoping he's wrong. 'Who is it, Lulu?' His voice rises.

'Calvin Mpete.'

Majola sighs loudly. 'How much?'

'R17 000.'

'How much?!'

'You heard right.'

'How much fucking cat do you have to snort to rack up R17 000 of debt?'

But she's already hung up.

Majola gets up hastily, closes the office door. He calls Lulu, pacing as he waits. She answers but doesn't say anything. Majola can hear her crying.

'When do you need the money?'

'Today. Or over the weekend. I'm not sure. He called and told us our time is up.'

'Who's "us"?'

'Me and Christine.' Lulu starts to sniffle.

Majola presses the phone to his forehead, closes his eyes. Then he checks the wall clock. It's almost 4 p.m.

'Does Mama know?'

'No. Of course not.'

'Okay. I'm coming through. It's too late to go to the bank. I can withdraw R5 000 on my credit card and R2 000 from my personal account. The rest will have to wait until I can increase my limit at the bank.'

'You can do it on the internet,' Lulu says.

'I'll see it if I can tonight. Is he there?'

'Who?'

'Mpete, who else?'

'He's always there. Day and night.'

Silence.

'Thank you, David.'

'I'll be there asap, Lulu.'

He takes his z88 out of his top drawer, checks that all his bank cards are in his wallet. This is the last thing he needs right now.

Alexandra's streets are bustling as everyone prepares for the weekend. Men are already drinking beer on the pavements, and the air is filled with the smoke from fires lit against the approaching cold of night. The ground is dotted with puddles and pools after the rains.

Majola is nervous. He doesn't know what to expect of Mpete. What he does know is that he'll have to stay calm and keep his distaste for Mpete in check. And leave his gun at his mother's house. They won't let him into the house with a weapon anyway – that is, if they even let him in.

He's stopped at Campus Square in Melville to withdraw the cash. The R7 000 lies heavily in his jacket pocket. He had to keep R3 000 back to see him to the end of the month. After going into debt to feed his own addiction, he can't really lend any more. He owes almost R90 000 on his credit card, and the bank won't give him any more leeway. He'll have to come up with something else.

A battered white bakkie comes to a sudden stop; Majola honks the horn. The driver gives him the finger.

'Gotta keep calm,' he says to himself.

He parks in front of Mama Thadie's house. He sees something moving at the small kitchen window, then the curtains close again. Lulu emerges from the front door.

'Where's Mama?' Majola asks as he gets out.

'She's not here yet. She went to work in Sandton today. She'll probably be back around six.'

Majola walks past Lulu to the door, then lets her walk in ahead of him. Looking helpless, Lulu heads to the kitchen. Majola stands at the table and puts his gun down in front of him.

'Sit,' Majola orders.

Lulu pulls out a chair and sits down. She doesn't look at him, keeps her eyes downcast.

'How long?'

'How long what?'

'How long have you been using?'

'A few months.'

'A few months?'

Lulu starts to fidget. 'About a year.'

Majola shakes his head in disbelief. 'How did it start? Was it Christine?'

'Does it matter?' Lulu asks, crossing her arms.

'Well, if you want me to cover your ass, it had better start mattering.'

Lulu looks at Majola, the obstinacy draining from her. She looks down at the table.

'We were at a party one night in Randburg. One of Christine's friends had cat, so we tried it. After that, me and Christine started buying for ourselves. Sometimes coke too, if we had enough money.'

'Well, your money didn't last very long, did it?'

She avoids his eyes, fiddling with an invisible stain on the table.

'And in Mama's house too. What were you thinking?'

Lulu doesn't reply.

'Look. I don't have R17 000. I have my own debts to pay off. I'm going to give him R7 000 and see if I can negotiate. Let's hope he cuts me some slack. Does he know who I am? Did you tell him about me?'

'No. I just said my brother may be able to help. He doesn't know you're police.'

'You'll have to make a plan. Get an extra job. Maybe you can waitress somewhere in Melville. Pay off your debt.'

'Melville?'

'Yes. You're coming to stay with me, like it or not. We'll have to make up a story to tell Mama.'

'Melville is far from the college and the salon.'

'You'll have to get used to it. And I thought you desperately wanted to get out of this hellhole?' Majola says, taking out his wallet and ID and placing them on the table. He feels his jacket pocket to check the money's still there.

'Stay here. If Mama comes, I'm at Uncle Tony's, hearing how his leg is doing.'

Majola walks out the door, turns back to her. 'You know, Lulu …'

Lulu turns in her chair and looks at him.

He turns away shaking his head.

Majola stops around the corner from the drug house in Mike Diradingwe Street and makes sure the car alarm is armed. Twilight is deepening and the smoke hangs thickly in the streets. He can hear the dull thud of music coming from one of the houses nearby.

Majola zips up his leather jacket, does one more check to see that the money is there.

Calvin Mpete's house has large steel doors, a six-foot grey brick wall and two heavies wearing thick jackets and beanies. They turn to him as he walks up the street, taking position in front of the door, hands shoved into deep pockets. The man on the left, wearing a military coat, is the taller of the two.

'I'm looking for Calvin Mpete. I'm Lulu Majola's brother. I need to speak to him,' he says before they can speak.

The men regard him coolly. One turns his back, takes out his phone and makes a call. After a short conversation, he nods at his associate, who unlocks the door with a large key. The guy with the phone motions at Majola to walk through, then follows him inside.

The courtyard is littered with junk, paper bags and broken beer bottles scattered across the paving. One of the doormen indicates that Majola should lift his arms. He frisks Majola, from his ankles to his middle, then under his arms. His hands stop when they feel the money in his inside pocket. The man raises an eyebrow.

'A gift for Calvin,' Majola says.

'That's Mr Mpete to you,' the other one says from behind him. Majola can smell the alcohol being breathed down his neck.

'Follow me,' the one in front says, unlocking the security gate at the wooden front door. He waits for Majola to enter before closing the door behind them. Majola hears the security gate slam and the key turning.

The house smells like weed, mixed with something sour. It's like the sunlight hasn't penetrated in ages. Music plays from different rooms, none in sync. As the doorman leads the way down a long passage, his boots crunch on the tiled floor. The walls are covered in red graffiti, mismatched lettering as if done by a child.

A low light comes from the end of the passage. All the doors on either side are shut, except for one.

As they pass, Majola sees a dimly lit sliver of the room. A naked girl on a bare mattress on the floor, her back to the door. Beside her, crumpled clothes and a smouldering bottleneck. A sweaty man in his underwear sees Majola and slams the door.

Majola can hear a thudding sound from the rooms upstairs, and a woman moaning in the throes of noisy sex. They're definitely selling more than drugs here. Majola wonders where they hide the supply. There are plenty of rooms here; easy to keep it away from outsiders. Or does Mpete have the police's protection and not give a shit?

The doorman stops at a door and knocks lightly. He opens it and allows Majola to enter, then closes the door and walks away.

The room was clearly once the master bedroom of the house, but now serves as a kind of office. The only light comes from a tall lamp in the corner and a small one on the desk. Heavy black curtains cover one window, brown blinds the other. An air conditioner blowing heated air has turned the room muggy and uncomfortable. The desk is against one wall, with two leather couches opposite it. A soccer game between two European teams is playing on the big-screen TV. From one of the couches, two bald heavies, even heavier than the doormen, are watching the game with the volume turned down. One is wearing only his boxer shorts. An overflowing ashtray and fast-food leftovers cover the coffee table in front of them. On the green carpet at their feet, there's a bottle of whisky and a 12-gauge shotgun. They don't even look at Majola as he walks to the desk.

A blonde is stretched across the other couch, doing her nails. She has dark circles under her eyes and her hair looks dirty. She gives him a bored look, then turns back to her nails. Bare feet, and no bra underneath her black dress. A good body. She's young, looks barely eighteen.

The desk is cluttered with papers. There's also a large computer screen and three thick white lines on a mirror beside a rolled-up blue bank note. Majola's mouth starts to water. Not now. Focus.

A revolver is poorly concealed between two magazines, the silver barrel pointing in his direction. The man in front of him is sitting on a high-backed office chair, his back to Majola. Majola can see only the top of his shaved head, as he's absorbed by the other TV screen on the wall. He's playing *Grand Theft Auto*.

Calvin Mpete. Drug boss with his claws dug into his sister. Majola wishes he could see his face. He needs to look into his eyes. So many rumours surround him. Bad ones: intimidation, abduction, murder. He's been running the drug game in Alex since forever.

Majola feels naked without his gun. And it's not like there's police backup waiting outside.

The sound of the game is deafening. Mpete picks up a remote, turns the volume down, but continues playing. It's suddenly way too quiet. One of the heavies picks up the bottle of whisky.

'Do you have the money?' Mpete asks, without turning around. His voice is harsh, raspy like a lifelong smoker's. Probably been smoking his own stuff. And judging by the lines on the desk, snorting it too.

'I do. I'll bring the rest later.'

'The rest? What rest?'

Mpete pauses the game. The image freezes on a man who has just lost his arm to the swing of an axe. He turns around slowly. His eyes are pitch black, but his complexion is paler than those of the rest of the men in the house.

'I told Lulu and that crack whore I want my R24 000.'

'R24 000? Lulu told me R17 000.'

'The extra R7 000 is what Christine owes. Your sister said she would vouch for her.'

'I've got nothing to do with her. Her debt is her problem,' Majola protests.

Mpete swivels his chair from side to side, crosses his arms. 'You'll have to sort that out with your sister. That's your problem.'

The men glare at each other.

'Where's the money?' Mpete asks without breaking his stare.

Majola unzips his jacket, takes out the stack of cash, and tosses it onto the desk. Mpete picks it up and throws it to one of the heavies on the couch, who catches it in one hand. He leans forward and starts to count it out on the table.

'Do you think I made it here by doing favours? Do you know how hard it is for a Xhosa in this line of work? Nigerians on every corner trying to fuck you up and take your territory?'

The man counting the money stops for a moment to look up at Mpete. Then goes on counting.

'What can you do? Shoot back or recruit them to your side. Right, Frank?'

Frank gives Mpete a smile, then continues counting.

Mpete leans forward with his elbows on the desk. Majola feels uncomfortable, exposed. He no longer has the money, his only bargaining chip. He considers his options. None of them looks very promising. The only possibility would be to go for the gun on the desk, but it's easily within Mpete's reach. Bad idea. A shotgun blast from one of the heavies at this distance would certainly be fatal. The other option is to try to hold Mpete hostage with his own gun, but that doesn't inspire much confidence in him. And to run for the door, down a straight, narrow passage with two heavies behind him and two more waiting behind a locked gate ... he'll just have to hope to make it out alive.

'You look familiar. What's your name?'

'Lulu's brother,' Majola answers, putting his hands in his pockets to help him keep his cool.

'Funny, man. You look like someone who walked around Alex in the Nineties, someone I knew.'

Majola doesn't answer. Mpete looks him up and down. Majola takes his hands out of his pockets, pulls his collar higher. Mpete narrows his eyes.

The girl gets up from the couch and slouches her way to Mpete's desk. Majola's eyes follow her. She moves like a cat. Her black dress only barely covers her bum. There are bruises on her shins and one of her knees is scabbed over. She could be a model; she's skinny and pretty enough: a model with a debilitating addiction.

Mpete sees Majola looking at her and smiles. She stops in front of Mpete, slowly bends over the desk, picks up the rolled bill and does a line. She rubs her nose. Then she bends for another. Mpete leans forward and puts his hand between her legs, feels her up slowly. The girls groans as she does the next line. When she walks away, Mpete smells his fingers.

'Straight outta Sandton.'

The girl smiles and winks at Mpete.

Majola avoids Mpete's eyes. His gaze is nailed to the last remaining line of cocaine.

'Go right ahead. It'll be the best line of charlie you've ever had. Uncut, from Colombia,' Mpete says smugly.

One of the heavies starts laughing.

'Looks like it runs in the family,' Mpete tells Frank.

The blonde girl smiles at Majola from the couch, her legs spread, one finger lightly running up and down her thigh. Frank signals to Mpete that the money is all there.

Majola forces his gaze away from the line on the desk. 'I'll bring the rest next weekend,' he says.

'Okay. I'll do you a favour. Next Saturday at the latest. Otherwise me and my two Nigerian friends will go pay a visit to Lulu and your mother, in that house with the broken Cressida on the bricks.'

Majola takes a step closer. Mpete's hand shoots out for the revolver, but he doesn't pick it up. Frank aims a Heckler and Koch MP7 at him without getting up. His associate has already picked up the shotgun and is standing with it aimed at Majola's chest. Where did the MP7 come from?

'Ooooh, cowboys!' the girl taunts the men.

'Easy now, big boy. Don't be mad at me; go take it out on your sister,' Mpete growls. 'Don't ever try shit in my house. Now get the fuck out of here. I'll see you soon enough.'

Majola walks backwards to the door. The weapons are all still pointed at him. The door is locked.

'Easy!' Mpete yells at the door. It opens and one of the doormen is there, ushering Majola out. A door down the hall opens and a young black girl who looks barely twelve years old comes running out, screaming at the top of her voice. She's wearing only her panties. A thickset man runs after her, throws her over his shoulder and takes her back to the room.

'Feisty thing,' he says to Majola.

The girl looks straight into his eyes. He'll have to put that moment away in the box of nightmares he keeps inside, just like all the others. One of the many he couldn't save.

'Let's go, baba,' the doorman says, shoving him towards the front door.

Majola is fuming. He's punched the steering wheel so hard his hand is still aching. He doesn't see how he can face Lulu, much less his mother.

He tosses his dirty shirt into the overflowing laundry basket, opens the bath taps. To the kitchen, where he picks up his phone. He had turned it to silent before going into Mpete's place. Four missed calls from Lulu. He calls her, and she picks up immediately.

'Why didn't you answer your phone?!' she asks, almost hysterically, but trying to keep her voice down. Probably so Mama Thadie won't hear.

'You have to start making your arrangements. I'm coming to pick you up this week. I just have to get a few things ready here.'

'What did Calvin say?'

'Calvin? Are you and that asshole on first-name terms?'

Lulu ignores the question.

'We've got until next Saturday. I don't know what I'm going to do; I'll have to talk to the bank tomorrow. You still owe R17 000. Apparently you vouched for Christine too.'

'He's lying. I told Christine she has to pay her own debt.'

'Well, it won't help arguing with him. That's what he decided.'

'What are we going to do if we can't get the money?' Lulu asks, concern in her voice.

'Well, then Mama will have to come stay here too. But let's not think about that right now.'

Lulu makes no reply.

'Another thing. You stay away from Christine. And you stay away from Mpete. I don't know how bad your addiction is, but you stay away till I come get you. Tell Mama I got you a better job at a salon in Melville. We can't break her heart.'

'Okay,' she says softly. 'Are you still mad at me?'

'No, Lulu. I'm just disappointed. Maybe I should have brought you here earlier. But there are drugs here too. At least I could have kept an eye on you. Or maybe I should have visited more often. Then I would have noticed in time. Now we have to work with what we've got and get out of this mess.'

'Thank you, David.'

Majola pauses. 'Good night, Lulu.'

'Sleep well, brother.'

He puts down the phone and opens the fridge. The milk has gone sour. The bread rolls are hard. He hasn't eaten today. On his fridge, he finds the menu for Mr Delivery: a pizza will have to do. After ordering, his battery dies and he plugs the phone in to charge.

Before Majola can lower himself into the warm bath, he sees Mpete's black eyes. The white lines on a mirror. The past still haunts him. He laughs at the thought that he was feeling somewhat overwhelmed three weeks ago and had considered taking a few days' leave to go to KwaZulu-Natal.

He closes his eyes and tries to let the warm water start working on him, but that little girl from Mpete's house won't stop staring at him.

15

A screaming siren from outside wakes Majola. He reaches for his phone to check the time but remembers he left it in the kitchen. He slept like a rock. He gets up quickly.

It's raining again; he can hear the water splashing in the gutters. But it's too dark to guess the time. Majola berates himself for forgetting his phone.

The kitchen floor is cold. Majola turns on the phone. Two voice messages. As he dials his voicemail he takes a bite of the cold pizza on the counter. It's six o'clock: he's had a good nine hours of sleep. He feels better, rested.

He was hoping Davids would call him with the registration number, but nothing. The first message is from Kappie. *Come and see me immediately, David. I tried calling. It's the numbers. You're not going to believe me if I tell you. I don't know how I missed it. Come right away, please.*

There have been eight missed calls. The last one was three o'clock in the morning. Shit. Majola calls Kappie's number. He picks up within seconds.

'What kind of detective's phone is on silent during a murder investigation?'

Majola is caught off guard. 'It was charging in the other room. Long day. Long week.'

'Did you get my message?'

'I did. What about the numbers?'

'When can you be here?'

'Give me half an hour.'

'Okay, I'll be waiting.'

A silence follows, then Kappie clears his throat.

'And, David …?'

'Yes?'

'Come with an open mind. You might not believe me,' he says before ending the call.

Majola stares into space. Will this be their breakthrough? The numbers? Have they been focusing on the wrong thing all along? He'll have to tell Ramsamy he won't be at the parade.

The retirement village is quiet when Majola arrives just before seven. The rain is still falling softly.

Majola tries to sidestep the puddles as he pulls the hood of his red raincoat over his head. The gardens are dreary, grey and sombre. The wire-mesh lawn furniture in the rain makes this place look like some European no man's land. Mother Nature has lost her mind, as has this city.

It's been exactly a week since they found the girl on the M1. And within a week his life has fallen to pieces. Lulu. The taxi murderer. It never rains, it fucking pours, baba.

Last night he dreamt he was doing cocaine again, with one of the girls he met months ago in Melville. And then Martie Bam came walking into the room and joined them. She was busy undressing beside the other girl, who was a few items of clothing ahead, when the sirens outside woke him up. His nose was runny when he got up, probably from the cold.

Before Majola reaches Kappie's place, the glass door opens. Kappie is already dressed in a grey tracksuit and trainers. His hair is still messy, though.

'Jis, jis. I thought it was you when I heard the car door.'

Kappie stands aside for Majola to enter.

'Morning, Kappie.'

'Morning, morning. This bloody weather – in Johannesburg we're drowning while Cape Town is turning to dust. The world is on its head.'

The apartment is cold as usual, but mercifully warmer than outside. Majola takes off his coat and sits at the round table. Here, in its brown file, lies the copy of the report, and beside it the autopsy photos of the numbers carved into the girls' backs. And beside that, the Bible, opened somewhere in the middle.

Kappie closes the door and puts the kettle on. Kappie looks around the room, avoiding Majola's eyes.

'How's the case going?' Kappie asks hesitantly.

'So-so. We have one or two eyewitnesses, but they haven't brought us any closer to catching him. And Radebe won't let us put up roadblocks. The taxi associations are blaming one other. We have a licence plate, but I'm not going to get too excited just yet. For now, we wait. How are you feeling?'

Kappie's attention is on the kettle, however, and he doesn't hear Majola, as if he isn't listening at all.

'Kappie?'

'Yes? Yes. Excuse me. Let me just pour these. Two spoonfuls of sugar, right?'

'Yebo.'

Majola's eye catches one of the photos. He picks it up: Jane Semenga. The colour image has a demonic allure.

Kappie pulls up a chair and sits down, handing Majola a steaming cup of coffee.

'Did I ever tell you I was in Koevoet?'

Majola nods.

'Do you know about the stuff that happened there? In the early Eighties?'

'I heard some stories,' Majola says, putting the picture down. 'Of soldiers tied to the bumpers of Casspirs, and torn to pieces by being driven through the bush. And men shot with cannons for the hell of it. And Eugene de Kock was there, wasn't he? Prime Evil.'

'Yes, he was.'

'What does that have to do with the dossiers? I'm sure you didn't call me for a history lesson.'

Kappie fidgets uncomfortably. 'No, I didn't. I just kind of want you to know where I'm coming from. And how things were back in those days.'

'I know it was rough, Kappie – not just for you guys, but for the people on the receiving end too. I grew up in the township, remember.'

'Yes, I know.'

Kappie takes a sip of coffee. He still can't seem to look at Majola.

'It's the numbers,' he says.

'You said so, yes. What about them?' Majola asks, somewhat impatiently.

Kappie looks at one of the pictures. 'They're docket numbers.'

Majola frowns. 'Docket numbers? We thought about that. But the letters and the numbers don't make sense. They would have had CR in them, right? Crime register? Or CAS, Crime Administration System. And they don't have the station names. So far, all of the letters in front of the numbers have been "ON". Or a zero and an "N".'

Kappie doesn't take his eyes off the pictures.

'ON stands for *ondervraging*.'

'Ondervraging as in "interrogation"?'

'Yes, that's right,' Kappie replies almost inaudibly.

'Well, that's news to me. And very strange. We don't have that any more.'

'You wouldn't. That was from before, during the State of Emergency in the Eighties. They were special dockets.'

'Okay, so someone is carving old docket numbers from the Eighties into girls' backs. That could mean we're dealing with a retired policeman, or one who's still around. Or someone who had access to the old dockets. How sure are you of your story?'

Kappie sighs. He slumps back into his chair. 'You know how good my memory is.'

'Yeah, like a lion.'

'Like an elephant, you mean.' Kappie smiles for a moment, then frowns. 'They were my dockets, David.'

It takes Majola a few seconds to respond. 'Your dockets?'

'Yes. I opened these dockets. These numbers carved into their backs were on my dockets. I was focusing on the wrong stuff when I first looked over them; otherwise I would have recognised them sooner.'

Majola shakes his head. Then he begins to smile. 'Are you pulling my leg?'

Kappie doesn't smile. 'No. Those are my numbers. I remember it clearly. This stuff haunted me for years.'

Majola's smile disappears. He can't tell if he's dreaming. He looks into Kappie's eyes.

'Kappie, what's going on here? Do you have something to do with these murders?'

Kappie doesn't answer. He stares at the rain pattering against the window.

'Kappie?' Majola says, with growing urgency.

'I'm going to tell you something, and I want you to listen until I'm finished talking. Then you'll understand this better. Don't interrupt me, please. Okay?'

Majola hesitates. 'Okay, I'm listening.'

Kappie readjusts in his chair. He still looks everywhere but at Majola. His eyes keep returning to the rain on the window.

'When I came back from Rundu, they needed people on the East Rand, to work in the riot squads. This was just before I met Deborah. We worked from Dunnottar; the staff in Benoni had become insufficient to deal with the situation. Back then, the riot squads worked with the Security Branch, acting on information we got from them. I was part of a unit who did home breaches. That was rough: I worked twelve-hour shifts for months on end. In the first few months we had several lawsuits filed against us for assault, but the senior state prosecutors dropped them all after being given information by the Security Branch. One of the officers from the Security Branch, I think his name was Barker, heard I'd come from Koevoet. And as fate would have it, he also heard that I was good at interrogations. Torture. I should say torture ... They roped me in, with a guy called Job Dimba, an old askari they'd turned to their cause. He was a Zulu and part of Inkatha, so he hated the Xhosas more than he hated us.'

Majola can see Kappie's mind is far away.

'He enjoyed the torturing. Women, children, old people: made no difference to him. As long as he could inflict pain, even if it was on his own people.'

Kappie smiles humourlessly. 'It was the perfect combination– the sadist and the specialist in interrogation and torture. I showed him the buttons, and he pressed them.'

He gets up and walks to the window.

'Most of the interrogations happened in Benoni or Dunnottar, but the officers started to get jittery. They didn't want blood on their hands.'

'I'm assuming most of the interrogations didn't have happy endings? Like with Biko?'

Kappie ignores the remark. 'There wasn't enough room in the Nissan Safari bakkies, and they couldn't afford to use Casspirs to do it. Then they suggested I use my own vehicle.'

'Your private car?'

'Oh, no. They got me a red taxi from the impound at Secunda.'

Majola's eyes widen. 'A red taxi?'

'I took the back seats out, left only one in the middle. Then I took it to Krugersdorp, to Malan's Upholsterers. They took out all the fabric and replaced with rubber. See, it would be easier to hose out the blood. You just pull up to a slight incline and wash everything away.'

'Fuck it.' Majola can't believe what he's hearing.

'We called the seat in the middle the "Seat of Death". That's where we got all our information: ammunition stores, informants, where they were planning attacks, planned rallies, that kind of thing.'

'What did the torture entail?'

Kappie looks at Majola for the first time since he started talking. 'David, I don't think it's necessary to go into the detail—'

'I think it fucking is. Your story is directly related to our murder case. Now is not the time to hold anything back.'

Kappie takes a breath, looks down at his hands.

'At the outset, just the usual. A tube over the face, later a plastic bag, because the tube immediately cut off the air supply. With a bag at least they could still hear our questions. Or Dimba would just go at them with his fists. If he hit them in the kidneys repeatedly, it didn't take very long for them to start talking. Sometimes we had two in the taxi at once. The other one would be cuffed in the corner. When he'd seen what we'd done to his friend, he'd sing like a canary.'

Kappie's voice has become softer, as if he's afraid someone will hear him.

'That wasn't all, was it?'

'Later, towards the end, we did it differently. It was clean and effective – no worries about swollen hands or bruised knuckles. Although we did use a truncheon too.'

'Yes?'

'We got this huge battery from an old friend of mine who worked on the mines. Installed it in the back of the taxi and attached it to the chair.' Kappie's voice is barely a whisper. His hands have started trembling.

'Then we took jumper cables to the guy's nipples. Or genitals. We shocked them. When they wet or soiled themselves, we knew they would talk. Or if we started smelling burning flesh.'

Majola drops his face into his hands. 'My God, Kappie …'

'We got all the information we needed. And perks: weekends off, rounds in the canteen, respect from the top brass. But things got out of hand. Dimba showed up one night with a blowtorch. That was the last one I did. We picked up a suspect at a shebeen in Katlehong. It was a rainy Saturday night, and I remember we were listening to the boeremusiek competition on Radio Suid Afrika. The suspect was tough; he didn't want to talk. The plastic bag didn't do the trick, and neither did the jumper cables. He laughed at us like a lunatic. Then Dimba pulled down the guy's pants, lit the blowtorch—'

'That's enough, Kappie. I've heard enough.'

Kappie stops talking, exhales slowly.

Majola gets up. 'That doesn't sound like something that belongs in a docket.'

'The methods weren't in the dockets, only the usual info. At that point, there was a lot of pressure from outside. That was the time when Helen Suzman marked the Casspirs and started counting the ammunition of the guys we sent into the townships. The station commander at Benoni, a young English-speaking guy from Natal, started to get nervous. He insisted we start opening dockets for the interrogations. That's why they were marked with "ON". The dockets you see here were the last ones I worked on in Tembisa, KwaThema and Katlehong. Afterwards, I left for Linden.'

'What happened to the station commander? From Natal?'

'The Security Police came for him one day. I never saw him or his family again.'

Majola shakes his head. 'I've heard some stories before. But Jesus, this is inhuman.'

'It was my job. I was following orders. It was a different time. We were all wrong in the head. Power-mad. Why do you think I asked to be transferred to Linden? I had to kiss ass till I was blue in the face; they didn't want to let me go.'

'That's easy to say – you were following orders, like you were some kind of robot,' Majola says without looking at Kappie.

'Fuck, David, it was war.'

Majola laughs cynically. 'War? Blowtorching the balls off a guy tied to a chair is war?'

The old man doesn't reply. Majola stares intently at him. 'Can I ask you something?'

Kappie looks at him, looks away. 'Well, now is your chance.'

'Did you enjoy it? Torturing them?'

Kappie looks at Majola, caught off guard. 'I resent myself every day. I was never there for my wife, or Lizanne. Not even when she was sick. I'm starting to make things better. I know it's too late now. You ask if I enjoyed it. You're still a child, David. You won't understand.'

Majola loses his cool. 'A child? You don't have to be an adult to realise that what you boere did was fucking evil.'

Majola picks up a photo and glances at it before tossing it aside.

'What's stopping me from arresting you right now?'

Kappie shakes his head in disbelief. 'You know me, young man. Look at me. I'm a broken old man,' he says with resignation.

'Do I really know you, Captain Loots? After what you just told me? Now you want me to feel sorry for you?'

Kappie's voice breaks. He's close to tears. 'Do you think I'm proud of what I did? Don't you think it still eats at me? Why do you think I take pills every day? It's so I don't lose my bloody mind. I knew it would come, that I would be punished.' Kappie slams his hand down on the table. 'I fucking knew it was coming!'

Majola says nothing. He almost pities the old man.

The ringing of Majola's phone breaks the silence. Kappie jumps at the sound.

Majola looks at the screen. It's Davids. He walks outside and closes the door behind him.

'Yes, Davids?'

'Morning, my captain. I've got good news. I got a match for the licence plates.'

'Let me hear it.'

'According to the traffic department, they belonged to one Daniël Loots. The number fell out of use in the late Nineties. He must be pretty old by now.'

Majola lowers his phone. He looks through the window, sees Kappie with his head in his hands.

'Thank you, Davids. I'll follow up. Will you send me the details?'

'On it, Captain. Shall I follow up myself?'

'No, it's fine. I'll check it out. Any other news?'

'Nothing yet. Hopefully we'll find something at the ranks today or tomorrow. Have a good evening.'

'Thank you, Davids. Good work.'

Majola can't believe it. What should he do now? Can it be Kappie? But why reveal everything now? He considers Basson's suspicions, and Kappie's setbacks that seem to coincide with the murders. It's right in front of him: Kappie is the murderer.

Or is someone setting him up? Is this case that complex? That ridiculous? Where does he hide the taxi? How does he abduct the girls? How do they climb in when a decrepit old white mlungu is driving?

Does the psychiatrist know something? Will he say anything without being served a warrant of arrest? If he does, all the other members in the team will know what he's up to. Majola will have to make a decision. Should he arrest Kappie or see what he can figure out by himself? Follow his gut? The more he thinks about it, the less it makes sense that Kappie killed all those girls. Then again, how many died on his watch during the unrest?

He realises the rain is getting heavier and walks back inside.

'Surprise, surprise. It seems like the plates on the taxi belong to one Daniël Loots. The vehicle was written off in the Nineties.'

Kappie is clearly shaken. 'Can't you see someone is busy framing me? That was the red Sentra I wrote off in Joubert Park.'

'Who's busy framing you, Kappie? One of the victims? Helen fucking Suzman? She's dead.'

'It could be one of the victims, someone who had access to the old dossiers. Maybe another policeman?'

Majola looks at the cupboard. 'The last time I was here, there were muddy prints at your back door. Your police shoes were covered in mud. How do you explain that?'

'Really, David? I wear those shoes all the time. And it's been raining all week.'

Kappie fidgets nervously in his chair.

Majola paces up and down at the foot of Kappie's bed.

'Okay. Let's say someone is framing you. Who? What happened to Dimba?'

'He walked in front of a train, ten years ago, in Springs.'

'And the victims? They would be roughly your age. Old men. What do you remember about them?'

'I tried to forget it all, to lock it out.'

'But you remember the docket numbers? Sounds like bullshit to me. What happened to your murder van?'

'Why would I lie to you? The van is scrap metal. Burger from Security Branch even mailed me a picture when they crushed it, as if the moment called for commiseration.'

'Okay. Let's say you're not the killer.'

Kappie lowers his hands to his lap in an almost childlike gesture of discomfort.

'Let's say he's recreating the murders,' says Majola. 'He would need access to the dossiers to get the numbers. Or he used to have access. I thought all you whiteys got rid of the evidence before the TRC could fuck you up?'

'Years ago, I called Sergeant Flip Swanepoel who worked at the Benoni archives,' says Kappie. 'I wanted to find out if he could get rid of the dossiers. He didn't want to; he said they were watching him. This was the early Nineties. I felt it was unfair, because a lot of the stuff on the Security Police just got lost. I went to sign it out myself, hoping that I could get rid of it. He wanted it back, though. Luckily, the dossiers never made it to the National State Archives in Pretoria. I never appeared before the Truth and Reconciliation Commission. I was one of the lucky ones. Or that's what I thought. Until now.'

'Why is he killing black girls? Why hasn't he come for you?'

'I don't know,' Kappie replies.

Majola looks at the report on the table. Jane Semenga's detail is on top. 'ON 345061986. So the docket was opened in 1986. And the 345? Is that the case number? The number of the interrogation?'

'There were more than that. Remember, I only started keeping records much later.'

Majola shakes his head in disbelief. 'And the letters below that?'

'That has nothing to do with the dossiers. That's something personal. It's a separate clue. I'll have to think about it some more. There's another thing.'

'Yes?'

'All of these dossiers: these are the last ten cases. One more is missing. I was involved in one more, according to these numbers. Then it would be eleven. 340 to 350. June 1986.'

'So one more girl is going to die?'

'I think so, yes,' Kappie answers despondently.

'What do you suggest I do now?'

'Call Flip Swanepoel. He's still at Benoni. He spent many years at the Archives before taking a desk job. I think he'll be retiring later this year.'

'And will he just give me access?'

'No one gives a damn about the stuff from the past any more. Tell him you're busy with research or something. Someone had to book out those dockets. Let's just hope it wasn't thirty years ago, and that everything is on the system.'

'Do you have his number?'

'He'll be at the station.'

Kappie gets up and turns to Majola. 'You have to believe me, young man. Do you think I would have said anything about the numbers if I killed those girls? Something sinister is going on here. I don't know why I have these setbacks when the murders happen. It worries me that I can't remember anything – not where I was, nothing. Is it coincidence? Please, David. Before it's too late.'

Majola tries to get his thoughts straight. 'Pack your stuff. Take only what you need. You're going to stay with Lizanne until I figure this thing out.'

'Excuse me?'

'You heard me. She's going to babysit you. And you don't put a foot outside that door. If it is you, I'm going to make it a bit harder for you,' Majola says, softening his words with a smile.

Kappie looks down, misses the humour in Majola's voice.

'I'll call her,' Majola says. 'Did that psychiatrist double your dose yet? Schoeman?'

'The nurse said he did.'

'Is there a nurse on duty?'

'There's always a nurse on duty.'

'I'll go speak to them. And I'll make sure Lizanne makes you take your pills every day.'

Majola gathers the pictures and papers from the report.

'You know I only have a few days,' he says. 'I'll have to hide this from Radebe and the team. Same with the licence plates and who they belong to. Let's hope they don't put two and two together. Hopefully I'll find something. But if there's another murder, I'll have to take you in. Let's hope, for your sake, I figure something out before that happens.'

'What about Basson?'

'What about him? He's been suspended.'

'Suspended?'

'Yes. That mess in Parkview.'

'That was him? I read something about it in the newspaper,' Kappie says, taking out a sports bag.

'That's for the better, though; he's the one who noticed your setbacks co-incided with the killings. Let's hope he hasn't dug further. Kappie?' Majola says, putting on his coat.

Kappie turns to him.

'I'm trusting you on this one. I'm putting my ass on the block here. Please tell me I'm not making a mistake.'

'Your head,' Kappie says, smiling.

'Huh?'

'It's your head on the block, or your ass on the line. And I know. Now we'll see if this old cop has taught you anything. Thank you for this, young man.'

'Good. I'll get to work. There has to be something I've missed. Are you nearly ready?'

'Yes, just need to grab my Bible.'

'Wait here. I need to go speak to the nurse and the guard at the gate.'

'Be my guest,' Kappie says, putting his glasses into his shirt pocket.

The guard hesitantly opens his window when Majola flashes his ID card.

'Can I see your logbook? How far back does it go?'

'About three months,' he says, handing the book over.

Majola takes out his phone to check the dates of the murders. He compares them to the vehicles that came and went that day.

'The madala at number fourteen: who comes to visit him?'

The man scratches at his cheek. 'Mostly his daughter. And the psychologist.'

'No one else?'

'Not that I know of. Why are you asking me this stuff again? That white cop also asked me about this. The one who came here with you last time.'

'Basson?'

'I can't remember. He was very rude to me.'

'That sounds like him.' Majola checks the dates again. On three of the mur-der dates, Schoeman had visited. He tears out the pages.

'Hayi!' the guard protests.

Majola hands him a business card. 'Let them call me if they give you any kak.'

'This is a fancy area. I've only been here once before, on a date, I think. How can a policeman afford to live here?'

Basson and Martie Bam are sitting at a coffee shop on the corner of Fourth and Seventh avenues. She points out the expensive cars in the parking lot.

'My father bought the property when it was still cheap,' Basson replies, tak-ing a sip of his brandy and Coke.

The waiter had given him a look when he walked in wearing tracksuit pants and a hoodie, the same clothes as yesterday.

'Fucking hell, you look like shit. Isn't it a bit early for a drink? It's not even eleven yet.'

'Thanks, but flattery will get you nowhere. It's happy hour somewhere in the world, right?'

Basson rubs the stubble on his chin with his bandaged left hand, takes another sip. The drink isn't strong enough by half. Their definition of a double must not quite match his own. He hasn't showered since the events at Zoo Lake yesterday. Delia hasn't left the bed since yesterday afternoon: she collapsed when she heard what Wikus did, and is now refusing to get up. She didn't even ask him where he was going this morning. Luckily their domestic worker is there today.

'What do you have for me?' Basson asks.

'Not really one for small-talk, are you?' Martie smiles curtly. 'Okay, the journo at the *Daily Sun* didn't give you the whole truth. There was an eyewitness. The cousin of the girl who was killed.'

'The one in Katlehong?'

'That's the one. She followed the taxi into the bushes. She gets hysterical when she talks about that night. But I went to find her at work, at the Checkers, and I cornered her. Scared her a bit with talk about obstructing justice, withholding evidence and so on.'

'I'm listening.' Basson looks at her red nails as her hands help her to tell her story. Her hair is tied in a bun. The white T-shirt under her leather jacket accentuates the curve of her breasts. She smells fresh. Unlike himself, he's sure.

'Will you please stop looking at my tits?'

Basson is caught off guard. 'Sorry. Easier said than done.'

'Look, I don't really mind; it's just that I want you to pay attention to what I'm saying,' Martie says, playfully. 'Okay, so she tells me she could hear her cousin screaming inside the taxi. Then it grew quiet. Then it started up again, as if he was torturing her. She ran away.'

'So he's killing them inside the taxi, as we thought. He doesn't take them somewhere else,' Basson says.

'That's right. Or that's what it sounds like if we can believe this girl. It didn't sound like she was lying. By this point I can pick up when someone is talking shit.'

Basson drinks deeply. 'It's always cheaper to drink at home. This is daylight robbery,' he says, trying to steer the conversation elsewhere, but she doesn't bite.

'Isn't that something to go on? I think that's some useful information.'

'Sure, it is.' Basson stares openly at her breasts, then up at her eyes. 'Just a pity I've been suspended. I have fuck-all to do with the case now.'

Martie looks at him in surprise. 'Suspended?'

'Yup. And one of these days I'm shipping out to Port Elizabeth to go do some PI work. Then I can catch fish every day.'

Martie treats him to a sugary-sweet smile. 'So, then you won't mind telling me everything you know, right?'

Basson calls the waiter over, looks back at Martie. 'That would be against the law.'

Martie's smile disappears as quickly as it had appeared. 'We had a deal. I didn't drive all the way to fucking Katlehong yesterday for nothing.'

'Double brandy and Coke, please. You know what, make it a triple.' The waiter frowns at Basson, then nods. Basson doesn't look at Martie.

'I know there have been more than three murders. You're hiding something. I'm going to find out,' she says, determination in her voice. Then her demeanour changes again. She leans forward, pushing her breasts towards him. She thinks for a second.

'Let's try something else. How about you and I go to my apartment in Melville. I'll show you what I'm hiding under this T-shirt, and answer any other burning questions you might have.'

Basson splutters and nearly chokes on the last sip of his drink. He can feel himself blushing. He can feel his lust awakening too.

Martie's phone starts to vibrate on the table. She looks at the number, smiles at Basson.

'Maybe that won't be necessary after all.'

Basson can't help but stare as she walks outside to stand on the pavement. The waiter puts his second drink down in front of him.

'Warrant Officer Davids. This is a nice surprise.'

'Lois Lane. What's cooking, good-looking?'

'Not much, until you called. I've been having some trouble with your friends.'

'Shall we trade some info, then? After this batch you'll owe me big time. It's about the taxi murderer.'

'I definitely have a few leads for you. Didn't you get my voicemail?'

'I did, my dear, I did. Okay, here goes.'

Martie listens carefully, doesn't interrupt him once. She can feel her excitement mounting the longer he talks. She can already see her story on the front page, and on all the breaking-news bulletins tomorrow night. It's the scoop she's been waiting for. After a few minutes he wraps up.

'And that's the story, Miss Martie.'

'You're a fucking star, Detective. I'll send you those numbers for the doctor and the model shortly, and set it up. I know for a fact they'll need your services, probably ask you to follow their husbands around. That's a perk of my job – I get all the juicy stories first.'

'Okay, Martie. But be careful. There's a possibility this whole thing is an inside job.'

'I will. Bye.'

Martie looks at the screen. It's her lucky day. If she knew Davids was going to contact her, she wouldn't have wasted her time on Basson.

Through the window, Basson can see Martie smiling as she ends her call. She comes walking back in, suddenly even more sure of herself.

'Sorry, Detective. It looks like you'll have to go home and take matters into your own hands. Ten murders, all over Gauteng, stretching over more than a year. One of your friends just spilled the whole bag of beans. Thanks for the story of my career. I'll make sure the papers are covered in this. With my byline. How the fuck did you lot think you could keep this from the public? All the young girls who could have been warned? Tomorrow, the police will be hauled over the coals again for your incompetence. As usual.'

'You're playing with fire, Martie,' Basson says quietly. 'You're digging in the devil's back yard. Not even those tits will save you if this guy is on your trail.'

'As I understand, he only goes for black girls.'

'But a white bitch getting in the way of his fun? How do you think he'll take it? I'm sure he'll make an exception. Maybe you should see some of the pictures from the autopsies. They're not pretty.'

Martie takes R50 from her handbag and puts it down on the table.

'And to think I would have let you put that dirty little thing inside me. Shame, here, take one last look at what you'll never have.'

Basson almost laughs as she walks out, exaggerating the sway of her hips even more, turning to wink at him as she goes out the door.

'Slut,' he says to himself and picks up his drink. 'I'm faithful these days.'

He realises his mind is already thickening. He'll have to stop at the liquor store for another bottle. Then he'll call Nigel October. They won't get rid of him that easily.

Majola stops in front of Lizanne's apartment complex. The windows are fogged up from the cold.

'I'll call Flip Swanepoel. I'm just going to grab something to eat. If he can help me today, I'll drive through this afternoon.'

Kappie nods, his bag of clothing on his lap. 'Go get something up there at Bikaner. You like curries, don't you?'

'I don't know if my stomach can handle much spice after a week like this.'

Kappie smiles, but quickly turns serious again. 'Your search could take a while. You know what the station archives look like.'

'I'll just dose myself with Red Bull or something. It's not like I can ask someone to help me. I'll have to lie.'

Suddenly, the image of the white lines on Mpete's desk comes rushing back. There's always that option. That could keep him alert and awake until he can get this done. There are a lot of reasons why he needs a boost: Lulu, Basson, the taxi killer, Kappie's confession, his week from hell, Busiswe. He's pulled back to the present by the sound of the sliding gate.

'There she is,' Kappie says with a smile when he sees Lizanne standing in her doorway, not wanting to come out in the rain. She's wearing a pink tracksuit and running shoes, her hair pulled back in a ponytail. She smiles when the Corolla pulls up in front of her door.

'How lucky can a girl be?' she says, rushing up to the car. She hugs Kappie tightly, then goes over to Majola to do the same. Her body is warm and her hair smells of fruit shampoo.

'Welcome. Is this your first time here, David?'

'It is my first time. You lot from Linden are way too hipster for me.'

'What's a hipster?' Kappie asks.

Lizanne rolls her eyes at Majola.

'They're kids who wear the same clothes as you do, Kappie. Then they think it's cool,' Majola jokes.

'Are you saying my style is cool?' Kappie laughs.

'Go inside, Dad. I just need to speak to David for a minute.'

Kappie picks up his bag and heads for the front door. Lizanne and Majola both watch him go, waiting until he is out of earshot.

'Should I be worried?' Lizanne asks.

'Not at all. I just don't want him to be alone. It's only for a few days. There's something I need to figure out. I would prefer it if you were close in case he has another setback.'

'I've been saying that for a while now, but he won't listen. Now he listens when you say it. Bloody typical,' Lizanne laughs. 'Good timing, too. I may only go back to work on Tuesday. I'm on call, but it looks like the weekend will be quiet. Maybe I can take him out to Cresta, or to that new bookshop up that way. We can walk; some exercise should do him good.'

'Great idea,' Majola says. He glances at the front door, but Kappie is inside.

'David, what's wrong? You were worked up when you called this morning.'

'Don't worry about it. It will only be for a short while, a week at most, until we figure out what causes these blackouts. His medication is in his bag. I know you will, but please make sure he takes it.'

'Look, I don't mind. My dad is always welcome to visit. But I want to know what's going on.'

'Do you trust me?' Majola asks seriously.

'Naturally.'

'I will tell you everything once I've got more of it pieced together. Just a few days. I promise.'

Lizanne nods.

'I'll swing by again tomorrow.'

'Can I give you something to eat? It's no bother. I was going to make some wors and mash for the old guy anyway.'

'Thank you, but I really can't. Tell Kappie I'll see him tomorrow.'

As he leaves the parking lot, Majola watches Lizanne in the rear-view mirror. She folds her arms and watches him until he rounds the corner.

Majola takes a table on the patio of the Bikaner restaurant in Linden. The smell of spices hangs thickly in the air, making his stomach rumble and his mouth salivate. The lonely pizza slice from this morning lost its efficacy hours ago.

Even though it's twelve o'clock, there's only one other couple on the patio with him. Maybe there are more people inside, hiding from the cold. He prefers the fresh air, though. He orders a Coke and a lamb curry. The streets are busy, vehicles rushing to and fro.

Maybe the curry will help to alleviate the sinking feeling in his stomach. It was easy to get Flip Swanepoel's number from the Benoni police station; the female officer barely asked why he wanted it. Flip answered his phone with a stern voice, the TV blaring in the background. It sounded like rugby. Flip wasn't overly enthusiastic about helping out and gave him hell for bothering him on his day off, and when Super Rugby was on, no less.

Not even the fact that he was calling from SVC could convince Swanepoel to go in to the Benoni station. It was only when Majola told him that he was a friend of Kappie's, and that he was trying to help him, that Flip agreed. He remembered that Kappie had mentioned Majola a few times, when he was still on the force. That made Majola feel a bit better about himself. Flip would only be at the station after five, though, because the Lions were playing the Crusaders at three. Majola has made peace with the fact that he'll be waiting out the rugby in this restaurant.

A lot will depend on what condition the records at Benoni are in. Many stations, especially satellite stations, have let their archives fall into complete disarray. There's no working system. He knows the National Archives in Pretoria is still in good nick, as he's had to go digging there before. All the documents since the turn of the millennium have been uploaded onto the electronic database. But even so, it isn't being utilised properly. That's why Radebe got so worked up: they would have picked up on this guy's pattern if the archives were being utilised properly.

What were the odds that someone had looked at those dossiers? And that he'd be able to find that person? Fuck, if they even still exist? He can only hope that one of those involved is still alive. It's been more than thirty years, so hope hangs by a thread. How can he track them down? It's going to take some footwork, backup, and time. He has none of those things.

The waiter brings his Coke, a placemat and some cutlery. The couple at the other end of the patio ask for their bill. Majola's phone rings. He really has to replace the theme from *The Exorcist*: it was funny at first, but recently it's been making him nervous when he hears it. He looks at the screen. Martie Bam. He silences the ringing.

He wonders if he'll ever enjoy watching horror movies again. They had never bothered him before, were always easy escapism. But this past week has changed that – the disappointment over Lulu and Basson, and Kappie's violent past. His life has started to resemble those movies too closely.

A message comes through from Martie Bam.

Did you really think you could hide this? Ten victims? You care nothing for public safety. Are you going to pick up when I call?

Majola can feel his face flushing.

'Shit,' he says, before his phone rings again.

Deep inside, he really hopes that Martie wants to negotiate.

'Martie.'

'Afternoon, Captain. I take it you have time to talk?'

Majola doesn't reply.

'Why did you lie?' Martie asks calmly.

'About what?'

'Don't play dumb. The taxi murderer. Zola Budd. Ten murders, all over Gauteng, all of them tortured, all of them electrocuted. All of them young black girls. Jesus, didn't you think the public could have used that information?'

'It's more complicated than that. The taxi associations are involved with this. Politicking. You know how it goes.'

'Of course. Politics, as usual. Fuck the innocents on the street, right? The story is already typed up. I'm filing it now. Not only with *Beeld*, but with *News24* and *Netwerk24*. Your media officer isn't picking up her phone. And my source is well informed, to say the least.'

'This will cause a shit storm, Martie. You need to think carefully about what you're doing.'

'That's not my problem.'

'Is there nothing I can do to convince you to wait a bit longer?'

'No.'

'Well, okay then,' Majola says and hangs up. 'Ngamasimba la!' he yells and throws his phone down on the table. The couple jump and look at him. Majola ignores them.

He grabs the phone again, looks through his contacts. He hesitates when he gets to Radebe's number. Who is the informant who slipped her the info? It has to be someone in his team. Mbatho? Maybe Basson, because he's pissed off about his suspension. Or Davids? Majola shakes his head. He can figure that out later. He makes the call.

'Captain Majola. Gee vir my good news. Have you arrested him?' Radebe sounds excited.

'No, Colonel.'

'What then? And where were you this morning? Waar was jy at parade?' The excitement ebbs with every word.

'I was following some clues. The investigation has been leaked; it will be in the newspapers by tomorrow.'

A silence follows, and keeps growing. Majola can hear Radebe's breathing.

'How? Who talked? Iemand from your team?'

'I don't know, Colonel. I'll try to find out.'

'Tomorrow the shit hits. We hid the information. Can we stop it?'

'If the information comes from inside, it will be accurate, Colonel. Then we can't do anything about it. And the journalist won't budge.'

There's a sudden, sharp sound on the other end. Radebe has either dropped the phone or thrown it. From far away Majola can hear him swearing in Zulu.

'I want a progress report by tomorrow morning. We'll have to knock up a press release. The commissioner is going to throw a shit fit.'

'Yes, Colonel.'

'Wie's die journalist?' Radebe asks, breathlessly.

'Martie Bam from *Beeld*.'

'That white bitch!'

Silence. 'Congrats. I guess that means you get your roadblocks and extra manpower,' Radebe says curtly. 'Ons kan begin implement by Monday. Figure out die routes where jy hulle soek. Jy's probably thrilled, nè?'

'No, Colonel.'

'Jy het one week, Captain. One more murder en ek bring in die Hawks.'

Radebe hangs up.

Majola is happy about the roadblocks. He doesn't have much to add to the report, only the testimony of Jacob Dube, the patrol driver, plus the licence plates, which he'll have to keep for himself, and the two sets of declarations and accusations by the taxi associations. Six of the drivers have criminal records for sexual crimes, all of them rape. Ramsamy and Rikhotso are working through the records.

A week's deadline doesn't help, though. And the next murder could be just around the corner, if Kappie is right. He can feel it. Then he'll be dropped from the case. And then it's just a matter of time before they lock Kappie up. Radebe will be so eager for an arrest that he'll rush the investigation. And if it's a white man, Radebe will make his life hell. Especially if it's Kappie.

Maybe it's what Kappie deserves, Majola thinks. Every dog gets its day. He berates himself for the thought. He has to focus. He'll have to get to Benoni asap. His time is running out.

'Takeaway, please; I need to go,' Majola tells the waiter as he brings the plate of steaming food. The waiter looks surprised, but takes the plate and walks back inside. Majola phones Flip Swanepoel. He'll have to record the game. For once, there's something more important than rugby on.

16

The parking lot at the Benoni police station is almost empty. A few personal vehicles, three police bakkies and a prison truck stand around as if abandoned. Most of the staff seem to have left for the weekend.

Majola takes in the squat, grey, four-storey building. The architects sure did their best to keep the style as unimaginative and grim as possible. Perhaps they intended to intimidate. He wonders how many have taken involuntary swan dives from the top of this one.

He locks the car and heads inside. Here, a drunk in blue overalls is causing trouble, screaming in Sotho while two spry constables drag him by the arms to the counter. Others look on with amused expressions; the policewoman behind the counter just keeps doing her paperwork, entirely unfazed.

On the wooden bench against the wall, an old balding man wearing a Lions rugby jersey, tracksuit pants and Crocs is looking at his phone screen. He seems completely oblivious to the ruckus around him. He has a red face, Majola notices, almost as red as the hair at his temples. A bushy ginger moustache hides his upper lip.

'Fokken poephol! Why can't he understand that running rugby doesn't always work? And then he kicks like a cripple, too.'

He jumps slightly when he notices Majola standing over him.

'Captain Majola?'

Majola nods.

'Excuse me, Captain. I'm just following the last few minutes on my phone.'

Flip Swanepoel gets up and shakes Majola's hand. 'Come, walk with me. The stuff you're looking for is in the basement beside the evidence room.'

Majola feels hope rising. Maybe, just maybe they've kept their records in some kind of order. Could he really be that lucky?

Right on cue, as if he's a mind reader, Swanepoel says, 'The place is a complete mess. They've had to fumigate twice since I've been gone. Damn rats started eating everything. After them came the termites. They had to move all the shelves from the walls to drill holes for the poison. And, of course, no one made the effort to move them back.'

Majola's hope drops as they descend the stairs to the basement. The passage smells like mould and damp concrete. When they reach the bottom, they find four doors on both sides of the passage, all of them shut. In the dimly lit evidence room, a constable is behind his desk.

Ignoring him, Swanepoel enters the room next door. He feels around for the light switch. The smell of dust is almost suffocating. Majola's heart sinks deeper as the fluorescent lights flicker on.

'Oh my God,' he says quietly.

'God hasn't been here in a while, Captain. Just the rats, unsolved cases and nightmares. And maybe a few ghosts if you can believe the sleeping constable back there.'

'I don't know – he was sleeping pretty deeply for a man who believes in ghosts,' Majola replies.

Swanepoel chortles, then sneezes.

'Gesondheid,' Majola says.

'You speak such beautiful Afrikaans.'

But Majola has stopped listening. He's overwhelmed by the disarray before him. The room is about twenty-five metres by five metres, and in the corner nearest the door is a desk with a tatty office chair pushed under it and an old computer on top. Only the flickering lights above them seem to be working. Ten metres ahead, the shadows take over. Everywhere around him are stacks of boxes. Some of the shelves, stuffed with boxes, have fallen over. Some of the boxes have torn and spilled their brown manila insides. Hundreds of boxes, big and small. The place smells like poison, and the air is sub-zero, for sure.

Swanepoel sees Majola's despair. 'I suggest you start looking on the computer.' He bends down and turns it on, as if he's too scared to sit in the chair. After a few seconds the screen flickers to life.

'From what date did they start backing up dossiers on the computer?' Majola asks.

'Everything from 1999; when I was here, anyway. I don't know how up-to-date it is these days. You know how it goes now.'

Majola doesn't know if Swanepoel wants him to agree. It feels like an insult because he's one of the new generation of police officers.

'They started shredding a lot of stuff after I left. Until the shredder broke. Then they stopped doing that too. The computer doesn't even have a password.' Swanepoel shakes his head.

'The dossiers I'm looking for are from before 1999. They're from the early Eighties,' Majola says, surveying the mountain of boxes.

Swanepoel frowns. 'Old SAPS cases? For what?'

Majola looks at the bald man. He'll have to take a chance, without knowing if he can trust Swanepoel. He knows he doesn't have a lot of time. Otherwise he'll be looking for a needle in a haystack the size of a soccer field.

'I'm looking for Daan Loots's old dossiers, from his time during the riots.'

'Fokkit.' Swanepoel thinks for a moment. 'That's about thirty years ago.'

Majola tries to remain optimistic. 'Specifically the cases where he … uh … did interrogations … in the van.'

Swanepoel is clearly shocked. He walks slowly up to Majola. 'Really? That stuff is ancient history, man.'

Before Majola can reply, realisation dawns on Swanepoel. 'Wait … my God … Does this have something to do with the Zola Budd killer? The one who's been fucking girls up in a red taxi?'

Majola is surprised anew by how many people know about this case. This is getting out of hand. Yet he's rather impressed that Swanepoel could make the connection so easily.

'Yes, Sergeant. It is related to that case,' Majola admits miserably.

'Do you think Kappie has something to do with it?'

Majola hesitates. 'I don't think so. I really hope not. But I'm here to find out. I think he's innocent. I think someone is trying to frame him, maybe one of his old victims. Or maybe someone else. But I don't have much time. After the next murder, they're taking me off the case. And tomorrow, the story goes to the press and everyone will know the gory details. The media will blow the investigation wide open.'

'Holy shit, man,' says Swanepoel. 'How well do you know Kappie?'

'Well, I thought I knew him well – until this morning, when he told me about the kinds of things he did back then.'

'But see, it was a different time.'

'That's what all you old people say.' Majola can't keep the bitterness from his voice.

Swanepoel smiles. 'Old Daan was a bit of a legend, you know. I don't want to say it too loudly; they'll give me shit no end.'

Majola lets him go on. 'He had the knack, God alone knows. One night I saw him break this smooth-talking lawyer in three hours, up there, on the fourth floor. The clown was so cocky he even wanted to defend himself. Kappie could get under your skin. Even the guys from Pretoria brought him in occasionally, that bunch from Vlakplaas – very hush-hush, but everyone knew. I've seen someone nearly beat a suspect to death, but the suspect wouldn't say a word. Kappie had other ways of making them talk, ways he must have perfected in that van.'

Swanepoel seems deep in thought. 'The two of us went out drinking a lot. But one thing about Kappie: he was never proud of what he had to do, not like the other bastards. I see they've started all these pages on Facebook these days, Koevoet, Unit 18, the 32 Battalion. The glory days. As if they can never forget, or never want to. As if that's going to help things. Old PW and Pik lied to the whole lot of us. The ANC became the "gevaar" they kept warning us about. Many just couldn't stomach it.'

Swanepoel keeps talking, as if he hasn't had an audience in ages. 'One day, just before the TRC shit started going down, in the early Nineties, Kappie came here to sign out his dockets. I warned him, said he had to bring them back, that we were being watched. They almost came down harder on those caught destroying dockets than on those named in them. And he actually brought them back. The TRC shifted focus to Pretoria, to the central archives. They probably realised there was simply too much to work through. The stuff should be here … somewhere.'

Majola takes off his jacket, and removes his gun and holster. He puts them down on a box and sighs heavily.

'You know, I agree,' Swanepoel says. 'It can't be Kappie. It doesn't sound like him. And the old son of a bitch deserves a fair chance.'

He looks out over the boxes. 'Your best bet is to start at the back there, in the dark. You'll have to spot-check for dates, otherwise you'll still be here come summer. I'm going to pop out and get two more fluorescent tubes to put in. They're the same size as those in my garage. Start pulling some of those boxes over. You'll see the difference between the dockets from the 1980s and the 1990s: they used to be bigger. There should be a list of all the dockets that were signed out back then, hopefully inside the box with those dockets. Or close to the box. Fuck, I don't know.'

Majola closes his eyes and breathes deeply.

'Do you have any idea what you're looking for?' Swanepoel asks.

'The dockets are from 1986. And they have the letters "ON" in front of the case numbers. I guess I'll start with the "ON" and the year, and take it from there.'

'Good idea. I don't remember them ever having "ON" written on them. But ja, that sounds like a good place to start.'

Majola rolls up his sleeves.

'I'll be back with the tubes. I'll bring some coffee for the night, and my old gas heater. Then we can tackle these boxes.'

'Excuse me?' Majola asks, surprised.

'I can't let you fuck around here in the dark by yourself, can I? I have a better idea of what's going on here than you do. And what if the ghosts get you? I just need to go tell my wife I haven't gone out drinking again.'

'Thank you, Sergeant.' Majola has to restrain himself from hugging the man.

'You can call me Flip, seeing as this is unofficial business.'

'Can you bring us some Red Bulls?' Majola takes his wallet from his jacket pocket. 'Wait, I'll walk you out. I need to go charge my phone in the car.'

Majola and Swanepoel walk out together.

'I bet you that jackass is still sleeping,' Swanepoel says, looking around for the guard.

'Wait – so did that blond kid die on the border or did he commit suicide?' Johnny Ackerman asks, confused, as he and Martie Bam descend the escalator at Rosebank Mall.

Martie wants to roll her eyes. 'That's not important. Christiaan Olwagen left it open to interpretation. You have to decide for yourself. The film has more layers than you think.'

'Christiaan who?' he asks.

'Olwagen. The director.'

Johnny takes her hand and shakes his head. 'I'm too young for the whole Voëlvry thing anyway.'

He takes out his wallet and pays for their parking ticket at the machine. Martie looks around them, suddenly feeling jumpy.

'Where is everybody? Where are all the other cars? And why did you park so far away?'

'I think everyone else parked on the other side, closer to the restaurant. And it's almost eleven,' Johnny says, offering Martie his arm. They head for the glass doors of the exit.

'How's your shoulder?' she asks, while her gaze flits around the parking lot. Basson's got her all paranoid with his bullshit.

'Better. I'll be able to play next Saturday. Sjoe, I had to glue myself to the bench today; I wanted to run onto the field so badly. I can't handle it when we choke like that. I've been a proud Lion all my life. Same as my uncle and my cousin.'

Johnny kisses Martie on the forehead. 'Next week, I'm taking you along. You can sit in the players' box. I might as well make my teammates jealous while I have something worth being jealous about.'

She smiles. 'We'll see.'

Martie has to admit that she's started to like this lumbering oaf. He's actually quite shy, with a soft heart beneath all those hard muscles. He compliments her every chance he gets. He might not be the deepest thinker, but she can take him under her wing and sharpen him up. She's just realised again how tired she is of being alone.

She couldn't wait to tell someone about her story in the papers tomorrow, and he was really excited: 'I bet you can't wait. Maybe I'll get up early and go steal you one of the posters from the lampposts.' That made her heart gush, she'll admit. She's going to give him a chance. Things seem to be slotting into place, finally.

'Why do you look so nervous?' Johnny asks her, concern in his voice.

Martie looks over at the section of the enormous parking lot that's in darkness, where the flea market takes place every weekend. No parking bays, no lights: it's as if the parking lot disappears over a cliff.

'Oh, it's nothing.' She tightens her grip around Johnny's waist. Johnny's white Hilux is parked just a few steps ahead. *Johnny Ackerman is proudly sponsored by Fourways Toyota.*

He opens the passenger door for Martie with a chivalrous flourish. 'It's still quite early,' he says, winking at her.

She smiles and gets in, her tiny handbag clutched on her lap. He closes the door and walks around the front of the bakkie, then suddenly comes to a stop. About thirty metres to the left, from the darkness of the vacant lot, two bright headlights have come to life.

Johnny's silhouette is starkly illuminated. He shields his eyes from the glare. 'What's this fucker's problem?'

Martie feels her blood run cold. The same feeling she had as a child when she thought there was someone outside her bedroom window.

'Johnny ...'

'I'll kick his ass if he's not careful,' Johnny says, walking towards the lights.

Martie hears the engine rev, low at first, then louder. She gets out of the bakkie. For a moment she can make out the shape of the vehicle. It's a taxi.

She hears tyres screeching.

'Johnny!'

He turns around, perplexed. For a fraction of a second, they make eye contact. Then the moving hunk of metal hits him with a dull thud. All she can see is a flash of red as it passes by. Where Johnny was standing, there's just more empty parking lot. Martie starts screaming.

Twenty metres away she sees Johnny roll out from under the taxi and come to a stop, face down. His arm is bent awkwardly behind his back, his neck twisted at an impossible angle. He's not moving. The taxi halts. Its brake lights shine and start pulsing crimson. Then it starts to reverse.

Johnny gets caught up in the undercarriage; he's dragged under and disappears beneath the vehicle. Martie can hear the sound of his body being pulled across the tarmac.

She can't move. Everything feels unreal. Basson's warning hits her like a physical blow: 'You're playing with fire, Martie.'

The taxi stops directly in front of her, a few metres ahead of the bakkie. Her field of vision is filled with its red gleam. The windows are blacked out and she can't see the driver. Johnny's arm is visible behind its rear tyre, where he got stuck. His hand lies lifelessly on the tarmac.

'What do you want? What do you want, you sick fuck?'

She looks to the right, quickly considers her options. She'll have to cover about eighty metres to get to the mall entrance and the escalator. There's the bakkie, but Johnny has the keys. Left is not an option – it's too far to the security boom at the exit. It won't help to get back into the bakkie anyway; he'll just destroy the car with her in it. Her phone is on the bakkie's floor in her handbag. There's not enough time. How is it possible that there's no one else around? There's no movement from the driver's side of the taxi. The only sound is the quiet idling of its engine.

Focus, Martie. Breathe. Think, goddammit. She backs up slowly, step by step, never taking her eyes off the taxi. The engine starts to rev. Once. Twice.

She turns and sprints for the door. She doesn't look around. All she can see is the entrance ahead. Sixty metres. She regrets wearing the high-heeled boots. Behind her she can hear the taxi's engine. He's gaining on her. She forces herself not to look around. Forty metres. Why aren't there kerbs here like the ones in the outside parking lot?

'God, please …'

About ten metres from the glass doors, there's a kerb that leads to the entrance. If she can make it there, he won't be able to follow. The engine roars behind her. She can hear her own heaving breath, the clack of her heels on the ground, the revving engine. Twenty metres to the kerb. Will she make it? She has to.

Then she feels the tremendous impact against her back and shoulder. She flies forward, falls face down. Her wrist is bent up painfully below her. Her chin scrapes against the ground and she can taste iron. She rolls over, groaning, lies on her back. The taxi is some way off, unmoving, engine at a low rumble.

It growls louder. He's taunting her. He's enjoying this. Martie tries to move her legs but a sharp pain stabs her hip. And her wrist is broken, of that she's sure. She starts to sob quietly. *Get up, Martie. You didn't make it this far to die in a parking lot. A fucking maniac in a taxi won't be the end of you. Get up. You're so close to the kerb.* She turns to the entrance.

Then she rolls over twice and picks herself up, out of the taxi's path. The pain in her hip is unbearable. By sheer willpower, she drags herself forward. She waits for the final blow that will knock the life from her. But it doesn't come. She stumbles to the kerb. So close now, so close to safety.

Martie hears a loud bang behind her. He's jumped the kerb.

Then another bang: her own body.

'God ... please God ... no ...' She's no longer moving.

Her arm is stretched out in front of her, touching the tiled floor of the entrance. In total agony, she turns herself around. Blood flows freely from her knees, where her trousers have torn.

He moves forward slowly. The taxi's bumper fell off on impact, but he drives over it. Gravel crunches under the tyres. Martie tries to inch her body backwards, but it isn't listening to her any more. She drops her head and stares at the bright lights on the ceiling.

She sees herself curled up with her dad beside the fire in Harrismith. He's brushing her hair. The winter sun shines weakly through the window.

'Papa ... I'm so ...'

Martie Bam's head bursts open like a ripe pomegranate under the weight of the taxi's wheel.

'What time is it?' Flip Swanepoel asks, rubbing his eyes. His flask of brandy was emptied long ago. The beanie on his head makes him look like he wandered in off the streets. The Lions jersey is blackened from the dust on the boxes.

'Just after midnight,' Majola replies. He's covered in the same black streaks.

He stops to look around them at all the boxes. 'Every time I see one from the Eighties, I want to jump for joy, but the next one is inevitably from the Nineties again. Nothing is where it should be.'

They've stacked the boxes they've worked through against one wall. Swanepoel regularly stops packing to thumb through some of the dossiers, often just with a shake of the head. Every now and then he smiles, as if taking a trip down memory lane.

Majola has checked only a handful of the dossiers. To him, this is an archive of forgotten nightmares. Mostly just information, but it's how that information was recorded that makes his skin crawl. He's listened to the tapes of the TRC hearings, but this is much worse. The secrecy – it's as if these harrowing accounts become all the more diabolical for being handwritten in blue ballpoint pen, riddled with spelling and grammar errors. As if the devil was writing in a rush.

Swanepoel tosses a dossier to one side, then kicks it further along so it doesn't lie against the heater.

'For your sake, I hope that when you find these dockets, they actually have something that can help you. Not just a name and a passbook number.'

'Me too.' Majola checks his wristwatch again. 'Shit, I need to go get my phone from the car. I'll be right back.'

Majola regrets not putting on his jacket: the wind cuts icily through the parking lot. He unlocks his car and gets his phone. Fourteen missed calls. Ramsamy, Davids and Radebe.

'Fuck.' He knows there's been another murder. And he's sitting in Benoni trying to save his friend's ass. He decides the safest bet is to call Ramsamy.

'Captain. The whole force has been looking for you for over an hour.'

'Yes, Ramsamy. Where did he leave her this time?'

'Rosebank Mall. The parking lot. But this is not our usual kind of victim.'

'No?'

'It's that journalist from the *Beeld*. Martie Bam. And her boyfriend. He made roadkill out of them, like dogs. Broke the bumper off the vehicle doing it.'

Majola is stunned. 'Roadkill?'

'Yes, Captain. Drove into and over them. We're struggling to keep the media away from the scene. There're a bunch of camera crews. It's a circus. We're so deep in the shit we'll need a shovel. Colonel Radebe is on his way too. How long before you can be here?'

'Probably about forty minutes. I'm not at my flat. Tell them I'm on my way.'

'If you come in from Bolton, take the turn-off into Cradock Avenue. We're at the parking garage on top. You'll have to stop at the bottom. The whole of Johannesburg's emergency services have congregated. I'll tell Radebe you're coming if he beats you to it. Where should I tell him you are?'

'Car trouble. Make something up.'

'Okay.'

'And tomorrow the newspapers will be running her story too,' Majola sighs.

'Isn't it a bit late for the Saturday papers?'

'Not the story about her murder – the one she wrote about Zola Budd. Her murderer.'

'Sorry?'

'I'll explain later. I'm coming.'

Majola immediately calls Kappie. His phone is dead. Lizanne's phone just keeps ringing.

'Where are you?' Majola says to himself.

Maybe he should go to Rosebank first, see if Kappie is still at Lizanne's. But he can't; he's already in deep kak for not being at the crime scene.

Majola takes a moment to be completely still. Then he gets out of the car and walks back into the archives to retrieve his gun and his jacket.

'I'll have to come back tomorrow, Flip. Thanks for the help, really,' Majola says, pulling on his jacket.

'Where are you off to so suddenly?' Swanepoel asks, surprised.

'Another murder. Or murders. The devil is on the loose.'

'Who? Where?'

'If you buy the papers tomorrow, you'll read all about it. First-hand info, leaked directly from my unit. It's a media circus. I have to go.'

Majola thinks he hears Flip say something just as he leaves, sounding like, 'Good luck.'

As the turn-off for the Rosebank Mall approaches, Majola changes his mind and keeps heading towards Linden. If Kappie is the killer, he won't be at home. He would have gone to hide the taxi somewhere. Maybe he'd be in one of his stupors again. He has to make sure. What's an extra thirty minutes when you're already this profoundly fucked?

It feels like an eternity before Majola pulls in at Lizanne's apartment complex in Linden, despite having raced there with lights flashing, jumping red lights as he went. He's so tired it feels as if he has sand in his eyes. The three Red Bulls have long since left his system.

He shows his ID to the security guard and drives up to her front door. The stench of car fumes hangs in the air from pushing the Toyota too hard. No lights are shining inside. Majola hammers on the front door. His hand moves to his gun. He knocks again. A light comes on and he hears rustling from inside. The moment of truth. He releases the safety on the z88.

Kappie opens the door. He's in his blue pyjamas, his hair is unkempt and his eyes are barely open.

'David? What are you doing here?'

Majola slides past Kappie and walks to his room. He stops in the doorway. Kappie's bed is unmade, the Bible open on the bedside table, beside a glass of water and his glasses.

'David, what are you looking for?' Kappie asks, confused, behind him in the passage.

Majola ignores him and turns the light on in Lizanne's room. The bed is made and there's no one there.

'Where is Lizanne, Kappie? I thought she's only going in on Tuesday?'

'She got called out. They had to do emergency spinal surgery. She probably left at about nine or so. And why is your pistol in your hand?'

Majola ignores the question. 'And where were you, Kappie?'

'At the whorehouse in Randburg. Where do you think I was? I was here. Have been since this morning.'

Majola gives him a piercing stare. He puts his pistol back in the holster. Then he walks back to Kappie's room and starts opening the cupboards. Everything is neat and tidy. No sign of a black outfit or anything out of place.

'You didn't go out at any point tonight?'

'No, David. I can even tell you which shitty artist was playing on *Jukebox*.'

Majola starts to relax. He sits down on Kappie's bed.

'What happened? Another murder?'

'Martie Bam, from *Beeld*. And her boyfriend, plays rugby for the Lions. Vehicular homicide in the parking lot at Rosebank Mall. Both of them dead.'

'Damnation ...' Kappie says. 'So that's why you came? To see if I'm asleep in bed and not chasing through the streets in a red taxi?'

Majola doesn't answer.

'I told you I don't have anything to do with this. Do you believe me now?'

'I don't know. This case is a complete mess. I don't know what to believe any more.'

'Have you tracked down the dossiers in Benoni yet?' Kappie asks.

'Still nothing. Flip and I've made some progress though. I'll try to go back tomorrow, if I have any time to spare, considering what's just happened.'

'Flip Swanepoel: did he help you?'

'Yes. It looks like you still have some friends.'

Kappie smiles, clearly touched. 'Do you have time for a coffee?'

Majola gets up. 'I have to get to Rosebank. It's probably after one already. I'm already in deep shit.' He walks past Kappie.

'Does this mean I can go back home?'

Majola turns around. 'No. Be patient. You just wait here until you hear otherwise.'

'David.'

Majola is at the car door. 'Yes?'

'Try to get some sleep, otherwise you're not going to make it. You have to focus.'

Majola nods.

'Do you believe me now?' Kappie asks again.

'I believe you ... Yeah, I believe you, Captain Loots,' Majola says before getting in.

It's half past one when Majola arrives on the scene. The ramp to the parking lot has been cordoned off. There are people everywhere: three media vans are parked beside the ramp, camera crews are bustling to and fro. A journalist from e.tv tries to stop him before he ducks under the police line.

'Captain Majola! Can you please tell us what happened to Martie Bam and Johnny Ackerman? Were they murdered by the Zola Monster?'

Majola shoots her a look. The Zola Monster? Really?

'No comment. The SAPS will have a press release ready by tomorrow.'

The journalist looks crestfallen. Two other journalists yell out questions at him as he makes his way up the ramp. The left lane of the ramp is full of parked police vehicles. He recognises Davids's BMW and Ramsamy's Honda, and sighs with relief when he sees that Radebe's black chariot isn't there yet.

Three police dogs and their handlers come walking by. The dogs yip and drool excitedly. What the fuck is the K9 unit doing here?

When he gets to the top, he sees the circus Ramsamy was referring to. Two pathology bakkies – why, he doesn't know; there are only two bodies. Two ambulances. About forty different uniformed individuals clutter the scene, busily performing their duties. Everyone has pitched up for the show. Ramsamy, talking to a security guard near the entrance of the parking lot, sees Majola and comes over. He smells fresh, as if he's just got out of the shower.

'Evening, Captain.'

'Sergeant. What the hell are the dogs doing here?'

'There are some units here that don't really belong. They're just as curious as the public. Now they're helping to keep the media out and so on. Two of the journalist's colleagues nearly came to blows with us when we wouldn't let them through. They have dogs at the mall escalators too, as more media people are trying to come in that way. We've arranged for them to close off all entrances to the mall. The lot over at the bar weren't happy with that.'

Majola looks out over the parking lot. There are two crime scenes, about sixty metres apart. The forensic unit has set up bright lights at both, and people in light-blue overalls are scurrying around. A camera flash lights up the tarmac every few seconds.

'Where do you want to go first? Ladies or gents?'

Majola looks from one scene to the other. 'Does it matter? Take me to where it started. Where is Sergeant Rikhotso and Warrant Officer Mbatho?'

'Rikhotso is at the security office checking the CCTV footage. Mbatho isn't picking up her phone.'

'Goddammit,' Majola curses.

Warrant Officer Davids, who has finished questioning a young couple, comes over to join them.

'Captain,' he greets him, and stands beside Ramsamy. 'Nice little bugger-up, eh?'

'A right shit show, I'd say,' Majola replies tersely. He doesn't have time for Davids's chatter.

Davids gets the hint and keeps quiet.

Majola ignores him. They stop at the body of Johnny Ackerman, a few metres in front of his Toyota Hilux. The passenger door is still open.

'Are the technicians almost done with the scene?'

Davids nods. 'Yes. Dr Lubbe is busy with the girl at the entrance.'

Majola is relieved that Dr Lubbe is here. On the other hand, he's ashamed that they haven't made any real progress since they last saw him. He hopes the doctor won't ask about Basson's suspension.

Majola kneels beside the body. Johnny's face is turned towards them, his eyes open, a gaping wound in his forehead. His tongue lolls out his mouth. His left arm is stretched out in front of him, bent in the wrong direction. His entire torso lies in a pool of blood and his clothes are torn to shreds.

'Which of you is going to give me the lowdown?'

Ramsamy and Davids look at each other. Then Ramsamy starts talking.

'According to the cameras, the bakkie came through the boom around 19:30. They don't have footage of where the bakkie is now parked. Bam and Ackerman then came through the entrance where Bam's body now lies.'

'Do we know where they were going when they came?'

'They went to see a film at the Cinema Nouveau.'

'What did they go see?' Majola immediately regrets asking. What does it matter what they saw? He must be more tired than he thought.

'According to the ticket stub in her purse, *Johnny Is Nie Dood Nie*.'

Davids snorts. 'Johnny looks pretty fucking dead to me.'

Majola gives him a humourless look. Ramsamy can't help smiling.

'Sorry,' says Davids, and drops his head. 'Kak joke.'

Ramsamy goes on. 'Just after eight, the red taxi came into the parking lot. Just before eleven, Bam and Ackerman came walking out. There's a camera at the pay point. Dr Lubbe thinks Martie Bam was standing at the car door. Ackerman was in front of the bakkie when he was hit. The taxi came to a stop about twenty metres further on.'

Only now does Majola notice the smear of blood where the taxi dragged Ackerman along the ground.

'He drove over him after hitting him – there's a lot of blood there, where it looks like he lay for a while. Then the taxi reversed over him and dragged him back here. That's when Bam must have run for the mall entrance.'

'Well, obviously she didn't outrun him. I warned her.'

'Sorry, Captain?'

'Tomorrow, or later today, the newspapers will run with the Zola Budd story. Martie called me yesterday. A reliable source of hers, one of us, leaked everything. Everything. And that source could only have been in our unit. Unless someone went and told someone else. So now, gentlemen, the shit hits the fan. I won't be surprised if Radebe takes us off the case.'

'One of us? Basson maybe? Because he's bitter for being suspended?' Ramsamy asks. Davids looks at the ground.

'I doubt it; doesn't sound like him. And how would that benefit him? What bothers me is that the murderer knew about it before the newspapers did,' Majola says as the forensic team zip up the body bag.

'It could be someone from the paper. The story would have been written up yesterday afternoon,' Ramsamy says.

'That's what we'll have to find out: whether the killer is one of our own.'

'One of us?' Davids protests. 'But we didn't know the story was going to be in the papers tomorrow.'

'Martie's source could have talked. For all we know, her source could be the murderer,' Majola says. 'You sure you two didn't speak to anyone?'

Ramsamy glances at Davids. 'No, Captain.'

Davids shakes his head.

Majola nods. 'Okay. Let's go hear what Dr Lubbe has to say.'

At the entrance, Dr Lubbe has covered Martie in a sheet. When he sees Majola, he steps back to make room for him.

'I covered her. The vultures on the escalator are starting to push their luck. If they get pictures of a headless Miss Bam, that's just more fuel on the fire.'

Majola looks at the black bumper lying a few metres away from her.

Dr Lubbe follows his gaze. 'He knocked it off when he jumped the kerb. There are some oil spills as well. I think he did some damage to the under-carriage.'

'So now we're looking for a red taxi without a bumper? How difficult can that be?' Davids asks.

The pathologist sighs. 'He doesn't seem to care if he gets caught any more. Or he knows exactly what your next move will be. This place is full of cameras. It's a Friday night; he must have known there would be eyewitnesses. He just doesn't give a shit any more.'

Majola looks at the pile of blood and gore where Martie's head should be. Her tiny leather boots stick out from under the sheet.

'Why exactly would he go for her? Does he know something we don't? Or did she know something we don't?' asks the doctor.

'She knows everything we know. That's why he killed her. Read the newspapers tomorrow.'

'He killed her for interfering in his game?' Davids asks.

'Could be. But we're also meddling in his affairs. Why not kill us?' Majola asks.

'Maybe he wants us to catch him?' Ramsamy says, looking convinced.

'If we understand the last message, he's almost finished,' says Dr Lubbe. 'Johnny was in the wrong place at the wrong time. I was just thinking this afternoon that the Lions wouldn't have lost if he was on the field. Unlucky bastard.'

Sergeant Rikhotso, smartly dressed in a brown suit and hat, has shouldered his way through the dog unit on the escalator.

'Captain, I've worked through the footage. You want to come take a look?'

'I'll be right there, Sergeant. Go make sure that footage doesn't go anywhere.

If the media get their hands on that, all hell will break loose.' Majola suddenly remembers the number plate.

'Did he have number plates?'

'Nothing, Captain. Not like last time,' Rikhotso replies.

Majola is relieved. That would have turned their attention to Kappie.

Dr Lubbe looks around him. 'Where's Basson?'

Then Majola sees Colonel Radebe walking over from the ramp to the parking lot. He sighs loudly. 'It's a long story, Doctor.' He turns to his team. 'Go on ahead of me to the security room. I'll meet you there. I just have to report to Colonel Radebe.'

Seeing Radebe approaching, the men disperse with renewed urgency.

'Good luck,' Davids says.

Majola turns to the pathologist. 'Now what, Doctor?'

Dr Lubbe pulls off his gloves. 'Well, now everyone will write about this, even foreign newspapers, because the guy was a rugby player. Everyone's going to bemoan how piss-poor we all are at our jobs. Then the top brass will give you the kind of support you asked for from the start. And then you'll catch him. He's getting reckless. Insane too. Or fucking brilliant. Good luck, Captain.'

He turns around and orders an assistant to bring the gurney and a body bag.

Majola waits for Radebe. He's wearing a long sports jacket with the Orlando Pirates logo on the chest, and black leather gloves. 'Captain, where were you?'

'Evening, Colonel.'

'Evening? It's fucking morning, sunshine. Bright and early.'

Majola ignores the comment. 'Car trouble. The cold isn't good for the battery.'

'Jy stay mos in Melville. Someone can pick you up. And what about your fancy BMW?'

'My phone was charging. I missed the calls.'

Silence. 'Are you busy with something I should know about, Captain?'

'No, Colonel.' Majola can feel the web tightening around him. The threads are still thin, invisible, but he feels them clinging to his skin.

'How did the mother-fucker know about the story she was writing?'

'I don't know, Colonel. It could be someone from the newspapers. It could be one of us.'

'I want you to get that bullshit out of your mind. It's not one of us. Wat dink jy people will say, after this shit show, when they hear you suspect one of our own?'

Majola makes no reply. Radebe looks at the gurney being pushed into the van.

'It had to be a white bitch too. You can mos kill a thousand darkies and no one bats an eye. Kill one Boer, then everyone grabs their pitchforks. And her boyfriend was nog 'n rugby player too. So wat nou, Captain?'

'Colonel, did you say I can get my roadblocks?'

'I don't have a choice, do I? The problem is, Metro will be picketing again on Monday. That means nothing much will happen tomorrow or Sondag. Weet jy what I suspect is going to happen?'

'No, Colonel.' Majola feels like a schoolboy again, being led to a hiding.

'I'm expecting a call from the commissioner tomorrow. Hy gaan ask ons moet 'n task force open. Get some guys from the Hawks, people who know their business.'

Majola feels something inside him catch fire, but he bites his tongue.

'They want to take you off the case. Maybe it's better that way.'

'Excuse me?'

'I put too much confidence in you. This case needs someone with more experience.'

Majola explodes. 'What the fuck were we supposed to do without back-up? With a team of less than ten?'

Radebe looks mock-surprised. 'Jy maak 'n plan. That mlungu teacher of yours would have.'

Majola doesn't answer. Fuming, he stares at the press assembled on the escalator.

'Call a meeting met jou team tomorrow. Check die video footage again. En ek soek daai report, the one I asked for yesterday. Maybe a miracle will happen.'

'Fine,' says Majola.

'What happened to the number plate? Jy het mos gekry on the previous footage?'

'It's an old number plate. The car was written off in the 1990s. It belonged to an old man. We checked it out.'

'Oh, did you now? Can't the old man be our murderer? Did you knock on his door? Het jy? Why didn't you mention this to me?'

'What, Colonel?'

'The number plate, Captain. Jy't my nooit gesê nie. I heard about it from Davids. Or did you think it wasn't important?'

Majola is stunned. The seed has been planted. Now all it needs to do is take root and grow into the tree that he'll hang himself from.

'Skryf dit op in jou report. The name of the owner too. And tomorrow I want see everything in that report, no gaps. Ek brief die press at ten. Then you'll see why I wanted to keep these murders out of the papers. Ek gaan bed toe. Sorry you can't do the same.'

Radebe turns around and walks away.

Majola balls his fists, his breath quickening. He's walked right into Radebe's trap. Tomorrow he'll find out that the number plates belong to Kappie. Then everything will fall apart. Then again, at this point, everything already has.

17

Majola only left the Rosebank Mall at around seven in the morning.

The murderer and his taxi had been caught on a handful of CCTV cameras. He had even paid for his parking, at the machine a few steps away from Martie's corpse. Dressed in black from head to toe, black hoodie, black balaclava, latex gloves: the whole get-up. He'd kept his face turned away from the cameras.

Majola felt sick when he saw him standing at the machine. The arrogance of the bastard, and his own helplessness, were almost too much to bear. When he left the parking lot, he had to help an overwhelmed constable prevent the morning-shift staff from going in. They couldn't understand how the whole parking lot could be a crime scene. He called in back-up from the uniform branches and got the mall manager to leave his bed to come and help out.

The newspaper posters tied to the lampposts served as a harsh reminder that this wasn't a dream. TAXI MONSTER LOOSE IN GAUTENG, according to *Beeld*. ZOLA BUDD DEVIL BUS! opined the *Saturday Star*. Fortunately, Bam and Ackerman's murders had happened too late to make the morning papers.

That didn't stop the radio and TV news bulletins from carrying the story though: how the police couldn't protect the acclaimed journalist, how they killed the best flank in the history of South African rugby. Fuck, they'd probably get the blame if the Springboks lost the next World Cup. Radebe also called and hauled him over the coals for missing the niece in Katlehong. Someone will have to go talk to her. And someone will have to go gag the fucking journalist from the *Daily Sun*. He would have done it himself, but he had the mountain of dossiers to work through in Benoni. His time is running out.

When Majola got home, he immediately jumped in the shower. He didn't have the heart to turn on the TV. He got dressed in his navy-blue tailored suit, white shirt and brown shoes. Might as well look good when they throw him to the wolves. Help though it did, the suit couldn't hide the bone-tired, world-weary look in his eyes. When he wrote up Radebe's report, he made sure he changed Kappie's number plates by a single digit. He hopes that Davids won't realise anything during the media briefing.

He's been awake for nearly twenty-four hours. The bright winter sun blinds him when he leaves the apartment.

Now, standing in front of his team, he admits to himself that he misses Basson. Outside the station, a crowd of reporters and their camera crews have begun to set up. Even CNN has sent a team. Radebe will have his hands full. At least that bastard has had some sleep.

'Alright then. Thanks for coming in so early. Mitchell will go over the CCTV footage from the mall again later. Sergeant Ramsamy has opened another dossier. But as you know, there aren't many similarities to the other murders.' Majola sits on the edge of the table in front of the board with all the victims' names on it.

'Sergeant Rikhotso went to Katlehong to speak to the victim's niece, the girl who saw what happened. The one we found out about in this morning's papers.'

Ramsamy shakes his head in disbelief.

'If her testimony is reliable, then we know the murders take place inside the taxi, just as Dr Lubbe suspected. The story is out there now. Now we can speak to the papers. Mitchell, will you be able to knock up as clear an image of the murderer and the taxi as you can from the footage? Maybe the public can help out with this one.'

Mbatho and Ramsamy suddenly jump to attention, looking at the door to the ops room. Colonel Radebe nearly fills the door frame. Davids and Mitchell stumble to their feet. Majola is the last to get up.

'Morning. Sit, please,' Radebe says. So he's speaking English this morning. He looks pretty smart in his dark-brown suit and green tie. He comes to stand beside Majola.

'Commissioner Nbele called me this morning. He's already spoken to the minister of police. We're going to assemble a task force, which will consist of some members from the Hawks and a few other units, until we take this guy down. I'll be in command. Captain Majola will act in an advisory capacity, and Sergeant Ramsamy will assist him. Later today, Captain Mathews Baloyi will conduct interviews with all of you, to get him up to speed. Thank you for your hard work.'

He walks out the door without another word. Everyone looks at Majola, who shakes his head, before following Radebe.

'Colonel.'

Radebe stops in the corridor and turns around.

'What should the rest of the team do?'

'Continue with their other cases – wat anders? I'm sure they have genoeg werk om te doen.' Radebe turns and walks to the lift. 'Jy en Ramsamy, I want you to look at possible locations for roadblocks. Begin with the areas where we found the bodies, then expand the net from there. I want to see the plan before you begin to implement it. Van môre af, the taxi associations will see the mense are too scared to take the taxis; they'll start feeling it in their pockets. Maybe help dit om hulle te convince to be more helpful. Maybe they've withheld information.'

Radebe gets into the lift. 'Dis nou out of my hands. This was a direct order from the minister. Now, let me go calm down the nation before we all lose our jobs.'

The doors of the lift close. Majola walks back to the ops room, crestfallen. In the corridor, he hears someone turn on the flat-screen TV.

Majola stops at the door to watch. A journalist is conducting short interviews with members of the public. A young black girl appears first.

'The police should have warned us. Why did they keep it quiet? They could have saved the other girls. I'll never get into a red taxi again.'

Majola mutters, 'And so it begins.'

An old black man is next up: 'I dreamt about him. It's the ancestors coming to punish us because we don't support the ANC any more.'

Davids laughs.

Last up is a blonde woman from Sandton wearing big sunglasses. 'Thank God I've never had to use a taxi. The police should arrest all the drivers while they're at it. They're all hooligans.'

Majola walks to the table, picks up the remote and turns the TV off. The team members turn around, watching him expectantly. He sits again on the edge of the table, crossing his arms.

'We did what we could, with what we had. You have no reason to feel bad – unless it's one of you who leaked the information, in which case fuck you.'

'Colonel Radebe clearly thinks we should feel bad,' Mitchell says.

'He's also just following orders. Worst of all, now that they have the necessary resources, they're probably going to catch the son of a bitch. Then everyone is going to wonder why we fucked it up.'

Majola gets up, wipes his hands on his trousers. 'I think that's that. Go work on your other cases. The sooner we forget about this mess, the better.'

Majola looks at Ramsamy. 'Sergeant, can I speak to you?'

Ramsamy sits back down. The rest of the team leave reluctantly.

Majola studies the map of Gauteng pinned to the board. 'Will you start looking at places to put up the roadblocks?'

Ramsamy nods.

'Radebe wants to start in the areas where he killed them. Start at the N1 and M1 highways. Put roadblocks with four vehicles at every large turn-off. Give them a stopper vehicle too, in case the fucker decides to make a break for it. In the west, start at Main Reef Road, Albertina Sisulu, Main, Gordon, 14th and Beyers Naudé. Take it all the way to Malibongwe. On the M1 side, start from Main Reef, Smit, Carr, Empire, Jan Smuts and take it to Grayston. Then put roadblocks with two vehicles at the major intersections between them. Consider Katlehong too. Maybe close up Kliprivier, Hennie Alberts and Vereeniging to the west. Look at Setai Street and Kaunda to the east. And if we have enough manpower, put people at the Golden Highway on the R553. And at the Soweto Highway too. I think that's a good start. Send the route outline to Radebe when you're done. He wants to see it. If he does his job, we could get these up and running by tonight with the units we have.'

'Captain, you need some rest.' Ramsamy raises his hands apologetically. 'When was the last time you slept?'

'There's something I have to sort out.' Majola looks at Ramsamy. He wonders if he should tell him about Kappie. Tell him he's on his way to Benoni, and that he suspects the taxi murderer is trying to frame Kappie. He wonders if he can trust Ramsamy.

No, Ramsamy does everything by the book. Straight and narrow. It's better to do this alone. The fact that Flip Swanepoel knows about this is already one confidant too many.

'I'll see you later,' Majola says.

Mbatho is waiting for him in the hallway. She has her handbag clutched in front of her like a shield.

'Can I help you, Warrant Officer Mbatho?'

'Yes, Captain … I just want to say … I'm quitting.'

Majola is caught off guard.

'Quitting? When did you decide this?'

Mbatho sounds suddenly relieved. 'I've been thinking about it for a while now. I'm going into business with my sister.'

'You'll have to put in your month's notice, I assume?'

'I will, yes. I just wanted to say … I know why you never liked me.'

'I'm sorry?'

'You've always been more like them than us. The abelungu.'

'I was unhappy because you didn't do your job, Warrant Mbatho.'

Mbatho shakes her head. 'What's worse, you're not just like the whiteys. You're just like the boere.'

Majola's jaw drops. Mbatho walks past him to the lift. He watches her go, too stunned to move.

Majola slowly pulls out of Johannesburg Central. He'll have to take a shower before going to Benoni; he can smell his own sweat.

Maybe he should stop at Café De La Crème bakery in Melville. He can barely keep his eyes open, and something sweet might give him some energy. In Napier Street he slows down, his gaze fixed on the road. He rubs his burning eyes. Passing cars flash by, almost hypnotically. He can feel his eyelids growing heavy.

The sound of a car horn brings him back into his body. He's in the wrong lane. His hands are shaking. Fuck, nearly took out another car. He can't go on like this. The day's just started.

At his apartment, he doesn't dare sit down in the lounge for fear of falling asleep. Earlier, in the office, he'd struggled to focus on the report for Radebe. By the afternoon, they'll release the screen grab from the Rosebank footage to the media. Tomorrow the picture will be in all the newspapers. The one showing the murderer all covered up probably won't help much, but the picture of the taxi might.

The twelve uniforms Radebe put on the switchboards will have their hands full fielding calls from the public. The majority of callers will have useless information, but they're hoping for those one or two calls that could put them on the right track.

Majola pulls on a black tracksuit and Nike trainers. His last meal was the takeaway curry he ate in the archive basement. He'd felt bad eating in front of Swanepoel, though he'd assured Majola that he was full from the braai that afternoon. He goes to the balcony, breathes in the cold winter air. The clouds have parted, allowing some struggling sunlight to come through. He takes out his phone and calls his mother.

'Hello, Mama.'

'David! How are you? I was just thinking about you.'

'I'm well, thanks. You?'

'Busy. Just busy.'

There's a silence.

'Where is Lulu, Mama?'

'She's taking a nap. She and Christine had a big fight yesterday. Lulu says they're not friends any more. I'm glad, to be honest. That girl was trouble.'

'I'm glad too.'

'What's wrong, David?' she asks, concern in her voice.

'It's just the work.'

'Are you sure?'

'Yes.'

'David, I had another dream. You need to watch out for that taxi, the one that was in the newspapers. All the people in Alex are talking about it. They say that taxi is cursed. Evil.'

Majola sighs. 'What else are they saying?'

'They say it's because our people are committing too much sin. Because we've forgotten our ancestors.'

'Tell Lulu I'll call her tomorrow. I'll come by this week to say hi.'

'I'll tell her. David ... please be careful.'

'Bye, Mama.'

Majola hangs up. He regrets making the call. He just wanted to hear her voice, feel somewhat normal for a moment. He's glad to hear about Lulu's argument with Christine. Seems like she listened to him for once. And that she hasn't told their mother about his plans to take her to live with him in Melville. One thing at a time.

He's out of ideas about what to do regarding Mpete and the money. The bank is only willing to extend his credit-card limit by R5 000. That leaves R12 000 to find. He can't borrow any more; he's reached his limit. And to approach a loan shark is suicide – you never dig yourself out of that hole. Then he'd just be in the same situation that he's in with Mpete anyway. He'll have to make a new plan. What that is, he has no clue. He's considered selling the BMW. And if that's the only recourse, he'll do it. But it will break his heart.

In the kitchen, Majola pours himself a glass of water. He looks at the blackboard propped up against the side of the fridge. 246 days. 246 days sober: no booze, no drugs. In all the chaos, he hasn't ticked off the other days.

The idea rears its head like a snake. It's been growing inside for a while; he just tried to subconsciously suppress it. But today the idea is hammering at the door. He's so tired. And there's still so much to do, so much resting on his shoulders. He knows of something that will keep him awake, see him through. Just for one more night, then he'll start over. Just one time.

He knows he's lying to himself. But the urge is strong. Kappie needs him. Tomorrow the captain of the Hawks will interview Davids and find out Majola wrote up the wrong info in Radebe's report. Then they'll do the maths and arrest Kappie.

Majola shakes his head, as if trying to dislodge the idea.

He picks up the phone, dials his sponsor's number. Andy's phone rings. Majola hangs up. Then makes a different call.

'Prince. Long time, brother. Can you help me out? Three grams. Coke. The good stuff … Yes, thirty minutes … At the usual place. Sharp, brother.'

His phone rings almost immediately. It's Andy. Majola doesn't answer.

Basson double-checks that he hasn't left anything lying around in the Mazda before he activates the alarm. It's Saturday night and this part of the city is unpredictable. It was dangerous even before the Nigerians decided to move to Berea.

He touches the gun tucked into the back of his pants, hidden beneath his windbreaker. Things settled down a bit at home today. Delia was also looking better, even cooked for them. He went to bed just after eight last night. At that point the brandy had taken its toll. He was tired of drinking, physically sick from the drinking. Delia had slept right through from the afternoon, not even waking when he got into bed beside her.

He's not really sure why he's here now. Maybe it's boredom, or the unsolved cases. Maybe it's one last chance to prove what he's made of. Maybe it's the suspicion that Daan Loots is somehow involved that's made him visit this hellhole. Once a policeman, always a policeman.

Basson considers the neon sign of Rihad's Electronics in Prospect Street. The 'R' died long ago. Now it's just *ihad's Electronics*. The shop is really just a front for organised evil, from computers to drugs. Stolen car radios are no longer in high demand, now that the new models come out with decent ones built in. That's probably what the robbed call the shop: 'I had's electronics'. Basson smiles at his own joke.

Nigel October has made himself at home in Berea. He knows everything about everything. There have been two attempts on his life but he's survived both. After the second attempt, he tracked down the drug gang behind them, killed their wives and children before their eyes, then shot them all in the stomach so they could die slowly. Nigel always says a gunshot to the stomach is the most painful.

Basson presses the buzzer on the security gate. There's a video camera above the door. The inside of the store isn't visible from outside; the windows are dirty and covered in old newspapers. The middle-aged Muslim woman behind the counter looks up from her book when she sees Basson.

'Can I help you?'

Electronics litter the shelves, everything from enormous sound systems to neon disco lights, and even a few old transistor radios.

'I'm here to see Nigel October.'

'Send him through, Paz,' a voice says before she can reply. It's coming from an open door to her right. Basson walks down a narrow passage that leads to a larger room. On both sides of the hall, generators of various sizes are stacked from the floor to the ceiling.

Nigel October is sitting behind a desk. He's wearing a checked shirt and a black coat, and his shaved head shines under the fluorescent lights. He looks up from his laptop.

'Look what the cat dragged in. Schemed I wouldn't see you again any time soon, detective. You're looking … worse for wear. Did you lose your razor?'

Basson points at the generators. 'It's all the load shedding. I don't like to shave in the dark. But I see you've found a solution.'

October smiles. 'If some stuff falls off a truck, of course I'm going to pick it up.' He closes his laptop.

'I hear you nearly beat a Zimbo to death.'

'Somehow you hear just about everything.'

October motions for Basson to take a chair. Basson pulls one over.

'Well, maybe not quite everything. Have you come to do business, or are you looking for a favour? You're certainly not here on police business. As I understand, you've been suspended.'

'What do you know about this mother-fucker killing girls in a taxi?'

'Jesus, detective. I know a lot, but I don't know much about serial killers. If we were on the Plain, that would be a different story. Then it might have been my neighbour's fucked-up kid. Or the butcher's retarded brother. But here in the city, I have no idea.'

'You spent some time working with the taxi associations, didn't you?'

'I did. Once in a while they ask me to sort out a pirate. But I can guarantee you, I haven't heard anything about him. Not even from the patrol cars.'

'Will you let me know?'

October nods. 'I'll do that.' Basson takes another look at the generators.

'Are you in the market, my larney? Maybe one of the small ones.'

'How much?'

'R2 000. Special price.'

'Fuck off.' Basson gets up.

October bursts out laughing. 'You drive a hard bargain, Detective. Anyway, that five o'clock shadow suits you. You can throw away that razor. You haven't made anything disappear from the evidence room lately, have you? You know where to find me, right?'

'That's not going to happen again any time soon. You'll let me know if you hear anything about the taxi?'

'I promise. Cheers, Detective.'

Outside, he takes out his keys. A guy in a beanie is busy tampering with the driver's-side door.

'Hey! You, fuck off!'

The man looks up, but keeps trying to jimmy the lock.

Basson draws his father's z88. He removes the safety and fires two shots into the air. The man jumps, sprints off, ducking as he goes. So do a couple of men standing on the corner. Basson lowers the gun. October is at the door, looking out.

'What the fuck are you doing, Detective?'

'You need to employ some car guards,' Basson says, without taking his eyes off the car. He takes out a cigarette and lights it.

'Fucking crazy boere,' October says, locking the gate again.

Majola is working twice as fast as he did the previous night. The fact that Swanepoel isn't here doesn't bother him. He's already worked his way through seven boxes, now all stacked up against the wall. Swanepoel had informed the uniform upstairs that Majola would be coming around again, so she didn't hesitate to give him the keys.

After meeting Prince at McDonald's, he went back home. His sense of guilt was overwhelming. But when he poured out some of the whitish, yellowish powder onto the counter, his mouth started to water. He crushed it with his bank card, then took out a brand-new hundred-rand note. The last thousand in his bank account will have to see him through the rest of the month. He had to repress the thought of Lulu and Mpete. He couldn't look at the blackboard up against the fridge.

The first line burnt his nostrils, but seconds later he couldn't remember why he had ever quit. For the first time he realised how different the feeling was when you didn't drink beforehand. Better. Sharper. He took off his jacket and did two more lines. Then he put on a St Germain album.

David Majola was back. He calmed himself down, focused on what needed to happen. He put his jacket back on, got his keys, wallet, ID and the CD. Instead of the Corolla, he got the BMW out of the garage.

At the Benoni station, he shut the door to the archives behind him so the constable in the evidence room wouldn't suspect anything. He did his fourth big line and zipped the coke safely back up in his jacket pocket. That would have to last him a few hours.

He opens another box, starts checking the dates, then moves the box aside. He doesn't even think about Lulu, Mpete or the wrong information he gave Radebe. His attention is on the boxes only. He brought two litres of water to help with the worst of the thirst and cotton-wool mouth. His appetite is gone.

He checks the time: it's almost eleven. He's been here for more than eight hours. Majola removes his jacket again, folds it carefully. He's perspiring heavily.

In the far corner, about twenty boxes are still waiting to be unpacked. He starts with the row in front, dossiers from 1988 and 1989. He hopes he'll find their sign-out registers as he did in the older boxes.

Everyone who signed out dossiers was required to write their name and police ID on a piece of A4 paper. Majola is tired of stacking the boxes neatly. When he's finished with a box, he tosses it to one side. He picks up the next box, checks the dossier on top, then throws it on the pile with the rest. Majola comes to a sudden halt. He looks at the dossier he's just tossed to the floor.

He takes out the next dossier and carefully reads the cover. *Sergeant Daniël Loots.* ON 113 02 1986. He can't believe his eyes. He puts the dossier down and drags the next box over. MS 121 02 1988. Same as the ones that follow. This can't be. He pulls the box aside, pulls the next one closer. ON 318 06 1986.

'Yes!'

It's strange to hear his own voice after so many hours of silence. He starts paging through the dossiers. ON 341 06 1986, ON 345 06 1986 – until he has all ten dossiers that coincide with the markings on the girls' backs. All the case numbers: 340 to 349.

As he turns to take the dossiers back to the table, a sheet of paper comes loose and floats to the ground. It's the sign-out register. Majola drops the dossiers to the floor and grabs the document. Two inscriptions mark the yellowing paper: *Signed out: 1992/04/29 – Badge number – 63027M – Sergeant Loots. Undersigned: Constable S. Mdusi.* This must be from the time Kappie tried to make the records disappear. The second inscription logged reads, *Signed out: 1997/02/10 – Badge numbers: 653127 – S.B. Nbete. Undersigned: Constable W. Badini.* Is it Nbete or Npete? The handwriting is too sloppy to be sure. But the badge numbers are clear enough.

He's the one I'm looking for. Twenty years ago he came to pull the records. Twenty years later he's looking for revenge. It's him. Majola folds the form in half and puts it aside, with the other files.

Why only now? Why twenty years later? And why black girls? His thoughts are all over the place.

He sits at the desk and drinks some water. To reward himself, he cuts another line on top of one of the dossiers and snorts deeply. He kicks back in the chair. *Now we're getting somewhere, David; now we're getting somewhere. But wait, Kappie said there were eleven dossiers.*

He goes back to the boxes to continue looking.

18

Majola eases the BMW into the garage. He almost forgot to turn down the volume again. He doesn't have the energy for an argument with the neighbours right now.

He can't find the final dossier. The eleventh one that Kappie spoke of, the last murder. After more than three hours of searching, he hid the other dossiers under his jacket and left the station in a hurry. He asked the constable upstairs if she could look up an officer named Nbete. As usual, the system was down. She had also never heard of a Constable W. Badini. He doubts anyone will complain about the mess he left behind. He decided to save the last two grams of cocaine – he has to get some sleep tonight, if only a few hours.

Tomorrow he'll call Michael Mponyane from Home Affairs and ask him to look up the two names. Some of the numbers are old passbook numbers, as Swanepoel said they would be. It's not going to help him much. He'll have to work through the police database to track down the details for these Nbete and Badini characters.

As he kills the engine and turns off the lights, Majola closes his eyes for a moment. His ears are ringing from the music, his heart beating arrhythmically. If he wants to, he can pull another all-nighter. But that would be stupid; he needs to be sharp tomorrow. He still has some cocaine left.

He checks the time – 4:23. 'Almost there, Kappie, almost there.' His phone rings and he jumps.

It's Radebe. 'Ons taxi left us a gift at James and Ethel Gray Park in Melrose. Ek's nou on my way there.'

'But how? Friday he kills two people in a parking lot; now he drops another victim?'

'He's playing us for the fools we are, Captain. First he played you, now he's playing me. Ek begin dink jy was reg: this could be an inside job.'

'And the roadblocks?'

'I had to use what we have. They didn't pick up anything. Van tomorrow af, Metro will be able to help out, then things should go better.'

Too fucking late for the girl he just dumped. She could have used the Metro's help today, Majola thinks.

'Is Sergeant Ramsamy there by jou?'

'No, Colonel.' What the hell would Ramsamy be doing at his place at this time of the morning?

'Kry jou gat to the park. The task team is on its way.' Radebe hangs up.

Majola views the apartment complex in his rear-view mirror. All the residents are warm in their beds, tucked in tight. Tomorrow they'll get on with their day. It'll be a topic of conversation in the tea room or the smokers' corner for a day or two. At most.

He wishes the rain would wash away the last two weeks. Or that he could turn back time to the morning he and Basson were drinking coffee in the restaurant in Mayfair. But the city keeps trudging its own path. Johannesburg doesn't stop for anyone. It wipes its golden ass with everyone. Nose in the air, a broken kind of bounce in its step, leaving bloody footprints behind it. All you can do is try to keep up and dodge the broken glass, hot coals and black shit it leaves in its wake. Majola turns on the cabin light and takes out the second gram from the cubbyhole.

This is the only way.

It takes a few rings before Ramsamy picks up.

'Captain,' he says, sleepily.

'Another victim. James and Ethel Gray Park. I'm heading there now.'

Ramsamy remains quiet, then says, 'My Honda is busted, sir.'

'Drop me a pin and I'll come pick you up.'

Next, Majola calls Lizanne.

'David? What time is it?' she asks, bemused.

'It's early, Lizanne. I'm sorry. Is Kappie there with you?'

Silence. 'Where else would he be?'

'Will you please go double-check?'

'Why? I can hear him snoring.'

'He didn't go anywhere last night?'

'David, what aren't you telling me? Is he involved in something?'

'No, it's not that serious,' Majola says.

'He didn't sleep well. He went to the kitchen once or twice during the night. But I can assure you, he was here.'

'Thank you. Tell him I'll swing by later today or tonight.'

'David?' he hears her ask as he's hanging up.

Ramsamy is waiting outside his townhouse in Northcliff, his raincoat hood pulled over his head.

'Jesus, about time this rain cleared up,' Majola says as Ramsamy gets in.

'It reminds me of summer in Durban. Everything's wet all the time. You can't get the towels to dry. At least Durban isn't as cold as this. It's global warming, I tell you,' Ramsamy says.

They drive in silence until they get to Jan Smuts, the only sound the hypnotic back and forth of the wipers. The drugs make Majola talkative, and he wants conversation, but he's scared Ramsamy will notice something. Then he can't hold back any more.

'So, what's your story, Sergeant? What are you doing in this city? I don't know very much about you – we always just talk about work. I know you're from Durban, and that you used to be in the Flying Squad.'

Ramsamy shifts uncomfortably in his seat. Then he starts to talk.

'My whole family is still in Durban. My brothers and sisters work in my parents' textile factory. It belonged to my great-grandfather.'

'What did they say when you wanted to become a policeman?'

Ramsamy smiles wryly. 'I'm sure you can imagine. My dad wanted me to take over; my other brothers didn't care too much for it. But hell, day in and day out with textiles and fabrics? I would have lost it.'

'So you decided to become a policeman?'

'Yes. Of course, I wanted to go to Bollywood first, but they said my hair wasn't slick enough.'

Majola laughs. 'Do you regret doing this?'

'Not at all. I enjoy being a detective. The Flying Squad was a bit heavy for me. I'm sure there are people who get their kicks from being the first on a scene, but I'm more the kind who picks up the pieces after things have settled down.'

'svc fits you like a glove. You'll go far here. Just hang in there. You're sharp, good eye for detail.'

Ramsamy looks at Majola. 'You think so?'

'I do. But don't let the job get to you. I think Basson has been in the service too long. It got to him. That thousand-yard stare they always talk about in movies? He has that from time to time. He's seen too much.'

'Warrant Officer Basson is a racist.'

'Maybe, but his heart is in the right place.'

Ramsamy shakes his head.

Majola continues. 'How many Afrikaners do you know who aren't racist? It's in their blood. Doesn't matter how hard they try, how friendly they try to be, you always see that sense of superiority somewhere behind the eyes. Or you see the inferiority they see in you. As long as they treat me with respect, I look past it. Captain Loots was the same. You can see the softer side, the caring, but he struggles to show it. That racism, from his father and his grandfather, it keeps him back. I've seen that side of him a few times, especially when he gets angry. That's when it comes out. The former government fucked up a whole lot of people – not just the black people, the whiteys too. But the wheel has turned; it's our turn now.'

'You're pretty damn liberal for a darkie. Was Mandela your hero or something?' Ramsamy remarks cynically.

'Fuck, man, I was hoping he'd announce that we could all run into the white neighbourhoods and go grab ourselves a Mercedes. I'd already staked out a house in Sandton with an slk out front. Then it was peace for all. Simunye, we are one.'

'It's never going to change. Not in my lifetime, at least. The racism,' Ramsamy insists as they turn into Melrose Street.

'Live and let live. If you don't fuck me over, I won't fuck you over. At least your people can visit the Free State for more than a day at a time.'

'Who the hell wants to go to the Free State anyway? Worst province in the country, hands down,' Ramsamy says.

'You forgot about Limpopo.'

Just after 5 a.m., they stop at the park in Melrose's Westwood Avenue, beside the children's play area. Majola has never been here, but he's driven past many times. It's an open field with trees along both sides. A paved path runs around the perimeter, where people from the affluent neighbourhood come to jog or jog or walk their dogs. The high-rises of the city centre are clearly visible from this vantage point, higher up the plateau. Majola can see the SABC tower and Ponte in the distant fog.

'Why are there so many people here?' Ramsamy asks.

'Probably Colonel Radebe's people. The case has been given priority status.'

Majola pulls up the hood of his raincoat. The scene has been cordoned off to keep the public at bay. The media are already circling, trying to move closer, but are deterred by the barks of the uniforms corralling them. Camera crews from ENCA are here, and something like thirty uniforms. Two forensics teams are clicking away with their cameras. They've put up a gazebo to stop the rain from messing up the scene. Majola notices two white Golf GTIs with blue lights fixed to the top. The Hawks are here. And he sees Radebe's BMW. He must have raced from Mondeor to beat them to it.

'Royal treatment,' Ramsamy says, without humour. 'Funny that the FBI isn't here.'

The rain has abated somewhat. Majola and Ramsamy duck under the police line a uniform raises for them. Six men under umbrellas huddle around the body of the naked girl. She's been propped up in a sitting position against the railings around the play park. A female pathologist whom Majola doesn't recognise is working on the victim.

'Ah, Captain. Let me introduce you,' Radebe says to the other men. He's speaking in his perfect English, not the broken Afrikaans he always insists on using with Majola.

'Colleagues, this is Captain David Majola from SVC. He's at your disposal.'

Radebe gestures to the men in turn. 'This is Captain Mathews Baloyi and Captain Steve Tlokwe from the Hawks. You know Captain Bok Louw, and this is Dr Steven Muller, a psychiatrist and criminologist from Pretoria.' A quick round of handshaking follows.

'May I introduce Sergeant Rahid Ramsamy,' Majola says, seeing that Radebe decided he wasn't important enough to deserve an introduction. Only Bok Louw steps forward to greet him; the others merely nod in his direction.

'And the pathologist over there is Dr Mieke Pienaar from Wits University,' says Radebe.

Dr Pienaar looks up and nods at them.

'She's already started going over Dr Lubbe's reports. We should get the results much faster now. This case is the highest priority from now on,' Radebe explains.

'Good lord,' Dr Pienaar says, almost inaudibly.

'What's wrong?' Baloyi asks.

'It's just ... the cruelty behind these injuries. I've never seen anything like it.'

Majola shares a look with Ramsamy. *Welcome to the big league, honey. You with all your degrees and references.* He wonders why Dr Lubbe has been taken off the case.

'Read out that number to Captain Majola,' Radebe instructs Bok Louw, who takes out a notepad.

'ON 350061986,' Majola says.

Everyone turns to him in unison. 'How do you know that?' Bok Louw asks.

'This is the one that brings the death toll up to eleven. The numbers follow in some kind of sequence. You must have seen that in the reports, surely?'

Ramsamy smiles at Majola's thinly veiled barb.

Mieke Pienaar turns to the other men. 'Show him the park's sign board.'

'Come and look,' Mathews Baloyi says. They walk up to a large white sign bearing the name and rules of the park. Across the board, in sloppy red letters, is the word SEKWEPHUZILE. A uniform is protecting it with an umbrella.

'"Too late",' Majola translates. 'In Zulu.'

'He wrote it in her blood,' Radebe says.

'It looks like he used his finger.'

'At the previous murder he wrote "very soon". Now "too late". Were there letters under the numbers?'

'No, just numbers this time,' Baloyi says.

'Then that riddle has also expired,' Majola speculates. 'He feels like he's given us enough clues. We've let this one slip through our fingers.'

'We? Who do you count among this "we"? *We* are only just taking over. Nothing is done yet. This is just the beginning for us,' Bok Louw says, excitedly.

Majola can feel his blood rising, fired by the drugs and the lack of sleep.

'Fuck you, boer! What do you think is going to change here? Now that you have all the resources, you think you're special? We did all the legwork, not you. Fucking mlungu asshole.'

Louw looks at Radebe meaningfully, waits for him to say something.

'Captain, come, walk with me,' says Radebe.

Majola glares at Bok Louw, who smiles but avoids his eyes. He follows Radebe. Ramsamy stays at the scene.

'When was the last time you slept?' Radebe asks quietly. 'Go home and get some rest. Ons sal hier aangaan, wrap things up. Ramsamy will be able to answer whatever questions we have.'

Majola stops walking. 'Why wasn't there a roadblock at the Glenhove turn-off? It's not even a kilometre from here.'

Radebe looks surprised. 'There was one at Atholl Oaklands. And another at Corlett Drive. I thought that made more sense: it's close to Alexandra, in case he lives there.'

Majola shakes his head. 'Very convenient. I'm sure he took that turn-off. How did he know there wouldn't be a roadblock?'

'Gaan slaap, Captain. Take the day off and we'll talk again tomorrow. Did you listen to the morning news bulletin?'

'No.'

'Two taxi owners have been shot in Diepkloof. Their taxis were torched.

Over in Snake Park, they stoned one taxi driver's wife to death. Accused her of witchcraft. Can you guess what colour their taxis were?'

Majola gives no reply.

Radebe smiles. 'I told you the shit storm was coming. Well, it's here now. That's why I waited with the press. Dis net die beginning. Tomorrow, no one will get into a red taxi. The day after that, they'll burn all the red taxis. See you tomorrow, Captain.'

Majola walks to his car, fuming. The murderer knows everything. They're not going to catch him like this. And now Radebe's acting as if it's all Majola's fault. Then that amateur Bok Louw starts mouthing off too! That's probably what everyone's thinking: when the darkies have finished fucking up, give it to the boere to sort out the mess. Fuck, now he's getting paranoid.

He walks past the yellow tape where members of the public are gathered beneath their umbrellas.

'When do you think you'll catch him?' a grey-haired, white man asks. 'I mean, how difficult can it be? It's a goddamn red taxi.'

Voices murmur in the background. Majola doesn't look at any of them.

'Captain,' Ramsamy comes up from behind. Majola stops.

'Don't you miss Daan Loots?' another voice asks from behind the line.

Majola turns to the man. He recognises him, one of Martie Bam's colleagues. Youngish guy, wearing a black cap. Bester, if he remembers correctly.

'Excuse me?' Majola asks.

'Weren't you guys ebony and ivory? Salt and pepper. Our very own *Lethal Weapon*. Even the criminals knew about you guys. But now that he's gone, you're useless on your own.'

Majola grabs the man by the collar. 'Fuck. You.' He spits out the words, then raises his hand to strike.

'Captain!' Ramsamy pulls him away from the reporter.

'Leave him!' the guy yells. 'Let's see how much worse the police will look when they start beating the press.' He straightens his jacket. The rest of the crowd has grown silent.

'Leave it, Captain,' Ramsamy says. 'It's not worth it.'

He leads Majola to the Corolla. 'Get some sleep. I'll call you tomorrow before lunch if you're not in yet. I'll ask one of the uniforms to take me home.'

Majola nods. 'Call me if anything important crops up.' He hesitates before getting in. 'Will you do something for me? Something that has nothing to do with the case?'

Ramsamy looks at him quizzically. 'Sure. What's that?'

'I'll give you a police ID. Can you check the internal database to see who it belongs to? And if the person is still on the force? It's an old number, from the 1990s. It's very urgent. Call me as soon as you find anything.'

'I'll do that. I'll have it done by the time you wake up.'

'Don't wait; call me immediately.'

Ramsamy nods. 'And Captain?'

Majola turns to Ramsamy.

'I don't know what you're on, but I don't think you need reminding of how hard you're going to crash when you come down.'

Majola is stunned.

'I wasn't always as innocent as you may think. I was a regular on the Durban rave scene when I was younger. I suggest you drink a lot of water and get some Rehidrat for when you wake up.'

Majola smiles, then gets into the car as Ramsamy walks back to the crime scene.

Majola checks the rear-view mirror to see if his nose is clean.

The road home felt too long. The rain had rumpled the headlines hanging from the lampposts. Now sitting in the kitchen with his laptop open, Majola knows he's going to fall apart if he doesn't go to bed soon. The wall clock says it's after six in the morning. He looks at the sign-out list he hid between the dossiers and sends Nbete's number to Ramsamy. Then he types in Michael Mponyane's name.

Hey baba

I need a favour. I'm looking for the last known address for the following ID numbers. There's a bottle of Glenfiddich in it for you if you can get it to me today. And a night out in Melville, on me, with all the bells and whistles. I'm done with the boring life.

P. Molefe 5609116001077
B. Mobane 6208095027073
F. Bemba 6103096029071
O. Motake 4509025540077
C. Witbooi 5407116776073

All five are male. That's all I have right now. I'm counting on you.
David

Five numbers. Five surnames and initials. That's all he has to go on. Three of the numbers in the dossiers were passbook numbers. The other two were so poorly written that he couldn't make them out.

After sending the email, he goes to his bedroom, kicks off his wet trainers and drops his coat to the floor. He places his pistol on the bedside table, beside his phone. He's out before he can even pull the covers over himself.

19

'Please fill out your details,' the girl says, cheerily smiling at Basson.

She's astoundingly attractive, he thinks to himself. Tall, pretty face and an ass that could pull off any pair of pants. And Afrikaans. Strange to find that in Parkhurst. Look, it's in a man's nature to notice these things.

Johan Schoeman has done well as a clinical psychologist, Basson muses as he takes in the consultation room, built onto Schoeman's house. A Mercedes c-Class and a Toyota Cruiser are parked in the driveway. Basson wonders if the receptionist receives anything other than patients.

Basson decided he'd take a long shot. Maybe Schoeman would be able to offer some more info on Loots. He went looking around the internet. Now he's convinced Schoeman is going to help him.

He had to drop Nonnie at crèche this morning. He felt less pissed off when he woke up this morning, perhaps because he didn't drink last night. Delia was relieved when he came back from Berea. She was probably thinking he'd gone back to Reza. She let him do his thing; she knows he's busy with something. It was with wide eyes that they watched the morning news. Another murder. The newspapers were still covering Martie Bam and Johnny Ackerman with front-page headlines. He didn't tell Delia about his meeting with Martie on Saturday morning. Delia kept glancing at him as they watched the news.

'I know you're still digging around in this case. I won't be able to change you. But please just be careful. Promise me?'

'I promise,' he answered quietly.

Now he's sitting, clean-shaven and hopeful, in Johan Schoeman's waiting room.

'Mr Schoeman says you can go in. You can leave the forms here. I'll let you know if anything is missing,' she says, with a smile. Her green eyes are quite hypnotic.

Schoeman's office is stuffy and overheated. Two plush leather chairs stand in one corner, Schoeman's large desk in the other. The room is softly lit. Basson wants to laugh – it's just like in the movies. Tranquil is the word. The patients have to feel at ease.

'Sergeant. My goodness! I didn't think I would see you again so soon, and for a personal appointment as opposed to police business. I'm honoured. Sit down, please.'

Basson takes a chair in front of his desk. He's already irritated by the man.

'I haven't been a sergeant in years, actually, but who's counting? Maybe you can help me with my skeletons, though.'

'Any time. Can I get you some coffee? Has Jenna offered you some?'

Almost like Jenna Jameson, the porn star.

'She did, thank you. I'm fine for now.'

'What can I help you with today?'

'Daan Loots,' Basson says, bringing an end to the pleasantries.

'Daan Loots? But I thought this was a medical appointment? A personal one?'

'It is. If you tell me what I want to know, I'll feel much better about myself.'

Schoeman smiles. 'You know very well about doctor-patient confidentiality. Unless someone's life is in danger, I'm not obliged to tell you anything. This can't be new information to you, surely?'

Basson ignores the question. He scans the framed pictures on the wall. Hunting photos hang beside university degrees. Shots of Schoeman next to a dead lion. Schoeman and some large, strange cat, definitely not local. And Schoeman next to a crocodile, rifle in hand, the reptile's jaws propped wide open.

'Why the fuck would you hunt a crocodile?' Basson says, not even trying to mask his disdain. 'Isn't that like shooting a Coke can in a swimming pool with a .22? If you killed it in the water with a Leatherman, that's a different story. But this, this just looks like you're waving the gun around to hide your impotence.'

'Well, *officer*, I shot it because I could afford it. That may be something you have little experience with. You also said you don't hunt, so I don't expect you to understand. I think this session is over.'

Basson looks him straight in the eye. 'You misheard me. I said I only hunt people.'

This unsettles Schoeman. He leans back in his chair.

'I went digging around, as I do,' says Basson. 'About something you said the other day. You spoke of all the white policemen you sorted out back in the Nineties; those you had declared unfit for duty, with full medical and pension; those who didn't want to work under the new government, who pretended to have been broken by what they'd been through.'

The colour drains slowly from Schoeman's face. He crosses his arms. 'Your point being?'

Basson selects a sweet from the bowl on the desk, puts it in his mouth. 'See, when I thought about it this morning, I remembered something from that time: a court case where a psychologist was found guilty of fraud. Apparently, for their lucrative discharge papers, all these poor idiots had to do was pony up three percent of their pensions. One of the patients ended up getting cancer and decided to rat on him. Other psychologists later found there was nothing wrong with any of them. Every policeman on earth has a spoonful of PTSD. My only question is, how did that psychologist end up practising again? According to the article, he was disbarred from the Professional Board of Psychology and the HPCSA. Was he accepted again? I doubt it. Did he bribe his way back in? Quite possibly. So, tell me, Johan Schoeman, since it was your name and picture I saw in the article, how did you pull it off?'

Schoeman's face flushes. 'That was more than twenty years ago. Who would you report me to?'

'How I figure it, what with that whole Life Esidimeni scandal and the loonies being placed in the wrong care facilities, the government would probably like to take some of the focus off their own fuck-ups for a while. And what better than a money-grubbing, sneaky Afrikaner pretending to be a psychologist?'

'I am a psychologist.'

'Who isn't supposed to practise any more. We can argue about this all day, or you can help me. What do you want to do? If you hadn't tried to be a smart-ass that day at Loots's place, I would never have suspected a thing. You'd think a sea-soned hunter like you would've had better aim than to shoot himself in the foot.'

Schoeman sighs long and loud, glances at the door.

'What do you want to know about Daan Loots?'

'Have you heard about the taxi murders?'

'Of course. It's everywhere.'

Basson takes out a cigarette and lights it.

'You can't smoke in here.' Schoeman waves his hand to disperse the smoke.

'Open a window if it bothers you.'

Schoeman does that. Then he puts a half-empty bottle of mineral water down for Basson to use as an ashtray. He sits again.

'I want you to check something for me. Is Loots's file in that filing cabinet over there?'

'It is.'

'Well, go pull it out for us, Johan.' Basson exhales across the desk.

Schoeman fetches the file and places it in front of Basson. Basson moves it back to Schoeman, taking out a notepad.

'Look up the dates of Daan Loots's setbacks, then write them down for me.'

Schoeman pages through the folder, takes out an A4 sheet and starts writing. When he's done, he hands the paper to Basson.

Basson places the notebook beside the sheet of paper and starts comparing dates.

'Mother-fucker. All ten of them. No fucking way is that a coincidence.'

Basson folds the paper and puts it in his pocket. 'Do you think Loots is capable of murder?' He points at the notebook. 'Every single one of Loots's setbacks coincides with one of the taxi murders.'

'Good God,' Schoeman says. 'You know, when I read about the taxi murders, something about it made me think … of …'

'Think of what?'

Schoeman shakes his head. 'I've done hypnotherapy with Daan Loots a few times. The first time it didn't help much. But after that … he had trauma in his youth, his mother committed suicide. His father was very strict, almost mili-tant. Then came the whole Border War. Loots was in Koevoet, or Operation K, in the early Eighties. That's when his problems really started.'

'Go on.'

'I could infer that he had specialist training in interrogations, and that he used it later when unrest broke out on the East Rand. I've seen a lot of patients with PTSD, especially old policemen, but his case was extreme. I guess it's unsurprising, considering what he had been through.'

'I'm not hearing what I want to hear, Johan.'

Schoeman sighs. 'He tortured people. Informants. Insurgents. Mostly people in the townships. A lot of them. Even committed murder.'

'That's nothing new. The old guard really got their hands dirty. You're still not telling me why the news reports made you think of him.'

'During our last session, it came out that he had ... tortured people in a van. A red van.' Basson leans forward in his chair. 'He assaulted and electrocuted them.'

Basson can't believe his ears. 'Just like the taxi murderer. And you didn't think the police needed to know about this?'

'It could just be coincidence. That was thirty years ago,' Schoeman argues.

'Do you think he's capable of committing murder?'

Schoeman shakes his head. 'Unlikely. Look, he clearly regrets the things he did. Physically he wouldn't be strong enough any more, at least judging by what's been described in the newspapers. And where the hell would he hide the taxi? He doesn't even drive these days. He never goes anywhere, and only his daughter and Captain Majola ever visit him. And let's say for a moment he wasn't on medication: something would have to trigger him. Something from that time, like the incident in his last year of service, before he started taking the meds. But I promise you, he's taking the pills. I regularly check with the nurse from the retirement home.'

Basson drops his cigarette into the bottle. It falls with a quiet hiss.

'How do you explain the setbacks, then?'

'That I don't know. I really wouldn't be able to tell you.'

'I think it's time for me and him to have a conversation,' Basson says icily.

'Can I say anything to convince you that's not a good idea? If he knows I spoke about our sessions with someone else, I can get into trouble.'

'Not as much fucking trouble as you'll be in if I take your story to the papers,' Basson says, getting up.

Schoeman also gets up, fidgeting with his collar.

'Um ... what will your silence cost me? How do I know you won't still go to the newspapers?' he asks, a tremble in his voice.

'Well, you can start by asking your receptionist to give me a blow job. That should get you some of the way.'

Schoeman gapes. He starts to stammer. 'J ... J ... Jenna is my daughter.'

'All the better. Then it should be easy to convince her,' Basson says, smugly.

'Please ... I ... please ...' Schoeman is on the verge of tears.

'I'm just joking, Johan. We poor policemen aren't like you filthy-rich folk. You know, this is the second time in as many weeks that I've sat down with someone who thinks they're better than me because they have money. Let this be a fucking lesson to you.'

Schoeman stares at the carpet.

'I guess everyone deserves a second chance. Goodbye, Johan.'

Basson leaves the door open as he departs, and makes a show of winking at Jenna on his way out.

'So, he hasn't been here since Saturday?'

'No. The policeman came to pick him up.'

'The one with the Corolla?'

'Yes. Majola,' the security guard replies.

Basson glances over the grounds of the Rosewood Retirement Village. 'What the hell are you up to, David?'

'Sorry?' The guard asks, nervously.

Basson shakes his head, rubs his stubble. 'Where does the caretaker live?'

'Number two, that row on the left.'

Instead of going to the caretaker's house, Basson heads back to Kappie's place. He tries the door, but it's locked and the curtains are drawn. He wonders if the guard will notice if he forces the door open. It seems to be held in place by a small latch at the top, and there's no security gate. He listens to determine if anyone is nearby. He grabs the door handle, readies himself.

'Hey! What are you doing over there?'

Basson jumps, pulling his hand back as if he's been burnt.

'Excuse me?'

'What are you doing at the old man's apartment? Hanging around looking for trouble again?' says the old lady.

Basson takes out his police ID. 'I'm from the police, ma'am. I'm busy investigating a murder.'

She shuffles closer to inspect Basson's ID. She smells like bird seed, Basson thinks. Her white slippers are almost as dirty as her pink dressing gown.

'Why aren't you in uniform?'

'I'm a detective. I don't wear a uniform.'

'Do you have a gun?'

'I do, yes.'

'Can I see it?'

'Why do you want to see my gun?'

'I want to shoot the pigeons who eat the feed I throw out for the little birdies.'

Something has clearly gone a bit screwy with her. Basson decides to go to the caretaker's place instead.

'Why don't you wear a uniform?' she asks again. Ignoring her, Basson walks briskly down the path.

'You should come visit again, sweetie. You look like a handsome Columbo!' she calls after him.

Basson knocks on the caretaker's door. A man in a tracksuit and slippers opens up, about seventy years old.

'Afternoon. Can I help you?' he asks suspiciously.

Basson shows his ID. 'Good afternoon. Warrant Officer Basson from SVC.'

'SVC? What does that stand for?' the man asks as he brings the ID close to inspect it.

'Serious and Violent Crimes Unit.'

The man hands back his ID. 'They have so many different units these days, I can't keep up. Sergeant Ben Kotze. I used to be with SAPS Equestrian. Many years ago, of course. Come in.'

Basson's spirits drop. He remains standing in the doorway.

'I don't want to bother you. I want to know if I can get access to Daan Loots's apartment. I'm busy with a murder investigation.'

'What? Did something happen to Daan?' Kotze asks, shocked.

'No, no, nothing like that. I just need to take a look around,' Basson says.

'Thank goodness. I haven't seen him in a while. Almost had me worried there.' Kotze puts his hands on his hips. 'What are you looking for then?'

'I am not at liberty to share that information with you. We're at a sensitive stage of the investigation. You probably know how it is, don't you, Sergeant?' Basson says, trying some flattery.

'Mm ...' Kotze's not convinced. 'Do you have a search warrant?'

His chances of getting anywhere have just hit a wall. He might as well pack this in and go.

Basson tries one last tactic. 'There wasn't enough time. I had to come here urgently.'

'Well, I guess you'll have to make some time then. Come back with a warrant. Until then I don't want to see you here again. Or I'll call your commander.'

Kotze slams the door in Basson's face. Basson stands there, dumbfounded for a few seconds. He walks back to his car. After such a promising morning, he's been humiliated by a geriatric sergeant and a pigeon-crazed old bat, dolled up in pink.

In the car, he takes out his phone. He has Majola on speed dial, and calls the number. But no one answers. It goes straight to voicemail.

'David, what are you up to? Are you hiding Loots? I know what he got up to during the unrest. The tortures, the red van. His setbacks all coincide with the dates of the murders. You'd better call me as soon as you get this. Or I'll blow this goddamn thing wide open.'

Mama Thadie's house smells like chicken-and-vegetable soup. She's humming to herself as she bustles between the kitchen table and the oven. A freshly baked loaf of bread is already on the table.

Every now and then, she sits on one of the chairs. She watches the clock: it's just past seven. She's glad she got off work a bit earlier today. Tim, her employer in Sandton, asked her to come and help out when his sister's domestic worker called in sick. Luckily her townhouse is only two blocks from Tim's. Some extra cash is always welcome. That's why they're having chicken soup tonight.

Her thoughts keep wandering. She's worried about David. He sounds tired. More than tired – hopeless. She could hear it; he should know he can't hide it from her.

Mama Thadie hears the key turn in the lock.

'Lulu!'

'Mama,' Lulu replies miserably.

'Come, sit. I made some delicious soup.'

Lulu drops her bag on the table and plops down on the chair closest to the heater. She holds her hands up to warm them.

'Do you want some tea? The soup won't be long now.'

Lulu nods.

Mama Thadie picks up the kettle.

'Mama?'

She turns around to face Lulu. 'Yes, my child?'

'I've got something to tell you, Mama.'

Worry creeps over Mama Thadie's face. She takes the dishcloth from her shoulder, drops it on the counter beside the stove, then sits down opposite Lulu. 'What is it, Lulu?'

Lulu keeps her eyes on the floor. Her hands are fidgeting in her lap. 'David wants me to move in with him, in Melville. He says there's more work there, that I'll be able to get a job at a salon there. He doesn't want me to stay in Alex any more. He says it's dangerous here.'

Mama Thadie looks at Lulu. 'If he thinks it's better, then maybe it makes sense to go. You've been wanting to move to that side for a while now.'

A tear runs down Lulu's cheek. 'But what about Mama? I can't just leave you here.'

Mama Thadie smiles. 'I've lived here almost my whole life, my girl. Where would I go? I can't watch over the two of you forever. I knew this would happen some day. I was blessed when David came back. But I knew the time was borrowed, from Jesus.'

The tears are now streaming down Lulu's face.

'Ai, Mama ...' Lulu gives her a long hug.

'What aren't you telling me, Lulu? Come, out with it.' Lulu turns away, shakes her head.

'Ag, Mama. It's just Christine. We're not friends any more.'

Mama Thadie hugs her close. 'You'll make new friends. Friends are like the rain: they come and go. Sometimes they allow you to grow like a tree; other times it's not enough, and you don't grow. Then you have to wait for new rains.'

Lulu sniffles.

'David said he would come by this week. We can discuss all of this then. But don't worry about me. You still have your whole lives ahead of you. I've lived mine. You are more important than anything else to me. You are my children.' Mama Thadie kisses Lulu on the forehead. 'Go dry your tears, then we'll eat.'

The harder he jabs the needle into his leg, the more crooked it becomes. Then he has to straighten it again. He's sitting on the only seat in the taxi.

Daan Loots is driving. 'If you can't remember your pass number, I won't stop,' he says every few seconds without turning around. Beside him sits the sangoma from the M1. The taxi comes to a halt.

Ramsamy and Basson are outside. Into the taxi they're tossing the bodies of naked girls, who flop on the floor like fish on the deck of a boat.

'Lulu!' Majola screams when he recognises his sister, but his hands are nailed to the armrests.

'Just like Jesus,' one of the dead girls says from the floor. A moth flies out of her mouth as she talks.

'Lulu! No!'

Majola jerks awake. He is drenched. The bedding is on the floor. There's a terrible throbbing in his head and he's struggling to get his eyes to focus. His hand searches for his phone, finally finds it, but the screen is a blur. He stumbles to the bathroom, opens the taps and waits for the water to warm up. He sees his face in the mirror. He looks sixty years old. His skin is grey, his eyes glassy.

'What goes up, must come down,' he whispers at his reflection.

He panics for a moment when he looks out the bathroom window. It's already dark outside. He checks his watch: it's after 7 p.m. He's missed the meeting at the station. Oh well, he tells himself, nothing to be done about it now.

With a wet cloth he wipes his face. His heart feels as if it weighs a metric ton. He wants to go back to sleep for another week. In the kitchen, he takes three painkillers, swallowing them down with big gulps of cold water from the fridge.

He wonders why he snapped at Bok Louw like that. Was it about what Mbatho had said to him? He was so high he couldn't help himself. He opens his laptop. Just for a moment he thinks of the remaining gram of coke in the BMW. And what's left of the second one in the pocket of his raincoat. No, tomorrow the heavy depression will hit. Today is like a rough hangover. Today is uncomfortable, tomorrow will be utter hell. He'll reconsider his options when he gets there.

Majola gets his phone from the bedroom, pulls a blanket over his shoulders and puts on his slippers. He nearly trips over the shoes in the hallway, then puts them out of the way. He adds boiling water to his coffee, decides against the milk. He needs something stronger. The kitchen light is too bright. He takes his phone, laptop and the fresh coffee to the living room and turns on the lamp.

Five missed calls on his phone. Luckily nothing from Radebe. Two from

Ramsamy, one from Michael Mponyane and one from Basson. Basson? There are three voicemails. He decides to talk to Ramsamy first.

He answers immediately.

'Captain. How are you feeling?'

'Shit. But I'm awake, at least. What's happening there?'

'Everyone is hustling. Colonel Radebe has roped in almost the whole of Metro to help with the roadblocks – all the spots we chose, and a few more in Soweto. Even if the murderer knows about the roadblocks, he's going to have a hard time moving around. Captain Mathews Baloyi sat down with each of us to find out what we know. He was impressed by how thorough the reports were.'

'Was Warrant Davids also there?' Majola asks, concerned.

'Yes, he was. The picture of the taxi was printed in nine of the papers, and it's still being circulated on several TV stations. A whole team has been assigned just to work through the information being called in. But it's a madhouse. Everyone has seen the taxi. Everyone claims they know the taxi driver – usually someone's ex-husband or a debt collector or something. Some of the loonies even claim the tokoloshe is driving the taxi.'

'Okay, we expected this. Did Radebe say anything about me not being there?'

'No. He said I should leave you to your rest. Like a concerned parent,' Ramsamy jokes.

Majola tries to laugh, but it sounds hollow.

'What could you find out about that police number I gave you?' Majola asks.

Ramsamy hesitates before he answers. 'It's a dead end. The number exists, but I can't get access. "Access denied": that's all that pops up on the screen. Do you know what that means?'

'It could mean it's an old number, someone who belonged to the old Security Branch. Or even National Intelligence. That's strange, I've never seen anything like that myself. Maybe you don't have the necessary clearance.'

'Do you want me to ask Colonel Radebe if he has the required clearance?'

'No, no, that's unnecessary. I'll try to find out what's going on tomorrow,' Majola says, aiming to sound untroubled. He changes the subject. 'Nothing yet from our superstar pathologist?'

'Nothing. Maybe she wants to make sure she's being thorough. Are you coming in tomorrow?'

'Yes, I am. I might have to run an errand in the morning, but I'll be there,' Majola says, opening an email from Michael Mponyane.

'Okay, we'll talk then. I think I'll also go to bed now; it's been quite a day.'

'Thank you, Sergeant Ramsamy. I'll see you tomorrow.'

Majola grinds his jaws to suppress his irritation and fatigue. He's hoping desperately that Michael has figured out something with the ID numbers.

Heitada David. I had to spark today. Choose the date. The Glenfid-
dich will be on you. Can we do a couple of lines again? ☺ I found
this great dealer with the best gear in Jozi.
P. (Peter John) Molefe 5609116001077 - *Deceased: 2014*
(age 58)
B. (Bengu) Mobane 6208095027073 - *Deceased: 2009 (age 47)*
F. (Felix) Bemba 6103096029071
Last known address:
11 Moka Street, Zone 5, Pimville, 1818, Soweto
Note: He renewed his ID book three years ago.

O. (Oliver) Motake 4509025540077
Last known address:
Magagula Street, Inxiweni, Tembisa
Note: He has renewed his ID twice, both times giving
the same address.

C. (Catherine) Witbooi 5407116776073
Deceased: 2011 (age 57)
NOTE: She was female, not male.

Hope that helps.
We'll talk soon. You can start pouring.
Michael

Only two names to work with. But that's better than nothing. Majola listens to
his voice messages, deletes those from Ramsamy and Mponyane. Basson is
next up.

A coldness grips Majola. The son of a bitch. He went digging on his own.
Thank God he's been suspended and decided to call him first. But how did he
find out? Schoeman? Has he been to see Kappie? But Kappie would have told
him if he had. And Schoeman wouldn't have told him; that would be unethical.

He'll have to call Basson. Majola takes a deep breath.

'Hello, Jason.'

'Hello, David. I take it you got my message?'

'I did.'

'Are you going to tell me where you're hiding Daan Loots?'

'He's staying with Lizanne.'

Basson didn't expect honesty, Majola thinks. Now he knows he's got nothing to hide.

'Will you let me explain?'

'Okay. I'm listening.'

'It's not him. I was there Saturday night after Martie Bam and her boyfriend were murdered. I called this morning and spoke to Lizanne, after the last murder. He was sleeping all night and didn't go anywhere near Melrose.'

'How do you explain his setbacks on the dates of the murders?'

'Fuck knows. Really. Listen, I'm fucking starving. Come, meet me at Picola in Linden. I'll buy you a pizza. How does that sound?'

'I've already had dinner.'

'Jason, please. You have to listen to me. I'll bring the dossiers of the people Kappie tortured in the Eighties.'

'Where the hell did you find those?'

'Benoni. So, in half an hour?'

'Okay.'

He'll have to play his cards right. He would rather have Basson on his side than in his way. But he's angry at himself for almost pleading with him.

'Fucking hell,' says Basson. 'Were you hit by a train?'

Basson is wearing a red Adidas tracksuit. If it weren't for the tan, Majola would have sworn he belonged in the old Eastern Bloc. 'Are you playing soccer these days?' Majola asks, sitting down at the outdoor table.

'Sometimes Delia thinks I'm younger than I am.'

Besides the two of them, the seating area outside the pizzeria is empty; only a handful of patrons sit inside. Out here, gas heaters burn warmly and canvas screens have been drawn across both sides to keep the worst of the cold out. Majola knows Basson is outside so he can smoke. He's also nursing a glass of brandy.

'Are you struggling to fall asleep again?' Basson asks.

Majola remembers that's the excuse he used to give when he showed up to work in this condition.

'I am. I don't know why, though. I'm off the case, acting in an advisory capacity only,' Majola says sarcastically.

'I thought that's what Radebe was going to do when I saw him on TV yesterday. Now he's gathered all his cronies to work on the case,' says Basson and takes another drag of his cigarette. 'He's not waiting between murders any more? Sunday morning's was on this evening's news again.'

Majola studies the menu and orders a Coke. He's glad he has the self-restraint not to order a beer right now.

Basson smiles at him. 'So, tell me what you've got, so that I can try figure out how Loots is doing it.'

Majola decides to be honest. That's the best way. He tells him about the investigation. About the eyewitness in the patrol car, Kappie's number plates on the taxi, Kappie's confession about his work during the unrest, about Flip Swanepoel and the Benoni dossiers. The only thing he leaves out is Lulu's problems.

'Holy shit. All of that in a week? Looks like everything falls apart when I'm gone. No wonder they don't have time to investigate me.'

Majola smiles wryly. Basson orders a Picola Special pizza and another brandy and Coke. Majola goes for a spaghetti Bolognese.

'Let me get this straight,' Basson says. 'We have the setbacks aligning with the murders, and the plates from Kappie's old car on the taxi, and you still don't think it's him?'

'Do you think Kappie would be stupid enough to use his old plates on the taxi? It doesn't make sense. And he wasn't anywhere near the last three murders.'

'He could be working with someone,' Basson responds.

'Who? That crazy old bird lady in the pink dressing gown?'

Basson laughs. 'Fucking hell. Then there wouldn't be any pigeons left in Johannesburg.'

Majola places a finger on the pile of dossiers. 'The answer is here somewhere. It's one of them. One of them wants revenge. Or someone who knew one of his victims. The chances are that it's another policeman, the owner of the goddamn police ID that no one can access. Or maybe that policeman, Nbete or whatever his name is, accessed it for someone else. Don't you know anyone in Pretoria who could help?'

'Unfortunately not. Everyone I know went private.' Basson's gaze rests on the dossiers. 'You said there were only two of them left alive?'

'Yes. According to my source at Home Affairs.'

'Okay.' Basson takes another sip. 'I'll listen to what you're saying. And what Schoeman told me. I'll give you the benefit of the doubt. Let's say Loots is innocent, that it looks too much like a Hollywood movie. Give me that address, then I'll go find out tomorrow – as long as it's not Tembisa: that's too far to drive when I'm paying for petrol.'

Majola smiles. 'Thanks. But be careful. Do you still have your dad's z88?'

'Naturally.'

'Let's hope the murderer gives us some breathing space. And that his message means what we think it means. Meanwhile, to keep you happy, I'll have Kappie stay at Lizanne's.'

'Maniacs like him don't let up. He'll have to kill again soon,' Basson says.

'Kappie?'

'No, the murderer. I think you need to get some sleep. Oh yeah, and Schoeman said something about a trigger. Some kind of trigger seems to be causing the setbacks.'

'Like what? Something from the past?' Majola asks.

'Probably something like that. For all we know it could be something he's reading in the Bible. Revelations.'

Majola cracks a smile.

'How are Delia and Nonnie?'

'Better. Delia is seeing a psychologist again. We're considering taking Nonnie too. She looks okay, but you never know.'

'And you? Not thinking of seeing one yourself?'

Basson laughs. 'I saw one this morning. But he didn't want his daughter to give me a blow job.'

'Huh? What did you do to Schoeman to make him talk?' asks Majola.

'Don't worry. That's a story for another day. I still have your *Stranger Things* DVD.'

'Have you watched it?'

'Not yet.'

'You can return it when you're done.'

Nomvelo Lesufi falls out the sliding door of the taxi. There is grass around her, and trees, but she can see street lights. Her vision is blurry from the blow to her nose. She can still taste blood in her mouth.

She runs towards the street lights. Her naked lower body is in pain. She's wearing only a torn T-shirt; the rest of her clothes are in the taxi.

'Ndincedeni!' she screams, but she doubts anyone will hear her; it must be after eleven.

She's expecting a hand on her shoulder at any moment, to drag her back into the dark. But it doesn't come. She hears the taxi door slam shut behind her, the engine coming to life, the taxi reversing quickly.

In front of her she sees a road. She's in Dippenaar Street; she can see the sign on the pavement. She must be in Diepkloof, not far from her home. She runs north. To her right is the Diepkloof Xtreme Park. That's where the monster raped her.

She runs without looking back, her feet stinging on the tar. When she can't run any more, when her lungs are burning so much that she has to stop, she looks around, just in time to see the taxi turn into Ingwenya Street.

She staggers on, wondering if she should seek refuge in one of the houses along the road. Dogs are barking everywhere. As she starts to feel light headed, as the pain in her lower body becomes unbearable, she slows down. Then she feels her legs go numb. She hears a vehicle approaching at speed.

'Please, Lord, please …' she whimpers.

She drags her body forward on the road, using every ounce of energy she has left. In front of her she can see the light pooling in the street from the approaching vehicle. He has to be close. She hears the engine rev. Then it slows down and pulls in beside her. It's larger than a normal car.

God, it's a taxi.

She collapses, protecting her face with her hands. She feels her bleeding knees burning. Nomvelo turns onto her back. Two men loom over her. One shines a flashlight into her face.

'Makhe ndikuncede, sisi,' she hears him say before she loses consciousness.

20

A scruffy brown dog sniffs at the door as Majola stops in Magagula Street in Tembisa.

It's in the old part of the township, where some of the gardens have large apricot trees. The homes look older and shabbier than some of the RDP houses he passed earlier, but they're sturdier.

Basson was right. He does feel like he has been hit by a train. The whole morning was a battle with himself not to do coke again. And a struggle to get up. He knows he needs more sleep. To reassure himself, he stowed a gram in the Corolla's cubbyhole.

He hates himself. He'd forgotten what it feels like to come down after so much of the stuff. Was it always this bad? He's feeling dangerously reckless, but also more depressed than he thought possible. Today, he swears, is the day he kills someone – if he doesn't kill himself first. Now he's in this godforsaken township too.

The headlines on the lampposts and radio news bulletins haven't helped his mood.

Another victim for Zola!

SAPS *must answer for serial killer.*

The radio painted a particularly bleak picture: chaos at the taxi ranks all over Gauteng, no one wanting to board a red taxi; three buses torched in Soweto, presumably because the taxi drivers are angry that commuters have started using them instead. The head of Faraday is apparently threatening a strike if the police don't catch the killer: that would be a disaster, as more than a million people use their taxis daily.

The only people cashing in are the panel beaters. A picture has been doing the rounds on the internet, showing a row of red taxis lined up outside a panel beater's workshop to be repainted – any colour but red. Radebe is probably losing his shit from all the stress.

Majola opens the cubbyhole and stares at the cocaine on the CD case. It'll have to get him through the day. Fuck knows, fighting it isn't helping, not now. The idea excites him: the feeling of looking forward to life again after one line. He'll check into rehab after this, he promises himself. He opens the cubbyhole again. His nose keeps running and his mouth is dry.

Majola gets out and chases the dog away. The dirt road has turned to mud. The little house at number 1287 is in a state of disrepair, the washing line in front drooping from two rusty poles. His mother's place in Alex looks like Buckingham Palace compared to this shanty.

A middle-aged woman with a brightly coloured headwrap opens the door and greets him hesitantly in Xhosa.

Majola immediately takes out his police ID. 'Afternoon. Captain Majola from the SAPS. I'm looking for Oliver Motake. According to Home Affairs he lives here.'

The woman frowns. 'Is this about what happened to Lizzie?'

Majola looks surprised. 'No. It's about another case. He's not in trouble; I just want to talk to him.'

The woman looks disappointed. 'Wait here. I'll go ask.'

She walks through the kitchen and out the back door, where Majola can hear her talking to someone. In the modest living room, the couch is covered in plastic. The small TV advertising Verimark products is bothering Majola; the volume's too loud and the people too fake. There's a framed photograph on the wall, of the woman, a teenage girl and an old man, all in their Sunday best.

'My dad says you can come on through. You'll have to speak up, as he can't hear very well. And he's blind. Diabetes.'

Majola's heart sinks. Clearly this isn't the murderer. This day is getting worse. He walks through to the small back yard, where a grey-haired old man, neatly dressed in a brown suit and hat, sits on a garden chair with a blanket over his legs. A wooden pipe hangs from his mouth, and an orange bag of Boxer tobacco, a box of matches and an ashtray lie on the ground next to him.

'Sorry, there's only one chair,' says the daughter before going back into the kitchen. The old man turns towards Majola but continues gazing out at the small patch of grass in front of him.

'Madala.' Majola greets him politely. He must do his best to keep the anger, depression and recklessness inside.

'What do the police want with me? Never thought I would see you again.' The old man's quiet laughter turns into a coughing fit.

'I only have a few questions. It's about something that happened long ago. In the 1980s.'

'The 1980s? I don't remember that well any more, but ask away.'

'Those times, with the riots. The police regularly questioned the comrades.'

'The boere?' the man laughs again softly.

'Yes. The boere. Did they ever have you in a taxi? A van? Where they questioned you?'

The man's face turns to stone.

'How do you know about that?'

'I read the cases, Madala. I want to talk to you about that. It's important for an investigation.'

'Does he ride again? The devil?'

'Excuse me?' Majola feels a chill run over his skin.

Motake shakes his head, then lifts his unseeing eyes to the grey sky.

'There were a lot of stories about that taxi. The people back then believed the devil himself drove it. Others said there was no one behind the wheel, that it drove itself. But if it picked you up, you never got out again. I was one of the lucky ones.'

'What can you remember?'

'They came to pick me up one night, the boere, at this house. Three of them, from the Security Branch. When they took me outside, the van was standing there. I almost wet myself. Sophia started crying hysterically; she had also heard the stories. She thought she would never see her husband again. The people in the street started throwing stones. Then the boere drove off with me.'

'And then?' Majola urges him to continue.

Motake's brow furrows. His hand reaches shakily for his tobacco, puts it on his lap.

'That Zulu tied me to a chair in the back. We drove around a bit. Then they stopped.'

His face contracts into a grimace. 'I remember, they had boeremusiek playing on the radio. Horrible. The Zulu kept asking, "Uyakuthanda lokhu? Do you like this music?" Then he would laugh. A boer also climbed in the back. I'll never forget his eyes – baby blue, like that Paul Newman at the bioscope.'

Motake fills his pipe from the pouch, lights it. He drags deeply, then slowly exhales the smoke. 'A boer would ask a question. If I didn't answer, the Zulu would hit me in the kidneys. I pissed blood for a week. He talked a hole through my head with all his questions; eventually I had no idea which way to turn. After a while, I sang. Like a bird.'

'What did you sing about?' Majola asks.

The old man's grey eyes tear up. 'We were hiding three comrades in Malawi. Freedom fighters. I told those dogs where they were hiding.'

'What did they do then?'

'They tossed me out. Without stopping, of course. I hurt my leg badly, but the diabetes got my foot. Three weeks later I heard the three comrades in Malawi were dead. I never forgave myself.'

'You must know it wasn't your fault. All the blood is on their hands.' Majola wants to put his hand on the old man's shoulder.

Motake takes another puff of his pipe. 'You know, just last week they raped little Lizzie on her way to school. The police haven't even been here. She's just going on as if nothing happened. Do you think it's better now? Than in those days?'

Majola is caught off guard. 'Well, at least the police are not treating people like animals.'

'The boere made no secret about how little they thought of us. They didn't lie to us the way today's bunch do. Promises, promises; they don't care. What did I fight for in the struggle?'

Majola doesn't answer.

'With the first election, with Mandela, I stood in the line for fourteen hours. We had hope that things would change. After a few years, I realised that everything was still the same. People like me, we have no luck. No luck under the boere, no luck under the ANC. I was born in the wrong country, on the wrong continent. I was cursed. Cursed right down to my pitch-black bones.'

Motake drops the matches beside the chair. Majola kneels to pick them up.

Motake grabs him by the arm. 'If you see him, tell Blue Eyes I'll see him in hell one of these days.'

Majola takes a step back, reeling at the old man's words. 'One last question, Madala,' he says, composing himself. 'Did you know any of the other people who were questioned in the taxi? Did you fight together?'

The old man thinks for a while. 'There were many, especially from Tembisa. There was one who became a policeman later on. I saw him in a shebeen one night, just around the corner from here. No one could believe it, not after what they'd done to him.'

Majola's heart starts racing. 'Can you remember who he was?'

Motake is quiet for a few moments. 'No, I can't. I really can't.'

'Will someone know? Who will remember?'

Motake shakes his head. 'It's been too long. They messed him up badly. Electrocution, cut him up, left him for dead at the side of the highway. I can't remember.'

'Madala, please, think carefully. His name, where he lived, anything.'

Motake whips his head towards Majola. The tobacco falls to the ground. 'I told you, I don't remember!' he yells before being overcome by another coughing fit.

Motake's daughter appears in the doorway, concern on her face. She gives Majola a stern look.

'Thank you, Madala.'

Motake doesn't respond.

Majola walks to the front door, Motake's daughter following him.

'Please don't come back. The past just breaks his heart,' she says.

'Here's my card,' Majola says apologetically. 'Please call me if he remembers anything.'

She nods and closes the door.

Back in the car, he takes in the little house. Motake's words turn in his head: 'I was cursed. Cursed right down to my pitch-black bones.' Majola considers the old black men begging on the street corners, with their grey hair, crooked backs and weather-beaten faces. Nothing ever came of their hope. Wrong country, wrong continent.

Majola opens the cubbyhole. His phone rings. Basson.

'It's definitely not Bemba,' Basson says without so much as a hello. 'He's riddled with AIDS, can't even get out of bed. And he can't remember a damn thing.'

Majola sighs. 'I've also hit another dead end.'

'So, what now?'

'I really don't know any more. Maybe I'll have to ask Radebe about that number.'

'Then you'll be cutting Loots's throat. And your own. Then perhaps we can go start that PI business in PE. PE PIS.'

Majola is too dejected to laugh. His phone vibrates against his ear. Another call from Ramsamy.

'Thanks, Jason, I'll let you know if I think of something else.' He hangs up and takes Ramsamy's call.

'Where are you, Captain?' Ramsamy sounds out of breath.

'I'm on my way. What's going on?'

'One of his victims got away. He raped her in Diepsloot, at Xtreme Park, then she ran away. A security company picked her up on the side of the road.'

'Slow down. How do you know it was him?'

'Radebe is convinced. Red taxi. Siyaya. It has to be him. She's in Baragwanath but she's badly traumatised. The doctors don't want us to speak to her. But Radebe said he'd deal with them.'

Majola is still doubtful. 'And the taxi? What do we have?'

'A number plate. There are four cameras in the park. The last one caught him before he drove off. We're trying to find out who it belongs to.'

'What's the plate number? Does the vehicle fit our description? Tinted windows? Missing reflecting strip?'

'Not sure; I'll get back to you. I'm still catching up myself. I have to go. I'll see you soon.'

The dog he'd seen earlier is sniffing at his wheels again. Why let the victim loose? Why move away from where the earlier murders were committed? Or was he just feeling bitter this morning? Will this nightmare finally come to an end? Something isn't quite right. Majola takes out the CD case and the packet of powder.

The ops room looks like someone kicked an anthill. Majola doesn't feel he belongs here: everyone is excited, as if a fire has been lit inside them. Everyone except him. The last two lines did precious little to lift his mood. The next one will get him where he needs to be.

He sniffs softly and self-consciously. Colonel Radebe is in conversation with Captain Mathews Baloyi while Bok Louw studies the map of Gauteng. Radebe spots Majola and motions for him to wait. When his conversation ends, he comes over.

'Looks like Lady Luck is on our side,' Radebe says. 'This is the break we needed. And just in time, before the taxi associations lose their shit.'

'How sure are you it's him?' says Majola.

Radebe gets worked up. 'Red taxi. Siyaya. Dark windows. Jong girl. Not close to a roadblock. What more do you want? Even a copycat would be stupid to try something with this much heat out there. Dis hy, I'm sure.'

Majola doesn't reply.

'I want you to join Captain Tlokwe, go to Baragwanath to talk to the victim.

Threaten them with obstruction of justice. She gave a short statement yesterday, which Ramsamy has. Why is your nose bleeding?'

Majola touches his nose. There's blood on his finger. 'I've got a cold; it's probably from all the nose-blowing.'

A constable hands him a roll of toilet paper from a desk.

'Thank you,' Majola says, unspooling a length and dabbing at his nose.

Ramsamy whispers beside him. 'Everything okay?'

'Yes, I'm fine,' Majola says shortly.

A uniform talking on the phone suddenly jumps up and looks around for Radebe. He puts down the phone and comes walking over, all fired up.

'It's the traffic department. We have him. Jacob Sibewu. He has a commercial licence. The vehicle is registered in his own name. 17857 Modisa Street, Diepkloof.'

'A Xhosa who carves Zulu names into girls' backs?' Majola says under his breath, so Radebe can't hear him. Ramsamy shrugs.

'That's it!' Radebe says excitedly. 'Okay, gather round.' He indicates the map on the wall. 'Captains Louw and Baloyi, go to that address immediately. Take back-up, but keep them on standby. First recon the street and the house; chances are he won't be there. Try to find out if he's alone. If not, see if you can find whoever lives with him. Take him or her to Diepsloot Zone 1 police station. The more we know about the house and the suspect, the better. But be careful – we don't want him to get spooked. Captains Majola and Tlokwe, go speak to the victim. If this is our guy, we must take him down today. It won't help messing around on the taxi routes; things are tense enough as it is. Good work.'

Radebe starts clapping and the others follow suit.

Just as Majola and Tlokwe are about to go, Radebe calls him over.

'You don't look impressed,' says Radebe.

'I don't know. Something doesn't feel right, Colonel.'

'As jy wil quit, Captain, just say the word. I don't have time for your kak now.'

'It's not that, Colonel. Yesterday's girl was physically raped. Why start now?'

'Well, we'll go find out,' Radebe says. 'When you're done at the hospital, come back immediately. Or find out where I am.'

When Majola turns to go, Radebe says, 'O ja, by the way, the previous licence plates you gave me were incorrect. Davids gave me the correct ones: the last numbers had been swapped around. You wouldn't believe who they belong to. Or maybe you would.'

Majola doesn't answer. It feels like the walls are closing in.

'Your Captain, Daan Loots,' says Radebe. 'If that's not a coincidence, I don't know what is.' Radebe smiles, steps closer to Majola. 'What are you up to, Captain? Are you hiding something?'

'No, Colonel.'

'If we conduct the raid tonight, bring Loots along. I want to finish this case. Klaar. When we're done, he can see if we've missed something. Even if he doesn't find anything in the dockets, he might find something in the house. And that's an order. If you know what's good for you, you'll do as I say, niks meer terugpraat.'

'Yes, Colonel.'

Why the hell does Radebe want Kappie there? Does he want to embarrass him in front of the Hawks? Is that his revenge? He has the Hawks to help out – why bring along an old man? But he doesn't ask any of this. He's in enough shit as it is.

Radebe turns and goes back to the uniforms behind him.

Majola realises he isn't high enough to deal with the absurdity of the morning.

'You don't look convinced, Captain,' Tlokwe says. They're driving in the Hawks' white Golf GTI with red-and-yellow stripes along its sides. Tlokwe is wearing his big black jacket, HAWKS printed large on the back. They probably stole the idea from the FBI.

Tlokwe is a little older than he is, with a trimmed grey beard. He has an air of superiority, as do most of the Hawks when they're around ordinary detectives. Majola was relieved when Tlokwe offered to drive. He's tired of driving. At least he can try to get his thoughts in some kind of order.

'It's just too easy. The rape, the fact that he let her get away, the messages we got wrong. On the other hand, no one would be stupid enough to rape a girl when everyone's looking for a red taxi. He'd have to be blind to miss that one.'

Tlokwe looks at Majola. 'Colonel Radebe seems sure of his story.'

'Colonel Radebe wants an arrest, no matter what. I can see the tension taking its toll, the pressure from above. He can handle the media, but if the taxis go on strike and the people can't get to work, then he'll be in trouble. Then the brass will come down on him like a ton of bricks. But let's hope he's right. It would just be a bit of an anti-climax if he is.'

Tlokwe smiles. 'You're one who likes action, then? You want a climax?'

Majola smiles for the first time in what feels like days. 'Yes. That's why I'm in SVC and not with the Hawks.'

Tlokwe laughs.

It feels like an eternity before they stop at Chris Hani Baragwanath Hospital. The place is colossal, and surprisingly clean inside. They flash their police IDs at the ICU counter, and the nurse makes a call. Seconds later a woman arrives, introducing herself as Doctor Gomez.

'I told the police this morning that she's still too traumatised and weak to speak,' she says.

'We are not the police,' Tlokwe says, 'we are the Hawks. And it's an emergency. Unless you want to be on the first plane back to Cuba, please do not fuck with us.'

The doctor gasps, then frowns. 'Be quick. She won't be awake for long. I just gave her another dose of Fentanyl. And try not to upset her.' She turns and walks down the long passage, having instructed a nurse to take them to the girl.

'She's pretty,' Majola says to break the silence.

'She is. But not enough ass for my tastes.'

The ICU is cramped. The last line of cocaine is starting to wear off. The dejectedness clings to Majola like a tick drinking its fill. Everything smells sharper. Most of the patients are sleeping, and orange curtains are drawn around some of the beds. At the end of the ward lies Nomvelo Lesufi. She's on her back, staring at the ceiling, her eyes half closed. A drip runs into her right arm.

'Nomvelo?' Tlokwe asks softly.

Slowly she looks at the men.

'We're from the Hawks. I'm Captain Tlokwe and this is Captain Majola. We need to ask you a few questions. We won't be long. Is that okay with you?'

Tears start running down her cheeks, but she nods.

'Can you tell us what happened last night?'

'I was working,' she says in a faint voice, 'at Hamisi's Cash and Carry. We did stocktaking. The first taxi was full and drove past me. I got into another taxi at Mofokeng Street. There were three other people in the taxi, and they got out before me. They all struggled to open the sliding door.'

'And then?'

'Then I told him I wanted to get off at Letsatsi Street. I realised something wasn't right when he started driving in the wrong direction. I got scared. I'd read about the Zola Budd who's killing young girls.' Nomvelo starts to sob. 'It got dark around me; there weren't many street lights. I didn't know we were in Xtreme Park.'

'Take your time,' Tlokwe says gently.

The woman next to Nomvelo starts coughing loudly. Goddamn, I'm on edge, thinks Majola.

'I tried to open the door but I couldn't. He climbed over the front seat and held me down on the seat. Then he took out a knife and held it to my throat.'

'What did the knife look like? Was it a long knife? A scalpel? Like doctors use?'

'No, it looked like a bread knife.'

So it's not a scalpel, Majola thinks. First discrepancy.

'Go on,' Tlokwe urges her.

'Then he told me in Sotho that if I did as he said, he wouldn't hurt me. He told me to take off my clothes. I was so scared.'

He's Sotho, Majola thinks. Second discrepancy.

Nomvelo starts to shake. She takes a deep breath and goes on.

'I had my T-shirt on. He cut the bra off underneath it. Then he pulled down his pants … After a few seconds he stopped, pushed my legs together, and … went in the back. It hurt so much. He kept the knife against my throat the whole time.'

'And then?'

'Then I thought, if the other passengers could get out, so can I. I just have to pull harder. I grabbed his hand with the knife and kicked him between the legs. Then I pulled hard, twice, and the door opened. Then I ran.'

'You're very brave, Nomvelo. So he didn't tie you up? He just held you down against the seats?' Majola asks quietly.

'Yes.'

'I know this is a difficult question, but did he put anything inside you? An object?'

Nomvelo looks shocked. 'No. I don't think so.'

'What did the man look like?'

She thinks about it. 'Big. He was wearing black clothes.'

Majola makes the first tick on the list in his head. He feels rather light head-ed, but there's nowhere to sit.

'Was he wearing gloves?'

'No.'

'Did you see anything else in the taxi that was out of the ordinary? Like a battery? Or a power box?'

'No, I don't think so. Not that I can recall.'

'Did you notice anything strange about the seats? Clamps? Leather straps?'

'No, they were normal seats.'

Majola looks at Tlokwe, shakes his head.

'Do you think it was him? The Zola killer? Could he come back?'

'No, Nomvelo, he won't. We have his address,' Tlokwe says. 'We don't know if he's the taxi murderer, but the man who hurt you we're going to catch very soon.'

Nomvelo's crying has abated somewhat. Majola feels like crying himself.

'Thank you, Nomvelo.' Tlokwe says, turning to go. Majola nods and follows him.

'What do you think?' Tlokwe asks.

'Well, unless he decided to do everything differently, this is not our mur-derer. Maybe he's discovered Viagra since Sunday night.'

Tlokwe cracks a smile. 'Just don't tell that to Radebe, or he'll use it to pin the murders on Sibewu.'

'A lot has happened since this morning,' Majola tells Basson on his way to the Diepkloof Zone 1 police station. It's nearly five o'clock; he left later than the others. He didn't take Tlokwe up on the offer to ride shotgun again. He doesn't like the guy that much. Today he doesn't like anyone. He takes two big gulps of water and feels a bit better. The black-heartedness is at bay, thanks to the two lines he did in the Corolla in the station parking lot.

'They're grasping at straws. They may lock him up for the rape, but what will Radebe do when the real murderer kills again in a week?' Basson asks.

'Maybe he's just playing for time with the media, hoping to shut them up while we catch the right guy,' says Majola. 'But I can assure you, he'll make certain the guy from last night takes the blame. The pressure is too much. How's your hand doing? I forgot to ask yesterday.'

'It's better today,' Basson says.

'Will you go over those dossiers I gave you again? Maybe you'll find something else.'

'Cool, I'll keep you posted. I'm itching to see the show Radebe's circus puts on.'

Majola pulls into the station parking lot. Radebe's BMW and two Golfs are there too, as well as Ramsamy's Honda and what he suspects is Louw's Hilux. What else would he drive? It's funny the prick doesn't drive a Fortuner – that would actually suit him better.

Radebe wasn't interested in their suspicion that this wasn't the murderer. 'Minor details. That means fuck-all. Red taxi, rapist, black clothes. Do the maths. There could be logical explanations for all your objections,' he said.

And it obviously fuelled his fire when they found out Sibewu had two prior convictions of rape and assault.

A sergeant leads Majola to the interrogation room. The Diepkloof station with its fresh brickwork looks relatively new compared to Johannesburg Central.

The sergeant knocks surreptitiously on a wooden door before opening it. Inside is a long, narrow, dark room with a large two-way mirror stretching across one wall. Radebe, Tlokwe, Baloyi, Dr Muller and Ramsamy are watching an interrogation in progress. Radebe turns as they enter, sees Majola. So this is where the Hollywood interrogation room is, Majola thinks.

On the other side of the glass, Bok Louw is sitting with a young woman at a metal table in a brightly lit room. Her arms are crossed defensively. The station must be new. This is the first time Majola has seen an interrogation room with two-way mirrors. A scrunched-up, bloody tissue lies in front of the young woman. Her lip is swollen. Louw is rubbing his hand.

Radebe motions for Majola to leave the room with him.

'She's a tough one. We're struggling with her,' Radebe says.

'Is that why her mouth is bleeding?'

'She put up a moerse fight at the salon. They had to calm her down.'

Majola doesn't ask about Louw's hand.

'What's her story, Colonel?'

'Kathy Morake. She's been living with Sibewu for four months. The criminologist says he can see she's scared of him, and that's why she doesn't want to talk. He works most nights, weekends too. For Dorljota, actually. On Monday, he got home very late, ruik soos alcohol. He also worked Saturday night. He spent all of Sunday morning in the garage fixing up the taxi. The pieces are starting to fit together. According to her, he's home early on Tuesday nights. I already called Warrant Officer Blignaut: his response team is ready for tonight. We also have crime-scene people on standby. Everything has to go down smoothly. I'll organise a search warrant before five. You and Loots can be there at seven; we're expecting him at eight o'clock. Tonight we'll take this asshole down.'

'And the numbers? Did Louw ask her about the numbers on the girls' backs?'

'He did. They don't ring a bell.'

'Are you sure Daan Loots has to be—'

Majola is interrupted by the door opening. It's Ramsamy.

'You need to come hear this,' he says, smiling. It's clear that Ramsamy is enjoying the interrogation. They follow him through.

Kathy has started crying. She wipes her face with the bloody tissue.

'Yes, but different. Different from other men,' she answers.

'Bok's magic is starting to work,' Baloyi says. Majola rolls his eyes.

'How? Sexually? What does he do that's different?'

'He likes to dominate.'

'Does he hold you down? Does he choke you? What is it?'

'He ties me down, to the bed. He has stuff under the bed he ties the ropes to. Then he opens my legs and ties my hands above my head. There's a rope around my neck too; he pulls it tighter and lets it go. Sometimes I faint. When I wake up, he's busy having sex with me.'

Louw glances at the mirror, gives a knowing look.

'Has he ever … uh … pleasured you with other objects?'

'Yes. He struggles to get it up, so he does all this stuff beforehand. He gets hard when he hurts me. Then he crouches over me and masturbates. He comes in my face.'

'What does he use?'

Kathy starts to cry. 'Whatever he can find. A bottle. His fist. A broom. Why do you want to know this stuff?'

Kathy keeps crying.

'It's him. You have him, I'm sure,' Dr Muller says.

'Did he ever shock you with something, Kathy? A battery? Jumper cables?' Louw asks.

'What? No. He never did anything like that. What kind of a question is that?'

Bok gets up and leaves the interrogation room without looking at Kathy. He opens the door and joins them.

'A broom. That could explain the injuries to the victims,' he says.

'It could also be coincidence,' Majola replies. 'What about the electrocution? The marks on their breasts? The pathologist said they were from clamps.'

Louw raises his eyebrows. 'Oh, come on, Captain, do you still think it's not him? He was working during the last three murders. He's a sexual sadist. He can't get it up. The ropes under the bed could explain the bruising to the victims. He drives a red taxi. He has a record for past offences. That's enough for me.'

Dr Muller nods in agreement.

'They even have a dog in the yard.' Louw smiles triumphantly.

'A dog?' Majola asks.

'Yes, a dog. That explains the hair on the victim's eyeball from Westpark.'

Majola disagrees. 'The murderer is methodical; everything is carefully planned. You never see his face on the CCTV footage. But last night he spoke to the victim? He drives over people in a mall parking lot for getting in his way, and then lets a victim run away? It just doesn't add up.'

Tlokwe nods in support.

'Well, we'll have to work with what we've got. I'll see you at the Caltex in Makura Avenue at eight,' Radebe says.

'What do we do with her?' Louw asks, indicating Kathy.

'Keep her here for now, as long as he doesn't get suspicious if she's not home,' Radebe replies.

Majola sees Ramsamy looking at Kathy.

'Let's get out of here, Sergeant,' he says. 'It's going to be a long night.'

It's just gone six o'clock. Majola is tired, and the cocaine is nearly finished. He was deliberating whether to call Prince but decided against it. He was afraid of being late again. Maybe he'll call tonight, or tomorrow morning. He knows he has a problem. This time he'll have to get proper help. This time the alcohol isn't the trigger; he'll find any excuse to use again. Luckily there was some left in the last bankie, which will have to last the night. Lulu's dilemma keeps gnawing at the back of his mind.

Kappie leaves Lizanne's apartment, wearing a thick black coat and black trousers and carrying his bag. He's even combed his hair.

'Where are you going?' Majola asks when he arrives at the apartment.

'Well, I thought that when we're finished at Diepkloof, you can drop me off at my place. You know I don't take taxis. The street in front of Lizanne's complex is too busy. The cars go past all through the night; I can't sleep.'

Majola smiles and starts the car. 'Okay, you have a point. Are you excited about tonight? Your old friend Bok Louw will be there too.'

'God help us. As long as he doesn't shoot himself in the foot.' Kappie inhales loudly. 'I didn't want to come at first, young man. But if I can do anything to help wrap this thing up as quickly as possible, then I must. It's been eating at me. Radebe's request does bother me, though.'

'Hopefully everything will be over by tomorrow. It looks like Radebe has a lot of trust in you,' Majola says.

'I was surprised he asked, especially after I couldn't make anything of the dossiers.'

'You're sure you don't remember an Npete or Nbete?'

'Quite sure. I went over your new dossiers too. That last one from Benoni, the one that's missing, bothers me. The key to everything could be in there. This suspect … I'm not sure about this, young man.'

'I hear you,' says Majola. 'But you know how it goes. They're looking for someone guilty. And perhaps it's not bad if this sick bastard gets taken down too, whether he's the taxi murderer or not. He's guilty of rape. If you feel things are getting too heavy, you go wait in the car. Radebe said you'll come in when they search the house after the raid.'

'How are you feeling?' asks Kappie. 'Your eyes are darting around tonight. You look nervous. And you're talking very fast.'

'The last two weeks have been rough. It's starting to get to me. Let's hope everything ends tonight,' Majola says, nervously touching his nose.

Kappie sighs. 'Yes, let's hope.'

For a while all is silent in the car.

'Thank you for everything, young man. I mean it.'

Majola is caught off guard. He glances at Kappie. 'No worries.'

Two unmarked white 320 BMW 3-series are parked at the Caltex in Makura Avenue. Tlokwe approaches from the shop, holding four take-away coffees. His breath fogs in the night air. The other men wait in the BMWs. Majola pulls in behind them.

Two petrol attendants look suspiciously at the convoy of white cars.

'Well, okay then. Let's get this over and done with,' Kappie says, opening the door.

The doors of the other cars open.

'My goodness, Captain Loots! I never thought I'd see you again,' Louw says, shaking Kappie's hand. Kappie greets him awkwardly. Ramsamy follows with a handshake, then Tlokwe. Radebe takes his coffee from Baloyi without shaking Kappie's outstretched hand.

'Captain. Glad you can help us,' Radebe says.

Kappie lowers his hands and nods.

'How are things between you and Jesus?'

Someone coughs uncomfortably. Kappie frowns. 'We've sorted out our shit, Colonel.'

Baloyi looks at Majola. Then everyone bursts out laughing. Radebe too.

'Alright then. Let's get this party started.' Radebe nods at Ramsamy, who fetches the map from the BMW. He unfurls it on the bonnet and everyone gathers around. Radebe points out number 17857 Modisa Street on the map.

'The response team is waiting here, two doors down from his,' says Radebe. They're in a panel van, *Mama Moholi's Plumbing* written on the side.'

Baloyi snorts. 'The SAPS always have time to crack jokes, huh?'

Ramsamy laughs. Radebe gives him a stern look: 'Please act as if you're used to this kind of operation, Sergeant.'

'Sorry, Colonel,' Ramsamy says, embarrassed.

'If he arrives home, the unit will let us know. Then we'll go and wait here,' Radebe continues, pointing a finger at Thibogang Street. 'It won't help us to be there now; we don't want him to notice anything on his way home. We've got an ambulance ready in Morokwen Street, which runs parallel to Modisa, in case anything fucks up. The forensics team is here, at Bopanang Primary School. If the response team has him, we move in.'

'What about LCRC?' Majola asks.

'I want to do it myself. I want to make sure everything goes by the book. Fok LCRC,' Radebe replies tersely.

Majola looks at Tlokwe.

'Warrant Officer Blignaut will let us know when Sibewu gets home,' says Radebe. 'We'll wait for him to settle down, then move in. I want him alive. I don't want to hear a single shot fired.'

'Why don't we take him in the street?' Kappie asks.

'The houses are too close together. If there's a gun fight, we'll have a lot of collateral damage,' Radebe replies.

Majola glances at Kappie. Kappie shakes his head in disbelief.

'Dr Muller says it's likely that he keeps souvenirs from the girls. Clothes, bank cards, even pictures. We have to keep our eyes open when we go in. We have to treat the whole place like a crime scene,' Radebe continues.

'Where is Dr Muller?' Majola asks.

'He wasn't available tonight. He'll join us again tomorrow.' He pauses. 'Captain Loots, are you ready? I know you haven't been in a situation like this in years. But we need your eyes and ears.'

Kappie nods.

Majola checks his watch. 19:46. Radebe's phone beeps.

'He's just pulled up. Let's go. Captain Majola, you and Captain Loots come with us.'

Majola arms the Corolla's alarm. He gets into the BMW with Radebe and Ramsamy. Kappie sits beside him after taking his bag out of the Corolla. Majola smiles at his paranoia. Baloyi, Tlokwe and Louw are in the other BMW. The men are quiet as they drive, the tension tangible. Majola looks out over the homes to the dark patch of an old mine dump.

He wonders if Sibewu's neighbours know what he's up to. Everyone's probably watching TV over dinner, unaware of the six armed guys from the response team waiting outside their homes with their fingers on the triggers.

Two minutes later, Radebe turns into Thibogang Street. Baloyi pulls up behind him. Both turn off their cars and kill the lights.

'Now we wait,' says Ramsamy into the silence.

'You probably never thought you'd be chasing another serial killer, did you Captain?' Radebe asks, watching Kappie in the rear-view mirror.

'What makes you think he's a serial killer? From what I hear, it sounds like he's just a rapist.'

Radebe gives Majola a look. 'I know Captain Majola has his doubts. But you'll see. My gut feeling is never wrong.'

The tension between Kappie and Radebe hangs in the air. Clearly nothing has changed. Why did he want Kappie here tonight?

Majola surveys the houses along the street, none with more than two rooms, three at the most. All are surrounded by high wire fences. Almost all of them have corrugated-iron shacks in the yard, where other people live. He wonders what Sibewu's home looks like.

South Africans are touchy about land. Every time he drives through Houghton or Melrose and sees the palatial homes there, Majola feels his gall rising. That much space for two or three people! And here they are, packed in like sardines. When will the people decide they've had enough?

He wishes he could do another line; he had to leave the last of the coke in the Corolla. And Ramsamy already suspects something is up with him, surely. So does Kappie. Everyone saw his nose bleed earlier. Fuck, he's so paranoid. He has to get out of the car. He can't breathe—

Radebe's phone beeps.

'He's in his bedroom. It's time.'

The men get out of the car, as do the three in the other BMW. Carefully, they close the doors. A dog in one of the nearby yards starts barking.

Radebe opens his boot and hands everyone a packet of latex gloves. He looks at Kappie.

'I don't want everyone's prints everywhere.'

Kappie takes the packet and pulls on the gloves.

They follow Radebe to the street corner. About sixty metres ahead, they see the white panel van. Radebe motions for them to stop. It's unnaturally quiet. Even the dog has stopped barking.

The panel van's door opens and four black figures wielding R5 assault rifles get out, aiming at the house in question. From the van's front doors two more emerge. Even in the dim light, Majola can see how heavily padded they are. Six beams of light shining from the barrels of their rifles lead the way to the small gate. The figure in front opens it, and they disappear into the yard.

Everyone waits in quiet suspense on the street corner, alert to the slightest sound. A woman from the adjacent house peers out of her window. Majola makes eye contact and slowly shakes his head at her.

Then the front door of Sibewu's house is smashed in. Loud voices ring out. Majola is still looking at the woman in the window. Seconds tick by. Then they hear two shots. Another one. The woman in the window quickly closes the curtains.

'Fuck!' It's Radebe. 'Fuck, fuck, fuck! Come on!' He storms ahead. Kappie stares at Majola, his eyes wide.

At Sibewu's gate, Radebe orders them to wait. He approaches the front door. Majola can see the red taxi in the doorless garage.

'There she is,' says Louw, noticing the taxi. 'Zola.'

'How does Colonel Radebe know it's safe to go inside?' Tlokwe asks.

'I think he's so pissed off he doesn't care,' Baloyi replies.

'Shouldn't we wait for LCRC?' Majola asks.

Baloyi shrugs. 'It's his call.'

They can hear Radebe's voice coming from the house, then someone responding in a low voice, then Radebe again. A light goes on in the house, and another light. After a few seconds, Radebe comes out the front door, a member of the response team behind him.

Radebe's on his phone. 'Bring uniforms from Diepsloot Zone 1 to close off the street. Call in LCRC. And the body-retrieval van.'

The detectives enter the gate to join Radebe. He turns to a member of the response team. 'You're supposed to be trained for these kinds of operations. You don't shoot someone in the fucking head when they reach for their gun!' Radebe hisses.

The guy lowers his head. This must be Warrant Officer Blignaut.

'Sorry, Colonel.'

'Sorry? Fuck "sorry". This is not the last you'll hear from me.' He walks back to the door, then turns to the detectives.

'Tlokwe, you check the taxi. Majola will join you shortly; he's first coming with me. Baloyi and Louw, take the bedroom; Ramsamy, the bathroom; Loots, the kitchen. I'll take the back yard. Just don't fuck up the place before LCRC get here.'

Majola realises that everyone's ranks have disappeared in the glare of Radebe's rage.

'Colonel, Kappie is a civilian. Shouldn't we wait—'

'Do your fucking job, Majola.' Radebe turns and enters the house.

'As if it's our fault,' Baloyi says, when Radebe is out of earshot.

'Good work,' Louw says to Blignaut as they pass him.

'Fuck off,' Blignaut replies, his eyes still downcast, as three of the response-unit guys come out.

The house is small, without a hallway. To the right is the bathroom, left is the kitchen, and beyond that is a small lounge, sparsely furnished. At the end of the short passage is the bedroom. Two members from the response team are standing beside the bed. Sibewu is lying on his back, his chin on his bare chest, arms outstretched. The wall behind him is splattered with blood. Pieces of brain matter fleck the pillows. There's a hole where his left eye used to be, and another hole in his neck.

'Why are you standing around like that? Get the fuck out of here!' Radebe roars at the response team.

They get the hell out of there. Majola peers past Louw: on the green carpet next to the bed is a black pistol. Louw kneels down beside it.

'She was right – there are hooks under the bed, and nylon ropes too. The same as you found at the M1 murder. Other than that, it's just trash.' Louw crawls in further. Then he pulls out a bunch of magazines.

'*Broken Girls. s&m Maids.* Like Kathy said, he had strange tastes.'

Baloyi opens the only cupboard in the room. Nothing but clothes and shoes.

'See if there's anything else under the bed. The rest of you, let's go check the taxi,' Radebe says.

LCRC have arrived at the scene; three men in light-blue overalls are taking gear from their vehicle. Sibewu's curious neighbours have gathered across the street, where a few uniforms are already hanging the yellow tape. The whole street is rhythmically washed in the blue lights from the various emergency vehicles. The body-removal van isn't here yet. Tlokwe has flicked on the garage lights and yellow light spills out onto the driveway. Radebe and Majola go to stand in front of the taxi.

'Did you ever think this moment would come, Captain?'

Majola doesn't answer. The first thing he sees is that the windows aren't tinted, as Davids's informant had described. It is the right model, though. Toyota HiAce Siyaya.

'She looks even scarier than on the CCTV footage,' Radebe says, smiling smugly.

'I don't want to mess around too much before LCRC get here,' Tlokwe says. There's about a metre of space on either side of the taxi, and three more metres at the back. The garage is separated from the back yard by a metal gate. Four tyres are stacked in a pile next to a locked metal chest and a workbench. Various car parts and tools are scattered over the workbench.

'Get someone to break open that chest,' Radebe orders Tlokwe.

Majola looks into the right-hand side of the taxi. The front row of seats looks completely ordinary, as does the rest of the interior.

'Apparently we were wrong,' Majola remarks. 'The murders were committed in Sibewu's house. For all we know, Kathy Morake was also involved. That still doesn't explain the short intervals between the murders and where he left the victims, unless this taxi can hit speeds of up to 300 kilometres per hour.'

He checks the taxi from the rear.

'This taxi has reflecting strips. The tyres aren't whitewall. The rims are white. The side windows are tinted like the one in the CCTV footage, but that one didn't have a Dorljota sticker on the back.'

Radebe looks inside. 'Two of the tyres back there are whitewall. And how hard is it to stick up some reflecting strips?' he says, clearly irritated.

Majola looks at the front side window. 'And where's the dent we saw on the footage? Where would he have got a new mudguard so quickly?'

Radebe walks to the front, right up against Majola.

'Move.'

Majola steps aside.

Radebe braces his back against the wall and gives two hard kicks against the mudguard, denting it.

'There's your fucking dent! What more soek jy, huh? Kathy Morake told us he spent the whole of Sunday working on the taxi. You still don't believe me?' Radebe is breathing heavily.

Tlokwe, who has just appeared at the garage door, looks on with wide eyes. Majola shakes his head in disbelief.

Ramsamy hurries closer.

'Colonel. I've found something. In the kitchen.'

Radebe gives Majola a dirty look.

Kappie is in the front room. Beside him, a member of LCRC is holding up a black canvas bag. Carefully, he opens it. Inside is a scalpel, pair of scissors and a black police truncheon. The scalpel and scissors are flecked with a dark substance.

'Loots, you bastard. I knew we should have pulled you in.' Radebe's face brightens.

Kappie smiles. LCRC carefully carries the bag to their van.

'Where did you find it?' Majola asks.

'In the kitchen, under the sink. There were some planks between the pipes and the wall. It's not the first time I've seen something like this. I called the LCRC guys over to get it out.'

'See, Captain? You can't buy that kind of experience,' Radebe says, arrogance dripping from every syllable. 'Now we have him. Hey, jy daar!' Radebe calls to one of the LCRC members. 'I want you to wrap up here. Let the team get on with it. Take that bag to the biology unit in Pretoria immediately. I don't care if you have to work through the night – I want to know whose blood is on those implements. Also check for fingerprints, everything we might need. I want it as soon as possible, otherwise I'll let you guys explain to the minister why you're dragging your feet.'

Majola sighs. Now Radebe wants to tell LCRC how to do their job.

'Can I go home now?' Kappie asks wearily.

'Yes, you may, Captain. If we had a chopper here, I'd have flown you home. Captain Tlokwe will go drop you at Majola's car.'

'Thank you,' Kappie says and joins Majola as he walks to the gate.

'Congratulations, Captain,' Tlokwe says to Kappie.

'You're very quiet, young man,' Kappie says before they get into the BMW. 'It's too easy. And where's the fucking dog Louw kept going on about?'

The Corolla turns into Main Reef Road. According to the clock on the dashboard, it's after eleven. The roads are quiet; every now and then a private security vehicle cruises by.

Kappie breaks the silence, speaking for the first time since Tlokwe dropped them off. 'What's bothering you, David? Talk to me.'

'There's just too much that doesn't fit,' says Majola. 'The docket numbers. Even the taxi. And what did he use to electrocute them? Radebe is so bloody thick-skulled that he doesn't want to listen to reason.'

'All the pieces don't always fit perfectly,' Kappie says. 'You know that. But you can't deny that there's a lot of evidence that does line up. For all we know, Sibewu is the last dossier missing from Benoni. Maybe it was his father we had in the taxi.'

'You're grasping at grass, Kappie.'

'Straws. You're grasping at straws.' Kappie smiles.

'All we can do now is wait. Louw will press Sibewu's girlfriend for details again. They'll take the taxi to Johannesburg Central to do a proper forensic sweep. They'll turn the house upside down through the night. And then we'll wait for the DNA tests from Pretoria.'

Kappie rubs his head. 'Look, I'll work through the dossiers again tomorrow, if it will put your mind at ease. That's the problem with these high-profile cases: no one has the time to investigate everything properly. It's a PR nightmare. They'll frame people or screw them over just to get an arrest. Maybe the docket numbers will never even come to light. With Sibewu dead, it could go to the grave with him.'

'That's how it goes. Politics,' Majola sighs. 'Let's hope the docket numbers died with him.'

'Go think some more about your connections,' says Kappie. 'There must be someone in Pretoria who can help us with that last number, who can get you the required access. My gut tells me someone is trying to hide something.'

'I've thought about it before. No one there will risk it. You know how seriously the officers take that kind of thing.'

'Will you do me a favour?' asks Kappie. 'Will you take Symons Road and stop at the Brixton Tower? I want to see the lights.'

Majola pulls the Corolla into the tower's parking lot, keeping the car idling. Behind them a security vehicle stops in the street. Majola flashes his blue lights and they pull away again. Only then does he turn off the ignition, bringing quiet to the night. They gaze at the artificial galaxies on the horizon, with the Hillbrow Tower and Ponte City rising above the other buildings.

'Did I ever tell you I grew up in Brixton?'

Majola looks at Kappie. 'No, you didn't. Close to here?'

'Yes. About six blocks back, in Caroline Street. My father worked for the railways as a shunter. My mother cut hair in the city centre. On Sundays we'd go window-shopping. That was before my mother died. Can you imagine that? Window shopping in the city centre?' Kappie smiles.

'Every time, around eight o'clock, we'd go for ice cream in Fietas. Then we'd come and park here, and my father would always say, "Hulle noem haar die Goudstad, the City of Gold. She has a lot of stories, a lot of history, but it's not she who has the heart of gold – it's the people. They give her heart." The rest I can't remember.'

Majola can hear Kappie's breathing.

'I was thinking the other day,' Kappie continues, 'that it's you lot, the good ones who are left, who have to drive the disease from this heart. Otherwise she's heading for a heart attack. Otherwise our heart stops beating.'

Majola smiles.

'Let's go,' says the old man. 'I'm flipping freezing. I can't wait to sleep in my own bed again.'

'You think I'm one of the good ones, Kappie?'

'Yes, yes I do, young man.'

21

Majola is glad to see the lift at Johannesburg Central is working again. It's Wednesday morning, just past nine. Every newspaper has covered the taxi murderer, Jacob Sibewu, who was shot. The taxis are back on the road, the taxi ranks calm again. The press officers for Faraday and Dorljota are overjoyed. The joint funeral for Martie Bam and Johnny Ackerman is this afternoon. They're expecting a full church in Centurion. And they're expecting load shedding again tonight.

The world goes on.

He feels slightly light headed. Yesterday he threw the last of the cocaine out the window after dropping Kappie off. Maybe it was Kappie's words at the Brixton Tower that did it. Maybe it was the death of Sibewu last night.

It's certainly a load off his back. He's going to pull himself together. When the dust settles, he's booking himself into rehab. He's going to see Andy this afternoon, just to keep him motivated until he can see a doctor. After that he'll see Basson. He wasn't able to dodge the comedown, although today he's feeling more melancholy than depressed, which is a small step in the right direction. He'll just have to push through.

'I see you lot are famous. They had to stop the presses for the news. Maybe it's just the Gauteng edition,' Bok Louw says when he walks into the ops room.

He hands Majola the *Daily Sun*. On the cover is a picture of him and Radebe, standing beside the taxi in Sibewu's driveway. ZOLA IS DEAD!

'Now you can frame it and hang it up along with your UJ-Rapist headline.'

'It's not much, but it's better than that picture of you and the donkey that made the cover of *Landbouweekblad*,' Majola jokes.

Louw is not amused. Clearly, he's not someone who handles criticism well.

Majola regrets his juvenile response. 'I'm just teasing, Captain. You guys did the hard work.'

Louw's frown lifts instantly. 'It was your legwork; we just wrapped up.'

Majola nods. He's not in the mood to stand around trading compliments with Bok Louw.

The ops room is noisy, more upbeat than yesterday. Radebe is on his phone in a corner, snazzily dressed in a black suit and sky-blue shirt. He's barely taken the phone from his ear when it rings again. He walks towards the door.

'Minister! Good morning, sir,' he says for everyone to hear, beaming.

'We must have done something right if he personally called Radebe,' Baloyi says from the table.

Captain Tlokwe enters the room. He starts speaking to Majola, keeping his voice down.

'Louw spent the whole night with Kathy Morake. Even Dr Muller came in to help with the questioning. He says she's talking the truth. She knows nothing about other girls in their bedroom. She says Sibewu had his weird quirks, but he wasn't a murderer. They sprayed every possible surface in his bedroom and the garage with luminol and Bluestar, without finding anyone else's blood. Nothing in the steel chest in the garage. There were a few drops next to the bed, but just as everyone got excited, it tested as a match for Kathy Morake. The taxi is down here in the garage – I've just been there, and it's not looking much better. LCRC are working their asses off. There are hundreds of fingerprints from all the passengers – under the seats, on the windows, against the panelling. It's going to take them days.'

'And the evidence we sent to Pretoria?'

'The doctor called earlier. She'll get back to us this afternoon to tell us if the blood on the scalpel and truncheon comes from any of the victims. She found fingerprints on the scissors too, so we should get that back tomorrow after she's run it through the database. It takes time.'

'How the hell did Radebe pull this off? It usually takes weeks,' Majola says glumly.

'What's bothering you, Captain? What are you thinking?' Tlokwe asks.

Radebe has returned to the ops room, still on the phone.

'It doesn't make sense,' says Majola. 'The girls bled so much that there has to be something in the taxi. Even if he used OxiClean, the chances are slim that there wouldn't be any trace of it. And the last murder was Sunday morning. I just don't buy it.'

'You think the real murderer is still out there?'

'I don't want to say it too loudly, but yeah. Problem is, if we understood his last message in Melrose correctly, he's done. Or at least for now. I don't think he'll be able to stop forever.'

Baloyi gets up and turns the volume up on the TV. Majola notices Ramsamy for the first time, sees him nodding and smiling. A journalist from e.tv is conducting interviews with people on the street.

'I'm so glad they caught him. I knew it. All the crooks live in Diepsloot,' an old woman opines.

'Now I can feel safe sending my daughter in a taxi to school again. The police did good work,' says a man in blue overalls.

'Yesterday everyone treated us like we were covered in shit; today we're heroes,' a uniformed officer says, shaking his head and turning to the television.

The journalist talks to Sibewu's neighbour. Majola recognises her as the woman he saw standing at the window.

'I heard people yelling,' she says. 'Many nights. I never thought there were girls being killed in his house. I never knew I was living next door to a monster.'

But not everyone interviewed is so easily convinced.

'It's not him. The police are covering it up. He's way too clever to get killed,' a young black man says.

Tlokwe and Majola share a quick look.

'They must bring the taxi to the kasi so we can burn it. We must burn all the evil spirits inside it so that the girls can be set free,' says an elderly man without front teeth.

Radebe turns off the TV. All eyes are on him.

'Morning, everyone. I know most of us are extremely tired after last night. But it was worth it. We got him. We're still busy processing everything and should have all our results by the end of the day. And tomorrow we'll have the results from the murder weapons we found on the scene. I want to thank all of you: the Hawks, those of you from Pretoria, the Metro police.'

Everyone applauds. Radebe raises a hand. 'Take the rest of the day off. You all deserve a break,' he says, smiling. Another round of applause breaks out.

Majola claps along half-heartedly. There's a storm coming and it looks as if he and Tlokwe are the only ones who can see it. Majola is considering discussing the Benoni dossiers with him. He may just believe him.

'Captain Majola?' Radebe winks him over before he can leave.

'Colonel.'

'Dit lyk my you had a good night's sleep.'

'I did, Colonel.'

Radebe takes Majola gently by the arm, leads him to a corner.

'What were you doing at Benoni station on Friday night, for eight hours?'

'Colonel?' Majola's heart skips a beat.

'Jy't reg gehoor. Did you forget that police cars have tracking devices?'

Majola can't think of an answer.

'I asked around and I was told you spent the whole night in the archives. What were you looking for?'

'Research, Colonel. Previous cases where taxis were involved in murders.'

'Come on, Captain. I know you're dedicated, but give me a break. Wasn't Daan Loots working at Benoni during the riots?'

'I don't know, Colonel.'

Radebe smiles. 'I'll ask again. Are you hiding something from me, Captain?'

'No, Colonel.'

Radebe keeps his eyes fixed on Majola for a few seconds; Majola holds his gaze.

'That's good. Sien jou tomorrow. I'll let you know if we hear anything.'

Majola's legs feel like jelly as he walks to the lift.

It has to be after two, Majola thinks. The mall's parking lot is full of school kids and their parents going to shop at the Spar. He comes here often. He frequented the DVD store until it closed a few months ago. There's a public pool too, but he's never gone to see what it looks like.

Andy comes tearing into the Wild Bean Café, jersey hanging loosely over his bleached jeans and his sandals slap-slapping as he walks. He's unshaven and his hair hangs to his shoulders. The round spectacles scream Melville artist. He smiles when he spots him.

'David! Good to see you, man.'

A computer programmer, Andy works from home. He doesn't know office hours.

'I haven't seen you at the meetings in a while,' Andy says, pulling out a chair. 'Has work been keeping you busy?'

'You don't understand – it's all I do.'

'Americano, please,' Andy tells the waiter. 'You must excuse me – I have to see a client at three. Work is quiet these days; I have to take what I can get.'

Majola nods. 'You probably saw I tried to call you.'

'I did, yes. Saturday. But then you didn't answer when I called back. Have you been using since Saturday? Or was it a once-off?' Andy talks like he's asking about the weather, as if it's the most natural thing in the world.

'I threw the last of it away last night.'

'How do you feel?'

'You know how I feel: like gnawing through my wrists.'

Andy smiles. 'That's the thing. She gives so little for such a short time, but she asks a lot. A few hours of pleasure for a few days of hell. That's why it's called a drug. What drove you to take a drink?'

'Nothing. I wasn't drinking. I was sober when I bought.'

Andy's eyebrows shoot up. Majola adds more milk to his coffee. Andy frowns.

'What made you decide that, David? To buy coke without the trigger?'

Majola sighs. 'I needed to stay awake. I needed to focus to help a friend. It was the only option. Or that's what I told myself.'

'And how did it feel?'

'Well ...' Majola looks at Andy. 'Great. So much better than when you have a few drinks in you. So much better, so much clearer. Your thoughts are ordered. But the guilt is worse.'

'At least you feel guilty for doing it. I was going to suggest you go back on the medication for the drinking, but it's a different story if you're using sober. Are you still jogging?'

'No, I haven't in a while.'

Majola shakes his head when Andy doesn't respond. 'Almost 250 days. But goddammit, Andy, these past two weeks ... I just couldn't.'

Andy smiles. 'You know, I avoid watching movies where they take drugs. I google the movies before I watch them. It just makes me crave it again. This fight never stops. The fact that you know enough to feel guilty is good news. The fact that your inhibitions weren't down when you bought, not so good.'

Andy reaches into his back pocket and takes out a slip of paper. 'Here's the number for someone who started a film club in Melville. They get together twice a week, then they watch a movie and hold a discussion afterwards. She's a great chick, Debbie, and she's also a recovering addict. I told her you might be joining them.'

Majola takes the slip of paper, puts it in his jacket pocket.

'Thanks. I think I need to go to rehab for a week or so,' he says.

'If you think it's necessary, then do it. I want you to come to the meeting on Sunday anyway.'

Majola nods quietly.

'David, don't be so hard on yourself. You had a good clean stretch. Many people I know last a week before going back to square one. Go back to your old routine. Run. Eat better. And join Debbie's club. You won't find me there – you film buffs are too nerdy for me.'

Majola smiles.

'And call me,' says Andy. 'Any time. Even in the middle of the night.'

'Thanks, Andy.'

Majola walks up the grassy incline to the Greenbriar apartment building. The wind is cold and the clouds seem to be assembling. The glass of Coke is cool in his hand.

Delia and Nonnie were glad to see him. Delia was looking a bit run down, probably because she had to help with the funeral. He's glad to be on a better footing with Basson. The remark from the other day still rankles, though.

'Is that a bag of charcoal I see?' Majola asks when he joins Basson.

'Sadly, yes. The wood at the garage was shit, and I didn't feel like driving all the way to Tyrone's.'

Basson is wearing a thick red jacket over his tracksuit pants. His black beanie makes him look like a fisherman. A cigarette hangs from his lips and he's got a drink in his hand. Majola stands beside him to stare into the glowing embers.

'I decided I might as well braai,' says Basson. 'Sounds like tonight there'll be more load shedding. And Delia has her hands full with the funeral.'

'Yeah, she mentioned.'

'So, you think you got him?' Basson asks, raising his hands to the heat.

'You know what I think. It's all well and good to make Sibewu the scapegoat, but what's going to happen when the real murderer kills again? Because then I won't have a choice – I'll have to implicate Kappie. I'll have to explain every-thing. It bothers me. There are things that fit, but more that don't.'

Majola pushes his hands deep into his pockets. 'You know, the taxi looked so ordinary, like any other that would stop beside you at a traffic light. I thought I would feel something, something weird, when I saw it, that it would be like something from a horror movie.'

Basson chuckles. 'Like from *Christine* by Stephen King?'

'Exactly. There are so many stories about the thing.' Majola sighs, gazing out over the beautiful gardens around the complex. 'Are you putting your apart-ment on the market?'

Basson raises his brandy and Coke then pokes around in the coals. Sparks shoot up and get carried off by the wind. 'I am. No reason to keep it, although it's not really a seller's market right now. Are you interested in buying?'

Majola smiles, shakes his head. He sits on the bench beside the fire.

'What's bothering you, David? Is there more to this case?'

Majola takes a deep breath. 'It's Lulu. She got mixed up with drugs in Alex. Now she owes Mpete money. He wants it by Saturday or the worst will happen to her and my mother. I don't know what to do.'

Basson looks at him. 'Mpete?'

'Yes.'

Majola gets up again to stand near the heat.

'I can't borrow any more. I reached my limit with the bank. And I can't get to the money in my pension fund fast enough; the admin takes a while.'

'How much are we talking here?' Basson asks after a moment.

'R17 000.'

Basson makes no reply, then takes another sip.

'I blame myself. I should have kept an eye on—'

'I'll transfer the money tomorrow. Just send me your banking details,' Bas-son says.

'Seriously?' Majola can't believe his ears.

'Yes. No worries. Pay me back when you can. It's money we saved up, but we're only going to need it later, when we go to PE.'

'No, Jason, I can't. It's your savi—'

'I don't want to hear it. Just take it, okay? You're going to pay me back, right?'

'Jeez, Jason, you don't understand how much I appreciate this. Thank you.'

'No worries,' Basson says again.

'You know, we've known each other for more than two years. I don't have a lot of friends. To be honest, I don't really have any fucking friends, only a couple of drinking buddies. You're the closest thing I've got. I'll gladly help.'

Majola smiles. 'Even if I'm a … black?'

Basson shakes his head, ashamed. 'Fuck, I still feel bad about that. Real bad.'

Delia comes walking over with Nonnie on her hip, wrapped in a blanket. In her other hand is a dish of meat.

'You men have to be pretty stupid to be out here in the cold. How are we doing?'

'We're just about ready to braai, Mamma.'

Delia sticks out her tongue. 'Don't you "Mamma" me.'

'How do you like your steak, Captain Majola?' Basson asks, taking the meat from Delia.

'Cooked, please. And please don't mention the word "parrilla" at any point.'

Basson and Majola laugh. Delia looks at them quizzically, then she laughs with them.

Majola feels guilty. He feels guilty because it looks as if things are going to work out. The case. Lulu. Him and Basson. He feels guilty because he couldn't stay clean.

He puts the Tupperware of leftover steak that Delia gave him on the kitchen counter. The lines from the other night still mark the countertop. He quickly wipes them away with a wet cloth. Then he wipes the little blackboard. Day one.

He smiles to himself. Back to square one. But he's hopeful. His phone rings. Tonight he'll change this creepy goddamn ringtone, he tells himself. It's Ramsamy.

'They have him,' Ramsamy says without greeting him. 'The DNA belongs to Mariamo Mokweng, the girl from Melrose on Monday. Her parents came to identify her this morning. There are also traces of blood from Ayanda Mcayi from Westpark on the scalpel and the baton. It's over, Captain.'

Majola almost feels like crying but holds back. 'Fingerprints?'

'They're still waiting. But the chances are slim, seeing as he wore latex gloves on the CCTV footage.'

'Thank you, Sergeant.'

'Captain, now that Basson and Mbatho aren't on the team any more, who's going to be working with you?'

Majola smiles. 'We can talk about it.'

'Thank you, Captain. Sleep well, Captain.'

Majola sits down. It's like a monstrous weight has been lifted off his shoulders.

'That's it,' he says out loud. 'Yaphela indaba. Not with a bang but with a whimper.'

He walks to the bedroom, gets out his trainers and places them next to the bed. Then he calls Kappie and Basson to tell them the news.

22

Majola feels good. He ran for three kilometres this morning. His lungs burnt every step of the way, partly because of the cold. The first kilometre was hell, but after he found his rhythm he started to get back into the swing of it. After a piping-hot bath to relax his muscles, he put on his best suit, the tailored black one, with a new white shirt and a black tie.

He had breakfast at the Wild Bean Café in Melville. Then he pulled out the dossier about the murder of the old couple in Mayfair and questioned their son. Now he's in the Corolla, with two samoosas for lunch.

He takes out his phone, which he always has on silent during interrogations. He wants to check whether the bank has released the money that Basson transferred. Five missed calls an hour ago. One from Kappie, four from Ramsamy. Two messages. He reads the first, from Kappie.

Fuck David. Look under my mattress for letter It's @

The message cuts off there.

Majola can feel the anxiety mounting. He reads the second message. It's from Lizanne.

Hi David. I'm on my way to my dad. He sounds upset. Let me know if you can come.

Majola calls Kappie's number but there's no answer. He calls Lizanne but her phone just rings and rings. What could have happened to Kappie? Is he confused again today? Was the action the other night too much for the old man? Majola tries to suppress the feeling creeping down his spine. Then his phone rings. Ramsamy.

'Captain, where are you? It's Daan Loots. The fingerprint results came back. Daan's fingerprints are on the scalpel and the baton. The police are at his place now. I'll meet you there.'

Majola drops the phone. Everything around him goes dark. It feels as if worms are wriggling around in his skull, prising loose questions. Perhaps Loots's fingerprints got on the scalpel when he found it in Sibewu's house? But he had gloves on, like the rest of them. This has to be a misunderstanding. Besides, why would someone with so many years of experience leave his fingerprints on the murder weapons? And be the one to bring them to the police's attention? This must all be a big mistake.

Majola tosses the bag of samoosas onto the passenger seat and turns the ignition. An oncoming truck has to slam on its brakes when he comes tearing out of the parking lot, tyres squealing. He turns on the sirens and emergency lights. At the intersection, all cars stop to let him through. He fumbles for his phone beneath the seat, then calls Kappie again. Still nothing.

Then he calls Lizanne. No answer.

'Just answer! Fuck!'

He comes to a screaming halt in front of the retirement home in Westdene. Four police cars and a white Golf GTI are already there. The boom at the front gate is open, and there's no sign of the security guard. He parks the Corolla at an angle behind one of the police bakkies.

Leaving the car door open, Majola runs to Kappie's apartment. Lizanne's Conquest is parked outside. An old man and three uniforms are gathered around a body covered by a sheet, two dirty slippers sticking out the end.

'God. He shot the old womn,' Majola says.

An officer lets him into Kappie's apartment. Majola is out of breath and feeling faint.

'Where is he? Where's Loots?'

Two officers look at him in surprise. The apartment has been turned upside down, clothes and documents strewn everywhere. Captain Tlokwe, standing before the single bed, barely looks around when he hears Majola enter. 'Fuck. Can you believe it?' he says. 'Captain, you'd better see this.'

Slowly, Majola steps closer. On the bed is the box that was at the top of Kappie's cupboard. The one that was empty when he last checked it.

Basson turns on the Mazda's alarm after locking his pistol in the boot. Maybe it's time to start using internet banking. Everyone does these days. To stand around and queue like an idiot isn't much fun, plus he's taking chances leaving his gun in the car. He smiles at the irony: the money he made from selling the drugs is now being spent to save a friend who owes drug money.

He's about to enter the bank in Melville when his phone rings. It's Nigel October. Basson looks around him, then takes the call.

'Brother. You've got the wrong cat,' October says.

'What are you talking about?'

'That taxi sicko. You've got the wrong dude.'

'I'm listening.'

'He's parked in an alley in Melrose Street in Marshalltown. Cherry red, tinted windows, no bumper.'

'Don't talk shi—'

'And a whitey's driving it. An old guy.'

'How the fuck do you know this?'

'I don't rat on my connections, my brother.'

Basson ends the call, nearly knocks over the security guard as he runs back to his car. He tosses the phone onto the passenger seat.

'I knew it. Loots, you mother-fucker.' He slams the car into reverse and guns it.

Move your ass, my man, he thinks as he roars down Empire Road.

'There are four green ID books in here, a black hoodie, balaclava, and two un-opened packets of latex gloves. Could you have guessed? Did you ever suspect it was him?'

Majola doesn't answer. Realisation hasn't sunk in yet.

'There's fresh blood at the back door. Looks like there was a struggle. Maybe the neighbour?' Tlokwe asks.

'It's his daughter. She sent me a message when she was on her way here. We need to find her,' Majola says, heading to the back door.

The wooden door isn't locked. He walks down the narrow strip between the wire fence and the apartments, makes his way to the service entrance. The lock is open. Blood has splattered the paving. He turns around and jogs back.

'They went out this way. How could I have been so blind?' he says to Tlokwe, who's standing at the back door. 'They can't have gone far.'

Majola suddenly remembers Kappie's text message. He goes back into the apartment and flips the mattress off the bed. The box of evidence falls to the floor. Nothing.

'Fuck.' Majola turns around, searching. Then he pulls one of the uniforms closer. 'Alert everyone. The taxi is out there. He can't be far. They got the wrong murderer. And he has his daughter with him.'

The sergeant looks confused. 'Everyone?'

'Yes, fuck, everyone: Colonel Radebe, head office, Metro, the aerial units, fucking everybody!'

The sergeant is startled, but runs for the police bakkie.

'Did you suspect something? About Loots?' Tlokwe asks.

Majola is struggling to stand still. 'Yes … no … I don't know.' Majola crouches down, tries to order his thoughts. Now he has to help. Lizanne's life depends on it.

'How could I have been so stupid?'

Basson is cutting through the streets of downtown Johannesburg, wishing he had a police car. He slows down at the intersections, then jumps them. Every-where drivers are hooting at him, giving him the finger.

He checks his watch. It's been fifteen minutes since October called him; he hauled ass to get here this fast. The bus lanes have helped. He shoots to the right, past a parked bus, and narrowly avoids colliding with a Volkswagen Polo. Both their side mirrors are smashed off. The Polo comes to a stop. A man on the pavement yells at him with flailing arms. There goes my insurance premium, Basson thinks. Ahead, he can see the sign for Melrose Street. He slows down.

What if October was lying? But how would he know about Loots? There's no reason he could have known the old man. Basson's palms are sweaty. He can feel his heart thundering in his chest.

The taxi is parked between two warehouses about twenty metres from the entrance of the alley, beside two large skips. It's pointing away from him. There's a wall at the far end, so he'll have to reverse if he wants to leave.

Basson looks ahead, reluctant to draw attention to himself. He parks the Mazda about thirty metres from the alley and kills the engine. Here it is. This is what he's been waiting for. Breathe. Think before going in there. He looks at his phone.

'The only thing that makes sense to me is that he planted the scalpel and the truncheon. When he was in Sibewu's kitchen. I remember thinking his coat looked a bit too big for him. That's how I thought he got his fingerprints on them, but we were all wearing gloves.' Tlokwe is trying to piece everything together.

Majola shakes his head. 'I don't know. I don't understand,' he says faintly. 'He wouldn't be that stupid.' Then he remembers the bag Kappie took out of the Corolla.

They're standing beside Majola's police car. The coroner's van arrived mere minutes ago. Kappie's neighbour is being lifted onto a gurney. On the lawn, pigeons are having a ball in the bird-bath.

His phone rings. It's Basson. Majola considers not answering. He's trying to make sense of things, to figure out where Kappie would have taken Lizanne. The Brixton Tower? Maybe the East Rand? To where the bloodshed started. Why Lizanne? Why take her? What does she have to do with anything?

He takes the call. Basson starts talking immediately.

'He's in Melrose Street, in Marshalltown. Loots. I was right all along. Red taxi, with a crazy old man driving it. I'm going in.'

Majola's heart misses a beat. 'Lizanne is with him, Jason. Wait for us to get there. We're on our way. Don't do anything stupid. Calm down. Just a few minutes, then we'll be there.'

'By the time you get here, he'll be gone.'

'Wait, Jason, please! Just give me a few minutes,' Majola pleads.

'Bye, David.'

The call ends.

Majola yanks open the car door.

'Now what?' Tlokwe asks.

'He's in the city, in Melrose Street. In an alley.'

'Who?'

'The fucking taxi. Loots.'

Majola drops the keys when he tries to start the car.

'Come, I'll drive. The Golf will get us there faster. Then you can radio in, request all units,' Tlokwe says, running to the Golf GTI.

'Get everyone to Melrose Street. Put roadblocks on Mooi, Albert and Durban streets. Make sure he has nowhere to go,' Majola yells at one of the officers before getting into the car.

Basson opens the boot and takes out his father's z88. For a moment he sees Wikus back at the restaurant. He regrets not having a bullet-proof vest right now.

He takes off his windbreaker and rolls up his sleeves. He tosses the holster back into the boot before closing it gently and turning his phone to silent mode.

Hugging the wall, he makes his way to the mouth of the alley. The street is uncommonly quiet. Further down, some workmen are unloading boxes from a truck. There's no one close by.

Ten metres.

He releases the safety catch. Wipes his hand on his trousers. If Loots comes driving out, he's going to empty the magazine into the taxi.

Five metres.

He wonders how far away Majola is. His hands are shaking a bit.

An engine starts. He picks up his pace, sticks his head around the corner, then slips into the alley.

There it is. Zola fucking Budd. The myth. The ghost story.

He can barely see through the blacked-out rear window. Smoke gusts from the exhaust.

Now Basson regrets coming alone. For a moment, he considers turning back, but he realises it's too late. He's come too far already; he has to see this through.

He walks slowly, his back to the wall, his gun aimed at the taxi's rear window. Shit, he'll be visible in the side mirrors. The alley is so quiet that all he can hear is the low rumble of the engine and the sound of his own footsteps.

He considers his options, and decides to smash the passenger window with his pistol.

Four metres from the taxi. Still no movement. Does the bastard know he's here? What's he waiting for? Is he actually in the taxi?

He's next to the taxi now. He tries to see inside but it's too dark. A car rushes past the mouth of the alley; Basson doesn't turn to look.

Got to stay calm.

There's a sudden noise from the taxi, a mumbling, as if from someone whose mouth has been gagged. Basson sees the passenger door isn't closed properly.

He yanks it open in one quick motion, his gun pointing into and around the cabin, finger on the trigger. He checks the front seats, relaxes for a split second.

'What the—'

Shots are reverberating down the alley, the echoes ringing against the brick walls. Pigeons scatter from the rooftops and disappear into the blue winter sky.

He realises he's already on his back.

Tlokwe has to lean on the horn every now and then for cars who don't get out of the way in time. Majola is surprised by the car's power; he gets slammed back in his seat every time Tlokwe floors the accelerator and pushes the needle into the red.

Tlokwe knows what he's doing. He weaves nimbly from the bus lane to the right lane, into oncoming traffic and back. The blue lights reflect off the shop-fronts and windows as they race past.

'They're on their way, the helicopter too. I spoke to Ramsamy – he's calling Colonel Radebe. He's not getting away this time. Take a right here. We're near-ly there,' Majola says, returning his phone to his pocket.

The Golf drifts dangerously around a corner, sending a flock of pedestrians scattering out the way when it hits the kerb. Tlokwe wrests back control and speeds on.

'Now I know why everyone complains about the blue-light brigade!' says Majola.

'Oh, they're a bunch of amateurs,' Tlokwe says. 'I passed my advanced-driv-ing course twice, flying colours both times.'

'Why twice?'

'I killed a pedestrian after the first course. Had to retake the test.'

'Take a right up there. This is the street,' Majola says.

They see Basson's red Mazda 3 almost instantly.

'There's his car. The alley has to be close. Stop behind him.'

Tlokwe comes to a stop and kills the engine. They get out simultaneously, close the doors with care.

'Hold on – the jackets are in the boot. You can never be too careful,' Tlokwe says.

He pops the boot and lifts the bottom panel. Beside the bulletproof jackets lie a twelve-gauge Mossberg 500 shotgun and an R5 assault rifle.

'Take your pick,' Tlokwe says with a smile.

'I'm happy with the Z88, thank you,' Majola replies. Tlokwe takes the shot-gun and chambers a shell. Majola removes his black parka. Both pull on the Hawks jackets. Majola draws his Z88 and inspects it.

Tlokwe walks in front, his shotgun raised to the mouth of the alley. He raises his fist, motioning for Majola to wait while he checks around the corner.

'Shit … we're too late.' Tlokwe lowers the shotgun.

Majola walks around him and looks down the alley. There's a man lying on his back and nothing else.

'Jason!' He holsters the gun as he runs.

It doesn't look good. Basson's shirt is covered in blood, his face turned away. His pistol lies a few metres from him. Majola drops to his knees at Basson's side.

'Jason! Can you hear me? Jason!' Majola tries to find a pulse in his neck. There's barely a flutter.

'Jason? Basson? Can you hear me?'

Basson doesn't respond. His chest is pumping out a slow stream of blood. If he's lucky the bullet missed his heart. He'll need help fast.

'Four minutes. They're on their way,' says Tlokwe, putting his cellphone away.

'Do you know him?' Tlokwe asks.

'He's my partner. He's my friend,' Majola whispers. He sinks down, sits beside Basson and lifts his head onto his lap. He can hear the sirens approaching in the distance.

'He might make it but we'll have to be quick.' The female paramedic with the thick plait stands aside as the two men carefully load the gurney into the ambulance.

Majola looks at his bloody hands, his white shirt smeared with red.

'Why didn't the idiot wait? Stubborn asshole.' Majola sits with his back against the wall. Tlokwe comes to stand beside him. The ambulance pulls away, lights flashing, sirens wailing.

'Captain!' A Metro policeman comes running over. 'They have him. They're on his ass in Troye Street.'

Majola jumps to his feet and follows him.

'Keys?' Majola asks the officer. 'The keys to the Ranger!' The man hands him the keys and Majola gets behind the wheel of the 4×4.

Tlokwe jumps in the other side. 'What? My Golf's not good enough?' he asks.

Majola ignores him, throws the car into reverse and backs up, sending a dustbin flying. Then he spins the wheels forward.

'I take it back. Rather fuck up Metro's car,' Tlokwe says drily as he grips the handle above the door.

'If we go down Von Wielligh Street, we might just cut him off at Main. The traffic is heavy in Troye,' Majola says.

Tlokwe peers out the window, up at the sky.

'The chopper is here too. That taxi is going nowhere,' he says as the sound of the helicopter starts cutting through the air.

Majola dodges through traffic, sometimes jumping the kerb with two wheels. A man pushes a trolley full of recycled refuse in front of the Ranger; Majola sends the whole plastic mess soaring through the air.

'Yehlisa isantya! We don't want to kill anyone!'

Majola shifts gears. 'No, not again.' He grabs the two-way radio. 'All units, all units. Wait for the suspect to leave the city centre. He has a hostage with him. I repeat, do not engage.'

The Ranger's engine is keening so loudly that it sounds ready to lift off. Majola smashes three parking meters out of the ground; one breaks the windscreen and tumbles across the roof.

'Slow down! Fuck! You're going to kill us.'

In Main Street, the traffic is so heavy that they can't move. Majola considers passing via the pavement but there's scaffolding on both sides.

'There he is!' Tlokwe points.

A few cars ahead, just past the traffic light, they can see the taxi on a slight incline. Four cars behind it is one of the SAPS Audis.

Majola grabs the radio.

'I repeat. Just follow him, do not engage. We have to get him out of the city.'

The traffic pulls slowly forward. Something in the Ranger must have come loose, as it's dragging at the wheel while Majola accelerates. The taxi takes a right into Main. The Audi follows close behind.

'Well, at least he's not trying to make a run for it,' Tlokwe says.

Majola jumps the light and follows the taxi. The motorists around them bash their horns. Tlokwe checks his shotgun. Majola wipes the sweat from his forehead, sees in the mirror that he's smeared some of Basson's blood across his face. The taxi turns into Mooi Street, away from the city. Majola picks up the radio.

'All units, block him off at Wemmer Pan Road, just before the highway. There's a taxi rank to the right: force him in there.'

'Do you think that's a good idea?' Tlokwe asks. 'The helicopter won't be able to see anything from above the highway.'

'If we don't get him there, he'll get onto the M1. There shouldn't be many people at the taxi rank at this time of day.'

The Ranger is two cars behind the Audi. A BMW 320 from SAPS slowly pulls up behind Majola. The Audi switches on its lights. Another Ranger from Metro falls in behind the Audi.

'Now we've got him. There's nowhere to go.'

Majola can hear the blades of the helicopter. About six hundred metres ahead, the police have blocked the road. He keeps his eye on the taxi.

It slowly moves across the tarmac of the taxi rank, coming to a stop at one side of a raised section with a two-metre drop to the left. The Ranger and Audi pull in diagonally in front of the taxi; Majola drives in beside the Audi. The taxi is about twenty metres away. Two more vehicles join them. Officers jump out and take up positions behind their vehicles, and two officers with assault rifles take up firing positions across the car's roof. Everyone is waiting tensely for Majola's orders.

'What do you want to do?' Tlokwe asks.

'Our highest priority is his daughter,' says Majola.

He and Tlokwe get out. Tlokwe ducks behind the Ranger's bonnet with his Mossberg.

Majola can still hear the helicopter above the noise of the highway. The taxi looks strange in the daylight with its tinted windows.

'Let's see what you do now. Your move,' Majola says and takes the radio from the Ranger, setting it to microphone. He can feel his heart race.

'This is the police. You are surrounded. Come out with your hands in the air.'

Silence. Only the dull groaning of traffic above their heads.

Majola looks at Tlokwe, then back at the taxi. 'Daan Loots, this is the police. Come out with your hands in the air. There is nowhere to go.'

One of the officers glances nervously at Majola; another one shifts his position against the side of the car. Then the taxi comes to life.

'Turn off the engine! There is nowhere to go. Come out with your hands up. This is your last warning.'

Majola turns to the men to his left: 'Don't shoot. He has a hostage.'

Three of them nod.

A shot is fired from the taxi. Then another shot, which hits the Ranger's front tyre.

Silence.

Then lead fills the air as everyone opens fire.

'Don't shoot! Cease fire!' Majola yells futilely.

Tlokwe is looking at him, shaking his head as he lowers his shotgun. The taxi is being torn to shreds. Two tyres explode, all the windows are shattered. The sound of the assault rifles and pistols is deafening; the acoustics under the highway make it sound like a warzone.

Everything goes quiet.

Majola's ears are ringing.

He hears the traffic again, underscoring the sound of the wrecked taxi falling to pieces. Glass crashes to the ground, metal clangs.

Majola drops the radio. He walks slowly towards the taxi, drawing his gun. If there's anyone in the taxi, they're dead for sure. The other officers follow him, their weapons raised.

Through the holes in the side windows, Majola can see a figure slumped in a seat, head lolling forward.

He steps closer. He stops.

'Lizanne.' It's barely a whisper.

Majola holsters his gun and walks around the taxi to open the sliding door. Lizanne's head is on her chest. Her mouth is gagged with a piece of cloth. Blood is running from her nose and dribbling down her cheek.

There's a hole in the right side of her head. Her hospital uniform is drenched in blood.

Majola throws open the driver's door.

'You sick fuck. Your own daughter.'

Tlokwe comes to stand beside Majola.

Captain Daan Loots's jaw has been blown off; blood drips from the wound. His eyes are open, his hands in his lap. On the seat beside him lies a Parabellum pistol. He's wearing his blue police uniform.

'Bastard's wearing his step-outs,' Tlokwe remarks.

Majola slams the door and walks away. He pulls off the bulletproof vest and tosses it aside.

'Where are you going?' One of the officers picks up the jacket.

'Leave him,' Tlokwe says.

Majola and Captain Tlokwe are standing beside the Golf in front of Milpark Hospital in Parktown. Majola's still wearing his bloody shirt, his hands still shaking. He was wandering around aimlessly in Dennis Street when Tlokwe picked him up.

'Are you sure you don't want me to wait?' Tlokwe asks.

Majola shakes his head.

'No. I'll find my way. Tell Colonel Radebe I'll call him. Thanks for the lift.'

'Sharp. That Ranger wouldn't start. You fucked it up good and proper.' Majola stares at the doors of the emergency ward, barely hearing a word.

Today started so well. Now he has almost nothing left – perhaps not even his job. They'll have questions about Loots, his visits to Benoni, the licence plates, about Basson. They'll blame him for Lizanne's death, maybe Basson's too. If he'd spoken up sooner, maybe today's bloodbath could have been averted. And his mother and Lulu are going to …

Majola raises a hand in greeting as he drags his feet across the emergency ward to the operating theatres. He's been here before, to question people whose loved ones were fighting for their lives.

'David?'

At first, he doesn't realise he's already reached the waiting room. Delia gets up immediately and hugs him, and bursts into tears.

The comfort of Delia's warm embrace shatters Majola's defences, and he can no longer hold his own tears back. He doesn't care who sees him. They stand like that for minutes. Delia slowly pushes him away. Her makeup is smudged.

'The doctor says the bullet missed his heart, but it looks like it went through one of his lungs. They wouldn't say more. Now I'm praying.' Delia stiffens, her eyes on Majola's shirt.

'Is that … Jason's blood?'

Her hand goes to her mouth, and she starts crying again. She sits down.

'I'm sorry. You shouldn't have seen that.' Majola is uncomfortable; maybe he should go, he thinks.

Then Delia talks through her tears: 'What was he doing there? He said he was going to the bank this morning. The next thing I heard, someone had shot him. What was he doing?'

'I don't know. Someone tipped him off that Loots was there.'

'Daan Loots? That old captain of his?'

Majola can't believe he has to say this. 'Yes. He's the taxi murderer.'

'What? But how?'

Majola sits down next to her. 'I suspected it. Actually no, I didn't. I thought someone was framing him for the murders. I should have spoken to someone about it.'

'Did Jason know about this?' Delia asks. She wipes her eyes but she can't stop the tears flowing.

'I told him, yes. He went to question someone in Soweto for me. But I didn't know what he was doing this morning.'

'Where is Loots now?'

'Dead. His daughter too.'

Delia lowers her head into her hands. 'What a mess.'

'I'm so sorry.' Majola's voice shakes.

'I knew Jason was still busy with the investigation. I let him do his thing. I know I can't change him. I think he wanted to leave something behind, a legacy like his father's, that old bloody racist, but he didn't want to hear anything bad about him.'

'It was his dad, after all,' Majola replies, hoping to console her. Family is family. And Lulu … The thought makes Majola get up. 'I have to go.'

Delia looks up, her eyes radiating compassion.

'He made his own decisions, David. He's an adult.'

Majola nods. 'Let me know as soon as he's out.'

Delia waves without saying anything. She starts crying quietly.

'Curiosity kills the fucking cat, young man,' Majola says to himself as he walks down the hall.

Having fetched his car from the retirement home, Majola stops at Liquor City in Melville. He doesn't have much left in his account but there's enough for a bottle of Bell's.

At the apartment, he strips off the bloody shirt and tie and tosses them in the bin. He'll burn them. He washes his hands and arms over the sink until he's scrubbed the skin raw, but still he doesn't stop.

He turns on the heater and sits at the kitchen table in his vest and underpants. The room heats up and makes him sweat.

The TV is blaring from the living room. The first sip of whisky quenches his thirst; the tenth numbs his conscience. His phone rings.

'I've found someone to help with that number,' says Ramsamy. 'We went to police college in Pretoria together. He'll have access.'

Silence.

'Captain?'

'Yes, Ramsamy. How will that help?'

Ramsamy hesitates. 'I actually just wanted to hear how you are. Everyone's looking for you at the station. Even Colonel Radebe is concerned.'

'Radebe? Radebe is a dog, like all the mother-fuckers with their ranks and their magoshas on the side.'

'I can hear you've been drinking, Captain. You'll have to come in tomorrow. It's a mess. Everyone is running around like headless chickens. Now the people want justice for Sibewu's death.'

'Drinking? Udakiwe? This morning I was one day clean. Tonight, I am no longer.'

'Should I come fetch you tomorrow?' Ramsamy asks.

Majola tosses the phone onto the table; it slides over the far edge.

He smiles cynically at the thought of everyone suddenly concerned about his well-being. Everyone's looking for him.

The bottle is half empty. His pistol is on the table in front of him. The holster's on the kitchen floor.

With every sip, he dissolves more of his resistance to putting the gun in his mouth and pulling the trigger. He takes another long swig from the bottle.

He picks up the pistol and stares down the barrel. Is this how it feels? To realise you're not strong enough? A coward? Maybe Busiswe was wrong – maybe he is just like his father: someone who walks away from everything.

There's something that keeps bothering him. He has an urge to return to the scene where Kappie and Lizanne died. It's as if he's being pulled back there. Why, he doesn't know. There's no doubt that Kappie was guilty.

He puts the barrel in his mouth, tastes the gun oil. It's cold on his lips. He bites down on the barrel. His hand starts to shake. He moves his finger to the trigger. Lulu. He can't save her. Majola closes his eyes.

A loud knock on the door makes him jump.

He takes the gun from his mouth. 'Hamba la!'

Three more loud knocks. He looks at the gun in his hand, puts it down on the table. A tear runs down his cheek.

Wiping his face, Majola walks to the front door. He unlatches and opens it.

'I'll be waiting forever if I have to wait for you, baba,' Michael Mponyane says, holding out a bottle of Glenfiddich. He walks past Majola. 'Where's your shirt? Are you crazy?'

Mponyane goes to the kitchen. Majola is perplexed and panicky.

'Heat us up a plate; I've got some good stuff. Class A, baba.' Mponyane drops a black baggie onto the table. 'There's more where that came from.'

Majola looks at the gun. He can't believe what almost just happened here.

'Why is your gun here? Are you planning on shooting somebody? Come, baba, put that plate in the microwave. We're going to Greenside. You can pay me back later for the Glenfiddich.'

Too tired to argue, Majola surrenders to Mponyane's orders. He takes out two glasses and warms a plate in the microwave.

After the first line, he feels better. After the third one he puts on his denim jacket and coat and forgets about the world. Two hours later, around eleven, he's in Greenside, passed out in his own vomit in the back seat of Mponyane's Mini Cooper.

23

Majola wakes up. He's wearing only his underpants and his body is cold. For a few seconds he doesn't know where he is. Then he sees he's in his own bed, and the duvet and blanket are on the floor. He tries to remember where he was last night. Fragments of memory come back to him, bringing with them a piercing headache. He remembers the club in Greenside, the drugs in the bathroom stall, the nausea and Mponyane helping him outside. The Mini Cooper. And that's all.

He drags himself from the bed. He wants to throw up every time he moves his head. His stomach is turning and his nose is blocked, but that doesn't stop him smelling the vomit on himself. When he walks past the living room, he sees Mponyane and a blonde girl under a blanket on the couch. They're fast asleep, their clothes on the floor.

On the coffee table is a plate with a rolled-up hundred. Beside it, a folded black bankie. His gun is still in the kitchen, beside the bottle of Bell's. He rushes to the sink and vomits. Last night's poison splashes over the dirty cups and glasses. He slumps to the floor with his back against the cupboard. This is rock bottom for him. He can't go on like this. But sitting there, eyes closed, he begins to feel faint hope.

Today is the day; better not to wait until tomorrow. He'll have to bring Lulu and his mother to safety. He reaches out and takes his phone off the counter. It's already ten o'clock. Eleven missed calls: Delia, Radebe, Ramsamy and Tlokwe, and one from his mother. Four voice messages, two texts. The first is from Delia.

Jason is in ICU. *He's still critical. The doctor says we have to be patient. The operation went well.*

Majola feels like crying. He phones his mother but she doesn't answer. Lulu's phone is off. Then he remembers his mother works on Fridays, and Lulu must be at college. He gets up and grabs a chair. Stares at his gun. He's been given a second chance. If Mponyane hadn't come round last night, his brains would be splattered all over the kitchen floor right now. It's as if he was sent.

He gets up slowly, goes to the bathroom, opens the shower taps. Then he puts a finger down his throat and throws up in the toilet. After showering, he dresses in his black tracksuit and parka. He pockets the cocaine in the living room; Mponyane and the girl don't wake up. He shuts the door on his way out and walks to the Corolla. He can't shake the feeling. He has to go check.

'Where is Colonel Radebe?'

Everyone in the ops room stops what they're doing and looks up when Majola speaks.

'Where were you, Captain? The whole world is looking for you. We came to your apartment twice last night,' Baloyi says.

'I'll ask again: where is Radebe?'

Ramsamy and Baloyi exchange a look. 'He's downstairs, in the garage, with the taxi. Forensics is busy with it,' says Ramsamy.

Majola heads to the lift, Baloyi following him.

'You'd better come back here when you're done. You owe us an explanation, Captain. We know about the trip to Benoni, about the dockets you took, and about Loots's plates on the taxi. Your tickets to the shit show have been booked, Captain.'

Majola lifts his arms and presses his wrists together. His eyes bore into Baloyi's. 'Then arrest me.'

The lift door closes.

Radebe is standing beside the destroyed Toyota Siyaya, arms crossed. Large lights illuminate the taxi, which is surrounded by a collection of cars used in hijackings and robberies. The garage smells of oil and loss. Majola's eye catches a Range Rover with a baby seat in the back. He doesn't want to think about what happened there.

Sibewu's taxi is here too. But all the attention is on Kappie's murder-mobile. No one from forensics is working on it now; maybe they're taking lunch, Majola thinks as he approaches Radebe. Radebe turns to him sharply, then looks again at the taxi.

'You know, this thing is genius. Pull this lever, the seats fold up. Flick that switch, the clamps lock down. A modified Siyaya killing machine. Some of the guys have been taking selfies; others are too scared or superstitious to even come into the garage. The devil's taxi. It's ridiculous.'

Majola stands beside Radebe. 'It sounds like you admire him.'

Radebe smiles. 'Well, you must admit, a lot of effort has gone into this. How gaan dit met Basson?'

'He's in the ICU. He's going to pull through.'

'How did Basson know so much about the investigation?'

Majola shrugs. 'Beats me.'

Radebe turns to Majola. 'Captain, you'll have to start talking. This is obstruction of justice. We found the old dossiers in Loots's apartment – his old dossiers, from when he worked the riots. He did things back then that he's been doing again this past year. My question is, why did you go find the dossiers for him in Benoni? Did you think you could help him, or maybe that he was being framed? Or were you trying to help him hide the evidence?'

Majola snorts. 'Please. I'm not so sure it even was him. He was with his daughter the night Martie Bam died. He was at her apartment on Monday morning too, when the last victim was found.'

Radebe laughs. 'After yesterday? Nog steeds, you're not sure? Your scepticism is making a fool of you. He was completely off his rocket, Captain. And conveniently his daughter has now died too, without confirming his alibi.'

'Rocker. Off his rocker,' Majola says, taking a transparent bag from his pocket. He hands it to Radebe.

'These are two Parabellum shell casings. Did LCRC get the shells from Loots's pistol? The two he apparently used to fire two shots from the taxi, before we opened fire?'

Radebe shakes his head. 'No, nie wat ek weet nie. What's your point?'

Majola slowly walks up to the taxi. 'See, I went to the scene this morning. Something was bothering me, or maybe I was just fucking drunk. If Loots was in the front seat, and opened fire from behind the wheel, how did the casings get outside the taxi? Down by the wall?'

'You know the shells fly through the air, often several metres,' Radebe protests, exasperated.

'But through a closed window?' Majola walks around the taxi and opens the passenger door. He tries to wind up the window but it can't go up any further. Then he turns around and does the same to the driver's window. It too doesn't move.

He says to Radebe, 'The window was closed the whole time. We broke it when we opened fire, which came after the shots Loots supposedly fired. How did those two shell casings make their way outside the taxi, to the bottom of the wall? If he'd fired first, through the driver's window, the shells would have been on the floor, at his feet.'

Radebe smiles. 'One of the LCRC guys could have closed the window.'

'Why? There's not much window left to close.'

'What are you getting at, Captain?'

Majola takes in the taxi. The front seat is covered in blood. Glass shards are strewn everywhere. He shakes his head, as if trying to shake loose something that keeps eluding him.

'They weren't alone in that taxi. There was someone else, someone who fired those shots from outside the taxi. That's what's been bothering me. When the two shots were fired, I didn't hear glass breaking. I came from behind the taxi, from the ditch, where I found the shells. The bullets hit low, at the tyres of the Ranger. That person decided he wanted to go to that taxi rank, not us. It was part of his plan.'

'Why did no one see him? The bystanders? The chopper?' Radebe asks triumphantly.

'The bystanders left when we arrived, to get out of the way of a possible shoot-out. The highway was blocking the chopper's view, so they wouldn't have seen anything.'

'You're the one who's off your rocker. This case is over, Captain. Finished en klaar.'

'Yes, Colonel. A closed case is more important than the truth.'

'Careful now, Captain. Moenie forget who you're talking to.'

Majola walks to the exit. 'I'll have my report ready by Monday.'

'No, Captain, I want it done today.'

'Then I'll tell you what I told Baloyi: arrest me.'

Majola turns around. 'And another thing: where is the apparatus for electrocution? The crocodile clamps?'

Radebe gives him a surprised look as he departs.

Majola's phone rings before he reaches his car. The weather forecast was right: judging by the clouds, more rain is coming. He picks up immediately.

'Mama?'

'It's Lulu, David. She didn't come home last night.'

Majola holds the phone against his forehead and clenches his eyes tight. He's too late.

'Did Mama try to call her?'

'Her phone just rang. I thought she'd slept over at a friend's house.'

'And Christine?'

'She's not picking up either.'

Majola quickens his pace, unlocks the Corolla and opens the cubbyhole. He takes out a pen and notepad.

'Look up Christine's number for me on your phone, please.'

'Okay,' she says. Majola can hear how worried she is. 'It's 074 165 8283. What's going on? Where is she?'

Majola shakily takes down the number. 'I'm going to find out. I want Mama to go to Gladys. Call a taxi.' Majola shudders at the word.

'But it's so late, I can't go over now. Her children are there for the weekend too.'

'Please, Mama, just trust me.'

For a moment she doesn't say anything.

'Okay. Are you coming too?'

'Later. First, I have to find Lulu. Bye.'

Majola slams the door. He unzips his parka and takes out the cocaine he took this morning. He opens the baggie and uses his driver's licence to scoop up a corner of the powder. He snorts a large quantity. Then another equally large mound.

A policewoman in uniform walks past and stares at him with wide eyes.

'What? You've never seen a detective using coke before?' he asks with the card held aloft, powder on his nose.

She shakes her head in disbelief and walks on.

Majola types in Christine's number. 'Pick up!'

Christine rejects his call after a few rings.

He opens WhatsApp and starts typing.

Call me, Christine. Or tonight I'll throw you into the men's cell at the Alex station. Then we'll see how desirable you'll be tomorrow.

Majola sees the two ticks go blue. Then his phone rings.

'Where is Lulu? You have twenty seconds.'

'I'm not her mother – how should I know where she is? We're not even friends any more.'

'Is she at Mpete's?'

Silence.

'Christine, I am not playing around. You're going to start talking, or I'll come find you at your mother's house and tell her what you've been up to.'

'Yes.'

'Yes, what?'

'She's there. I heard that two men in a BMW picked her up at the taxi rank last night. I tried to call her but she's not picking up.'

Majola's blood runs cold. 'What's his number?'

'Whose number?'

'Sweet Jesus! Mpete. Who else?'

'I'll send it to you.'

'I'm waiting.'

Majola can hear her pressing buttons, then he hears the message come through.

'David? Please tell her she has to call me.'

'You stay away from Lulu. I'm not going to warn you again or they'll find your body in a ditch.'

Majola hangs up. His legs are numb. It's after 2 p.m. What will he say to Mpete? He'll have to try to remain calm, despite being as high as a kite and feeling as if he could tear Mpete to pieces. He doesn't have the money. He has maybe R1 000 left. Delia, maybe? He can't. Not with Basson possibly on his deathbed. There's no one else to ask.

A thought has been turning over in his head for a while, though it comes to mind when he's high. The confidence he's feeling helps him make the decision. It's his only option. He calls Mpete.

'Yes.'

'I told you I would have the money ready. What do you want with Lulu?'

Mpete laughs. 'Call it insurance – making sure you're a man of your word.'

'I'll see you tonight.'

'Good boy. I thought you were coming tomorrow. And, brother? You should have told me she's a virgin. Then I wouldn't have had my two dogs play with her last night.'

Majola feels something fundamental break inside him. He'd suspected something like this might happen but hadn't wanted to think about it.

'Brother, are you still there? Don't worry, I took her first. I was a gentleman. And she was on some of my good merchandise. I think she liked it too.'

Majola bites his fist and tries to stay calm. 'I'll see you later.'

Majola slams the phone down on the dashboard. He starts hitting himself against the side of the head.

'Stupid fuck! Stupid. Stupid.'

Light rain has begun falling. All he can hear are the drops on the roof and his own heartbeat. The grey mass of cloud has blotted out the rays of the sun.

Maybe this is Judgment Day. For him, at least.

The rain is coming down in sheets. And as he expected, there have already been two accidents on the way to Windsor East. Mogadishu – that's what everyone calls this part of Randburg.

He's thirsty again. His tongue is sticking to the roof of his mouth. He finished the whole gram of cocaine after the call with Mpete, in the car, in his apartment's garage. It gave him new courage. But no amount of cocaine can blot out the image of Lulu with those two sweaty Nigerians on top of her.

Mponyane was already gone when he got home. Majola's on the war path now. The streets of Alex will run red. The filth will be washed into the gutters along with the rats.

Through his drugged trance he can feel the grip of fear. He's just one man. But the cocaine helps him keep the fear at bay. The dopamine his brain is churning out is helping him to stay awake. It gives him courage. Makes him reckless.

If he could just get his head straight. But he's thinking about everything at once: Basson, the cinema from his childhood, Busiswe's body on top of him as they're having sex, the red taxi. Always the red taxi. Omnipresent, just like Jesus. As if it has taken up a permanent position in his brain.

He turns into Beatrice Street.

'You can rent, bossa,' John Madondo had said. 'It's cheaper. But if you lose it, you pay triple. You won't get much for R1 000. You'll owe me.'

Majola agreed, thanked him profusely.

He pulls the Corolla up in front of one of the red garage doors of Viscount Mews. Number 97, if he remembers correctly. He sends a message to John. He raises the hood of his parka and makes sure he has his z88. You can never be too careful.

The garage door swings open slowly; Majola can see a bulky figure through the wet windscreen. He opens the door and gets out, walks briskly over with a glance over his shoulder. The man, whom Majola does not know, is probably a head taller than him, and twice as broad.

'That way,' he says, pointing Majola to a security gate.

The garage is empty. The man follows and locks the gate behind them. The townhouse is dark, all the curtains drawn. John Madondo is sitting on a couch, still as fat as the last time Majola saw him. Beside him is a big bag of biltong. He knows the rolls at the back of his neck are still there, stacked up like brown hairless worms. Or turds, maybe? Focus, David, focus. Every few seconds, Madondo's hand makes an autonomous trip from the bag to his mouth.

Madondo motions for Majola to sit. He can smell the leather of the lounge suite, and old sweat. The giant behind Majola remains standing by the gate, his arms folded. Majola is nervous; his eyes flash across the room like they're mirrorballs.

'Do you have the money?' Madondo asks when he realises Majola isn't in the mood for conversation. Majola gets up and unzips his parka, reaches into an inside pocket. The giant sees the z88.

'Ho,' he says, drawing a 357 Magnum revolver and training it on Majola.

'Easy now,' Majola says. 'The money's in my inside pocket.' His heart is racing. Slowly he pulls out the money, holds it out to Madondo, who takes it with a stern expression. Then Madondo smiles and turns at the giant. 'Steady, Clinton. I've known the captain for many years.'

Madondo counts the money and nods at Clinton. The giant disappears up the stairs to the top floor.

'I don't have cocaine, but I have cat. I put four grams in the bag,' Madondo says.

Majola nods. He's past caring about the quality. He just has to get through the day, get this over with.

'This whole package is worth R5 000. So you owe me four K.'

Majola nods and rubs his nose. Clinton comes down the stairs with a Nike sports bag.

'I got you a Glock 17. Two clips with seventeen hollow-points.'

Clinton places the bag on the table.

'Your four grams are in the side pocket.'

Majola opens the bag and takes out a black pump-action shotgun.

'It's a Remington 870 tactical. I couldn't get you a Mossberg at such short notice. I removed the butt. It takes seven shells and it has a Hogue pistol grip, for those sweaty hands of yours,' Madondo jokes.

Majola tests the pump action, then looks down the three-inch chamber for dirt. The shotgun is practically brand new.

'Thirty shells in the bag. But I doubt you'll need that many.'

Majola smiles.

'Or will you? I need to know if I'll ever see my merchandise again.'

Majola returns the shotgun and inspects the Glock. The serial number has been filed off.

'I wonder how much trash this pistol has killed,' he says as he releases the magazine, checks it, and slams it back in. He cocks the gun three times in quick succession.

'I only know about its owner: his junkie of a wife came to sell it after he shot himself.'

Majola is suddenly filled with a deep unease. 'That's bad luck.'

'Not if you only have R1 000. Then it's a blessing.'

Majola puts the pistol back and closes the bag. He gets up.

'Thanks, John. I'll square this with you.'

Madondo nods. 'Don't go dying now. And bring it back by next week. And David?'

Majola turns around.

'Did you ever think, back at school when we went to watch those movies in Alex, that we would be here today?'

Majola can feel another part of his heart breaking. He just shakes his head.

Clinton unlocks the gate.

'Good luck,' Madondo says, putting more biltong in his mouth.

Majola walks out without another word.

People are on their way home, Majola notices from his apartment's balcony. People with prospects. Families ready to sit down to dinner, then go lie by the fire or the heater and read a book or watch a movie. Maybe they'll discuss the week's events.

Majola's shoes are getting wet from the rain. It's starting to drip from his hoodie. He's lost all faith in this city and the people who make up its heartbeat. The heartbeat took Kappie, Lizanne, Busi, Martie Bam and that rugby player, rhythmically pulverised them until there was nothing left. Just like it did to eleven young women.

But he'll cling to his thread of hope for all it's worth. He won't end up in the shit with all the others. From this thread, he'll climb his way back up, back to the heart. And he'll destroy every chamber. Bring the heart to a stop.

Majola drinks the last sip of Bell's from the bottle, then flings the bottle across the street. It shatters on the pavement. The motorists don't notice a thing. Typical – blind, deaf and dumb.

He goes inside and sits down on the couch. The bulletproof jacket is heavy and uncomfortable. He grabs the plate Mponyane used to cut lines off the table, sends it shattering against the wall.

'Stop acting like you're not coming back.'

He feels around in the Nike bag for the hole he made. It's big enough. He just has to make sure it's pointing in the right direction. He regrets not asking

Madondo for a holster for the Glock. Majola leans back on the couch, laces his hands behind his head and closes his eyes.

He runs through the steps. It's easier now that most of this morning's cocaine has lost its effect. Go in, save Lulu, get out. He's counting on there being five guys, same as last time: two at the entrance, three in Mpete's office. Hopefully the Sandton model isn't there. Everyone will be armed. Only five, hopefully no more. And please don't let one of Mpete's horny customers try to be a hero.

His prospects aren't very promising. But this is the only chance he has. If only he could come up with a plan to get into Mpete's office without the two guys at the door realising it. But that won't work – they'll ask to check his bag and will see the shotgun. Or search him and find that he's wearing a bulletproof vest. All he has to do is get through the gate, the first gate. Best-case scenario, he makes it out of there with Lulu and some broken bones. Worst-case scenario, they shoot him in the head and get rid of Lulu when they're done with her.

He picks up his phone and looks up Ramsamy's number. He starts typing.

If something happens to me, ask Basson. He knows what I'm doing. If something happens to Basson, you'll just have to figure it out for yourselves. I still don't believe it was Loots. If you go digging, you'll find it.

'The minister of police has said that IPID, the Independent Police Investigation Directorate, will begin their investigation of the Johannesburg Central police station on Monday. This will shed more light on the information that was leaked, the wrongful death of Jacob Sibewu and the procedures that led to the death of the murderer Daniël Loots and his daughter, Lizanne Loots. He asks members of the public to please be patient.'

Majola turns the radio off. He takes the Glock and the extra magazine from the cubbyhole and slips them into his right pocket. The parka's pockets are deep; hopefully no one will notice the bulge in the dark. In his left pocket he stashes nine extra shotgun shells.

Majola feels something under his nose, wipes at it with a finger. More blood. The cat he did minutes earlier burnt his nose. So be it, he thinks. The drug woke him up and all his nerves are firing at once. He can feel the cold from outside through the windows, his sweaty hands, the texture of the steering wheel beneath his fingers. He's ready for whatever comes his way.

He adjusts the rear-view mirror to look at himself. The parka's hood casts a shadow over his face, yet he can see the unshaven beard, the cracked lips, the dilated pupils.

'Yeah, you mother-fuckers. I said I would bring the plagues crashing down upon you. Well, here I am, David Majola, the Zulu plague.'

He smiles to himself. He picks up the bag, starts walking in the rain to Mpete's house.

The closer he gets to the house, the faster his heart races. And his stomach is burning. When was the last time he ate? He can't remember. He transfers the bag to his left hand. It's raining harder and the streets are abandoned. That's good. Stay in your homes, he thinks; you want no part in this.

The two heavies who guarded the door last week aren't there. He takes a deep breath, crosses the road and rings the bell. Where's the padlock the guy unlocked last time? Up and to his right, a small white camera points a green eye at him.

After a few seconds the gate opens. Majola enters the courtyard and stops. The two men are a few steps higher, near the front door. Majola immediately recognises the big one with the military overcoat. The other one is smaller, wearing a yellow raincoat.

The smaller one motions to the large one. 'Go search him.'

'In the rain? You're the one with the raincoat on. You go search him.'

The man hesitates, then walks down the stairs. 'Fucking desperate junkies, in this rain.'

'That's a big bag for such a small amount of money, baba.'

Majola can see the dark recess of the passage beyond the front door. The door isn't closed. Luck is on his side. Majola turns slightly to the side, plants his feet on the ground. He brings the bag to his chest, sticks his hand through the hole.

'The bag, baba. Open it.' The man puts his hand on the zip. He looks up into Majola's eyes, suddenly afraid.

The blow from the shotgun knocks the man off his feet; he lands splayed on the stairs with a gaping hole in his chest. The big man isn't fast enough, can't draw his gun in time. He realises this and changes tactics, diving into the passage. Majola pulls the shotgun from the bag and reloads as he runs for the stairs. He catches the man a few metres from the door at the end of the passage. Smashes the butt of the Remington into the back of his head. The man falls to his knees and raises his hands.

A semi-naked man comes out of one of the rooms, sees the shotgun with Majola behind it, and makes a beeline for the front door. Two more men and a woman follow suit. Where is Lulu? He can see more clearly now that some of the doors are open.

He presses the shotgun up against the man's back, takes the pistol from the guy's belt. Then he tosses it into the doorway after releasing the magazine.

'Get up. We're going to visit Calvin.'

The man gets to his feet and slowly walks to the end of the hall. Majola grabs the man's belt with his left hand; with the right he keeps the shotgun to the back of his head. Another woman screams behind him and run to the front door.

'Okay. Easy. That's your name right, Easy?'

'Yes.'

'You're going to unlock the door for me. And then we're going in together.'

'You're crazy. They'll shoot me!'

His words have barely been uttered when the door is yanked open by a man wielding an MP7 machine gun. For a moment the man hesitates when he sees Easy. Easy tries to duck for cover but Majola keeps him upright. The man starts to shoot. One bullet pushes Easy back – Majola can feel the bullet hit him in the vest. It must have passed straight through Easy. The second bullet hits nearly exactly the same spot and Majola feels the blow. Easy crumples to his knees; Majola dives for the wall.

The man follows Majola with his gun, but Majola is too quick and fires the shotgun. The man swears loudly, drops his gun and grabs his hand. He's lost three fingers. He stares aghast at the bloody stumps. Majola reloads and blows half of the guy's head off. He falls onto his back in the doorway.

Immediately, Majola gets up and sprints for Mpete's desk, looking neither left nor right. As he runs, he reloads the shotgun. Bullets graze past him and hit the wall. He hears a window break. One bullet knocks the gun from his hands with a dull *thwack*. Then he feels the sting in his shoulder. He dives over the desk and crashes into the wall, rolls back under the desk. He rolls into the foetal position to protect his whole body. Another volley of shots hits the desk. Majola covers his head with his hands, but the bullets don't penetrate.

Then it stops.

They're at the couches to his right. He could see them in the corner of his eye when he ran in.

'I knew I shouldn't have bought the imbuia. That fucking wood is as hard as rock,' Calvin Mpete says.

There's a silence. Mpete breaks it. 'Your shotgun is fucked, Lulu's brother. Or, should I say, Captain David Majola. You can come out. And if you have any more weapons, put them on the desk now. It's two against one.'

Majola doesn't respond.

'If you come out, we can talk. Like men. We can make a deal. If you don't come out, we'll kill you. Then turn your sister into a free-for-all until there's nothing left of her. Then I'll tie bricks to her feet and throw her in the Jukskei. What do you say?'

Majola throws back the hood of his parka. He pulls out the Glock. The weapon feels comfortable in his hand, like an old friend. He turns onto his back and listens. He can hear Mpete whispering something. There's nowhere to go. If he makes a run for it, they'll shoot him. His shoulder hurts but it doesn't feel too serious – the adrenaline is probably dulling the pain. He can still use the arm.

He turns his head slowly. At the front of the desk there's a small gap between the floor and the wood. He turns quietly onto his other side, holds the Glock in his left hand so he can see through the gap. Two feet are approaching, legs visible up to the knees. Majola inches back to move his arm into position; he clenches his jaw as his shoulder protests. His right hand is also throbbing, from the shot that hit the Remington. Satisfied with the angle of his gun, Majola pulls the trigger a few times in quick succession. In this small space, the shots are deafening. Only the first shot misses. He sees blood fountain from the man's calf, how he falls forward onto his knees, then down onto his face, dropping his shotgun. Majola takes aim and fires two more shots. The first hits the top of the man's head, the second lands just below it. A dark hole appears in his shaven scalp. He doesn't move.

Majola can see Mpete coming closer. He fires two more shots but misses his legs. Lightning fast, he turns on his back, raises the gun above the desk and takes blind aim at Mpete. He pulls the trigger. The slot on the Glock jumps open; he's out of bullets. He expects to see the barrel of a gun reach across the desk any second but it doesn't come. The room has gone completely silent.

He turns his body again, looks through the gap. He can see the black soles of two shoes on the carpet. Mpete's on his back. He got the fucker. He releases the magazine, gets the spare from his pocket, rams it home and chambers a round. He takes two deep breaths, then rolls out from under the desk.

He rises fast to his feet but a shot hits him in the chest. The steel plate of the vest knocks the breath out of him. His back hits the wall; his head hits the TV, which falls from its wall mounting. He drops hard to the floor.

For a moment he and Mpete look at each other. Then Mpete, covered in blood, drops his gun to the floor. His torso falls back. Majola wonders how many of the hollow-point bullets hit him. He breathes in deeply, gets painfully to his feet and walks over to Mpete.

Mpete's breathing is ragged and convulsive. Blood flows freely from wounds on his chest and stomach. He stares into Majola's eyes. His eyes are unfocused, glassy.

'Not bad, Lulu's brother. Now I remember where I know you from. That ...'

Majola shoots him between the eyes. Mpete's leg kicks once, and then he becomes lifeless.

He walks over to pick up the other guy's gun. At the desk, he fires two shots into the computer. The box blows apart. He destroys the hard drive with the butt of the shotgun.

After leaving the room, he enters the first doorway. No one there. He crosses the hall and kicks open the door opposite. Lulu is on the bed, wearing only a vest and panties.

'Lulu!'

Her response is sluggish. 'Calvin?'

'No, it's David. We have to go. We don't have much time.'

He helps her up, then squats beside the bed.

'Get on my back. I'll give you a piggyback, like when we were little. You remember?'

Lulu clambers slowly onto his back, wrapping her arms around his neck. Majola nearly collapses from the dead weight but pushes on, out of the room.

In the passage in front of him stands a little girl. Majola recognises her from the previous week. He stops to look at her. She's wearing only a filthy red T-shirt.

He holds out his hand. 'Come, sisi. It's over. Let's go.'

She looks up at him without reacting.

He walks past her and looks back. 'Are you coming? I'm with the police.'

'Isethembiso?' she asks, terrified.

'I promise. Cross my heart. Let's go home.'

Majola steps over the guy in the front doorway. His blood is running down the stairs in small rivulets, dispersing in the rain. The girl, frightened by the sight of the body, tiptoes fearfully past.

The gate is still open. Majola rushes down the street towards his car, the girl on his heels. Then his knees give in. He drops down hard, busting his knee on the tarmac. Lulu slips from his back. The girl stops.

'Lulu, you'll have to walk. I can't carry you further. Lulu!'

Majola slaps her across the face, startling the girl.

Lulu gets up slowly. Majola puts his good arm around her waist. The girl hooks in on the other side. His lungs are burning when he gets to the BMW. He fumbles for the keys in his pocket, unlocks it. He puts Lulu on the back seat, where she lies down immediately. He opens the passenger door for the girl.

'You sit in front.'

She obeys him instantly. Majola gets in, and just sits there for a moment. He's breathing too fast. His eyes want to close. He doesn't have an iota of energy left in him. He can feels himself drift off.

The girl tugs at his arm. 'Policeman, wake up.'

Majola wakes up. He takes the packet of cat from the cubbyhole, rips open the bag and throws the contents in his mouth. He drops the packet on the seat between his legs. His jacket is sprinkled with the powder, his lips and chin covered in white. Then he looks intensely at the girl.

'I told them the plague was coming for them. You remember, Busiswe? I told them!'

The girl shrinks away from Majola. 'My name is Lucy.'

He starts the car and tears off with tyres screaming.

'What's wrong with her, David? Where are her clothes?' Mama Thadie frowns. 'And why is she bleeding?'

Gladys watches, arms crossed, while Majola sits Lulu down on the couch. She hands him a blanket to throw over his sister. Lulu moans softly.

Gladys turns to the small figure at the front door. 'Who is this child, David?'

David and Mama Thadie look up in unison: there Lucy stands, drenched by the rain.

'Come in, child. What are you doing there?' Mama Thadie calls out.

Gladys fetches a towel from the bathroom. Mama Thadie takes Lucy's hand

and settles her in front of the heater. Majola, shivering from the cold, sits on the arm of the couch.

'Call the police,' he instructs his mother. 'Tell them the girl just showed up here. Her name's Lucy. Go put Lulu in bed. Don't tell the police about her. Let her take a bath tomorrow, then take her to the clinic. I'll explain later.'

'That's all you ever say! You'll explain later!' Mama Thadie is close to hysteria. Gladys sits beside Lucy and starts drying her hair with a towel.

Majola gets up slowly, groaning, his hand clasped to his chest. It feels like a vein in his right eye has burst. 'I have to go.'

He stops in front of Lucy. 'Sisi, please listen carefully. You mustn't tell the police about me. Tell them people started shooting and then you ran. You walked here because you were scared. Then you knocked on this door. Okay?'

'Okay, policeman,' Lucy says in a quivering voice. She stands up and throws her arms around him.

'Don't worry, sisi,' Majola says, pulling away from her grip.

'Where are you going, David? Talk to me!' Mama Thadie implores.

'Thank you, Gladys,' Majola says before heading out into the pouring rain. Gladys nods. Mama Thadie stands in the doorway as he drives away.

Majola wakes up with a start. He's hungry. His shoulder is throbbing. The pain in his chest is making it hard to breathe. But he's thankful to have woken up again. He's not sure why, yet; it hurts like hell when he moves. He struggles to focus, then realises he's on his living-room couch. He looks for his phone on the carpet beside him, but it's not there. His parka and the bulletproof vest are, though. He raises his head, squints through his left eye. His shirt is stained dark red.

'When Colonel Ramdiwa called me last night, I knew.'

Majola's heart skips several beats. Across the room from him sits someone in a dark suit. He tries to focus. It's Colonel Radebe. He's poured himself a whisky, has the drink balanced on his knee. He takes a sip. Wasn't his whisky finished?

'Colonel. What time is it? How did you get in?'

'Your front door was open. And it's almost five o'clock.'

'Five? But it's light outside.'

'Five p.m., Captain. It's Saturday.'

Majola sighs. Last night's events are starting to come back to him. The drive home, how he scratched his car on the guard-rail on the M1 en route, how he threw up from the pain in kitchen. He doesn't know how he got to the couch.

'You left your BMW unlocked too. And you forgot this on the back seat.' Radebe drops the illegal Glock on the table after sliding out the magazine.

'Will you listen to what I have to say?' Radebe asks.

'Yes, Colonel,' Majola says. He doesn't know what's going on, but he might as well listen. He's in such deep shit that a crane wouldn't be able to lift him out.

'They thought it was gang related. Five dead. The computer was shot to pieces, probably to destroy the CCTV footage. But that was actually run through the computer in the top room.'

Majola breathes deeply. This is the end.

'Then I checked the footage. And wie sien ek daar, smiling for the camera? My very own, vigilant Captain David Majola. Black cape and everything. Shotgun-blaster.'

Majola stares at the ceiling. 'I'll come in.'

Radebe takes another sip. 'Can I finish?'

Majola makes no reply.

'I've always watched out for you – you just don't know it. When you applied to the police college, you didn't pass the psych test. I changed that; ek het jou gehelp. I hadn't made colonel yet; I was a sergeant. But I knew people from the struggle. Your promotions to sergeant, warrant officer, I helped. I even put you in a team with Loots – hy was die best in the field. You were supposed to take over from me: I told you this.'

Majola slowly turns his head to Radebe. It's like he's dreaming. But he also knows the nightmare is coming. Radebe isn't done yet.

'But this has been going on longer than you know. Ek was daar the night you lay in Joburg Gen. I saw the cut to your throat. I also saw what they did to your girlfriend, to her face. Rapists. Animals.'

'I'm not sure I understand, Colonel. Why—'

'I used to live on the East Rand, with my wife Rose. My first wife. Then I moved to Alex. We only had one child, a son. She wanted more but I couldn't. Maybe I wasn't home enough; the force wanted its pound of flesh. The child, hy was anders, always in trouble. I beat him, talked nicely, nothing helped. After school I got him a job, but he was more interested in gangs. The Alex Kids.' Radebe smiles, empties his glass.

'After the incident at the Jukskei River, I wrote him off. I even changed my surname, out of shame. Pretended to be a fokken Zulu. Do you know how rough that was? I didn't want to be associated with him.'

'What incident?' Majola asks, sitting up despite the pain.

'Your incident, David. My son and his gang tried to kill you and raped your girlfriend. My son is Calvin Mpete.'

Majola feels the world around him turning. He collapses back onto the couch.

'Mpete raped Busiswe? Your son?'

'Yes. And now you've killed him. I guess that's justice.'

'I ... I ... don't believe it.'

Radebe gets up. 'He got what he deserved. It's just funny that one of his victims got him in the end. One from nearly twenty years ago. How het jy geweet?'

'I didn't. I went to get my sister. He was holding her ransom, for drug money. He also raped h—'

'I've heard enough,' Radebe says. 'He was still my son. We'll say this incident was gang related. I won't let the footage get out. No one cares about a dead drug dealer anyway. Ek is jammer, David. All those years ago, I tried to smother your case when I realised it was Calvin. I knew the case officers. It cost me a pretty penny.'

Majola is speechless. Radebe sees the broken plate with the white powder on the floor.

'Drugs don't make for good endings. Ever. But you probably know this. If you go on like this, you'll end up no better than Calvin.' Radebe buttons up his jacket.

'This is your get-out-of-jail-free card. If you can live with your conscience, so can I. The Zola case is a different matter. I can't cover for you there. You'll have to come in. The investigation has been handed over to IPID. Get that wound on your shoulder checked out, then you come in on Monday. And go see someone about the drugs.'

Radebe walks to the door. 'And clean up the kitchen – there's puke everywhere.'

Majola hears him close the door. All the years of wondering and hope have just manifested in an unexpected way. Just like that. In the strangest, most obscure manner possible. What were the odds that he'd shoot Busiswe's killer twenty years later while trying to rescue his sister?

He doesn't know what to feel. He doesn't feel happy. Should he feel guilty? Everything is confusing. What a fuck-up. He shakes his head in disbelief. Justice for Busiswe, finally.

Majola wants to laugh. He wants to cry. He wants to tell someone.

David Majola breaks down weeping.

24

It's Sunday morning. A new day. Majola is sitting at the service-station restaurant across the road from his apartment; he had a couple of rand left for a coffee. He's clean shaven and wearing his dark-blue tracksuit. After showering, he bound the wound on his shoulder; he'll probably need stitches. The four painkillers helped somewhat. His sternum is bruised from the shots to the vest, but that'll heal.

He feels oppressively gloomy from the comedown. It's survivable, though, just about. He threw away the remaining packets of cat. Madondo sounded angry about the Remington, but he's glad to have his Glock back. The apartment clean-up will have to wait for later. First, he has to go to Andy's AA meeting in Melville. After that he'll go to his mother and Lulu, maybe even stop at Busiswe's grave. He hasn't heard from his mom this morning. Her phone's off. Maybe she's at the clinic, or at church.

Delia called to say Basson was stable. A bullet had gone through his lung, another through his shoulder. He'll have to quit smoking, she said. He's not going to like that.

Tomorrow Majola will walk into the station with his head held high, ready to answer IPID's questions. He'll be honest. He'll share his suspicions with them, that he still thinks Kappie had an accomplice. Then he'll take the consequences as they come. He'll see Radebe and they'll greet each other as if nothing happened. He's been given a second chance. He won't waste it.

He gets up slowly and walks to the church in Fourth Street. The fresh air should do him some good, despite the pain in his shoulder and chest.

Andy smiles when he sees him. Majola sits on one of the plastic chairs arranged in a circle, and blows into his hands to warm them. The walk was perhaps not such a good idea; his shoulder's killing him. Maybe he should go to the doctor in Milpark after this, though he doesn't know how he'll explain his injuries. They'll have to report him.

The rest of the group, seven in total, are standing chatting at the kettle and cups in the corner. Andy walks over to Majola, a cup of coffee in his hand.

'I'm glad you could make it,' Andy says.

Majola takes the coffee with a nod.

Andy calls the others over to sit down.

Majola scans the faces. He remembers three of the men from last time. A lawyer, a tennis coach and a restaurateur. The pretty woman and the short man in the blue suit he doesn't recognise, nor the black guy with the dreadlocks. He'd always thought it was only beggars and junkies who came to these meetings, for the free coffee and the chance to shed a tear. How wrong he was.

To start the meeting, Andy asks everyone to introduce themselves. Majola considers just listening today. Everyone will think he's lying if he tells them about the past few weeks anyway.

The lawyer goes first. He started drinking when he lost his job. Well, no one can blame him for that. The more emotional he gets during his testimony, the more Majola thinks he shouldn't be so hard on himself.

Majola checks his phone from time to time to see if his mother has called. Two missed calls from Ramsamy, probably to hear if he's still alive after Friday's message. He'll have to call him back, tell him to relax.

Majola is jolted from his reverie when the guy next to him begins speaking. The lawyer has finished his story.

'Hello. My name is Aneni Masimba. I'm an alcoholic.' Aneni is greeted by a mumbled chorus.

Majola's head is bowed.

Aneni moves around uncomfortably in his chair. 'I was doing well until last week.'

You and me both, buddy.

'On Tuesday I started to follow the programme again. Then I read some-thing on Friday that sent me off the cliff again.' Aneni hesitates.

'Take your time, Aneni. What upset you so much that you started drinking?'

'Okay. I've told you before that I do prescription deliveries on my motor-bike from Helen Joseph Hospital, mostly to pharmacies and old-age homes. In Friday's *Daily Sun* I read that they've killed Zola Budd. The real murderer. Then I read the name: Daniël Loots.'

Majola opens his eyes and fixes them on Aneni.

'I don't know if I should go on.'

'Everything you say stays between us, Aneni. You know this.' Andy draws him out. Majola's impatience is about to bubble over.

'Okay. For the last year I've been mixing up someone's order. Prescription medication. Every now and then, I would go to meet a man, then I would re-place Daniël Loots's medication with some other medicine he gave me. I think ... I think I'm guilty of those murders too. I messed with his medication.'

'Thank you, Aneni. So why did you—'

'Say that again?' Majola's voice is way too loud. 'You've been substituting Daan Loots's medication for the past year?'

'David, please.' Andy tries to calm him down.

Majola looks at Andy, motions for him to hold on.

Aneni is caught off guard. 'Yes. That's what I said.'

'How did you do it? Who brought the other medication to you?'

Aneni turns to Andy for help. Andy nods for him to go on.

'A black man. We met every few weeks, mostly in this area. I needed the money. I gave him the medication, then he gave me a different box. That's what I would give to the nurse at the old-age home.'

'What did he drive?'

'A black BMW.'

Majola shakes his head. 'Did you take down his number plate?'

'I did. I was scared something bad would come from the transaction, espe-cially because medication was involved. I have it on my phone.'

Majola gets up, feeling faint.

'Read it out to me, please.'

Andy gets up and walks to Majola. 'David, please. Can we go on?'

'Sit, Andy,' Majola orders.

Andy looks like he's been slapped, and sits back down. Aneni is busy on his phone.

'Sometimes he came in a Polo too. The number was CD 07 NS GP.'

'And the BMW?' Majola asks.

'VN 12 NC GP.'

'Jesus,' Majola says under his breath. He takes out his phone and goes through his pictures.

'Am I in trouble?'

'No … no, not at all …' Majola holds his phone out to Aneni. There's a picture of three men, Majola included, beside a fire.

'Do you recognise the man in the BMW?'

Aneni looks at the picture, then at Majola.

'Look closely.'

'The one in the middle.'

'Are you sure?'

'Dead certain. I've seen his face many times over the last year.'

Majola is shaking as he looks up Ramsamy's number.

'Sorry, Andy,' he says, 'but Aneni has just solved the Zola Budd case.'

Majola walks out, his phone to his ear.

'What happened to you, Captain? I've been looking for you since Friday!' Ramsamy says.

'Ramsamy, it's—'

'I've got the name that goes with that last number. It wasn't Nbete or Mbete. It was Mpete. The police member in question changed his surname, but the number stayed the same. It's Radebe now.'

'I know. It's Colonel Radebe.'

'What?'

'He's been switching Loots's medication. He pulled Loots's dossiers. He framed Loots.'

'But … but … how?' Ramsamy stutters.

'I'm going to find out now. Meet me at his house in Mondeor in an hour. Bring back-up. I'll record with my phone: if something happens to me, just listen to the audio file. Ramsamy, are you still there?'

'Yes, Captain.'

'Okay, see you in an hour.' Majola hangs up. As he leaves the hall, he remembers he walked here. He turns back.

'Andy. Sorry, can you drop me off at home? Right now? It's a matter of life and death.'

Majola smiles. What were the odds? The coincidence, that he would end up in an AA meeting with the right delivery guy. And that Ramsamy's breakthrough would come at the same time. The gods must be on his side, for the first time in ages.

Majola speeds down the express lane to the Xavier turn-off in the Corolla, and heads left to Mondeor.

He tries to put together all the pieces of the puzzle as he drives. This is why the murderer always dodged the patrol vehicles: he knew exactly where they were. That's why Radebe didn't want to agree to the roadblocks. That's why he changed the layout to remove the roadblock from the Atholl Oaklands turn-off near Melrose. It was all one big game to him.

But why? What did he have against Kappie? Jealousy, perhaps? Did he drive the taxi himself? How did he do it?

Majola turns slowly into Edenhurst Road and parks in front of Radebe's house. The double-storey with the six-foot wall is one of many in the street, expansive, expensive and well maintained. He takes out his phone, opens the recording app, and puts it back in his pocket. Then he checks his gun.

He doesn't know what to expect. Will Radebe deny it? Will he go free? Will he confess? Or will he fight back? Is he expecting him?

With the z88 concealed behind his back, under his jacket, Majola stands in front of the large wooden gate. There's a strange smell in the air. He presses the button on the intercom and takes a step back to try to see if there's anything happening on the top floor. He doesn't see any movement. Is Radebe even here? He presses the button again. Somewhere in the house he can hear the buzzer. He takes out his phone and calls Radebe. His phone is off.

Majola decides to wait for reinforcements, but the gate opens. He walks in cautiously. He takes out his phone again, presses the button to start recording, and returns it to his pocket. The garden is in a shambles, the grass long and the flowerbeds overrun with weeds. Radebe's BMW is parked in front of the garage. The car is dirty, covered in dust, with handprints on the doors and the boot. The front window is open. Majola peers in: the keys are in the ignition. Is he going to try to make a run for it? Paving stones mark the path to the front door. The smell is stronger now. He keeps his hand on his gun. The front door is open.

'Colonel?' Majola asks from the doorway. He's drenched in sweat beneath the bulletproof vest. 'Colonel? It's David Majola.'

No answer. Majola nervously walks in. There's no sound in the house. No TV, no radio, no voices. Silent as the grave. Basson mentioned that Radebe's wife had left him. Majola looks into the living room to his left. It's strewn with bottles, mostly empty, whisky and beer. No one has tidied up in months. The flatscreen TV lies broken on the wooden floor. Newspapers are scattered over the rug.

As he walks down the hallway, the smell gets stronger. It seems to be coming from the back of the house. The kitchen looks as if a bomb's exploded here, with old food all over the table and a mountain of dishes in the sink. Majola waves the flies away from his face. Is this the source of the smell? The back door is open. Majola can see a light on in the garage. Radebe has to be here somewhere; who else would have opened the gate?

The smell becomes sharper when he steps outside. He draws his gun, lets it lead the way. Drawing a deep breath, he opens the steel door that leads to the garage.

The smell overwhelms Majola, burning his throat and eyes. He covers his mouth and nose with his free hand. In the corner he can see a dead dog. The garage is brightly lit. To his left, someone starts to clap.

'Bravo! The captain has solved the riddle. That's my boy.'

Colonel Radebe sits at a wire-mesh table on a garden chair. He's wearing a dirty white robe and blue slippers. On the table lie his Glock, a dossier and an A4 sheet of paper.

'Sorry about the smell. It was my wife Angie's dog. He just became too much of a nuisance, what with all the blood. But you get used to the smell after a while.' Radebe is talking in his polished English, no trace of the broken Afrikaans he always speaks to Majola.

Radebe leans back in the chair. Majola realises that Radebe no longer has any intention of hiding anything. Or is this just part of his game? He looks around the garage. There's a chest freezer against the wall, beside a steel workbench with a portable CD player and a large battery with two crocodile clamps. Next to the freezer, a hose and a compressor. Clothing is strewn everywhere.

Now I've got you, you mother-fucker. He looks again at the badly decomposed dog.

'The dog hair we found on the victim at Westpark Cemetery?'

Radebe smiles. 'You can put away your gun, Captain. I've no desire to try anything.'

'Not with that Glock on the table.'

Radebe puts the gun down at his feet.

'Happy?' he asks with a smile.

Majola lowers his gun.

Radebe leans back in the chair. 'What was it? The service number?'

'Yes. That and the delivery guy you bribed to switch out Kappie's medication. He's in the same AA group as I am. If you hadn't told me to get help yesterday, I might not have gone to the meeting. Ironic, isn't it?'

'It's got nothing to do with irony, Captain. You're a good detective. '

'I suspected it was one of us. But I never thought—'

'You'd be surprised what you can accomplish with a bit of money and a high rank. For months I've been receiving all of your emails, messages and voice recordings from a private-security firm, like clockwork, every night at nine.'

'You knew about every—'

'I know that Mbatho has a clothing business on the side. I know that Ramsamy is obsessed with his ex-fiancée. That Davids plays PI in his free time. That your friend Basson and Nigel October stole a kilogram of drugs from the evidence room. And you and your coke, of course. It's only Rikhotso and Mitchell who aren't broken. It's a fucking wonder you could make any headway with a whole team of fuck-ups.'

'Basson ...'

'Yes, it was his oversight. Nigel October. Basson asked him to be on the lookout for the taxi. Unfortunately, he didn't know that October has been my informant for much longer than he's been his. I told October to tell him the taxi was in that alley. He was so shocked when he opened the door and saw me next to Loots that he didn't shoot. So I shot him. That day will go down in history as a work of genius.'

293

'And then Lizanne Loots also had to suffer?'

'That was justice, the balancing of the scales. I wanted that dog Loots to do to her what I'd done to all the other girls. With the truncheon. But he just sat there like a zombie, tears running down his cheeks. I couldn't believe how easy it was. He hears the trigger, he turns into a zombie. Putty in my hands. She fought like a hellcat when she arrived at Loots's place after I'd sent a message from his phone.'

'What did Loots do when you did that to his dau—'

'Looks like you're still lagging behind a bit, Captain. See, I got Loots's medical records. He was fucked up about what he did during the riots. Then I switched his medication for a year with a concoction of my own. He never killed, he just drove, took orders. There were things that triggered him. And with the potent cocktail of pills, it worked like a charm. Can you guess what his trigger was?'

Majola doesn't respond.

'Boeremusiek. Ha! Fucking boeremusiek. I walk in with the CD player and start playing some of the hits. Then he loses his shit. Then I give orders: put on your uniform, drive there, stop here. Then I go drop him off again, change his clothes, tuck him into bed. The next day he doesn't remember a fucking thing. As easy as that. I got his records from that quack Schoeman. That guy needs no convincing to start singing. And if you go digging around on the internet you find some interesting things. I took my opportunity. If that didn't work … well, I probably would have killed him right there in his little room. It was only with that journalist white bitch and the last victim that he didn't join in the fun.'

Radebe gets serious. 'But he knew exactly what was going on in that taxi when I had the girls there. He needed to feel what he did.'

Majola's composure cracks. 'What he did? Almost thirty years ago? You're the one who tore those girls apart. One of them was pregnant!'

Radebe gets up slowly, turns to Majola. Majola raises his gun.

'Easy there, Colonel!'

'What he did, Captain?' Radebe slowly opens his robe. Underneath he is naked. First Majola sees his chest, but his eyes fix on the bag hanging from his middle. He gasps.

Where Radebe's genitals should be, there is nothing. Only a dark purple scar, with a thin translucent pipe running out of it.

'Have you seen enough, Captain?' Radebe's voice trembles.

Majola looks away. Radebe closes the robe and sits down again.

'You were Loots's last victim? The one they burnt with the blowtorch?'

Radebe taps a finger on the dossier in front of him.

'Now you're getting it, Captain. This is the dossier you were looking for, the one I signed out at Benoni more than twenty years ago. It's my own dossier.'

Radebe's voice breaks. 'It's Loots's fault, Calvin turning out like he did. It's his fault that my first wife left me. And now Angie too. He took everything away from me. It was his turn. That Zulu dog that worked with him, I got him drunk years ago and shoved him onto the tracks in Springs – after I'd cut off his penis and hung it around his neck. And yes, I did enjoy torturing the girls. They made me think of Angie. She was the only one who accepted me. But it was all a lie. She also fucked off with another man. Those girls ... were all the women who saw me as broken, who laughed at me. They had to pay. What else could I do with such a wreck of a body? The girls were pleasure, the numbers were revenge on Loots.'

He pauses before going on. 'You know, I tried to find the original taxi. I so hoped they still had it. But I ended up buying Zola on Gumtree. It took two years to get her perfect. And she was perfect.'

Radebe smiles with deep satisfaction. 'And you know the biggest joke of all? I stored her two blocks from the station, right under your noses. I even bribed the night guard for the keys to the side gate at Loots's place. The Zimbos are so scared of deportation they'll do anything.'

Majola shakes his head. 'I've heard enough. You'll have to come with me.'

'Wait a minute, Captain. Don't you want to know more? What about Sibewu?'

Majola glances at the freezer and the pile of licence plates and clothing on top of it. Something's drawing him to it.

'Sibewu was luck. I wanted Loots there. I went into the house before you did. I planted the truncheon and the other things I'd hidden under my coat. Then I sent Loots to the kitchen. I've had his fingerprints for ages. Easy. And you know, your friend Basson and that white bitch? They were just fun. That's what you get for sticking your nose where it doesn't belong. You, Captain, had to figure it out. But now it's a nice touch, garnish to my story.'

'At the last murder you said you were done,' Majola says, taking another step closer.

'I am. My taxi is gone. Loots died with his daughter. You solved the riddle, you and Loots. There had to be a winner. And Loots eventually figured out the docket numbers and the letters. But you have to see what I did first – then you can decide if your side won.'

Majola doesn't understand his last statement. 'The letters?'

Radebe points at the sheet of paper beside the dossier. 'Oh yes. You were right about the Parabellum casings at the taxi rank. I was hoping you'd block me off at the rank under the M1; that's exactly where I was going. Before you started shooting, I got out, jumped over the low wall. Then I fired two shots under the taxi. You thought it was him and opened fire. So technically you killed him, not me. The helicopter couldn't see me, so I just walked off. Now that's how a plan comes together.'

'You think this is some kind of game. You're sick. Why wait thirty years?'

'I've been planning this since I signed out those dockets. But Angie ...' Radebe's voice breaks. 'Angie held me back. She kept the darkness caged up.

But when she left with that other fuck, she left the cage door wide open. This was payback. All the magoshas who laughed, all of it: Loots's fault.'

'And all this time I thought Kappie had problems,' Majola says.

Radebe rolls his eyes. 'Kappie this, Kappie that – as if Loots was your fucking father. Meanwhile it was I who got you where you are today. Even after I saved your ass last night.'

Majola can hear the sirens approaching.

Radebe snorts. 'The cavalry are here. And here I was thinking we're two friends having a conversation.'

'We're not friends, you sick bastard.'

Radebe bends over and picks up the Glock.

'Put down that gun!' Majola yells, taking another step forward.

Radebe still has the gun pointed at the ground. A deep sadness washes over him. His voice is soft when speaks.

'You and I are the same, David. We're a bit broken. It's this city. I tried to fight it but the broken part of me was too strong. I had to embrace it.'

In one motion, Radebe raises the gun to his temple and pulls the trigger. The shot reverberates around the garage.

'No! Ah fuck, no.'

Radebe's body tumbles to the ground. The robe falls open to reveal his mutilated body. Majola drops his gun, bends over and covers Radebe. Blood pools around the colonel's head.

Majola takes out his phone and stops the recording. He puts it down on the wire table. The steel door flies open and a bunch of uniforms come storming in.

Ramsamy rushes to his side. 'Fucking hell. What happened here? Captain? What are you looking at?'

Majola is staring at the workbench, the freezer. That jersey looks familiar.

Majola steps closer, Ramsamy following him, frowning. The response team lower their weapons. Majola recognises that jersey, green and white, with a ZCC badge.

'Captain?' Ramsamy asks again.

Majola lifts the freezer door, slowly. He holds his breath. Time stands still. The other men are approaching the freezer.

It is empty. He turns to the door, then runs out.

'Captain! Where are you going?' Ramsamy shouts, following him.

Majola stops at the driver's side of the BMW and takes the keys out of the ignition. He presses the button and the boot of the car opens. He walks around to the boot, drops the key. Lulu is lying on Mama Thadie's chest with her eyes closed. Almost peaceful, as if she is sleeping. His mother's eyes are closed too. They are both naked. Both their throats have been cut clean across.

TWO WEEKS LATER

Basson groans as he tries to get comfortable. There's droëwors and Energade on the bedside table, and a teddy bear with a police cap that Nonnie brought him.

'How do you feel?' Ramsamy asks from the chair.

'Better than when you were here last week. They've prescribed pills to dampen my nicotine cravings. They don't really help.'

Ramsamy looks uncertain for a moment. Then he says, 'They're going to cover it up. They're going to say it was just a suicide. The political backlash will be too heavy. The minister spoke to the team yesterday, IPID too. Everyone has to sign NDAs and promise not to say anything.'

'Mother-fuckers. Can you believe it? So the directorate turns out not to be as independent as its name suggests. And now Daan Loots will forever be remembered as one of South Africa's worst serial killers.'

Ramsamy nods, raking his hands through his hair.

'How's David doing?' Basson asks, concerned.

'Up and down. I was there two days ago. He didn't recognise me. The lights are on but there's no one home. The doctor says it's going to take some time. But he might come back.'

'I still can't believe it.'

Ramsamy takes a deep breath. 'You know, I dream about it often. I come walking in and he's just standing there in front of the car boot. The way he looked at me … I can't—'

'Why were they naked? Did the bastard torture them as well?' Basson asks.

'Not from what I saw. Maybe he only wanted their clothes to put with the other souvenirs. Who knows what went on in his head?'

'How are those fuckers going to cover that up?'

'The two women are reported missing. The lengths these guys will go to baffles me.'

'Maybe you should also go see someone.'

'I already am. It's been better. And I've got good news for you.'

Basson tries to push a pillow up behind his back. 'I'm listening.'

'IPID are dropping their investigation. They don't want to draw any further attention to anyone or anything to do with the case. Since you were involved from the start, and got shot by a serial killer …'

'That's fucking great news.' Basson exhales slowly. 'How are things at SVC?'

'Well, Rikhotso and I have been promoted to warrant officers. Davids was fired for leaking the information to the press. We might be working with Pretoria; apparently there's a serial making himself known over there. "Casanova Killer", they're calling him. Bok Louw is standing in for Majola. We're waiting for the new colonel.'

'Bok Louw. Fucking cowboy,' Basson snorts.

'I went digging around a bit,' Ramsamy continues, 'in Radebe's medical records. His psychiatrist wanted to have him committed three years ago. Disso-ciative personality disorder. That very same psychiatrist was gunned down in his own driveway a few weeks later. Makes you wonder, doesn't it?'

'Like Kappie. Do you think Radebe knew what he was doing? He seemed completely normal at the station. A fucking asshole, but a normal fucking ass-hole.'

'I have no idea,' Ramsamy says.

'I don't think we'll ever see another case like this. It's like something from a movie. They usually only come once in a policeman's life.' Basson drinks from the bottle at his side.

'Don't be so sure. "This is Africa," as the good Captain Majola always said.'

Ramsamy gets up. 'Have you made up your mind? Are you leaving? You talked about "we" policemen a moment ago.'

'Yes, that's just habit. As soon as I'm better, we're moving to J-Bay.'

Ramsamy hesitates before he speaks. 'You know, we've had our shit, you and I. And I still don't like you all that much.'

Basson smiles.

'You always made comments – said I was gay and all that shit.' Ramsamy pauses again. 'My fiancée, a Zulu girl, left me for my brother four years ago, two weeks before the wedding. That's another reason I go for therapy.'

Basson smiles. 'I know, I can be a fucking asshole sometimes too.'

Ramsamy puts two forms on the bedside table.

'That's the NDA you have to sign; the other is the letter Daan Loots left for Captain Majola. It explains the letters carved into the girls.'

'Where did you get that? I thought they were covering all this up?'

'I took it from the table in Radebe's garage. He doesn't refer to it in the cell-phone recording. Just in case this cover-up backfires, we've got something to cover our asses.'

Ramsamy extends his hand.

'Farewell, Detective. All the best.'

Basson shakes his hand. 'Goodbye, Sergeant ... excuse me, Warrant Officer.'

Ramsamy smiles and walks to the door.

Basson leans over painfully and picks up the letter from Loots.

Young man,

I tried to call you. Something is wrong here. The more I try to remember my setbacks, the more I see Radebe's face. I see him standing in my apartment. That made me look at the numbers again. It's the letters, actually. Do you remember I told you he always taunted me about my Christianity? The other night at the garage again he said, 'Can you remember the Commandments?'

'How are you and Jesus doing?' I think he has something to do with the murders. IT'S THE TEN COMMANDMENTS, DAVID. That was the riddle he set for me. I tried to remember if he was one of the people we had in the van back in the day, but my memory fails me. It's in English and Zulu. It's a long shot, I know. This is what I think – look at the letters and numbers:
MAMM 15 14 – That's the fifteenth (O) and fourteenth (N) letters of the alphabet.
Then it spells MAMMON – The first commandment – Thou shalt not worship any God but me.
SO 20 6 – SOTF – second commandment – Sons of the fathers will be punished if any idols are worshipped.
JISS 9 19 – JISSIS – That's the third commandment – Thou shalt not take the Lord's name in vain.
ISON 20 15 – ISONTO (Sunday) – fourth commandment – You must keep the Sabbath sacred.
ABAZA 12 9 – ABAZALI – fifth commandment – Honour your father and mother.
SHA 25 1 – SHAYA (Deathblow) – sixth commandment – Thou shalt not kill.
ANG 9 5 – ANGIE (Radebe's wife's name. Didn't she leave him?) – seventh commandment – Thou shalt not commit adultery?
BASS 15 14 – BASSON – eighth commandment – All I can think here is that Warrant Basson stole something? Stole something from Radebe?
BAMAN 7 1 – BAMANGA (False) – ninth commandment – Thou shalt not lie.
UMHA 23 21 – UMHAWU (Envy) tenth commandment – Thou shalt not covet.

That's what I think. Does this make sense to you?
David, if I don't see you again: it's been an honour. You were like a son to me, young man. I've got all the respect in the world for who you've become. Please take care of Lizanne if something happens to me.
And remember the following – it might be my last bit of wisdom: Apartheid had many engines and many operators. The exhaust fumes from those engines made everyone sick – not just those run over by them or chewed up by the gears, but also those who kept those engines turning. If only those in the road could see how broken the operators really were.

Love
Kappie

'Would you look at that? Daan Loots, you old bastard.' Basson says. He folds up the letter and puts it back on the bedside table. Then he tears up the NDA form and throws the shreds in the bin.

TWO MONTHS LATER

'Are you sure you want to go again? The last time he didn't even recognise you,' Delia says, putting her hand on Basson's knee.

'Well, it's worth a try. You sure you don't want to come along? It's warm in the car.'

'We'll put the aircon on,' Delia says.

'Say goodbye to David, Papa,' Nonnie says from the seat in the back.

Basson opens the door and gets out slowly, a plastic bag in his hand. His shoulder still gives him trouble, but it's already better than it was a month ago.

He walks across the underground parking lot at the Akeso psychiatric clinic in Parktown. He's glad summer has finally come around. It really was the winter to end all winters. For him, at least.

He presses the button for the third floor. He looks at himself in the lift mirror. 'You're one of the lucky ones.' He pulls his T-shirt straight.

Majola is in his room, sitting in an armchair beside his single bed, staring out the window. He's wearing a white vest and Adidas tracksuit pants. The scar on his shoulder is visible.

'Afternoon, David.'

Majola doesn't react.

Basson sits on the bed in front of him. 'I came to say goodbye. We're leaving for Jeffreys Bay this weekend. The furniture is coming next week.'

Majola blinks. He reaches into his pocket, then hands Basson a small, folded-up note.

'Ngithengele.'

Basson unfolds it. It's a list of groceries. Milk, chips, eggs, bread and a few other items.

'For Mama and Lulu.'

'I'll take it to them, David.'

Basson starts to choke up. He swallows the tears. 'You'd better get fucking better, David. Don't stop fighting, my friend.'

Majola shakes his head almost imperceptibly.

Basson stands. He upends the plastic bag onto the bed.

'Ramsamy brought a card that arrived for you at the station. It's from someone called Lucy. There's a drawing inside of a little girl and a policeman. Quite arty. And here's your *Stranger Things* DVD. I started watching the second season, and as usual it's not as good as the first one.'

Majola turns his head to Basson, then looks out the window again. He begins speaking in a whisper.

'They call this the City of Gold. She has lots of stories, a lot of history. But it's not she who has the heart of gold; it's the people. They give her heart.'

A tear rolls down Majola's cheek and falls onto his lap.

'Goodbye, David,' Basson says, and leaves the room.

ACKNOWLEDGEMENTS

To my wife Almerie, who put up with my moods as the story sucked me in. And to my mother, who dragged me off to the library with her as a teenager.

Special thanks to Sunell Wiehman for answering and ironing out medical queries, and Lizeri Mitchell for explanations of the legal process, as well as to Tertius Kapp who further fanned the writer's flame. And of course to Martin Steyn, for help with police-procedural issues and other advice. Thanks to Jaco Adriaanse for the translation.

Additional sources:

Unmaking the Torturer by Elaine Bing (LAPA Publishers)
Tydbom: 'n Polisieman se Ware Verhaal by Johan Marais (Tafelberg)
Voices from Alexandra Township – Where Rats Eat Babies and the Elderly
    (Media for Justice www.mediaforjustice.net)
A Day in the Life of a Durban Taxi Driver by Qiniso Mbili (www.sowetanlive.co.za)
Mobile Workplace: Work Conditions and Family Life of Taxi Drivers
    by Mpho Manoagae Mmadi (University of Pretoria)